Other novels by Julian Gloag:

Our Mother's House
A Sentence of Life
Maundy
A Woman of Character

Julian Gloag

HR
A Henry Robbins Book
E. P. Dutton / New York

for JACQUELINE, without whose
perspicacity, faith, and generosity
this book would not have been written.

For information contact: E. P. Dutton, 2 Park Avenue, New York, N.Y.
10016

Library of Congress Cataloging in Publication Data
Gloag, Julian.
Sleeping dogs lie.
"A Henry Robbins book."
I. Title.
PZ4.G5615Sl   [PS3557.L6]   813'.5'4   79-28204

ISBN: 0-525-20497-0

Published simultaneously in Canada by
Clarke, Irwin & Company Limited, Toronto and Vancouver

Designed by Barbara Cohen

10 9 8 7 6 5 4 3 2 1

First Edition

"An excessive preoccupation with individuals is heuristically sterile."

Mayer-Gross, Slater and Roth: *Clinical Psychiatry,* 3rd ed. (London: Baillière, Tyndall & Cassell, 1969), p. 4

One

1

Dr. Hugh Welchman put down his knife and fork and removed a kipper bone from his teeth.

"I'm afraid they're rather salty," Julia said.

"No matter." He coughed his sharp smoker's cough and drank some tea. For him, deboning a kipper was rather more intricate than performing a leucotomy or disentangling the origins of a compulsive ritual—and far less rewarding. A proper breakfast consisted of sausages or bacon or even just plain fried bread with plenty of ketchup. Fish was a Friday penance (and today was Tuesday); the guilt-conditioned reflex of his taste buds was all that remained of his mother's quiet piety.

"Hugh, try not to squeeze anyone in after seven, will you?"

"Ummm?" He reached across the ruined kipper for the box of fifty cigarettes Julia put at his place every morning. "Sorry—why not?"

"We're having dinner with the Semples."

"Oh." The Semples were their closest neighbours up The Lane. Mike Semple, historian and Senior Tutor of Carol College, was inclined to be a gossip and his wife . . .

"Don't worry, I'll take Reg off your hands."

"Good." He nodded. Regina Semple had no small talk and when she got on to her subject—some esoteric branch of linguistic studies—she was completely incomprehensible. Her cooking, like her conversation, was of a thoroughly indigestible French kind; and Hugh, who disliked wine unless it was sweet, would have swapped all Mike's carefully selected clarets and burgundies for a pint of bitter. But he didn't really object to the Semples—his one abiding nightmare was that someday Reg would ask to be accepted as a patient.

"Actually, it fits in quite well." He struck a match and lit a cigarette. "I wanted to have a word with Mike, anyway."

"About Alex Brinton?"

Hugh took his glasses from his breast pocket and put them on and stared at his wife. "How did you guess?"

"I do look after your appointments, you know." A faint smile lightened her habitually grave expression. "And he is an under-graduate at Carol now, isn't he?"

"Do you know him?"

"I did when he was a little boy."

"I see." He frowned. Except for her nurses' training in London, Julia had always lived in Cambridge—in this house, in fact—and knew, or knew of, a great many people in both the town and the university. But, just as he didn't normally discuss his cases, so he didn't encourage her to talk about her acquaintances; and he tried to avoid accepting as a patient anyone whom Julia knew or had been involved with. "Then you must know the family?"

"Not really, not since the accident."

"Accident?"

"Hasn't Alex told you?" Her tone was light, but the enquiry was clearly serious. Nothing now remained of her kipper but a neat skeleton.

"No. No," he spoke slowly, "though I suspected there might be something of the kind. The boy's G.P. was not forthcoming and—"

"Henry Stand?"

"Don't tell me you know him too?" He drew sharply on his cigarette.

"Of course. He was in partnership with Jonathan Brinton—Alex's father—at one time. He was our G.P. too, for a bit."

"Oh." So Stand evidently knew a lot more about young Brinton than he had passed on. Well, that was all right—Hugh could do his own case-taking. What troubled him a little was Julia's involvement. Although, on a social level, he often appreciated her knowledge of this middle-class milieu—of which he himself had no instinctive grasp—professionally he found the series of half-truths and unverifiable surmises on which such knowledge was fed to be largely useless, if not actually counter-productive. And yet in this case, perhaps . . . "Julia, I think I'd like to hear about the Brintons —about this accident."

"It was a long time ago," she said, frowning, as if seeking to excuse her knowledge.

"It's not your fault." But wasn't it in a way? Because of her, a vicarious element of nonprofessional involvement had inevitably crept into the case.

Julia shook her head with an impulsive movement that rippled

3

her short-cut black hair. "Are you sure Alex remembers nothing about it?"

"I fancy whatever *it* is, is part of the repressed material."

"I'm sorry, Hugh, but it's unlike you to ask."

"That's all right. It might be important. Perhaps this evening—"

"After the Semples."

"—after the Semples." He nodded, glanced at his watch—five to nine. The weak April sunlight, filtered through thin clouds, made the large dining room even starker than usual. With a single-barred electric fire, it was chilly too. In the series of mean flats and narrow houses he had been brought up in, the kitchen, where they ate, had always been warm, even during the war. He frowned: he hardly thought about his childhood once a month, and now he had done so twice in ten minutes. He shivered slightly in his heavy tweed suit. There was something faintly different about this morning—silence from the kitchen perhaps. "No Mrs. Nance?"

"She's having a bit of trouble with that daughter of hers. Same old thing. I told her to take the day off."

"I'm sorry." Tuesday was the most inconvenient time for Mrs. Nance to be out; it was his only day devoted entirely to private patients at home (and by the end of it he was often well into his second box of cigarettes). When she was not there, the automatic message-taker took over answering the phone, but organising the traffic of patients fell on Julia.

"I don't mind. At least I get a closer look at the clientele. I wonder what they make of me. Have you ever thought your patients probably assume you're married to Mrs. Nance?"

"That's unlikely if they've seen you—even if they haven't, as a matter of fact."

"Why?"

"Ummm? Oh—well, I assume we're talking about the females, and they'd lend my wife all the endowments of perfection: the *most* beautiful, intelligent, charming, and all that."

"Oh. I see. That's nice of them."

"Not very." He gave a short barking laugh. "Projective identification. You are them. The 'real' you would be subject to feelings of murderous hostility."

"You make them sound rather an unpleasant lot."

"Unpleasant?" He took off his glasses and rubbed vaguely with his napkin at a smear of grease across one lens. "I don't know.

4

Positive transference is a—" A movement of Julia's head stopped him in mid-speech. "Sorry." He smiled and put on his glasses and looked at her through a haze of grease that now extended across both lenses. No gossip from her, no jargon from him—that was their understanding, and he found it a useful discipline on the whole. From her he had learned, and trained himself to employ, a certain simple, nonprofessional exactitude of observation, both verbally and visually.

The bell rang and he stood up. "The Savage." He stubbed out his cigarette in the corpse of the kipper. "I'll take her straight up." He slipped the cigarette box into his pocket and went out to the hall.

He lit another cigarette before opening the front door.

"Hello, Caroline."

"Good morning, Doctor." Caroline Savage simpered—a good day for her. On bad days she grimaced. Simper or grimace, but never a true smile on the world. And if she did—smile an unstrictured smile—what then? Then perhaps he would be able to swallow his breakfast kipper. But the prognosis was poor in either case.

"I'll lead the way." He ran briskly up the stairs. Once he had let her go first and she had set a sultry, bottom-wiggling pace that had put her in a seductive mood for the entire session.

As he made for the desk and she for the couch, she said huskily, "Hugh, you smoke too much, I'm worried about you."

"Ummm." Recently one undergraduate patient had criticised his smoking, not because he was courting cancer or indulging in a substitute gratification of an infantile order, but because he was endangering the patient; a criticism that related very well to a recurrent nightmare in which the young man was being pursued along the edge of a cliff by a dragon with smoking nostrils. Hugh settled himself in the springy leather chair. "And how are you today?"

"Oh, something wonderful happened to me on the weekend. You remember I told you about . . ."

He thought fleetingly, as he invariably did, how ill Caroline's boudoir mannerisms sat in his shabby little hothouse of an office. Then he was listening attentively, remembering, connecting—he had an almost faultless memory (photographic for the written word), which did not permit him to forget the meanest trivia. An elephant—if not a dragon—among therapists. But beneath his attentiveness the problem of Alex Brinton circled smokily in his mind.

Dr. Stand's recommendation of Alex Brinton, a first-year undergraduate at Carol, had rather surprised Hugh. Stand had the reputation of being more concerned with the trick knees and pulled muscles of rugger players than with the emotional complications of students. But he'd been sensible about Alex (the boy did need help), though not forthcoming.

Alex was of middle height, slightly mesomorphic, well-built, a good chin, though otherwise rather delicate of feature. His reflexes were excellent. He had a mild stammer, hardly more than a hesitancy of speech, but no sign of aphasia. Father and mother both alive, mother in good health, father with a mild heart condition. One sister, six years older. Private school, Winchester, minor scholarship in history to Carol, rowed in the college second boat, played squash—a conventional background. Quite obviously intelligent.

"I gather from Dr. Stand that you've been having some difficulties with your studies." This after some minutes of silence.

"Not really. A b-bit perhaps." He smiled. "I had to tell old Henry something. Er, may I smoke, sir?"

"Yes, of course."

Alex lit the cigarette carefully, taking a lighter out of a small leather pouch to do so. He sat still, smoking, his deepset grey eyes cast down, as though examining his fingernails—which were cut close but not bitten. More silence. "I expect you want to know about my d-dreams and things, don't you?"

"Tell me about your dreams."

"I don't have any."

Hugh smiled.

Alex frowned, then smiled too—a slight flush on his cheeks. "Shouldn't I be on the couch?"

"If it helps."

"Oh. Well, no, I think I'll stay here." He patted the arm of the chair. "I'm sorry. This is a bit difficult. The tricky thing is . . . I mean, it seems really so trivial, you know. . . ." He pulled quickly on his cigarette and coughed. When the spasm was over, he sat still again, not brushing aside the flop of dark hair that had fallen across his forehead. "You see, I'm afraid . . . afraid. . . ." He stared at some point over Hugh's shoulder, his mouth was slightly open and there was a faint down of moisture on his upper lip.

"Just try to relax."

With a visible effort, he pulled himself together. "Well, the

6

truth is that I'm afraid of going downstairs." He gave an awkward little laugh, took a handkerchief from his sleeve and wiped his mouth. "I told you it was trivial, didn't I?"

"Isn't that what you're here to find out?"

"Well, I—yes. That's what I'm afraid of."

In that first session, quite a lot of detail had emerged. The phobia exhibited a remarkable specificity of response; it was only one particular flight of stairs that frightened Alex—the stone staircase leading to his second-floor set of rooms at Carol—and it was only going down that worried him, petrified him to the point where he had been driven to climb out of the window and drop onto the flower bed below when no one was looking. This took some courage, because he was a conventional young man. He had missed Hall and cut lectures to avoid the nightmare descent and, worse in his eyes, he had not turned up on the river.

"I miss the exercise and, frankly, it's getting d-damned awkward. I had the president and the secretary of the boat club up the other night, telling me it wasn't the spirit. And it isn't. Of course, Carol isn't much on the river and I'm only in the second boat, but we're hard pressed for oars and I . . . well, I've invented a tennis elbow, but they're not too convinced and, if something isn't done, I shall be dropped from the Bumps. . . ."

The social inconveniences were much on his mind, ostensibly. Making a fool of himself was an anxiety more easily dealt with than the actual terror of descent.

"I've tried everything I could think of, you know. I got myself stupefyingly tight one afternoon, put on the *Eroica* full blast and made a dash for it with my eyes shut. That was worse than anything —I couldn't do it. Then I thought if I went down backwards on my hands and knees, it might make it all right. The blasted gyp caught me halfway." He had blushed heavily at the memory. "I told him I had an attack of lumbago. Of course he didn't believe me, but he helped me down. I was sweating and shivering like a nonswimmer about to be ducked in the deep end. I'm beginning to get a bit confused myself with all these different medical explanations," he had laughed tremulously. "The truth is, I'm just a damned c-coward about it."

"It seems to me you have shown considerable resolve. But it might help if you tried to think of this as a simple disability to which no shame attaches—after all, a sprained ankle would have much the same effect. For the moment I think you should try to avoid the circumstances that provoke the trouble."

"Well, I could always go and stay with my people—our house is only a quarter of an hour away on the Newmarket road."

"Ummm."

"Or I could ask the bursar to shift me somewhere else. I expect he would, particularly if you—I mean, if I could produce a medical certificate."

"That might be possible."

"But would it really do any good? I mean, if you slam the door on a problem, doesn't . . ." he was suddenly confused, blinked rapidly several times, ". . . d-doesn't it c-come back and hit you on the head in some other way?"

"I'm not suggesting that you run away from the problem—merely that you avoid the distress of the symptoms. The problem we will try to deal with here."

"I see." A shake of the head. "Or rather, I don't see. I'll be quite happy if I can just get down those bloody stairs without screaming. That's the problem, as far as I'm concerned." Again the tremulous laugh. "You don't know what it's like. Every time I make it, it takes me two or three double whiskies at the Blue Boar to recover. I shall become a regular alcoholic if this keeps up." A curiously glazed look came into his eyes—and he stared out of the window as though surprised and puzzled to see the day still there. He came to with a start as the cigarette burnt down to his fingers, and he stubbed it out assiduously for a moment, then relapsed into his daze.

"What are you thinking?"

"Er? Oh—nothing." He shook his head. "All the same, one must keep trying."

At that, Hugh had decided against tranquilisers—they wouldn't go with the alcohol, and it was better that the boy had some inducement to get out, even if it was only whisky at the Blue Boar.

At a later session, Alex had said: "Phil's getting rather cross with me. Phil Cross—we share rooms. He complains I'm always there whenever he wants to bring a girl up—he's rather one for the girls, is Phil." He frowned. "He says I'm becoming a monk. Not a convivial one—a miserable bloody monk, he calls me." A cough, half embarrassed, half defiant. "Which brings up my sex life, I suppose—that's always important, isn't it?"

8

It had been unspectacular—a mild romantic attachment to a member of the school cricket eleven, some fairly heavy "snogging" (Alex's own uneasily disdainful word) with a schoolgirl from Newcastle when apple-picking in Norfolk, a failed assignation with a prostitute in Boulogne, and a rather more satisfactory affair, sustained for six days, with an Austrian girl on a ski holiday in the Valais. More important than this fairly light-hearted recital had been the frowning hesitation at the mention of Cross and his girl friends. That had been towards the end of the sixth session. At the seventh session, Alex had hardly been able to restrain his excitement as he came into the office.

"It's all right!" he had burst out, as he sat down. "I walked down without a tremor this morning." He leaned back with a self-satisfied smile. "I've found out what it's all about. Don't you want to know?"

"If you want to tell me."

"Well—where do I begin? You know you said that it might have been triggered by some incident, but I couldn't remember anything out of the way. I mean, it just came upon me, like the Lady of Shalot's doom, as it were. Well, you were right—there was an incident." He beamed.

Hugh regarded him steadily.

"Well, you see, it was Phil who reminded me. That Saturday night—you remember it was Sunday morning that it first hit me, when I wanted to go to chapel?—Phil had had one of his girls up, a nurse, I believe, he rather specialises in nurses. Well, we all got a bit tight, you know—and then Phil and the nurse went off into the bedroom. I mean, I don't mind that too much, as long as they don't stay all night. But when they came out Phil wanted me to drive the wretched creature home—I've got a car, you see, and he doesn't. Well, I wouldn't. I couldn't have anymore passed a breathalyser than I could have walked a tightrope. He got a bit shirty—he's quite unreasonable when he's drunk—but eventually barged out with the girl, slamming the door with an almighty crash." He was silent for a moment, breathing rather quickly, licking his lips with his tongue. "Slamming the door." It was not as easy as he had thought. He gave a strained smile. "Well then, a minute or two later, Phil came back and said—said there'd been a frightful accident. The girl had fallen down the stairs, and he was afraid . . . afraid she'd . . ." He got up abruptly and, turning his back to Hugh, looked out

9

of the window at the grey April day. "He was afraid she'd broken her neck or something." Jerky stop. "And I was a doctor's son—so would I—well, of course I said yes, but when I got to the top of the stairs, I couldn't—I mean, there she was, I could see her in a sort of heap there, at the b-bottom of the stairs. In a heap." His voice rose to a squeak on the last word, and he suddenly put his hands over his face.

"Sit down, old chap."

"What? Oh yes, yes, thank you." He sat down diffidently on the edge of the chair.

Hugh poured a glass of water and handed it him.

"Thanks awfully." Alex gulped it down, then braced himself. "Well, that's it really. I saw her there, but I couldn't move. Phil got halfway down the stairs, saw I wasn't following, and began calling me to come down. But I couldn't—I couldn't move. After a bit he began shouting at me—you bloody b-bastard, you snivelling little —well, that sort of thing. Then I just went back into the room and went to bed. The girl was all right apparently, twisted an ankle, passed out with the drink, I expect. They got home all right. Of course, it was quite unforgivable, but I didn't remember anything about it, till Phil made a row about it last night—and then it all came back. Just like that. Of course he thought I'd been too ashamed to mention it. And he wasn't going to—he was just going to let me stew in my own juice. I did realise in a vague way that he was a bit bitchier than usual, but he's never very genial, unless he's had a few, that is—Cross by name, cross by nature. But I was too taken up with —with the other thing—to notice it very much. So, well—there we are." He sat back with a sigh and a tired, uneasy little smile.

"And this is what you remember yourself, not what your friend told you?"

"Oh yes. It just came back to me. It's all quite clear now."

"Is there anything else you recall about that evening?"

"No. I don't think so. Oh well, one thing, yes—the whole place smelled of whisky."

"What place?"

"Well, the staircase, the room, I suppose."

"You'd been drinking whisky?"

"Well, obviously. I think so, I mean. That's—well, I seem to remember gin actually. Perhaps it was gin I smelt."

Hugh glanced out of the window at a deceptive patch of blue sky, which closed, shutting out the brief sun almost as he looked.

"So that's it, isn't it? I was just pissed and made a fool of myself. It's a bit shame-making, but I expect I'll get over it."

"There's nothing else that you remember specifically?"

"Well, there was the dog, of course, but that came after."

"After what?"

"Er?" He looked blankly at Hugh. "Oh well, I suppose, after . . . I don't know."

"Where was the dog?"

"By the door."

"The door of your rooms?"

"No, at the bottom of the stairs."

"There's a door at the bottom of the stairs?"

"Yes—no. I say, I've just remembered, I used . . ." He frowned.

"Try not to hold back."

"Well, I remember now I did use to have a dream. About a dog. I had it quite often. It was more of a nightmare really."

"Yes?"

"That's all. Just this black dog. But it used to frighten me."

"And the dog you saw that evening—was it the same kind of dog?"

"I don't know. I—I'm not sure there was a dog now. Phil didn't say anything about it. Does it really matter?" A touch of impatience.

"Perhaps." Clearly the boy was talking about an entirely different episode, probably a vital one; Hugh was encouraged to find it so close to the surface. He decided to probe a little further, cautiously. "Did you keep a dog at home?"

"Oh no, we don't like dogs."

"We?"

"Daddy and Mother—at least, I think Mother doesn't. Of course, Kate likes dogs."

"Your sister?"

"Yes. She often goes off to dog shows."

"And you?"

"Me?" The question caused him some difficulty. "Well, I—I don't know, really." He licked his lips and gave a weak little smile. "I don't think I do much, actually—I m-mean, they're always m-messing up the w-w-wicket, and that sort of thing, aren't they?"

Hugh nodded. There were only four minutes left. "Well now, Alex, I'm going to prescribe you some tranquilisers. You've had a bit of a hard time, you know. I'd rather you didn't drink while you're on them—the occasional glass of wine's all right, but no spirits. Then we'll see how you feel next time."

"Next time? But—but I thought, I mean, it's finished now, isn't it?"

"I shouldn't expect too much, you know. You've made a useful start, but we've got a long way to go."

"But I feel quite all right, perfectly fit, in fact."

"Good. But, all the same, I want you to take it easy—which is why I'm giving you these tranquilisers." He scribbled his signature and handed the prescription across the desk to Alex. "You should take one before each meal and a last one before going to bed." He stood up and came round to Alex's chair. "And, look, if anything's worrying you, don't try to sweat it out by yourself—ring me up. If I'm not in, you can just record a message and I'll ring you back. All right?"

"Well, yes—I suppose so." Alex looked puzzled and deflated and there was a sulky line about his mouth. He had taken Hugh's proffered hand almost reluctantly; Hugh noted the palm was slightly damp. As a rule, he discouraged patients from phoning, but in this case an exception was probably justified.

That had been last Saturday, and Alex had not phoned. But when he had come for yesterday's session, he had been in a state of considerable anxiety.

The staircase terror had returned, worse than ever, and he blamed Hugh.

"You and your b-bloody pills—I was perfectly all right till I started your pills." He had begun shrilly and had gone on for quite a long time, his voice trembling. He had taken the Librium, as instructed, on Saturday and on Sunday morning, but then had not been able to get down for chapel. He had stayed in his rooms all Sunday, finally letting himself down from the window very early on Monday morning before anyone was about. He had slept for a few hours on a friend's couch.

Gradually, he had wound down and had sat silent, depressed and exhausted. And then Hugh had begun to talk in carefully generalised terms of the theory of the unconscious, the function of dreams, repressed material, and anxiety. . . . He wanted to engage the boy's intelligence and draw his interest; in fact, both to prepare him for and comfort him against what might be to come. The one really significant thing that had been established in prior sessions was that Alex had absolutely no memory of anything before the age of about five and a half, at which time he was apparently living with an aunt in the North. He had only come home to live with his parents sometime when he was six, after, he thought, a year away. There was something very nasty in the woodshed there—or at the bottom of the stairs. Whatever it was would probably emerge gradually, but there was the possibility that some incident or connection might bring out an early traumatic event whole—that might be cathartic, but might be seriously counter-productive. No one could be easy with this type of hysterical conversion symptom. So Hugh talked slowly, after a while taking off his glasses, feeling his way, discarding the idea of recommending Alex to go back and stay at his parents' house—the nasty thing might well be there (was there a stone staircase in the house?)—finally suggesting that he continue to sleep on his friend's couch. "Who's your tutor at Carol? Semple, is it? I could have a word with him to regularise the position, if you like." Take it easy, take the pills, keep in touch.

He took Alex down to the front door. On the step, the young man, not looking at him, had murmured an apology, "I'm sorry, sir, about . . ."

"You never have to apologise for anything when you're here, you know, old chap." He recalled a remark Julia was fond of quoting. "Wasn't it some Oxford historian who said something about never apologising?"

"Jowett, but he wasn't an historian. 'Never apologise, never explain.' Though I don't think the last part of that's very appropriate in the circumstances, is it?" Alex had given a little, wry smile.

And Hugh had nodded and watched him skid out of the gravelled drive in a small scarlet car. It was a blustery day and the wind whipped the fledgling leaves of the few trees that were scattered down The Lane. It was a naked landscape with its high over-arching sky and Hugh, town bred, had never got used to the bleakness or to the barrenness of their flowerless garden. His mother, otherwise impoverished, had lavished much care on geraniums in window boxes and potted plants on the mantelpiece—the sills and lintels of life.

". . . but of course what really worries me is can he keep it up?" Caroline Savage blushed. "I don't mean that literally."

"Don't you?"

"Well," a throaty little giggle, "I suppose I do, don't I? Poor Reggie, I'd just do anything. . . ."

2

The Rover jolted uncomfortably over the Semples' drive, even though Julia skilfully avoided the worst of the potholes.

"Why doesn't Mike have the thing resurfaced?"

"I expect he thinks a touch of dilapidation is very nice and English."

Hugh grunted. "Well, what about all this floodlighting, is that English?"

Julia stopped the car and switched off. There was a vast expanse of immaculately striped lawn in front of the house, and the floodlights turned the gently falling rain to silver. "No, I expect that's Reg. But you must admit it's effective."

"Ostentatious."

"Some people might call it ostentatious to use the car to go a hundred yards up The Lane."

Hugh smiled. Left to herself, Julia would have walked even if it had been a couple of miles—or taken her huge motor-bike. "Why does the Englishwoman behave like a foreigner, and the foreigner like an Englishman?"

"Why does a psychiatrist ask such an obvious question?"

"Even a psychiatrist is human." Actually, Hugh had little eye for social nuance and relied a good deal on Julia's easy ability to observe and categorise. Socially she was his stable element—just as psychologically he was hers—but, despite her bridge evenings and tennis and her wide nodding acquaintance, he knew her real interest in this academically tinged, upper-middle-class world was probably as superficial as his own. Julia was essentially solitary—perhaps all poets were—and his somewhat unflattering function was to guard and cherish her solitude, hoping that one day he would be allowed to hear the hidden voice.

"I suppose you're thinking about the food."

"Er? Ah, if only I could escape that."

"Would you rather I turned round and drove us home? I can think up an excuse."

"Well . . ." He was tempted; Julia's white lies were remarkably convincing and suddenly he wanted nothing more than the silent comfort of her presence in front of the waiting-room fire. But he shook his head. "No—no, I'll go in."

"Good, because it's too late now."

The front door had opened, and Mike Semple stood on the threshold. He was a slightly dramatic figure, tall with a beautiful head of genuinely silver hair, bright blue eyes, and carefully dilapidated clothes.

"Good evening, Julia. Hugh, how are you?" He shook hands a little theatrically, lightly pressing Hugh's nicotine-stained fingers in his perfectly manicured paw.

"Fine. I need a drink."

"Of course, of course." Mike's tone was of concerned indulgence, as though Hugh might be infected with his patients' instability. It was a refreshing change from the wary deference he was accorded by some of their friends. Perhaps this was because, being an expert on Balkan history, Mike was thoroughly conversant with instability.

"Where's Reg?" Julia asked as they were led into the large living room—the Semples' house was even bigger than their own (or rather, Julia's), and a lot warmer.

"In the kitchen, I'm afraid," said Mike, with a faint smile. "What can I offer you, Julia? Sherry?"

"Yes, thanks. Pour it out, will you? I'll just go and see if there's anything I can do." She whisked quickly from the room.

"Martini for you, I take it?"

Hugh nodded. He sat down in a large wing chair by the fire—this was one of the few houses he knew where a good bright log fire did not automatically mean the central heating was shut off. The heat was stimulating, everything in the room arranged for comfort and ease. Nothing beautiful—except for a faded rug in front of the hearth that Julia said was valuable—but nothing obnoxious, unless one was to take offence at a large brown stain across one wall. Was that, he wondered, the inside equivalent of the potholes in the drive —one necessary flaw to prove the fundamental soundness of the rest? He took the proffered glass and looked through the clear liquid at the distorted dance of the flame in the grate.

"You're very meditative tonight, old man. What are you thinking, if I dare ask?"

"As a matter of fact, I was wondering how you got these martinis without bubbles."

"Gentleness, my dear fellow. You don't shake them—no, never, never shake them—you stir lightly, wait a little, pour slowly. Mustn't bruise the gin. A good tutorial technique—a little mild stimulation brings out the flavour of the individual mind, but over-excitation is apt to turn the intellectual juices rancid."

"And what is the function of the ice?"

"It sharpens the wit and provides the necessary historical detachment." Mike crossed his long legs, raised his glass and smiled. "Speaking of which, I've just been dipping into Milmeyer's little monograph on Ferenczi—do you know it?"

"No, I haven't seen it yet." Hugh drank to prevent himself smiling—Mike's dinner party technique was to read up on something, preferably rather obscure, in his guests' fields of study, so that they could jump intelligently through a professional hoop or two, if they felt so inclined.

"No? I was surprised at the extent of the bibliography. Am I right in assuming that there is something of a vogue for Ferenczi at the moment?"

"More particularly in the States than here, I think. There's a good deal of thinking—and polemicising—going on just now about the orthodox analyst–patient relationship. Obviously Ferenczi fits in rather well in a superficial way."

"Yes. Couldn't one call him the first of the behaviourists?"

"He always thought of himself as an orthodox Freudian, I believe. The analyst's physical response was essentially passive and only to be used strictly analytically, that is to stimulate or assist the transference. I'm afraid I'm a bit rusty—but it does seem to me that he was quite clearly against exciting any expectations in the patient of any relationship beyond the analytic one." He took a sharp draft of the martini. "A little mild and well-modulated stimulation, but no over-excitation."

"Good. Very good." Mike laughed.

They sat in silence for a while, looking at the fire. Hugh, savouring the cool bite of the liquor on his tongue and in his throat, felt an unaccountable reluctance to bring up the subject of Alex. He took out a cigarette and put it in his mouth without lighting it.

"In point of fact," said Mike suddenly, striking a match and touching it to Hugh's cigarette, "I believe we have a—er, a client in common, don't we?"

Hugh blinked away a curl of smoke that had crept under his glasses. "Brinton. How did you know?"

"No detective genius, I'm afraid. Dr. Stand told me he'd sent Alex along to you about a month ago. Do you know Stand? No?

Gruff little fellow, but competent, I believe. Actually he came round to tell me that Worrell would have to be scratched from the varsity crew—a pulled ligament or something. He was to have been our first rowing blue in a decade. A tragedy for the college. Bad luck on Worrell too, of course. Anyway, Stand just mentioned Alex in passing."

"These things are supposed to be confidential."

"I mentioned that, though I'm sure he was only trying to be helpful. But he worried me of course—I haven't got a maniac on my hands, have I?"

"No, of course not. All the same," he drew on his cigarette, "I wanted to bring it up to you. Alex is quite willing I should do so, by the way."

"I see. Not expecting trouble?"

"Have you any reason for asking that?"

"Only that there must be something serious to cause a breach in the impenetrable dike of your discretion." He gave Hugh a quizzical glance.

"Ummm." He shrugged and threw his cigarette into the fire. "Well, let me put it this way. There is an immediate problem, the practical aspect of which might come to your attention. You haven't, by the way, noticed any falling off in Brinton's work lately, have you?"

"Nooo. His work is remarkably even. On the other hand, he cut a supervision with me last week—and no word of apology. Unusual for him."

"That's easily explained." Hugh did so briefly. "So it's possible that he may want to change rooms, in which case you might smooth the way, if you would."

"Of course. Remarkable. And what is the other problem?"

"Other problem?"

"Your implication was surely that there is likely to be a future problem too."

"Do you know anything about his background?"

"A bit. Have a drink?"

"Thanks."

Mike took the glasses and began to mix another jug of martinis at the table against the wall. "He's a local boy, of course, you knew that? Yes—father's a G.P. out on the Newmarket road. He's got a sister, several years older, Katherine Brinton—one of the shining lights in seventeenth-century literature. She's a fellow at Lady Strange—a brilliant girl. Wait a minute, there's something else."

"Yes?"

"Nothing to do with the university." He stirred the ice with a meditative clink against the glass. "Must have been just about the time I became Junior Tutor. Some kind of tragedy . . . now what?"

"Tragedy?"

"Ummm." Mike held the glass stirrer poised, half closed his eyes and lifted his aquiline nose as though to catch an interestingly mysterious scent. "Brinton, Brinton—it was the mother, I think. Killed in some curious fashion, now . . ."

"But the mother's alive."

"Surely not? No no. It must have been the mother—at any rate a female. And there was a cat involved, the family pet, I believe. Did it suddenly turn savage and bite her throat out?"

Hugh took off his glasses, breathed on them and put them on again.

"Or was it a horse? No, I'm afraid it escapes me." He carefully poured the martinis. "But surely Julia would know?"

"Perhaps."

"My dear Hugh, you intrigue me. We must pump her!"

Hugh shook his head abruptly. "Tell me, Mike, what's your impression of young Brinton?"

Mike returned with the glasses and sat down, the same slightly quizzical expression on his face. "Alex is a throwback."

"A throwback?" He took a gulp of his drink—it seemed harsher this time. Had Mike absent-mindedly bruised the gin?

"I'll tell you—ten or twelve years ago, I had plenty of undergraduates like Alex, but I haven't seen one of quite his kind for some time. He has a good mind, not particularly quick, by no means profound, but he can produce quite adequate results, without, I feel, having to labour too long. He is polite but not deferential, punctillious but not pedantic, amiable without being consciously charming, and he has a sense of humour. He works moderately, exercises moderately, and, I imagine, drinks and smokes moderately. He is good looking, but his good looks are not as striking as one might suppose from the individual features. He dresses well, very well, in what is now a rather old-fashioned style, but without affectation. All in all, a good chap. I'm afraid this is rather superficial, Hugh."

"But you're getting to something."

"Well, I'm not sure how to put it exactly. He's an excellent example of a sound public-school education, from a comfortably-off professional middle-class background—but he's rather an out-of-date model. While other men play at what they imagine the undergraduate of the fifties to have been, Alex actually is such an undergraduate. He has no affectations and no rough edges—that's rare nowadays. His type used to be one's pleasure and one's despair, now he's a curiosity. He's all of a piece—almost too good to be true. And yet I have the feeling that there is something missing. Not just a contemporary quality, but some human quality."

"Interesting." Hugh took a sip. It wasn't a bad description of someone living their life in the shadow of repressed traumatic material, trying to disprove the one fatal flaw by the perfect equilibrium of all the rest. Julia's "accident" and Mike's "tragedy" were probably one and the same thing. Hugh had had second thoughts about probing Julia's memory further, but now he knew he'd have to, after all. He sighed. "Sorry, Mike—I was off. What did you say?"

"I said that he has a very good fluid style of writing—in marked contrast to that hobbled conventional manner of speech of his. Another thing in his favour is that he always hands in his essays typed—professionally typed. Of course, I suppose perhaps he's merely afraid his handwriting would give something away."

"Ummmm."

"Might one not take this staircase trepidation—climacophobia? —as an encouraging sign in the long run?"

"It's the short run I'm fri—concerned about now."

"My dear Hugh, you positively terrify me. Shouldn't I perhaps send the boy home?"

"I don't think so. It's up to him. I wouldn't advise it."

"Quite, but I have a responsibility to the college."

Hugh looked at the handsome, smiling face. "What Alex is suffering from is not contagious, you know."

Mike gave his mellow laugh. "Do you think our wives have fallen into the *civet de lièvre*?" He stood up. "I'd better go and have a look." But at the door he turned. "Tell me—*Is* there a cat in the picture?"

"A dog perhaps."

"Of course. How stupid of me. A dog. Quite appropriate."

Hugh drew the curtains across the French windows and lit the gas fire. The room was cold but, because of its size, could be heated relatively quickly. It was half of what had been a much larger room that Julia had had partitioned off, when her father died, to make a study for herself and this, a waiting room for the patients. With Hugh's professional library along the dividing wall and its heavy, old-fashioned furniture, it was the only place in the house, apart from his office, where Hugh really felt at home.

Julia came in from putting the car away. "Oh good, you've got the fire going." The soft rain that was still falling outside had made a fine glittering mist on her dark hair. "Would you like a drink?"

He glanced at her—they hardly ever drank after dinner. Three or four emergencies over the years perhaps, not more.

"Do you know, I think I would."

"Port?"

"Anything to take away the taste of that meal."

"Oh, Hugh, it wasn't so bad. As a matter of fact she brought it off rather well, I thought."

"What on earth were those little lobsterlike things with sauce all over them and nothing inside?

"Écrevisses à la Nantua—crawfish."

"I've never eaten anything so messy in my life."

"You've had rather bad luck with fish today, haven't you?"

Hugh grunted. He vaguely suspected Reg, knowing his physical clumsiness, had done it on purpose—but no, there was no trace of humour in Reg Semple, or, fair to say, malice. "Oh and Julia," he called as she went into the hall, "bring me another fifty, would you?"

He took out his last cigarette, lit it, and sat down with a sigh in the overstuffed armchair that sagged slightly from the weight of innumerable patients. The chair, just as the original patients, derived from his deceased father-in-law, sometime Professor of Psychiatric Medicine in the University of Cambridge and without whom Hugh would have had neither practice nor position. Or, at least, would have had to work a good deal harder for them. Sometimes, in his wryer moods, he felt that his life, his wife, and his domain were nothing more than bequests from old Professor Welling.

"Sorry it took so long, I had to decant the port." She put down the tray and tossed a box of cigarettes accurately into Hugh's lap.

He grinned as he took the glass. "Welling '47, I suppose?"

"You may laugh, but you know you like it. Actually, it's prewar. Did you check the message-taker?"

"Yes—nothing." He drank. It was agreeably sweet—unlike Mike's vaunted Pommard, which had tasted of nothing much more than old earth. "Excellent. What was Reg lecturing you about all evening?"

"Semiotics."

"Oh yes? I couldn't make head or tail of the odds and ends that came my way. Sounded like a foreign language."

Leaning against the mantelpiece—she was not a great one for sitting—Julia gave her serious, secret little smile. "It probably was. Reg said it was easier to understand in French."

"Was it?"

"No. But it was quite restful. I planned the redecoration of the sitting room."

"Ah. Well, I suppose it could do with a bit of livening up." He thought it a sad, characterless place.

Julia smiled again and drank some of her port. "Mike seemed to be giving you rather a hard time too."

"Yes. I had to listen to a long disquisition on how the history of post-World War One Europe might have been entirely different if Zita had married Zog. Curious, not Mike's usual form at all."

"Perhaps you said something to annoy him."

"To frustrate him, rather." So, reluctantly, he had brought himself round to it. "He wanted to pump you about the accident in the Brinton family—tragedy, he called it—and I rather headed him off."

"So he knows about it, does he?"

"He knows something—but it doesn't make a great deal of sense to me."

Julia nodded. "Well, I don't know that I shall be able to do much better." She opened a long ebony box on the mantelpiece and took out a Turkish cigarette and lit it from a book of matches. "It happened when I was in London. Father wrote to me about it, but I didn't—I didn't pay very much attention, I'm afraid."

The slight tremor in her voice surprised Hugh. "Should you have done?"

"Well, I—I *had* known them fairly well, the Brintons, before the accident, I mean."

"I see." Watching her smoking in her cool, self-possessed way, he again felt a shade of annoyance at her failure to warn him in advance of her involvement with Alex's family, however long ago. "Tell me about it."

"It happened one afternoon when everyone was in the house —the children too, I mean. Arabella Brinton was ill at the time, or convalescent, because there was a resident nurse. Somehow or other, she managed to fall down the stairs and break her neck or fracture her skull, I'm not sure."

"*Who* fell down the stairs?"

"Why, Arabella—Alex's mother."

Hugh put his glass down on the table. "I was under the impression that Alex's mother was alive."

"Good heavens, no. Oh, wait a minute, you must be thinking of the stepmother. Ellen—no, Elaine. She was Arabella's nurse. They—Jonathan and she—were married not long after the death. A bit too soon for some people, because I remember Father saying there was some rather unpleasant gossip. Father must have been upset too, I think, because he'd been rather fond of Arabella Brinton."

"Oh. Tell me, was there a dog involved?"

"A dog?" Julia took a puff of her cigarette. "They had a dog at one time, yes. A big black poodle."

"I see. You say Arabella Brinton was ill—what was wrong with her, do you know?"

"I'm not sure. She was always a kind of semi-invalid, but very —vital, for all that. She was dark and rather languorous; she had a marvellous Marlene Dietrich sort of voice."

"How did you come to know them?"

"Let's see—I think it must have been through old Dr. Anstey, Arabella's father, who was our G.P. at one time, I believe, until he handed us on to Henry Stand and later to Jonathan—although Father and I were never ill—not then. It must have been when I was fifteen or sixteen. I was very horsy at the time."

"You were?"

"I was perfectly normal, you know."

"Yes," said Hugh neutrally. This must be one of the areas in Julia's life posted PRIVATE: NO TRESPASSING—particularly by a psychiatrist. Respect for this prohibition had been an unspoken condition of their marriage; and as far as he could Hugh refrained from exercising his professional expertise on his wife, a limitation to which he not only felt morally bound but that also, not being an introspective man, in many ways suited his own requirements. He did not read—she did not show him—her poems. All in good time. Her women friends he hardly even knew by sight; but he guessed they were not of great importance to her. Her need for privacy—almost certainly adopted at an early stage as a measure of self-preservation against a widowed father's oppressive affection—was now a matter of deep habit. Yet he was reasonably confident that one day the ice would break—and he would be there when it happened—but meanwhile the rules were observed. There was nothing to do but wait—yet perhaps he could give her a slight nudge.

"Tell me about it," he said.

"About what?" she said with unusual sharpness. "About being normal? Surely you don't have to be told about that."

"About being horsy." He smiled.

"Oh that." Her momentary agitation died as quickly as it had sprung up. "Well, the Brintons kept horses then—only a couple of elderly hacks, but they needed exercise. So I used to go out there two or three times a week and groom them and exercise them a bit. Kate, that's Alex's sister, who must have been seven or eight at the time, was becoming interested in horses then and I taught her to ride. No one else in the family was horsy—as a matter of fact, I think the animals were left over from old Dr. Anstey's day. He used to do his rounds in a dog cart until he died, I believe. Jonathan inherited the practise of course." She stopped and stared abstractedly over Hugh's head.

He kept silent, busying himself with putting out his cigarette and lighting another and drinking the port—sensing there was more to come, for, despite her apparent abstraction, there was something watchful, almost apprehensive about her stance. A familiar symptom, but one that gave no clue as to the nature of the malady.

"They had, still have, I suppose," she went on almost dreamily, "a rather spectacular old house out on the Newmarket road. The New Inn—but it's actually sixteenth century. Used to be a coaching inn. We used to get back—Kate and I—in time for tea—a proper children's tea with boiled eggs and sardines and crumpets and paste and cake, the lot. We'd have it in a real old-fashioned kitchen with the nanny-*cum*-housekeeper presiding. What was her name? Wardy, that's it, very breezy, always telling stories about her daughters and her husband who had died suddenly after eating an entire jam roly-poly all by himself. She fascinated me—she was so very cheerful and unconcerned about it. Alex couldn't have been more than three then—he was a lovely little boy, very serious, but with a ravishing smile. Sometimes when Dr. Jonathan got back from his rounds he would come into the kitchen for a few minutes—he never said much, just stood there drinking a cup of tea, he had a rather sad, gentle face, but extremely handsome. I enjoyed all that. It seems a long time ago." She slowly put out her cigarette and stood pensively staring down at the glowing bones of the gas fire and gently stroking the pleats of her red silk dress, a gesture of comfort for the forlorn.

And it must have been, Hugh thought, a dreamlike world—unimaginable to him. At that time he was studying for his finals at St. Matthew's and nursing his father through his last illness—a giant of a man turned in a few weeks into an incontinent, disgruntled, withered wreck, filled with beady-eyed jealousy of his son's health. He shook his head.

"Occasionally I'd be invited into the drawing room to have a glass of sherry with Arabella. I would have to pour it, because she would always be reclining on one of those little satin-covered love seats. She smelled marvellous and had a big emerald ring on her left hand. She talked a great deal about places and books and plays I'd never even heard of—and music. I enjoyed that too, though I don't suppose I ever said two words. Poor thing . . ."

Hugh got up and poured himself some more port and came and stood by the fire next to his wife. "Why poor thing?"

"Oh, she had everything a woman is supposed to want—two very nice children, plenty of help, lots of money and leisure, a good, hard-working husband—"

"Hard-working and handsome."

They both turned at the same moment and looked at themselves reflected side by side in the mirror above the mantelpiece. Julia was thirty-four, but could have easily passed for twenty-five; Hugh was only eight years older, but with his bald head, straying grey tufts above the ears, pouchy cheeks and thick glasses, might well have been in his fifties and was not infrequently taken for Julia's father. They both smiled at the same moment.

"Hard-working and handsome. But I don't think it really—well, suited her."

"Ummm."

"I'm afraid I'm not being much help, am I?"

"You've given me a very good idea of the atmosphere."

"But you want facts?"

"I'm a little uneasy. There's something explosive there and I'd like to be prepared. The boy is rather—fragile."

"But, Hugh, are the facts important? I mean, I thought the important thing was the reaction of the unconscious—whether what it reacted to was real or imaginary."

Startled, he turned from her reflection to look at the reality and noticed that there was a faint flush on her ivory white cheeks. "It's always useful to know the elements of what one is dealing with. I think I shall have to have a chat with Stand."

"You won't get much out of him." She hesitated, smiled. "He used to be known as Dr. Hard-to-Stand."

Hugh laughed. His sense of uneasiness was suddenly subdued by a new urgency. "I didn't know you ever rode a horse." He took off his glasses and dropped them on the mantelpiece.

"I rode an elephant once—at the zoo."

He drew her to him, his senses stirring. He was still a little worried, but the bite of anxiety sharpened the tooth of lust—or should that be the other way around? He sniffed the faint scent of Turkish tobacco that hung about her, and, across her shoulders, he saw his own froglike features reflected blankly back at him.

"To hell with the elephant."

3

He was shown into a small room almost entirely filled by a large highly-polished table.

"Doctor will be with you in a moment, Doctor. Can I take your coat?"

"Thank you, Nurse. No, I'll hang on to it, thanks."

It was almost as cold inside as out. He spotted an ancient electric fire and switched it on. Through the window he could see the daffodils in Stand's neat little garden being tossed by the bitter wind off the Fens, and on his way in from the hospital he had noticed white caps on the river. And here he was in a cold room with cold feet waiting for what he could guess would be a cold welcome. "Well, all right, I suppose so, if I must," Stand had answered over the phone to Hugh's request for a few moments of his time, "although I can't see what's so urgent about it." Nor did Hugh exactly and, mindful of Julia's warning, *You won't get much out of him,* he had almost called it a day there and then. But he hadn't, partly because Alex was beginning to remember things, albeit patchily.

Yesterday the boy's hand had been clammy when he arrived for his hour, his face wan. "I've had a d-dream," he said in a shaky voice, giving a small smile and a sidelong look at Hugh, as if expecting to be congratulated on having at last done his duty as a patient.

Hugh had lit a cigarette and waited.

Alex's perturbation visibly increased. "I think I should explain something first." He fell silent again, blinking rapidly. It was several minutes before he nerved himself to continue. "I'm afraid I m-misled you. About Mother. You see, she isn't my real m-mother. My real mother's name was Arabella—I remember seeing it on my birth certificate when I went to get my passport." He drew a long breath. "Of course, I suppose I've always known in a way. But, you see, my real mother died before I was—before I can remember. Nobody ever talks about it at home and usually—well, I mean, I must have just forgotten about it when you asked about my parents, because for all practical purposes my stepmother *is* my mother; I mean, I call her Mother and all that. . . . Do you understand?"

"Yes. Do you know what caused you to remember?"

"It was this dream." He shivered. "A nightmare, you'd call it, really. I was in the dining room at home, and I was a little boy again —I had short trousers and long grey socks on. I wasn't wearing shoes—I knew that was because it was very important for me to be absolutely silent. I was quite horribly frightened. There was something I had to do—was terrified of doing, but must do. Because I was terrified of not doing it, too. And I had to do it without being caught. It was sort of like Grandmother's Footsteps, except I couldn't move fast—I could hardly move at all. I was—weighed down, with fright, I suppose. I could hardly breathe. And there was a patch of sunlight on the carpet and I stood there for a long time not daring to cross it, although I knew I had to hurry . . . but then I did cross it. I took one of the dining room chairs, it was terribly heavy, but I had to lift it somehow, because I knew if I dragged it across the floor it would make a noise. I had to get the chair into the corner. It was awful." His voice quavered and he clenched his hands. "But I did it at last. And then, just as I'd climbed up on the chair, I heard someone behind me—I knew there was someone behind me and I . . . well, then I woke up." He gave a long sigh. "Or rather Teddy woke me up—I'm sleeping on Teddy Taylor's sofa at the moment, he's a Wykehamist too. He was shaking me—apparently I was shouting the house down."

"And you made a connection with your mother?"

"Well, you see—Teddy says I was calling out 'Mummy, Mummy,' over and over again at the top of my lungs." He lit a cigarette with a trembling hand.

"And Mummy would be your real mother?"

"I think it must be, yes—you see, I call Mother, 'Mother.' I've tried to think about it—the dream, I mean. Was it Mummy who was coming up behind me? Or was I calling for her to come and rescue me? I don't know, I just know I was scared witless. There is just one other thing—I have the feeling that it was not the first time I was doing this—it was as if it was, well, a sort of secret, regular task, if you know what I mean."

"You don't remember ever actually having done such a thing?"

"Nooo. Yet somehow—even now—it feels kind of vaguely familiar—as though it *did* happen. But I can't remember."

"Do you recall what was in the corner?"

"Not in the dream, no—but I suppose it was what's always been there. A corner cupboard—fixed rather high up on the wall, high for a small boy. Oh I see. What's in the cupboard? I'm not sure —some old plates and things I think; I've the idea I've seen Wardy take a fruit bowl out of there. That doesn't make much sense, does it?"

Hugh slapped his hands together and blew on them. No heat came from the electric fire, only an odour of singeing dust. Stand must be performing major surgery, the time it was taking him. Hugh tried to see his watch, but it was high up on his wrist, buried under layers of overcoat, jacket, sweater. He glanced round the morbid little room for a clock. There wasn't one, but there was a corner cupboard. He looked at it—what did one keep in a dining room corner cupboard? He'd forgotten to ask Alex if his had been glass-fronted—this one wasn't. Skirting the polished round table, he moved towards the cupboard. It was locked—he turned the key, and opened the door. Yes—sherry decanter half full, glasses, and an unopened spare bottle.

"Help yourself."

Hugh turned slowly, having carefully shut the cupboard door. "Dr. Stand? It's very good of you to see me like this."

"Good? What's good about it? Didn't give me much option, did you?" He was a shortish, broad-shouldered, fiftyish man of grizzled belligerence. "I mean it. Have one. I generally do at this time of day."

"Thanks, I will." He went back to the fireplace and watched Stand pour him a generous glass of sherry. He detested the stuff and never drank at midday except on Sundays, but he took the glass with a smile. "Cheers."

Stand grunted. "Well, what can I do for you?"

"I'm curious to know why you recommended young Brinton to me."

"You are, are you? That's two questions. I recommended him to a psychiatrist because he told me that if I didn't he'd find someone who would. I recommended him to you because I was a friend of old Arthur Welling's and anyone who married his daughter can't be altogether a fool."

Hugh drank some sherry—it was ever viler than he recalled.

"But let me tell you, Welchman, I regard the whole thing as a lot of idiotic nonsense."

"Psychiatry?"

"No. I'm not altogether a fool, either." He gave a startlingly toothy grin. "But there's a time and a place—and a person—for everything. Alex is as sane as you and I."

"You may be flattering us."

"Oh quite, I've heard that sort of thing before. What d'you want to know?"

"I'd like to know something about the circumstances of the death of Arabella Brinton. I understand you were the family's general practitioner at the time."

"Still am. Who told you that? That's all over and done with, you know—that's better left alone."

"Look here, Stand, if you don't tell me, someone else will— someone who probably knows less about it."

"What are you, a doctor or a blasted detective?"

Hugh swallowed the remainder of the sherry and put his glass on the table. "Case-taking is part of my job."

"Oh, all right. Arabella Brinton fell down some cellar steps, broke her neck, fractured her occiput, died within five minutes. You know the New Inn? No, well the steps are stone, narrow and well worn, easiest thing in the world to slip, particularly for a woman in a weakened condition."

"Weakened condition?"

"She wasn't a robust woman at the best of times. But she'd had a bad bout of pleurisy. She was beginning to get over that when she got a particularly virulent form of influenza, followed by pneumonia."

"Pneumonia?"

"Yes." Stand took a swig of sherry and coughed. "I—she must have done something silly, opened the window or something. She was not—not an easy patient to treat. As I said, she was never robust, and, in addition, she was allergic to penicillin. But she was over the worst of it when this happened—of course, still very weak."

"When did it happen, by the way?"

"Fourteen years ago—almost to the day. A Friday afternoon."

"What was she doing in the cellar?"

Dr. Stand rubbed his upper lip with one finger. "Is it really necessary for you to rake all this over?"

"Frankly, I have no idea. Perhaps. Did you know that Alex has no recollection of his mother at all?"

"Not surprised." He swallowed the remainder of his sherry and made a grimace. "Good thing. Why not let it lie?"

"Alex came to me because he had developed a quite specific and, for him, crippling phobia." Hugh described it, carefully observing Stand, who had no visible reaction at all. "As you must be aware, this kind of focal hysterical symptom almost invariably relates to a traumatic incident in the past. It should respond fairly readily to psychoanalytic treatment, but all the same it would make my task a good deal easier if I had an accurate and impartial picture of the background of events—and the event itself, in particular."

"You saying Alex is a mental cripple?"

"He's a young man living half a life, if that. Now, I'd like to ask you again, what was Arabella Brinton doing in the cellar?"

"Oh well, if you must have it—she went down to get a bottle."

"A bottle of what?"

"Eh?"

"Did she get a bottle?"

"Yes." Stand frowned. "The whole place stank of whisky, if you must know. What's that got to do with it?"

Almost identical—*the whole place smelled of whisky.* So the boy had been close enough for that. He opened his mouth to ask, then changed the question at the last instant—he would have to be circumspect with this military little doctor. "Was she an alcoholic?"

"She had a history of drinking. She'd had a difficult time when Katherine was born—that's the girl. It started then. She was pretty much over it when Alex came along, but that was worse—postnatal depression and her father died about the same time. So it began again. But she'd made efforts to master it. I thought she'd done so. But of course she'd just been fighting a long and difficult illness, her powers were much reduced. . . ." He frowned again and put up a finger to rub his upper lip, then changed direction and tugged at an ear lobe.

"Who was in the house at the time?"

"Well, I was, for one. In a manner of speaking. I had a small flat over the stables. I was in partnership with Brinton in those days. I'd been back from my rounds for some minutes, when Brinton came running up. . . ." He turned slightly and looked out of the window—watching the daffodils. He and they, Hugh thought suddenly, would be used to taking the same sort of drubbing. "He found her, you see, like that . . . just got in himself, a bit panicked. She'd not been dead more than ten minutes when I examined her."

"And the children—were they there?"

"Oh yes, they were in the house. Katherine was a sensible little thing, took it well. Alex . . ."

"Yes?"

"Quiet little chap. Highly strung though. Not surprising, really. But you're right—he knew something was up. Couldn't help it. Ambulance, police in the house and all that sort of thing. I had to keep him under sedation. He and his sister were sent off to an aunt in Yorkshire for the rest of the year. Best thing."

"And nobody else was there?"

"Oh well, the housekeeper creature, Mrs. Warden."

"Wasn't there a nurse?"

"Nurse Trotman. Yes, but she was off—gardening. Got back just about the time I'd finished examining Arabella."

"And she afterwards married Brinton?"

"Yes." Stand put his hands together and cracked a knuckle with the sound of a pistol shot. "Frankly, I don't see what bearing this can—"

30

"There was an inquest, of course?"

"Eh? Yes. Yes, of course. Death by Misadventure. But I tell you, Welchman, you'd better let sleeping dogs lie. You're only stirring up trouble, and I don't approve."

"Trouble? How's that? Is there some mystery connected with—"

"Nonsense. I hope you don't listen to gossip. I'm talking about painful memories. You can only hurt the innocent. Let the dead rest." The knuckle cracked again sharply.

"I'm concerned with the living."

"And what good d'you suppose it'll do the boy to know his mother was an alcoholic? Tell me that, eh?"

"If that's the worst there is to know, I'd count it a gain. Besides, obviously the problems of the living take precedence over the reputation of the dead."

"Truth at any price, is that it? You talk as though you've never suffered a defeat in your life, Welchman." His face flushed an angry red.

"My concern is professional, not personal."

"You and your brethren, you know it all, you—"

"You've been most helpful." He moved towards the door.

"What?" A wary look came into Stand's eye.

"Please give my apologies to your wife for keeping you so long."

"Wife? I'm not married." He blew out his cheeks as he followed Hugh into the cramped little hall. "Never have been."

"Well, good-bye." He turned on the doorstep. "Oh, by the way, was the dog in the cellar?"

"Eh? The dog? No—she didn't get into the cellar." For the first time there was something tentative in the doctor's manner. "Tried to hard enough. Seldom seen an animal so frantic—like a filly at the smell of fresh blood. Shoved her in the stables—wore her claws down to the pad trying to make a hole in the door. Gave her a shot too." He raised his hand and pulled at his ear lobe. "Poor bitch. Had to be put down in the end, you know."

"No, I didn't know."

"Yes—yes. Animals, you know—tragic, tragic." He sighed. "Well, good-bye, Welchman. Give my regards to your good wife— nice girl."

There was a lull in the wind and for a moment the sun shone as Hugh walked down the garden path and got into his car. He lit a cigarette. In the rear-view mirror he could see Stand in the doorway, still tugging at his ear lobe.

Well, he had some facts now, but they seemed to complicate rather than elucidate. Clearly, Stand was no source of objective information. Obviously very emotionally involved in the whole business—yes, but perhaps just a little too obviously. The only impression of really genuine feeling Hugh had received had been when he talked of the dog—*tragic, tragic.* Not a stupid man; indeed, Hugh had the idea that he might be rather clever, or at least astute, but then what was he being clever about? *Better let sleeping dogs lie—*what did that mean? For someone who so firmly proclaimed there was no mystery, he was very mysterious. Alex had undoubtedly seen something—but what? For the moment he would have to assume the worst—but what was the worst? How on earth had Arabella Brinton been able to get downstairs to the cellar in a house full of people without anyone stopping her? And why had she gone to the cellar for whisky rather than to the corner cupboard in the dining room for whatever was there—sherry probably? And why...

With an impatient movement, Hugh started the car and put it in gear. After all, he was not a "blasted detective," and these sorts of considerations were probably quite peripheral to re-establishing Alex's functional integration.

"I've been remembering about Mummy. . . ." He was dressed as neatly as ever—white shirt, wool tie, grey flannels, beautifully pressed sports jacket—but had an air of distance, as though immersed in some sleepless dream, and a vein showed mauve on his pale forehead.

"Yes?"

"I think she must have been ill a lot. I only seem to remember her in bed—loose dark hair against the white pillow. And it always seemed to be the afternoon—she'd call me into her room after lunch. She had a ring with a big green stone—an emerald, it must have been—and she used to run her hand through my hair and sometimes the little spikes that held the stone in place would snag my hair, but I didn't mind that. She would talk and I loved to listen to her—she had a voice like, like honey, but husky too. But then sometimes she would hit me—hit me on the head with the stone turned round—a sharp rap on the skull. I remember her holding my wrist tight and her face would be close to mine and there would be a kind of hissing whisper. And then I was afraid of her. And I'd go back to my room and cry and cry till Wardy came and opened the curtains and she'd say, 'And have we had a nice bye-byes, Master Alex?' and I'd pretend to be asleep. I had to take a rest in the afternoons, you see." He paused, frowning.

"Another reason I think she must have been ill was that she was always asking for her medicine. But there was something secret about it—secret and frightening. Wait a minute, wait a minute. . . ." He blinked in rapid surprise. "Of course, I remember now— it all ties up with the dream. That's it, of course! I had to go and get her medicine—that's what was downstairs in the corner cupboard. That's what I was doing in the dining room! She had a plastic cup, like the ones on the top of a thermos bottle, and I'd go down with the cup under my sweater and I'd have to fill it, but from a different bottle each time. Of course, it couldn't have been medicine, could it? And that's when she'd be angry with me—when I was too afraid to go or when I couldn't get it because there was somebody there. Kate reading in the dining room window seat or Wardy on the prowl, or Nursey coming in unexpectedly from the . . ." He stared at Hugh.

"Nursey?"

"I mean Moth . . . Mother. Good God!" His hand went to his mouth. "I'm getting mixed up, I can't, no . . . no, wait a minute." He looked out of the window. "Nursey is Mother? Or, rather, Mother was Nursey . . . is that possible? Yes—that's it, of course." He was excited, trembling. "Mother was a n-nurse once, I think— I'm sure. She's very good at bandaging one up and all that sort of thing. But then when did she marry Daddy? It must have been after Mummy died—but I don't remember any of that. I suppose it all happened when I was living with Aunt Edith." He stopped and then added irrelevantly, "Daddy has always wanted me to be a doctor, you know." Then he sat quite still and silent for several minutes.

"Let me know what you're thinking, if you can."

"Ummm? Oh well, I was thinking . . . I had another dream last night. A nightmare too." But he said it as though it were a relief. He had been on a ski slope and a little way below him, crouched, ready to push off had been the Austrian girl Anna, with whom he had had his solitary affair. And suddenly he'd been afraid, terrified

—the same feeling as he'd had at the top of the staircase—afraid for her. He knew something appalling was going to happen to her if she skied down the hill, and he tried to call out, to warn her, but he couldn't. No sound came and he couldn't move. Paralyzed, he watched her push off, gather speed, turning and skimming down the long slope. And then she fell—a sudden break in the movement, a twist and a flurry of poles and skis and kicked-up snow that obscured her falling body. Then he woke up.

"The funny thing is that Anna really did have a skiing accident —she b-broke her leg. But it was before I came; I mean I didn't see it or anything. Actually, you see, that's how I met her—I twisted my ankle on the second day, so we both wound up sitting in front of the big fire while the rest of them went off. Of course it was a bit awkward at first, I mean she had this c-cast on her leg." He blushed. "I, well, I was afraid of hurting her, you see—but she said it would be all right, and she was the expert, and it was."

"The expert?"

"Oh, she's a medical student—third year, I think. Of course she was a bit older than me. But she wasn't at all like the nurses here —I mean, well, Phil Cross's nursing birds, they're just promiscuous, but then nurses always are, aren't they?" He gasped and blushed heavily. "I mean—I mean . . ."

"Your stepmother?"

"No! Of course not, M-Mother didn't, Mother couldn't . . ."

"But she did marry your father?"

"Yes, yes of course she did—she married Daddy, not Uncle Henry." He looked bewildered.

"Do you think there was ever anything between your step-mother and Uncle Henry?"

"I do wish you'd stop calling her my stepmother," he said petulantly. "No of course there wasn't—how could there have been? I don't know why I said that. Does everything have to be significant the whole t-time?"

Hugh smiled. "Tell me a bit about your relationship with Anna."

"Oh well—she was very attractive, in a blond sort of way. I mean, I wasn't in love with her or any of that kind of thing, but it was all so natural, so uncomplicated—even with her cast and my bandaged ankle," a fleeting smile, "and, you know, I didn't feel there was anything hole-in-corner about it. Perhaps because she

34

was a foreigner. How can I put it? It was clean and, well, d-decent. Not like Hilda in Norfolk. Anna was very undemanding. I mean, Hilda made me feel guilty and sort of dirty."

"But you didn't feel guilty with Anna?"

"Good heavens, no. Just comfortable—as though it was the most ordinary thing in the world."

"Yes. Let's just go back to your dream for a moment. Did you actually see the girl's face?"

"Well, no. Her back was towards me and she was wearing . . ." He frowned. "I say, that's odd. She was wearing a sort of cloak—I mean you'd expect her to have had on an anorak. . . ."

"What colour was the cloak?"

"Dark blue, with a red-lined hood—like a nurse's cape . . . I—I say . . ."

"The hood was down then?"

"No—no, but I just caught a glimpse of the edge of it and a patch of hair. That's odd—her hair was black."

"And Anna is blond?"

"Yes."

"And your mother?"

"She's fair too." Alex smiled. "That rather knocks that one on the head, doesn't it?" He hesitated. "I suppose all this m-means something, doesn't it?"

"Dreams are certainly the unconscious expression, yes, of 'something.' Something we wish to happen, something we are afraid did happen and want to prevent—an attempt to rewrite the plot, as it were. But they are often evasive indicators. There is certainly a relationship between the fall of your unknown woman in the dream—whoever she is or represents—and your own fear of falling down the staircase. As you said earlier, your mother—Mummy—had dark hair, so the unknown figure may be an amalgam. I don't have to emphasise the sexual connotation of the word *fall*—to fall is to sin, we fall into temptation, Adam and Eve fell. When we add your earlier dream and what you have now recalled about going *down the staircase* to fetch your mother's medicine and the fear that induced in you, then I think we have made a significant step in understanding some of the underlying factors in your immediate problem."

Alex blinked. "Then that explains—explains the stairs and everything?"

Hugh shook his head. "Let me put it like this. Our work here is not a matter of answering questions—in a mathematical sense. It is more like attempting to chart a largely unknown territory. I'm not saying that every valley and every hill are not important and germane, they are, and I think you have just reached the brow of one such hill. You may start recalling quite a bit now, you know, and when you do, the view you get, as it were, may be quite startling. But your final concern is the total picture a thorough mapping will give. Every time you traverse a mountain range, you mustn't expect to see the sea."

"Yes, all right. I see that. I suppose—I suppose Mummy must have been a d-drunk, mustn't she?"

"She was very probably alcoholic, yes."

"Daddy drinks too much sometimes—quite often, in fact."

"I shouldn't worry about that—alcoholism is not inherited, you know." Although, he refrained from adding, it may be a factor.

"Oh."

"You must remember, too, that your mother, Mummy, was obviously a very sick woman at the time you're describing."

"Yes, she must have been, mustn't she? After all, she died." He sounded suddenly bored.

"Have you talked to your father at all?"

"No. Oh, he knows I'm coming to see you. He disapproves, of course. Why, do you think I ought to?"

"No—I want you to try to take it as easy as possible. How is it going in college?"

"I'm still sleeping at Teddy's." Then with a quick spurt of energy. "But I'm going to move back to my rooms today. After all, I'm not a little b-boy anymore!"

"Well, all right. But don't be disappointed if the problem is still there—it's not the important thing, you know."

"It's important to me. Teddy's a decent enough chap, but I can tell he's beginning to think I'm a bit batty."

"You are not batty."

"Well, you can't say it's exactly normal."

"A lot of 'normal' people do some very strange things, you know."

"I suppose they do. I remember the maths master at my prep school used to take his cricket bat to bed."

36

Hugh smiled and stood up. "Our time's run out." They shook hands across the desk. "Until Tuesday then."

"Right-ho." At the door, Alex stopped. "You know, one thing strikes me as odd—if all this relates to the staircase at home, why don't I have any trouble with that, but only with the stairs in college?"

"Well, let's discuss it next time, shall we?"

"All right."

Hugh sat back and lit a cigarette. The answer to that was almost certainly because the college stairs were stone, like those of the cellar at the New Inn. And Alex was probably going to see that for himself at any moment now.

Hugh took off his glasses and rubbed his eyes. He looked out of the high windows at the greyness of the day. What sort of negligence had allowed a little boy to be subjected to such a daily ordeal at the hands of a chronically disturbed mother—in a house with a nurse, a housekeeper, and two doctors? And why on earth hadn't the woman been committed? They had been asking for trouble, and they had got it. Such a thing could not have happened in the cramped quarters of his own childhood. Even now, after years of practise among them, he found it hard to get used to the callous emotional negligence of some of these middle-class families.

There was the sound of the next patient's tread on the stairs. Hugh put on his glasses and turned towards the door.

4

The Sunday morning was clear and sunny. Ducks and drakes sailed cockily on the Mill pond close under the wall to snatch and gobble the sandwich crusts and bits of uneaten cheese roll tossed down to them. A fresh breeze puckered the surface of the water and gently stirred the willows on the other side of the pond. The late rains had given body to the flow of the Granta and the rapid rush of the river over the weir added its undertone to the undergraduate chatter. Hugh slowly drank his bitter and allowed himself the pleasure of not listening to the content of the voices—the general middle-Atlantic egalitarian twang now and again pierced by an upper-class yodel, *"I say . . . !"*

In his own days as a student at London, Hugh had had to struggle to overcome a powerful East End accent—a cockney G.P. might have passed, but a cockney psychiatrist, never. For already before the end of his first-year medical studies, he had been quite decided to become a psychiatrist. Ex-C. S. M. Welchman had taken it well on the whole—"I expect you'll be wanting sherry now, lad." But they'd settled for rum and finished the better part of a bottle that night, as Hugh tried drunkenly to explain psychiatry to a father who believed that "they're all a bunch of bleeding malingerers, take my word for it, laddie," and a mother who sat anxiously listening, torn between natural pride of her son in brass-buttoned blazer and striped tie and terror of what the neighbours would say. The neighbours hadn't said anything, except from a safe distance—they had just simply ostracised the entire family. Sergeant-Major Welchman, whose opinion of humanity was much the same as the Duke of Wellington's of the common soldier, hadn't given a damn. But his wife had cried a good deal in the night and gone about with red eyes in the day. The flowers in her window box wilted from lack of water, and one Sunday on the way back from church someone spat on her. She had died that summer, while Hugh was down in Sussex working as an orderly in a mental hospital. He had been a child of her middle-age—her first, a daughter, had died before Hugh was born—and had never had a chance to do anything for her.

Fortunately he had been bright, a brightness artificially enhanced by his unusual memory, which allowed him to breeze faultlessly through examinations. His only other recommendation had been an ability to play a rather brutal kind of soccer and to hold his own in a brawl.

Hugh got up from his seat on the wall and fetched himself another pint—he hardly had to struggle against the crowd of drinkers, who parted easily with "Sorry, sir" and "No, you go first, sir." He was beginning to feel hungry for his roast beef and potatoes and the cucumber and onion salad that he'd taught Julia how to make.

He had lost his seat on the wall to a girl in a flowered dress and a large pink summer hat, so he stood and stared upstream, past Scudamore's boatyard where the river curved glinting in the sunlight and two or three punts dawdled on the water. He had never been in a punt in his life—or indeed on any boat smaller than the troopship that had transported the family from India when he was a boy.

"Hugh, my dear fellow, what are you drinking there—beer?"

"Oh, hello Mike."

"You're looking a bit grim—no wonder, if you will insist on imbibing that stuff. Well, cheers." Mike Semple raised a glass of gin and tonic. He looked anything but grim himself in baggy trousers and a baggy sweater and an old jacket patched with leather—a calculatedly insouciant English look, Julia would have said. "Julia told me I would find you here."

Hugh was conscious of a spasm of irritation. "Oh yes?" He came to the Mill to escape talk.

"Seeing how the normal half lives, eh?"

"Ummm." It was annoyingly close to the truth.

Mike laughed and, as if on command, a puff of wind ruffled his thick silver locks. "You needn't worry, I didn't come here for idle chatter. I have a reason."

"That's what I was afraid of."

"Sometimes, my dear Hugh, you remind me inescapably of that old chestnut about the child psychiatrist who'd just had his drive-way resurfaced and the little boy next door who strays onto the wet cement. The psychiatrist leans out of the window in a great taking, brandishing his fist and shouting at the infant, which of course brings out an indignant mother who remarks icily that he of all people is supposed to love children, to which he replies, 'Madam, I do—in the abstract, but not in the concrete.'"

"Yes." Hugh sighed and gave a small dutiful smile.

"Well well. The point is, I wonder if you'd be free to dine with me tomorrow night at high table?"

"Well . . ." Hugh frowned.

"I've asked Charlie Mainwaring to come along. You know Charlie, don't you?"

"The criminologist? Vaguely. Why him?"

"Because he's fascinated, you know, absolutely fascinated."

"About what?"

"My dear fellow, haven't I been making myself clear? The Brinton case, of course. I just mentioned it casually, you know, and Charlie pricked up his ears immediately. It appears to be something of a *cause célèbre* among those in the know. I thought it would be a good idea to get you two together for a little pow-wow—I've got some Mercurey I'd like you to try, unfashionable, but interesting, I think."

"I can't discuss my cases, Mike, you know that."

"I'm not just talking about *your* case. I'm talking about the curious circumstances surrounding the death of Arabella Brinton—*that's* the Brinton case."

"I understood at the inquest on Arabella Brinton the verdict was one of Death by Misadventure."

"Ah, you know about the inquest then?"

"Not exactly, I know there was one, but—"

"Then I've got something for you." Mike took a large brown envelope folded in two from his breast pocket and handed it to Hugh. "There, that's something for you to 'bone up on,' as my American men say."

"What is it?"

"Transcript of the Brinton inquest—leaves a lot to be desired, but interesting all the same. Charlie had it in his files. He's hand in glove with the Cambridge C.I.D., of course."

Hugh looked at the envelope—scrawled across the middle was the one word, *Brinton,* and neatly in one corner, Property of C. W. F. M. Mainwaring. He had a sudden impulse to throw it into the river frothing over the weir and let it be sucked down under the notice, KEEP CLEAR STRONG CURRENT.

"So I can count on you?"

"What?"

"To dine. I might even be able to get hold of—"

"No. Sorry, Mike. This sort of thing is quite irrelevant to my professional interest in Alex—Mainwaring can't help me there, and I can't help Mainwaring in whatever his interest may be."

"Well, *I* have an interest. After all I am the boy's tutor and his director of studies."

"Yes, clearly. And I'll keep you informed of anything you need to know."

"That's encouraging. All the same, I think you're making a mistake." He shook his head dubiously. "Well, I must run off. I'm the cook on Sundays, you know. Here, Chris," he said to a passing undergraduate, "be a good chap and take my glass back to the counter, would you?"

"Right-ho, Mike."

"Good-bye, then." And to Hugh's surprise Mike actually did run off—a lazy, long-legged stride across the turf of Laundress Green.

Hugh stuffed the envelope into his pocket and finished his beer. He left his tankard on the wall and made his way along Queen's Lane, through Webb's Court and over King's Bridge. The clouds were high, and the sun shone brilliantly on the river and there were flowers everywhere—but he didn't take his usual pleasure in the stroll. Drinking at the Mill or wandering about Cambridge were the only times when no patient knew his whereabouts and when he didn't think of his work. But now the Brinton family revolved uninvited in his head, with a faint undertone of irritation at Julia for having told Mike where he was. He shook his head—that wasn't fair. Mike had almost certainly made a charmingly convincing case for reaching him. He was a clever man—and a perceptive one; but what flaw of judgement had allowed him to imagine Hugh could be persuaded to gossip about a patient? Lighting a cigarette, he glanced up at the ugly stub of the University Library. Julia said that books should be housed beneath towers and domes "for soaring spirits," not in an industrial turret "made for fat bottoms." He smiled—one of his patients, Sandra Dunwiddy, worked in the library and her bottom *was* conspicuously fat—and threw away the match.

"What are you grinning for?" an elderly gentleman said quaveringly. "You're littering, young man—littering!"

Hugh laughed and began to walk more briskly.

In ten minutes he turned into the gate of Hillside. The front garden was neat and reasonably decent—though nothing to the perfection of the Semples—but completely without flowers, which might have lightened the rather dour appearance of the grey stuccoed house with its black shutters. In his latter years, old Professor Welling had developed rose fever—almost coincident with Hugh's marriage to his daughter—with the result that no planting had been done and the magnificent old rose garden had been uprooted. It was a tradition of desolation that Julia had continued and Hugh, with little time and no gifts as a gardener, had done nothing to change. "An allergy to orange blossom would have been perfectly understandable, my dear fellow," old Welling had said with his dry cackle, "but what brooks it to gain a son if one must lose one's roses?"

Against the wall by the front door was propped an old-fashioned upright lady's bike.

Hugh frowned. Social calls were not welcomed before evening on Sunday and patients were actively discouraged. He ran over in

41

his mind possible violators of the rule—Caroline Savage had a Mini, George Pressman a mauve Rolls-Royce, Bernard Handley a motor scooter. Only Madge Platten had such a bicycle, but as her sole purpose would be a Ferenczi-like sexual assault, she'd be unlikely to present herself when Julia was in the house.

He sighed and pushed open the door—it was never locked. He sniffed at the fragrance of roast beef in the hall—he hoped they would not have to ask whoever it was to lunch. He dropped the transcript of the inquest on the letter salver next to the twin telephones on the hall stand and listened. Whoever it was was very quiet. That ruled out any of Julia's bridge friends—who, anyway, he vaguely thought, were usually entertained in the sitting room, which was empty. That meant the waiting room—so either an old friend or something serious. He lit a cigarette, braced his shoulders, and opened the door.

"Oh Hugh, there you are. This is Kate Brinton. Alex's sister."

"Hello." They shook hands—hers was cool and slim and ring-less, he noticed. He had half expected to find an emerald on her finger.

"That's the first time I've ever been introduced like that." She smiled and he at once saw the resemblance to Alex, though her hair was much lighter, her eyes wider set and without the boy's long lashes, and the boniness of her features had less elegance and more strength.

"I don't suppose you want any sherry, Hugh—would you like beer?"

"No thanks, I'm awash as it is." The sun shone in through the open French window and the room was not cold. The sherry decanter stood on the table and there was a lingering trace of Julia's Turkish cigarettes on the air—and something else, a certain quality in the silence between the two women. He glanced from one to the other.

"Do we pass inspection?" Kate asked.

"I was just trying to imagine you both on horseback—in jodhpurs and little velvet caps."

"Good lord, that was a long time ago. I haven't been on a horse for years."

"No—you've both changed over to bikes, I see, though of a rather different order."

42

"Oh, Julia was always the one to take risks."

"Come on, Kate—there was nothing risky about old Maria and Beauty." A faint flush tinged Julia's cheek and she stood up quickly. "I'll just go and have a look at the beef. Are you sure you won't stay to lunch, Kate?"

"No thanks, really—I've got to get back." But she made no move and, as Julia left the room, turned to Hugh. "I wouldn't mind a drop more sherry, though."

"By all means." He refilled her glass and sat down. The full glass of sherry, Julia's uncharacteristically abrupt departure, the girl's obvious nervousness—these were not good signs; it would be some time before he got to his roast beef, and his politeness was going to be stretched to the limit. Soon she would ask for a cigarette. He lit one himself, making rather a business of it to focus her attention. He noted that her nails were bitten to the quick—a pity, for she had good hands—and, although she could hardly be much more than twenty-five, her pale, clear skin was already marked with deep lines on the brow and about the mouth.

"I don't know how much Julia has told you," she said abruptly.

"About what?"

"About Mummy's death."

"Not a great deal—she was away from Cambridge at the time, you know."

"Yes—of course. Have you talked to anyone else?"

"I've had a word with the recommending physician—Dr. Stand."

"Good heavens, don't tell me old Henry's seen the light?"

"The light?"

"Recommending someone to a psychiatrist; I should have thought he'd as soon have sent him to an astrologer." She gave Hugh a critical look. "Still, as Julia's husband, I suppose he thought you were relatively harmless." She laughed—a clean, musical sound. "Good old Henry, loyal to the last ditch. Keep it in the family. Well, I don't suppose you got much out of him." She rubbed her fingers across her forehead.

Hugh waited, but she had gone off into a dreamlike state, staring out of the window, hands folded in her lap. Her body was quite still, as though she had learned long ago not to draw attention to herself by movement—she sat upright on the couch, like a small girl at a tea party.

"You wish to tell me something specific?"

She turned her head immediately. "Yes—I am prevaricating, aren't I?" She reached for her glass, drank some sherry, replaced it on the table. "Alex came to see me this morning—at home, which is unusual enough for him."

"You live at home?"

"No, I live in college. Lady Strange. But I often go home for the weekend, or part of it. My father . . ." She shook her head impatiently. "I'm afraid I'm finding this more difficult than I thought. Do you think it would help if I lay down?" An impish grin.

He smiled politely. "I'd be interested to know what Alex had to say."

"Not what I have to say?"

"Of course. Though you are not my patient."

"You're looking at me as though I were."

"That only means I'm listening attentively."

"Sorry. Well, he wanted to know how Mummy died—all the details."

"And did you tell him all the details?"

"God, no!"

"Ummm." Hugh nodded.

"I gather that meets with your approval?"

"It's generally better to allow repressed material to come to the surface without outside prompting."

"Oh quite." She gave him a sardonic smile. "Could I have one of your cigarettes?"

"Of course." He gave her one and lit it.

"Well, I'll tell you, if Alex remembers, you'd better be sure to have him in a safe place when he does. Like a strait-jacket."

"I take it you are referring to events surrounding the accident?"

"Yes." She drew a deep breath and coughed slightly—she wasn't a smoker. "Only it wasn't an accident. Alex pushed her."

"I see." He regarded Kate carefully—Alex had said very little about her, or their relationship together. The trauma that had afflicted Alex had been dealt with by the simple mechanism of total repression, but that method had probably not been open to Kate, who must have been eleven or twelve at the time. The nature of her evasion was suggested by her physical control and the academic intellectualism in which she apparently excelled. He needed to

44

know a great deal more about the family constellation. "Miss Brinton, do you know—"

"Kate."

"Kate—do you know this about Alex of your own knowledge?"

"I didn't actually see him, if that's what you mean, but I'm sure."

"Perhaps you'd better tell me about it."

"Well, it was a Friday," she was suddenly brisk. "About four-thirty, I should think—a nasty foggy afternoon. I was sitting in the dining room window seat, reading and dreaming—I'd just discovered Keats. . . ."

"Yes?"

"Actually, I was convalescing from scarlet fever and ought to have been resting in my room, but, at any rate, there I was, a palely loitering truant in the window seat, as it were, when I heard a kind of thump, a heavy sound, a cross between a thump and a crash. I remember wondering vaguely what it could be. I don't know how long it took for me to realise it sounded like someone slamming the cellar door. Not more than a couple of minutes, I should think. Well, that was peculiar, you see—because the cellar door was kept locked and no one was allowed down there except Daddy. There was a handrail, but the steps were worn and rather dangerous. Of course, anyone *could* have gone down there—the key was kept on a hook by the door. But it was strictly forbidden. And then I heard Maida whining in the back hall. Maida was our poodle bitch. She wasn't supposed to come back into the house till teatime, so I went into the back hall to investigate. Well, the back door was open, which it shouldn't have been—I suppose Elaine hadn't shut it properly—and there was—"

"Elaine?"

"My stepmother—but she was Mummy's nurse at the time, then married Daddy with somewhat indecent haste after the death."

"Good. Please continue."

"Well, Maida was trying to push through the swing door that opens into the passage leading to the front hall. So I let her through into the passage, and there was Alex standing at the cellar door." She leaned across and carefully stubbed out her cigarette. "Is that all clear?"

"Admirably. What happened then?"

"I said something like, 'Alex, you naughty boy, what are you doing downstairs? Go back to your room at once.' He was in a sort of daze, but then he woke up and looked at me and I've never seen anyone so—so terrified and guilty-looking in my life. He went upstairs without a word. I was having a hard time holding Maida who was struggling to get at the door—the cellar door. So I—I opened it." She took a trembling breath. "I wish to God I never had. Mummy was down there, all spread out at the bottom of the steps. There was only a naked bulb, but I could see her quite clearly—she wore a green silk peignoir with Chinese characters on it, and it had floated out on either side of her, like wings. Underneath she was naked. I still see that white body sometimes, the breasts . . ." She broke off. She bit her lip sharply and her eyes gleamed with tears. "I—I . . ." She turned her head away and gave a sobbing shudder.

The day had clouded over and it was suddenly chilly. Hugh got up and shut the French windows. When he came back, she was drying her eyes with a man's handkerchief; there was no make-up to go awry. Unlike her brother, she was an extreme ectomorph—and there was something particularly fragile and strained about her lean body in jeans and an old striped shirt slightly too large.

Hugh gave her a cigarette and filled her glass; on impulse he filled the empty glass on the tray too and immediately wished he hadn't when he took a sip.

"Now, tell me, Miss Br—Kate—what makes you assume Alex pushed your mother down those steps?"

"Isn't it obvious?"

"No. From what you relate, there was a time interval between your hearing the fall and your entering the passage and coming upon Alex. Why could your mother not simply have stumbled and fallen backwards of her own accord—which Alex may have observed and descended to investigate. Wouldn't that account for the shocked panic you saw in him?"

"The door was slammed shut, *then* she fell—that's what I heard. She couldn't have slammed the door on herself because there's no handle on the inside—nothing to get hold of. It was thump—crash, not crash—thump. The crash was the whisky bottle shattering, of course. I've thought about this a great deal, you know."

"Quite." The dog was accounted for, the smell of whisky inescapably suggested that Alex had at least opened the cellar door and seen his mother—the most necessary memory to repress—but there was the singular omission of the presence of Kate, a relatively harmless recollection surely . . . or not? "I see. So Alex went upstairs —then what did you do?"

"Well, I put Maida out—she was whining and clawing at the door until I couldn't bear it. And then—then I sort of stood there frozen. I knew I ought to go down and—and help her, to see if . . . but I knew she was dead. And that's how Daddy found me— standing there with my hand on the door."

"And you told him what had happened?"

"No—I never told anyone what really happened. He just said, 'Kate, what are you doing here? Why aren't you in your room?' Sharply—as though he had already guessed there was something wrong; he's usually rather gentle. Then he must have noticed something about the door, because he opened it and looked down and said, 'Christ!' So he sent me upstairs, and after a bit Uncle Henry came up—Henry Stand—and gave me a couple of little blue pills and told me just to say that I'd been in my room all afternoon if anyone enquired. I asked him if she was dead. 'Yes, she's dead,' he said in that gruff, kindly way of his, 'but she didn't suffer.' And then the next day Alex and I were packed off to an aunt in Yorkshire."

"I see." She was certainly far too clever not to see the resemblance between her account of coming upon Alex at the cellar door and her father's discovery of her in the same position. "And you never told anyone about Alex's presence, is that correct?"

"Yes. It's not really so odd, you know, the way we lived."

"And nobody ever talked about it?"

"No." There was a slight hesitancy. "Well, I did once ask Elaine if she thought it was an accident, but she just said, 'You of all people should not have to ask about that.' I don't claim any particular merit for not having spoken up. I just thought—I *knew*—no one would believe me. Among other things, I'm afraid I had rather the reputation of a liar as a little girl. So I just didn't say anything."

"Quite." Silence and lies—the most natural of defensive measures for a deprived child; the problem was, how far had those measures been extended into the present?

"The implication being that she thought *you* had pushed your mother down the steps?"

Kate nodded, sucked awkwardly on her cigarette. "The wicked stepdaughter—what do you call that, role reversal?"

47

"And your father—did he think the same thing?"

"Yes. But he's been very nice about it, you know." She spoke dryly, but he noticed the glitter of tears in her eyes. "He's never reproached me, never hinted any such thing in word or deed. Except perhaps that he treats me with a special gentleness—as though I were an invalid, or a little bit odd mentally."

"Yes." Whether rightly or wrongly, she had been chosen as the scapegoat—yet obviously she'd not been crushed by that, had even been able to play the role, however distortedly, to her advantage. Was it that role that Alex's possible revelations would threaten?

"Of course, he was well rid of her, so he wasn't likely to have made a fuss—on balance he was probably grateful."

"How's that?"

"Mummy was pretty awful, you know. She was an alcoholic and you know how nasty they can be. She had the money and always let Daddy know it—I think she made his life absolute hell. She tortured him—she tortured us all."

"Even Alex?"

"Oh yes—she used to make him steal whisky and sherry for her. She'd tried it on me, but I refused. But she'd hated me long before that—I think she always hated me. It was she who put it about that I was a liar. She was very convincing, you know, very charming, to outsiders. By most people—Wardy included, that's our housekeeper—she was always what is called 'much loved.' I hated her, loathed her. I would cheerfully have murdered her." For a moment her lips were hard and compressed, then she smiled. "Of course, you've only got my word for all this. I might simply be a neurotic bitch working off a bit of spite or envy."

"Of course." Envy of whom? The stepmother, perhaps—or Alex? Why had she come here—to attempt to establish Alex's guilt in his, Hugh's eyes? But she was not foolish enough to imagine that anything she said would in any way directly influence his professional judgement. "All right, now if I understand you correctly, your fear is that when—or perhaps I should say if and when—Alex recollects that it was he who pushed his mother down the steps, the knowledge will in some way prove too much for him."

"Well—yes, of course, I—"

"Now surely you are aware that the emergence of repressed material relative to a traumatic event is, if handled correctly, of therapeutic value, not destructive at all, whether that event is fictive

48

or real; that is to say, whether Alex was observer or actor is not of major importance. After all, we're not policemen."

"Oh yes—all Freud's young Viennese girls were raped by their fathers, and we're all murderers. Do credit me with some elementary intelligence. When you've stripped away all the unconscious foul-ups, you're not necessarily left in the Garden of Eden—you may well be stuck with something absolutely ghastly, and it's no bloody good then going about mouthing truisms about universal guilt. It wasn't particularly bracing for Oedipus, if you recall, when he found out the truth. And how do you think Alex's conventional little shrimpish soul is going to deal with matricide? He'll go under —he'll just collapse." Her cheek was tinted with anger.

"I doubt it. Our worst terrors have their origin in the unconscious. Reality is what saves us."

" 'Humankind cannot bear very much reality.' "

"Reality is not so bad, you know."

"Welchman's reply to the poet. Where have you been living lately?"

"Cambridge."

"Well, that probably explains us both."

Hugh laughed. For a moment Kate glared at him, then she laughed too. She stood up. "Well, I expect you're right. After all, I'm an expert on seventeenth-century texts, not twentieth-century people. I must be off."

From the front door he watched her ride away, stiff and almost stately on her staid machine, her long hair stirring gently behind her.

Julia looked up from the kitchen table with such a lack of recognition in her glance that he said involuntarily, "Are you all right?"

"Of course." She frowned; she disliked being asked about her state of health, or mind. "You must be hungry?"

"Oddly enough I seem to have lost my appetite."

"I'm not hungry either." She smiled—in the softening light she might have been as young as Kate, except that, unlike Kate's tense immobility, Julia's stillness had an ageless quality. "Well, we can have it later in sandwiches. Would you like a drink? Port?"

"Perhaps. Yes. Why not?" As she went down to the half cellar that Professor Welling had built to house his wine, Hugh looked around the immaculate kitchen—not a room he was often in. The roast beef sat cooling in a pan on the counter by the stove, exuding an odour of meat. Next to it was the cucumber salad. On the table lay the brown envelope Mike Semple had given him, and the transcript of the inquest was open. Outside, the lawn was cut by a complicated design of flower beds where once the rose bushes had stood. Nothing grew there now. There was a stone sun-dial on a patch of turf in the centre. It was as bleak as an untended graveyard in the grey afternoon.

As Julia came back and handed him a glass he nodded at the transcript. "Anything interesting in that?"

"I hope you don't mind—I took it off the hall table. Where did you get it?"

"Mike gave it me—he tracked me down to the Mill."

"Hugh, I'm sorry, you're not having at all a peaceful Sunday, are you?"

"It doesn't matter." He took off his glasses and slid them into his breast pocket.

"What did Kate want to see you about?"

"She didn't tell you?"

"No, we just discussed—old times."

"Really?" And yet there had been a definite tension between them when he'd entered the waiting room. "Well, she came to warn me that Alex had pushed his mother down the cellar steps."

"Oh no!"

"Why not?"

"Not him. That's wicked. He was an angel. It's impossible."

"On balance, I think it unlikely, but certainly not impossible."

"Well, it's not at all what it says here." She riffled quickly through the transcript. "Here we are. It's Henry Stand giving evidence:

Coroner: It's quite clear then that the broken neck and the fracture of the occiput occurred when the deceased's head struck the stone floor of the cellar. But what is puzzling is the extensive fracture of the frontal bones of the skull. Perhaps you have an explanation for how that might have occurred, Doctor?

Witness: The only possible way of accounting for such a blow is that the deceased was struck by the cellar door as she was practically at the top of the steps. This is consistent with the fact that, though the entire frontal bones were shattered, the skin of the temples was not broken. I may point out that while the door is a heavy old oak one, the wood on both sides is smooth and polished with age and use.

Coroner: Thank you, Doctor. Now I am going to ask you a question not strictly in your professional capacity. But I understand that you both live and practise in the house and that you are therefore in a position to be quite familiar with the household?

Witness: Lived there for several years and a couple of years before the war too.

Coroner: Very well. Now we have the problem of how the door of the cellar came to be shut or slammed with sufficient force as to precipitate the deceased backwards and at the same time fracture the skull. In your view, would it be possible for a sudden strong current of air to exert sufficient force to cause the door to shut?

Witness: Out of the question. Door's much too heavy. Besides where would the draft come from? Nowhere. Front door's almost never opened—anyway the wind would blow in the wrong direction. And between the back door and the cellar door, there's another door.

Coroner: I see. Well, in that case, we must look to some other agency.

Witness: Obviously.

Coroner: Quite. Now, we have heard from Dr. Brinton that when he entered the hall—the front hall, as it is called—the first thing he saw was the dog scratching at the cellar door. Indeed, that is what attracted his attention to it. We have also heard from Inspector Ply that the door carried quite extensive, fresh marks of a dog's claws. Now, in your opinion, would the dog in question have been capable of pushing the door shut with the force that the extent of the injuries leads us to suppose must have been exerted?

Witness: Absolutely. She's a strong, healthy young poodle bitch. Knock you or me over if she wanted to, if we weren't ready for her.

Julia laid down the pages. "That's it. That's all there is. Nothing about the children, except that someone says they were upstairs taking their naps."

"The dog did it?"

"That's what the jury thought. Death by Misadventure. Doesn't that rather invalidate Kate's version of events?"

"On the face of it, it does. But she doesn't say she actually saw Alex do it."

"Then how can she possibly know?"

"She can't. As a matter of fact, I have the impression she's playing a rather elaborate neurotic game, but to what end I'm not sure."

She sighed. "Kate was always good at games."

"Julia, have you got something against her?" He was puzzled.

She looked away, looked back at him. "No," she said in a low tone, "no—I've got something against myself. . . ."

Hugh drank some port and waited, watching her as she stared down at the transcript of the inquest.

She raised her head. "It's just that I'm rather ashamed of myself. I didn't do anything, you see—oh of course when I got Father's letter about Arabella, I wrote. But I could easily have come back— even for the weekend—and I didn't."

"Do you think it would have made very much difference?"

"It would—would have made a difference to me."

"How?"

"We could have talked. She must have desperately needed someone to talk to, to understand, to hold her hand—and all she got was Elaine!"

"She had her father. From what she told me, her father seems to have been her only reasonably successful affective connection in the family."

"He would have been useless in an emergency."

"Well, it's true he'd had a shock—a double shock, if he really did assume that Kate had pushed her mother, as she tells me he did, but—"

"She told you that?" Julia frowned.

"Yes. Granted that Brinton doesn't sound a very well-balanced person, I really don't think a visit would have been very productive. For one thing, Kate wasn't there—she was sent away almost immediately with Alex to a relative in the North."

"Yes, I think I did hear that."

"So what good could you have done? If anyone, it was Brinton who needed his hand held. Aren't you perhaps taking this a bit too personally?"

"You mean I'm only thinking about myself? Maybe." She gave a wintry smile. "But there was more to it than that. I suppose I ought to tell you, although it's silly—nothing at all really. But it might have a bearing. In those days—before I went to London—I had a crush on Dr. Jonathan. I didn't see him very often—I told you how he used to come into the kitchen sometimes while we were having tea. He *was* a handsome man—physically rather like Kate. But I don't suppose he'd said more than a dozen words together to me." She paused—as though listening to herself, for herself. "Then one day, after tea, my motor bike wouldn't start; as a matter of fact, I'd fixed it so it wouldn't. So Jonathan very nicely drove me home. I'd planned exactly what I was going to say—I must have been a rather designing young woman—and the astonishing thing was that it worked! More or less. He didn't laugh, or pat me on the head or talk to me like a Dutch uncle. I didn't recognise it then, but he put on the noble suffering male act."

"Act?"

"Yes, I think so. It came out in an easy, practised way, as if he'd done it often enough before. It had no particular reference to me. It was just because I was handy. He stopped the car and kissed me, and he unbuttoned my blouse and put his hand on my breast. I was overwhelmed—nobody had ever done that before." She raised her hand and touched herself for a moment. "And all the time he talked —about needing love and help and recognition, what a terrible burden Arabella was to him."

"Because of her drinking?"

"He didn't say that—and I didn't know about it. He was just the sort of man who always had to have someone else to blame his troubles on. But at the time it was all overpowering. I was half thrilled, half shocked—and a little frightened too. I remember stroking his head and calling him my poppet—when you're caught off guard at that age, the language of love tends to revert to the nursery level." She smiled. "But it wasn't funny at all. I was awkward and finally, I think, embarrassed, more than anything else. I never stayed to tea again, so I didn't see him—except once in Heffers when I hid behind the stacks. A month later I was writing an elegy about the divided heart and love's insuperable barriers. Soon after that I went up to London and forgot all about it."

"But you hadn't forgotten?"

"No, not really. Of course I'd taken up with Martin—Martin the great poet—but I hadn't really forgotten Jonathan. Not just Jonathan—everyone, everything at the New Inn. That's what makes it so inexcusable. . . ."

"Because Jonathan—rather than Kate—might have needed you, is that it?"

"No. Oh, he needed someone of course, but not necessarily me. Anyone would have done. If Elaine hadn't been handy, he might even have married Wardy." There was a bitter undertone to her words that surprised him.

"Look, Julia," he reached over and took her hand, "try not to let this worry you. You have nothing to reproach yourself with, believe me. In any case, it's all over and done with now."

"Is it?" She stared at him. Her eyes very blue. Her face totally concentrated. Then her hand relaxed in his. "You may be right," she muttered, "perhaps I've been making a mistake. But don't you think that . . ."

"I think," he said slowly, carefully, "that when and if Alex begins to recollect his role in all this, the air will be cleared. Obviously the Brintons have lived in an atmosphere of extraordinary misunderstanding and suspicion—a lack of trust that has caused the most appalling emotional deprivation. Anything would be better than that."

She withdrew her hand. "You have great faith in the healing properties of the truth, haven't you?"

"Well," he smiled, "truth is largely a matter of adjustment, you know—a way of looking at the facts that is satisfactory and not inhib—not impeding."

"You're very confident. But supposing, just supposing, the facts are not as it says here," she tapped the transcript, "and not what Kate believes. What if Alex remembers differently?"

"No revelation is likely to be damaging, not if it's handled properly. And, after all, I shall probably have something to say about that when the time comes." He leaned back and lit a cigarette. "Do you know, I think I'm hungry now."

As he watched her carve the beef and cut the bread in her quick efficient way, he felt encouraged. Even when it was ostensibly related to others, she did not often talk so clearly, and yet so tentatively, about herself. The sacrifices offered to old buried guilts—the self-inflicted deprivation of garden and flowers, of dogs and horses, even of warmth in the house, and, above all, of children—was she not in her own secret way at last beginning to be uneasy about their efficacy? *Perhaps I've been making a mistake.* The arrival of the last bus after a long wait in the cold. The first crack in the ice. It was perhaps a beginning.

Hugh looked down at the plate Julia put in front of him. And maybe one day she would come to call *him* "poppet" too.

5

He finished writing the last word on the day's case notes at the Clinic—a bureaucratic procedure that he rarely bothered with for his private patients. It was almost midnight and his little office was grey with cigarette smoke. He took off his glasses and rubbed his eyes. It had been a particularly beastly and difficult Monday, ending with a savagely hostile session with Sandra Dunwiddy. One more thing to be done—and then he could lock up, if Julia was back, and go to bed. He pressed the play-back button on the message-taker:

"This is Dr. Welchman's residence. Dr. Welchman is not available at the moment, but if you . . ." And then, "Hello, you old cocksucker . . ." He sighed, but listened patiently to Madge Platten's feast of obscenity. She often showed remarkable streaks of inventiveness, but the basic message always remained the same—an unrelenting nymphomaniacal hatred of the male. He was not touched by it anymore than he was by a patient's stifled words of love; not sharing grief or elation, never censuring malice or celebrating joy—the thin line of detachment could easily become a steel rail of dissociation, every patient being treated with an even-handed boredom. Yet, of course, one always had one's secret favourites, just as one would for children. . . . He was not often given to such reflections. He rewound the tape and, putting on his glasses, heaved himself out of his chair and went downstairs.

He stepped out of the front door onto the gravel and looked up; a light shone softly through the rose-coloured curtains of their bedroom—so Julia was home. He was glad. Sometimes her Monday and Friday bridge evenings lasted till one o'clock in the morning, or later, and then she would go and sleep alone in her own stark little room.

It was a fine starry night, no wind at all, no moon, and the darkness had wrapped away the bleakness of the landscape. For once he did not mind the chilliness of the air. He had a sudden longing for flowers, for the scent of bloom and blossom. Perhaps they could get a real gardener instead of a man once a week to mow the lawn. No, one day, perhaps, Julia would take up gardening of her own accord—an activity that she had always refused, probably because of its association with her one memory of her mother, a lady in a summer dress kneeling at the border's edge, who had deserted her by death. It was an issue that couldn't be forced. No more than the other issue—a child or children—that he'd always hoped for, but had not come. And perhaps now, after yesterday's crack in her impenetrability, an opening was possible. And yet there seemed to him a sadness on the air, a sadness in the house that made him reluctant to reenter.

Why? Down to his left the headlights of a car swivelled as it turned into The Lane. Because, of course, on his way out of the hospital this evening, he'd discovered that an old patient, Bob Lummis, was in the medical wing; Bantock had been unavailable, John Grantham "in conference," and there had appeared to be no one responsible on duty.

The car raced briskly up The Lane, then swerved suddenly into the driveway and came to a skidding halt in front of the house. Hugh hardly had time to register the impulse to dart back indoors before Mike Semple alighted from the driver's seat.

"My dear Hugh, I saw your lamp in the window, or door as it may be, and couldn't resist it. You're looking very squirearchal."

"Ummm." He made an effort, "Good evening, Mike." Despite the lightness of his tone, the Senior Tutor was unaccustomedly sombre in his dark suit and tie and long black gown.

"Do you have time for a word or two?"

"Well . . ." Mike was a well-known night owl, and Hugh felt rather like the mouse about to be pounced upon.

"No idle chatter, I assure you. About young Alex Brinton."

"Then, of course. Come in." He led the way into the hall. "Let me have your gown. What can I give you to drink?"

"Drink? What about some of your father-in-law's port—or is that sacrosanct?"

"Not to me. Come along, we'll see what's there." Wearily, he took Mike into the kitchen and down into the small brick-lined cellar with its sanded floor.

"I say, Hugh, what a splendid place—and he's got some treasures here too: '27, '48, '34—and '31! These are worth a fortune at today's prices. Of course, the old fellow must have *made* a fortune out of that book of his."

"*Elements of Modern Psychiatry.* Take your pick."

"Ah yes—Welling's *Elements.* A classic in its day." Mike spoke off-handedly, moving along the rows and racks, almost sniffing at the wine. " 'Britain's answer to Freud.' Do you remember the dreadful guff in the obituaries?"

"Yes. Come on, Mike."

"Dare we try the '31?"

"Why not?" Hugh reached forward to seize a bottle, but his hand was caught firmly by Mike.

"Good heavens, man—not like that. Allow me, do."

"Go ahead. The stuff's on the table there." What Hugh really wanted was a cup of tea. He watched with impatient admiration as the tutor carefully slid out the cork and decanted the port over a bright light on the table that made the wine a beautiful translucent crimson. He knew that he himself would be incapable of managing such a feat without shaking the bottle or mangling the cork—sometimes it was as much as he could do to light a cigarette. He lit one now. "What's all this about, Alex?"

"Ah." Mike took two large long-stemmed balloon glasses from the shelf, carefully wiped the insides with a clean white cloth and filled them half full. "This ought to be quite an experience." He lifted his glass delicately to his nose. "I've had a very interesting evening."

Hugh thought of his own warmed-up soup and bread and butter, case notes and too many cigarettes. He took a swig. "Shall we go up?"

"Let's stay here—it has rather the air of a crypt down here, the proper atmosphere for the act of reverence we are about to perform; which you have already performed, I see."

"I don't mind." He felt for a moment a stranger in the house —a not unfamiliar feeling; he had long ago accepted the fact that he only really felt at home in his consulting room or the waiting room. "Can we get on with it?"

"Alex, you mean? Of course, of course. You must forgive me. Well, I dined with Charlie—we missed you—and very interesting it was, as I've said. But the *pièce de résistance* was afterwards. Charlie had invited along the policeman who'd been in charge of the case all those years ago—a big bug now, Chief Superintendent of the Cambridge C.I.D.; as Charlie said, the horse's mouth."

Hugh grunted, but, despite himself, became more alert.

Mike took a half mouthful and slowly rinsed it and swallowed. "Ah! Well, the main point of it was that this fellow, Ply his name is, is convinced the first Mrs. Brinton was murdered."

Hugh took another large draft. "By whom?"

"That's the beauty of it—by anyone, apparently."

"Anyone?"

"Anyone in or about the house at the time—the good Dr. Brinton himself; his colleague Dr. Stand; the R.N. who was looking after Mrs. Brinton, Elaine Trotman, afterwards the second Mrs. Brinton; Mrs. Warden the housekeeper; and both the children, Katherine and Alex Brinton."

"Why?"

"Well, they all had motives apparently. The policeman, naturally enough, thinks it was money—and it's true that Arabella Brinton was extremely well off; she was an Anstey, you know, and they owned a great deal of property at one time, which she inherited from her father, who was a G.P. too, by the way. The bulk of it, including the house, had been left to Alex, in trust till he was twenty-one—that was in his Grandfather Anstey's will—the old man was rather old fashioned about women apparently. But Arabella still had a nice bundle to leave. Most of that went to Brinton, and of course, as trustee, he got control of Alex's share, which makes him the leading suspect. Then Dr. Stand got ten thousand— he'd once been engaged to Arabella, you know. Even Mrs. Warden got two thousand—sorely needed: delinquent daughters or something of the sort. And Nurse Trotman got Brinton himself, although from what I hear, apart from financially, he wasn't much of a catch. Still there's always something a bit fishy about the doctor-nurse business, isn't there?"

"Julia was a nurse."

"My dear Hugh, how inexcusably clumsy of me—but you know what I mean. . . ."

"All this isn't much more than local gossip, is it?"

"Gossip has a function, you know—several, in fact, some of them quite educative. But the point is—"

"All the same, I don't think I'm terribly interested in hearing about all this."

"Charlie had the deuce of a time getting the policeman chappie to come along—though once he realised I was Alex's tutor he was quite keen. Sniffed something in the wind, you know—he's not unlike a dog actually, an elderly retriever perhaps, whose teeth are going back on him but still has the old instincts. Wanted to know what my interest was—I had to get high-falutin' and throw Laing and Foucault at him."

"You didn't mention my name, I hope?"

"Coupled with Foucault?" Mike grinned. "Of course not, my dear fellow—give me credit for a little discretion."

"Mike, can you honestly imagine a five-year-old boy—or an eleven-year-old girl, for that matter—pushing his mother down the cellar steps for the sake of a few thousand pounds at twenty-one?"

"Obviously not. But there is more to it than that—a lot more. The woman was a chronic alcoholic and a nasty one—she probably made everyone's life pretty much hell in that house and—"

"But it emerged quite clearly at the inquest that the dog was responsible."

"Oh, so you've done your homework, have you?" Mike smiled faintly.

"I've read the transcript." Hugh emptied his glass and dropped his cigarette on the sandy floor and stepped on it. "Look, don't you think the police investigation—"

"The police investigation was quashed from the top. The Chief Constable at the time, or whoever it was, was a personal friend of the Anstey family. Ply says he was told not to push it, but there were some things about the circumstantial evidence that worried him, let alone the family situation. And that hasn't changed a great deal—Brinton himself is halfway to being an alcoholic these days apparently and—"

"Really?" Hugh slowly took out his nearly empty box of cigarettes and lit one. "How does your policeman know that?"

"A couple of cases of drunken driving, and several times he's been picked up in the streets practically insensible. There's also been some hanky-panky with female patients, though never any charges brought. Altogether a rather undesirable type. But then the stepmother doesn't sound very agreeable either—a rather dauntingly cold fish. And the housekeeper apparently had, and still has, very much an eye to the main chance. As for Dr. Stand, the policeman seemed to be sure he was concealing some sort of evidence. But that's hardly the point; I—"

"Quite."

"The main thing is the boy's memory."

"Only up to a point. Retrieval of unconscious material is only a part of the therapeutic process and—"

"But what about the others involved?"

"The others are not my patients."

"Hugh, I'm inclined to take this seriously." Mike set his glass down on the table. "I'm quite aware that the actual content of the memory is not necessarily the vital thing as far as the therapy goes. But what if the boy remembers having seen someone murder his mother? His father perhaps—or his sister? I suppose the members of the family are aware that Alex is undergoing treatment?"

"I believe so. But I don't see—"

"Isn't he a bit of a walking time-bomb? And mightn't somebody try to defuse him before the explosion?"

Hugh smiled faintly. "Aren't you being a little melodramatic? If somebody did shut the door in Mrs. Brinton's face and the boy saw it, we will probably have to try to analyse what actually happened—but my guess is that it would turn out to have been an accident and certainly no one would be able to prove otherwise; it certainly couldn't have been a premeditated act. Nobody is going to be, well, legally jeopardized by anything a five-year-old may or may not have seen—the only danger is to Alex's own mental stability, and I'm confident we can handle that."

"You're assuming all the other people involved are mentally stable but—"

"No, I'm not."

"—but supposing they aren't, then whether the danger is real or imaginary, they may still feel desperately threatened and could conceivably take appropriately desperate action. You've got to admit, Hugh, it is at least a possibility."

"I think it's largely academic." He frowned; he reached over absently and poured some more port into his glass. "Why exactly does your policeman friend refuse to accept the dog's responsibility for the death?"

"He's no friend of mine, but he's no fool and not being needlessly perverse, I'm sure. In order for the dog to have got to the cellar door, it would first had to have gone through a swing door from the back hall to the passage. When Ply examined that swing door it moved easily on its spring hinge, but he noticed that the door was covered with still-damp mud and several claw marks. Why should the dog have clawed at a door it could easily have pushed open? Because, Ply opines, in fact the dog could not have opened it at all —the spring, therefore, must have been loosened or readjusted between the time of the murder and the police's arrival on the scene. The dog was deliberately made the scapegoat, or, to mix the metaphor a bit more, the dog was a red herring. Somebody *did* let the dog through—but after the cellar door had been slammed and the deed done."

"I see." What had Kate said? *I let her through into the passage, and there was Alex standing at the cellar door.* That suggested that Kate was telling the truth . . . a confirmation that did little, however, to obviate the false tone of her anxiety on Alex's behalf. Her real fear probably related to a different suspicion, that—who?—her own father had done it? Had she allowed herself to be suspected—by her stepmother, perhaps by Stand too—in order to divert suspicion from him, and was not perhaps her accusation of Alex simply a continuation of that diversion? And if Alex had seen his father— Dr. Brinton, alcoholic, unstable, dependent . . . "Ummm? What, Mike?"

"I am concerned about my pupil, Hugh."

"Yes." He emptied his glass in two swallows. "There may be something in what you say."

"I thought you ought to be informed. I—I'm fond of that boy."

Hugh looked closely at the Senior Tutor, unwontedly serious, tired, his treasured wine untouched on the table, and he felt a sudden flow of sympathy, as from one childless man to another. How had Mike described Alex?—*an out-of-date model,* that was it, *almost too good to be true.* Not such a bad description of Mike himself —what could be more out of date than the type of academic English gentleman he strove so hard to be? The identification with Alex would be natural—and sad. Behind the façade, the bonhomie, the fondness for gossip and "keeping abreast," would lie a similar insecurity, perhaps an old, unresolved trauma too. As far as he knew Mike appeared to have no history—to have sprung into Cambridge already the bright youngish academic, now a valued committeeman and pillar of his college. "Yes, I see. Well, thank you."

"Good." Mike grinned, all his buoyancy regained. "And now we have another serious matter to discuss, eh?"

"What?" Hugh was suddenly dog tired.

"Why, the port, my dear fellow, the port!"

Julia was sitting cross-legged on the bed reading, the light of a small rose-shaded lamp falling directly onto the book and casting a pink radiance onto her face. It was a familiar position—the dark hair swinging forward onto the cheek, the long lashes unblinking, the hands still on the book—a position of tranquil concentration.

He was caught by a cough.

She looked up, and he went and sat on the bed beside her. He glanced at her book and she turned the spine so he could see: *The Poetical Works of John Keats.* She was reaching back into the past. He was encouraged—that could be nothing but good.

"You're being very traditional tonight." Usually it was poets he'd never heard of, women mostly with vaguely ecclesiastical names—Bishop, Plath, Sexton. . . .

She smiled and, as she leaned past him to put the book on the bedside table, he thought, with her warm fresh rosiness, her eyes bright, the hair shining thickly, she might have been seventeen—back from an afternoon's ride at the Brintons'.

"Who was your visitor—not a patient, I hope?"

"Ummm? No—no. It was Mike Semple." He took off his glasses and rubbed his face and sighed.

"Gossip?"

"Yes and no. I gave him some port." He stood up and removed his jacket and dropped it on a chair. The room was pleasantly warm —Julia must have turned on the heat. Nice of her, because she really liked a cold bedroom with a wide-open window. He hesitated— looking at her without his glasses, soft in her roseate pool of light, she was as beautiful, mysterious, and unchanged, as when he married her. He didn't want to talk, to break the moment; he wanted to take her in his arms. But she wouldn't react—and he wouldn't rest easily himself either, he realised—until he had told her. "Actually, he came to tell me about Alex. He'd been spending the evening with Mainwaring and with the policeman who'd been in charge of the Brinton case." He started to take off his tie.

"I see. What fun for Mike."

"I don't know. As a matter of fact, I've seldom seen him so

serious." The knot of his tie had tightened into a hard ball, he wrenched at it and it parted with a crack.

"About Alex?"

"Yes—and the others. You see, the problem is," he tossed the tie at the waste paper basket and missed, "the problem is that the policeman's convinced Arabella Brinton was murdered."

"Oh Hugh—but the inquest, the dog . . ."

"According to this chap, the evidence was almost certainly doctored to make it look as though the dog had done it. It's a bit technical, but when one puts it together with what Kate told me, it makes sense. In fact, I'm inclined, after tonight, to give a bit more weight to Kate's account of that afternoon."

"But she thinks Alex himself—"

"That's a conclusion that has its basis not so much in anything she saw, I believe, as in something she didn't see, doesn't want to face —or face the possibility of. The trouble is that anyone might have slammed the door on Mrs. Brinton—they were all there, or thereabouts. The children, the nurse, Brinton himself, the housekeeper, even Dr. Stand . . ." He took off his shirt and regarded his torso in the mirror—the thick mass of hair from throat to loins had begun to turn grey before he was thirty and was now almost white.

"Hugh, surely murder is rather far-fetched—why *not* an accident?"

"I agree. It might have been a simple reflex action—as one does tend automatically to shut an open door. Or a psychological accident—what the Germans call a *Kurzschluss-Handlung*—a sort of short-circuit action that's quite out of harmony with the normal personality." He kicked off his shoes, let his trousers drop and stepped out of them. "But whatever the degree of deliberation, the significant thing is the subsequent efforts at concealment—if this Ply fellow is right."

"You mean what Alex is concealing?"

"Repressing. Yes, that too." He removed his underpants and stood, naked, holding them dangling from one hand. "I think perhaps I'm going to have to try abreaction." As he spoke, he realised he'd already made the decision.

"Why?"

"Well, for one thing, the father—your charming Dr. Brinton— seems to be quite seriously unstable these days."

"You think there's some kind of danger to—"

"Mike thinks so, but then Mike's a bit of an old woman. All the same," he threw the underpants onto the chest of drawers, "one must try to avoid any possibility of risk, and I'd rather have whatever's repressed come out in a controlled situation at this point. Move over a bit, Julia."

She shifted to one side and he got into bed.

"Are you sure abreaction will work?"

"I'm not sure of anything. Might, might not—some patients abreact very little."

"He has an appointment tomorrow, doesn't he?"

"Yes, but it's too complicated at the house. I'll fix it up at St. E.'s later in the week—I'll want him under observation for a bit afterwards, anyway."

"I see," she murmured, her mouth close to his ear, her body warm against his.

He pulled her down and she made love with a strong but almost abstract intensity, as though she would absolve herself of all particular thought or feeling, bury the sharpness of her anxieties in his thick body, his stolid mind, just as she interred the old memory of roses in the present bleakness of the garden. It did not strike him as ironic that while his professional function was to evoke and focus recollection, for Julia he was the instrumentality of oblivion. His role was acceptance without analysis; if there ever was to be a flowering, it would not come through forcing.

Later, caressing her, he was aware of an unrelieved tension in her body. He said, almost tentatively, "I know you're worried about Alex."

She made a little grunting noise—of assent or protest?—and entwined her fingers in the hair of his chest.

"And the rest of them too, of course. It doesn't do to exaggerate, and I think . . ."

Suddenly her hand tightened on his chest and her whole body stiffened against him. "Oh Christ!" And she began to sob.

He touched her, stroked her, moved her. He could hardly remember her so demanding, so pliant—so suppliant.

"Oh God, Hugh, oh God," she cried out into the warm, close night of their bedroom.

That cry of naked anguish had exhausted her and she fell into a deep sleep. He pondered the nature of her pain, but—whether it was for Kate or for her own close-held self—it seemed to him that her tears, still damp on his flesh, were the first brief flutter of rain after a long dry season.

"Dear wife," he murmured and instantly slept.

6

Twelve twenty-four. Alex was a quarter of an hour late. Hugh stood up and looked out of the high window. It was a breezy, blustery day —he could just see the chimneys of the Semples' house up The Lane, smoke coming from one, shredded and dispersed almost instantly by the wind. He wondered if Reg kept a fire burning all year round. What were they doing—these childless couples in huge houses: Hillside, Hilltop, and what was the name of the Brinton place?—New Inn? And with only a beleaguered remnant of domestic service, like Mrs. Nance who'd been in the house twenty-five years, dutifully serving the "Old Professor," playing with the little girl Julia, whom she probably loved more than her own wayward daughter. For Mrs. Nance, Hugh was an intruder. Houses without life or warmth—no dogs or cats or horses or chickens. (The Welchmans had kept chickens once—in the married quarters at Aldershot. He remembered his mother calling, "chick-chick-chick!") No flowers. But even during the war there'd always been geraniums in the window box in Hackney.

He went back to his desk and automatically lit a cigarette. Twelve-thirty. It was quite unlike Alex to be dilatory. Had the boy been home? He recalled Mike's words: *Mightn't somebody try to defuse him before the explosion?* That was hardly the point, but all the same a highly-charged emotional catharsis at the scene of the—on the spot, was hardly to be desired. The light on the phone flashed and Hugh lifted the receiver instantly.

"Welchman speaking."

"Oh—Hugh? This is Kate—Kate Brinton. I just wanted to tell you that Alex will be along in a few minutes. He's been here with me—at Lady Strange—but I've just sent him off."

"Good. Thank you very much."

"He's all right, I think. There've been some developments."

"I see. Well, I'm sure we can deal with that."

"What a comfort you are." There was a pause and for a moment he thought she had rung off. Then, "Hugh—could you see *me*?"

Hugh hesitated. "Do you mean professionally?"

"I don't know—but I suppose I am sort of part of the case, aren't I? Although I must confess I hadn't actually thought of paying."

"Ummm." He smiled faintly. "Well, when did you have in mind?"

"Today?"

"I'm afraid I'm seeing patients until eight. But I suppose you could drop round, oh, say about nine-ish?"

"You couldn't come round here to Lady Strange, could you? I loathe riding my bike in the dark."

Again he hesitated—she was rather a tiresome young woman, and it was hardly part of his duties to go rushing round Cambridge comforting his patients' relatives. On the other hand, there was Julia's very definite anxiety about her, and it would certainly do no harm to know a little more about Dr. Brinton. "Perhaps that could be managed. Yes, all right."

"You're a poppet. Nine o'clock then? *Ciao.*" And she rang off.

Nine. A nuisance. He was going to have to miss his lunch because of Alex, and tonight he'd have to bolt his dinner for the sake of the sister. He pressed the buzzer that rang the patients' white phone downstairs.

"Julia? Alex will be here in a few minutes—show him right up, would you? And I'm afraid I'm going to have to skip lunch."

He stubbed out his cigarette and tried to clear his mind. The Brinton family was beginning to occupy too much of his attention, at the possible expense of the patient. There was a sea of Cambridge gossip surrounding this business, in which he must be careful his professional objectivity did not founder. He acknowledged to himself that Kate interested him in some curious and rather distasteful way—*poppet* indeed!

"I'm sorry I'm l-late."

"That's all right, old chap. Come in, come in." He got up and shook Alex's hand—firm but slightly damp. His face was flushed, but he seemed steady enough.

"I'm afraid I'm a b-bit of a mess," he said as he sat down, running his fingers through his usually immaculate hair and leaving it spiky and ruffled. His tie, too, was awry. "Did K-Kate phone you?"

"Yes."

"Well . . ." he began, then stopped.

"Take your time. I gather something has occurred?"

"Yes, that's it. The trouble is there's so m-much of it." He hesitated, frowned, then gave a little laugh.

"You remembered something?"

"Yes. No—I mean, yes, but that's not how it started." He took out a packet of cigarettes—he was smoking Hugh's brand now. He lit a cigarette, then carefully slid his lighter back into its pouch.

"There's no hurry—I'll run you over into lunchtime."

"Oh. That's very d-decent of you, sir." He took a deep breath. "Well, it started on Sunday—Sunday morning. I went home—to the New Inn, you know—I thought I'd have a chat with Kate and find out how Mummy actually did die. It seems that she fell down the cellar steps and, well, b-broke her neck, I suppose. It left me sort of dazed, yet it seemed to make sense—I mean, it explained why I . . . the whole staircase thing. In a way. I stayed at home all Sunday, then on Monday I went for a long walk and tried to puzzle it out —you see, it seemed to me that I must have known how Mummy died, I mean, at least unconsciously. I thought I would ask Daddy, but somehow I couldn't screw up the courage—I think really I didn't *want* to know.

"Then last night—I was still at home—I had a rotten night, I couldn't sleep for thinking about it, but I suppose I must have dozed off in the end. When I woke up it was just beginning to be light, and I suddenly thought, why not go and see? So I—I did." He drew on his cigarette, then went on in a voice that shook a little.

"I must have been half asleep still, b-because it was like a dream—a nightmare. I kept saying to myself, don't be scared, Alex, don't be scared—but I was t-terrified. All I wanted to do was to turn round and run up to my room and b-bury my head in the pillow. But I had to go on, I can't explain it. It took an age, but there I was at last. I took the key down from its hook and opened the cellar door —it was dark down there, and I could feel the cold coming up and the smell of d-damp. Then I leaned in and switched on the light, and it was as though—as though . . ." He gave a slight sob, shook his head. "It was as though I had switched on my memory. She was lying d-down there on her back, n-naked lying there . . . her hair was all spread out . . . I knew she was dead, but her eyes were open, you see and . . . and she looked so angry, so t-terribly angry. . . ." He shuddered and put one hand across his eyes. "And I stood there, I remember standing there and I heard myself saying, 'Oh please, God, no. Please, God, no,' over and over again. You see, I knew—knew it was my fault." He wiped the back of his hand over his eyes leaving a streak across one cheek. "And there was this smell, you see—this awful smell, Mummy smell—I suppose now it must have been whisky—and yet not so awful because when she smelt like that she was always m-much nicer. Her m-medicine. But I hated it then, and I shut the door to keep the smell away . . . and then . . ."

"And then?"

"What? Oh—and then . . . well, it all seems a bit confused, but Kate was there telling me to go up to my room and Maida—that's the dog, we had a dog then, you see—sort of growling and whining. I was frightened of Kate, she used to order me about an awful lot, but I was glad she was there then." He stopped, looked down at the cigarette in his hand, stubbed it out slowly in the ashtray. He sat on in frowning silence.

"Did you remember anything else?"

Alex nodded. "Yes. I shut the door, you see—this morning, I mean. Then I went into the kitchen and made myself some coffee —and as I was making it, I felt, well, almost happy, relieved. I mean I was awfully unsteady and shaky—I knocked the top off the perco-lator—but it was like, oh, like when there's some frightful ordeal and then you get it over with and somehow it doesn't seem so bad after all. Is that frightfully callous?"

"No, it's perfectly natural that when long-repressed material of such a traumatic nature comes to the surface and is faced fairly and squarely that there will be a feeling of relief, sometimes even of euphoria."

"Yes, that's it," he said eagerly. "I did feel sort of euphoric at first . . . but then as I sat drinking the coffee, I thought, but why did I think it was my fault? 'Oh please, God, no.' I remembered that —and then suddenly I began remembering other things, bits and pieces that seemed just to come tumbling into my head. I had prayed, you see—I remember kneeling beside my bed and praying that I wouldn't have to fetch Mummy's medicine anymore, that someone would find out, that something would happen to her even.

And when I saw her lying there, it was as though God had answered my prayer—so that's why it was my fault, you see.

"And I recalled something else too—the worst of it was when I *couldn't* get her medicine. Once I went down to the dining room and Kate was there reading in the window seat—she didn't see me, but I had to go back upstairs and tell Mummy I didn't have it, and she hit me and hit me with her ring, it was worse than ever, her face was all sort of screwed up and screeching. And I ran away to my room and hid behind the door. Then I heard her coming after me —she had green leather slippers that made a sort of clip-clop noise, very slow . . . clip-clop . . . and I could hear her panting. . . . Oh God, it was horrible." He clenched the arms of his chair and there was sweat on his forehead. "Horrible!" He swallowed convulsively.

"Take it easy, old chap."

Alex relaxed a little and shook his head. "But she *didn't* come, you see. I had the room at the top of the stairs in those days, and I heard her coming towards it, but then she went on and down the stairs—they creaked, you know, so I knew. And I peeped out of the door and there she was, halfway down, clinging to the banister, fumbling with her dressing gown—a kind of green silk thing—and making that dreadful hoarse sort of panting sound. I don't think I'll ever forget that awful noise—it was as if she were dying. . . ." He had gradually pulled himself forward on his seat, now he lay back and closed his eyes. "I don't know, I don't know," he murmured.

After a while Hugh said, "What is it that you don't know?"

Alex opened his eyes. "I don't know if it was all the same time —that's what I can't remember, you see. I sort of feel it was, but I don't recall her actually getting to the bottom of the stairs, and I don't remember going down the stairs myself—if it was the same afternoon, I mean—I was just there at the cellar door, looking down at her. So there's a gap, you see."

"Does that worry you?"

"Yes, I think so," he said uncertainly. "At any rate, that's what I was thinking about when Daddy came in. 'Hello,' he said, 'you're up with the lark, my dear.' He always calls me 'my dear,' you know," he flushed faintly, "I don't know why—he's not particularly, well, affectionate. I haven't really told you much about Daddy, have I? I don't know, I don't get on with him too well. He's always sort of watching me, and then he's always wanting me to do things—like become a doctor—which I'm really not particularly keen on doing. One feels that one could never really live up to his expectations, but on the other hand everything one does sort of irritates him. Do you know what I mean?"

"I think so. It's not uncommon in a father-son relationship."

"Isn't it? Well, I'm glad I'm not the only one. All the same, it really is a bit much. Not that he can't be generous—to me, that is. He gave me my car when I came up, you know, although I hadn't asked. But he wouldn't give one to Kate, though I said he ought to, she needs it much more than me really. He's much closer to Kate than to me, you know, but he said no, she had a perfectly good bike and anyway—and this is really extraordinary—anyway if she had a car, people would think she was rich and start running after her for her money. Good Lord, I'd like to see anyone try that one on with Kate. She's as cold as a stalactite." He stubbed out his cigarette quickly and neatly.

"And that's what he was like this morning—irrational. He looked absolutely frightful too—I don't think he'd been to bed at all. Sometimes he does that, you know—sits up in his study all night. He drinks a bit too much often—maybe that was it, he could have had a hangover. But I didn't really take it in at the time, I was just so full of what I'd remembered that I started to pour it all out without thinking. Oh, I suppose I did think actually—the whole thing has been a completely taboo subject in the house, you see, and I suppose I thought that if I talked to him, perhaps . . . well," he shrugged, "I hardly had a chance. I was just telling him about seeing Mummy at the bottom of the cellar steps, when he suddenly got absolutely furious, burst out in a rage, 'Nonsense, absolute nonsense—you were far too young to remember anything, a baby, besides you were in your room. Who's been filling your head with such rubbish—that head-shrinker of yours, I suppose? Or is it Kate? Well, you needn't believe a word she says, she's always been a liar.' He was actually trembling, and he went on and on, wouldn't listen to a word I said, so I got up and left. I suppose I should have tried to . . . but he was so absolutely beside himself. I've never seen him behave remotely like that before. I was angry myself, and I'm afraid I was rather rude to him—I, I told him to go and take one of his bloody pills and calm down. He's an awful pill-popper, you know. Well, anyway, I ran upstairs and got dressed—and then I began to think. What on earth was it all about? Why was he making such a fuss? Of course he must have been upset—but it was an awfully long time ago. And why had he got it in for Kate like that?

"Well, to cut a long story short, I buzzed down to see Kate. She was just off to give a lecture or something, so I had to hang about till she came back. And then when I told her—what I'd remembered and what Daddy's reaction had been, do you know what she said?" He stared at Hugh, his large grey eyes wide in puzzlement. "I can't believe it—she said that Daddy thought that she, Kate, had deliberately *pushed* Mummy down the steps!"

"I see." Hugh nodded. "Did she say anything else?"

"Well, yes, of course. But I was flabbergasted—I am flabbergasted. She says, yes, I *was* there. She says that it was an accident, and she said that, after I had gone upstairs, Daddy had come in and found her at the door and had just jumped to the conclusion that she'd done it. And then she said—she's awfully honest at times, Kate—she said that it was true that she had hated Mummy and had once threatened to kill her, but, I mean, one says these things. . . . If it was an accident, why should Daddy think it was Kate? After all, he actually rather dotes on her, you know. And if it really wasn't an accident—well of course, Kate did say that she was in the dining room, so I think perhaps it must have been the same afternoon after all. I suppose she could have come round and . . ." He blinked his long lashes rapidly. "Of course, Kate is a bit of a cold fish—I wouldn't put it past her. I mean, she's very decent and all that, but I bet she can be ruthless—and if she decided someone was better off dead than alive . . ." He shook his head again. "No, I can't really believe that—but why did she go on letting him think she had done it? I asked her that and she said, she said, 'rather me than you.' But it seems so hard. Can you believe that?"

"Can *you* believe it, Alex?"

"I don't know what to believe. I mean, Daddy's not a fool. He must have some reason. I can't help feeling that there's something else. I have wondered, you know," he gave a little lop-sided smile, "if after all perhaps I didn't do it myself. But then I don't remember anything—I mean, I remember seeing Mummy going down the stairs and then I remember being at the cellar door, but there's this gap. Is it—would it be possible to block something out like that?"

"Oh yes—if there is anything to block out. If it was the same afternoon—we don't know that. But it seems likely that you were —numbed with terror at the time. These are very frightening experiences for a little boy. But you must remember that you are not a little boy now. On the other hand, it's possible that you did hear or even see something that has still not surfaced. I think I'd like to try a little experiment—what we call abreactive treatment. It's a form of hypnosis, the aim of which is to bring back into consciousness a traumatic event—to, as it were, relive that event or experience. It's quite simple really, but it will have to be done at the hospital and I should like you to stay overnight. No one can say for certain, but I think it quite possible that if you consent to this treatment we may be able to clear the whole matter up."

"Well—if, if you think so, of course. I mean, yes." He nodded. "There's no good beating about the bush, is there? I'll have to know the worst one day."

"Well, the worst may not be so very bad." Hugh smiled, and suddenly his stomach rumbled for his lost lunch. "And what you must bear in mind is that, as you said, it did all happen a very long time ago. What haunts us very often is unrecognised past terrors, but once they are recognised, they cease to be terrors. They are, as it were, put into the context of childhood where they properly belong—and then we have to assess the damage that they have caused and begin the job of doing something about it. Does that make sense?"

"Oh yes, I think so. It doesn't sound so bad."

"No, it's not so bad. How about Thursday afternoon, four o'clock at St. Ethelbert's—you know it? Good—bring an overnight bag, pyjamas and that sort of thing. Just go in the front entrance and ask for me." He paused. "There's just one other thing. Do you intend to go home at all now?"

"Well, I don't know—I hadn't really thought. Perhaps I should talk to Mother. . . ."

"On the whole, I think it might be wiser to give it a miss and go back to Carol. But if you do go home, remember this: Your father, for whatever reason, has had a shock. It takes time to adjust to having our preconceptions shattered. Talk often helps. But be gentle. All right?"

"All right. But if I know Daddy he won't refer to it. We never talk much in our house, you know. Except about the weather and the garden and how Mrs. Grundy's rheumatism is getting on." He smiled.

"Good. But take it easy in any event." He stood up. "I'll see you on Thursday afternoon at four."

They shook hands gravely, and, from the doorway, Hugh watched the boy run lithely down the stairs.

Fifteen minutes to go before the next patient. He was undecided. He was not really hungry, but he ought to have a word with Julia. At that moment she came out of her bedroom door farther along the landing.

"Was that Alex?"

"Yes—didn't you let him in?"

"No, Mrs. Nance did. Did he—has something happened?"

"Yes, in a way." He moved towards her, and she stood aside to let him pass into her room. It was a room he was not often in; but whenever he was, he was struck by its bareness—a chair, a table, a chest of drawers and built-in dresser, a shelf of poetry, a single bed, a lithograph of a curiously deformed little girl on the wall. There was an odour of Turkish tobacco; he was surprised—Julia usually disapproved of smoking in the bedroom. He turned to look at her—she seemed, he thought, wan.

"What is it?" she asked. "He's remembered something, hasn't he? He saw someone?"

"Yes, but . . ." He frowned. "It's all right, Julia. What he saw was his mother—going down the stairs, then after the fall, on the cellar floor."

"You mean—then he didn't do it?"

"It's not likely. But there's a gap—a gap in his memory at precisely the crucial moment, and that can't but be significant." He felt for his cigarettes, then desisted. "He saw Kate."

"Kate?"

"Yes, just as she said—I think perhaps I've not been giving sufficient weight to her account. By the way, I'm going along to see her tonight after dinner. It may be important."

"Why?"

"Ummm?" He looked out of the window at the scudding clouds and a tree—one of The Lane's few—bent by the wind, held at bay like a quivering animal. It was not only important, but also it might be urgent—did Kate know what had occurred during that blank period in Alex's recollection? "I'm afraid she might have a bit of a problem on her hands with her father."

"Why?"

"He sounds even more unstable than I'd imagined—in fact I'd say there is a rather typical element of paranoia present."

"Oh Hugh, she'd die if anything happened to him."

"Would she?" He glanced at her in surprise. "I wasn't thinking of that. A paranoiac's danger is at least as much to those about him as to himself, perhaps more so."

"You think *he*'s going to do something dreadful!"

"I don't know—I'm not a prophet, I'm a psychiatrist." And then, as he saw the tears slipping from her eyes, he instantly regretted his irritability. "All I mean is that there was a bit of a blow-up between Alex and his father this morning. I don't take it too seriously, but I don't think the New Inn is the place for the boy at the moment. I've sent him back to his college. We'll do the abreaction on Thursday. Julia, my dear." He took her in his arms and felt her body quiver against his. "You know," he murmured as though they were words of love, "I can't help feeling that it was probably an accident after all."

She stiffened, moved away a little. "You're just trying to cheer me up, aren't you?"

"No." He looked at her, puzzled. "All I mean is that, if it was due to a human agency, it was an accidental one."

"Oh."

"You're not feeling up to much, are you? Is it your per—"

"No. I'm all right. You know I'm never ill."

"I wasn't thinking of that." She hardly ever was, it was true—though she had been quite badly stricken by some unknown virus not long after he'd met her. It was, in fact, by that chance that he had really come to know her and love her. "Look, I'm going to get you a Librium."

"You know I don't care for those things."

"Don't I." He smiled. "Come on. It's indicated." He went to the bathroom, opened the medicine cabinet, and shook out the capsule into his hand. Hugh had no qualms about dosing himself and he also kept a back-up supply of psychotropic drugs, which he used to replenish the cabinet in his office—Soneryl, Tuinal, Thorazine, Ativan, Sinequan, Prothiaden, Tofranil, Vesprin—in addition to everything from codeine to Gelusil, paregoric to syrup of figs. The cupboard was crammed.

Back in the bedroom he handed Julia the pill and a glass of water. She took both and swallowed without further protest.

"Why don't you have a bit of rest?"

"Oh no—I think I'll go for a ride."

"Well, all right, but take it easy—that'll have a slight effect on your reactions, you know."

"That's the point of it, isn't it? Anything for peace." She smiled wryly.

It was cold—a bitter wind swept across the Fens and into Cambridge. Even the short walk from his car through the two courts to the new extension of Lady Strange College chilled Hugh: *Pleydell Court*—chastely carved over the stone lintel. Kate's living room was chaste too—cool blues and greens and white-topped surfaces. He moved directly to a raised stone fireplace with a conical steel hood and held out his hands to the fresh yellow flames. He shivered, though the room was in fact quite warm. Hillside looked cold and was cold.

"A drink?"

"Oh, I don't think—"

"How about a hot toddy—you're chilled to the bone, aren't you?"

"Well—all right. Thank you." He'd misjudged the weather and left his overcoat at home.

"I shan't be a moment—the kettle's on the boil."

In that case, he almost said, "I'd prefer a cup of tea," but she had already disappeared. He took off his glasses and rubbed his eyes —night driving was always a strain and his head ached slightly. In the dimness of his uncorrected vision the room was soft and watery, and Kate seemed to swim rather than walk as she came back from her pantry. He moved to put on his glasses and they fell out of his hand onto the stone fireplace.

"Broken?"

"Left lens cracked." He squinted through it—a glittering hairline divided the room, Kate in two. "Good enough to get me home. I've got a spare pair at the house." He put them in his pocket.

"Bad luck." She set the tray down. "I've brought rum, but I could make it whisky if you prefer?"

"Rum for me, please." He watched her as she mixed the drink —brown sugar, a clove, a dollop of rum.

"Hell." She made a small hissing sound. "Hope you don't mind a drop of blood in the grog, I've sliced my finger instead of the lemon."

"Let's have a look."

"It's nothing." She sucked at it. "We both seem to be rather clumsy tonight."

"It's a character trait with me, I'm afraid."

"A maladroit medico?" She dropped a slice of lemon and poured boiling water into the rummer and handed it to him as he sat down beside her on the couch.

"It doesn't operate professionally, only in my private life."

"Oh."

Close as he was to her, Hugh couldn't see her expression—it was going to be a handicap to conduct this interview without glasses. He sniffed at his drink and sipped it, and the slightly sickly scent stirred in his mind memories of his father seated in the confined kitchen getting steadily sozzled on a bottle of army rum slipped him by a complaisant quartermaster. "Sorry—what did you say?"

"I said, was your father a medical man?"

"No." That was instinctively clever of her—or had she made the connection: rum/army/father? She would probably have read —these people did—the announcement of his marriage to Julia in *The Times*:

WELCHMAN-WELLING: The marriage between Hugh Welchman, D.P.M., only son of the late C. S. M. Welchman and the late Dorothy Welchman, and Julia Judith, only daughter of Arthur Ashcroft Welling, sometime Professor of Psychiatric Medicine in the University of Cambridge, and the late Helen Welling . . .

"No. My father was a warrant officer in the infantry."

"That's a curious background for a psychiatrist."

"Why?" Hugh recognised the necessary prevarication—but the topic of fathers would eventually lead them round to Dr. Brinton, which was what, he suspected, they both wanted.

"Well, I mean—it can't have been very comfortable."

"Life in the raw, is that it?"

"No—well, yes, perhaps I did mean something as idiotic as that. But what I really mean is—people like me seem to have had it so easy. The best schools, the College, piano lessons, riding, summers at La Hyère and in the Engadine, trips to Paris and Venice and Vienna, skiing at Chamonix—it was all so, *is* all so cushy."

76

"Is your life cushy?" He put down his rummer and lit a cigarette.

"No!" A vehemence instantly reversed with laughter. "But I didn't bring you here to talk about myself."

"Didn't you?"

"Perhaps, in a way—but not this way. You might have expected the patient would be resistant."

"Calling in the doctor is hardly an expression of resistance."

"No, I suppose not." She got up quickly and took two long logs from under the fireplace and laid them across the still-crackling sticks. Then she turned and stood, her legs slightly apart, her back to the fire—a masculine stance. "I expect Alex told you, didn't he, about Daddy's reaction to his remembering this morning?"

"Yes."

"The way Alex put it, he sounded pretty irrational—almost out of his mind. It's what I've been afraid of. And what he said about me—all that talk about my filling Alex's head with ideas. I couldn't bear . . ." She turned her head for a moment. "I thought, I must have it out with him. I couldn't let him think that I was trying to shift the blame onto Alex. I knew what he'd feel about that—it would be like putting it on himself. I mean, if it were true—or he came to think it was true—that Alex pushed Mummy down. It would destroy him."

"I don't think I quite follow. You say that all these years he has thought that *you* killed your mother—and *that* has not destroyed him."

"Oh, he'd forgive me. I mean, I'm sure in a way he blames himself for what happened, but the effect is blunted so that he can live with it—because he chiefly blames me. But he could never shift that to Alex. He'd have to take the full guilt on himself. And I think it would crush him."

"You're saying that *your* having taken on the guilt—having accepted the role of scapegoat—is what has kept your father from having a breakdown?"

"What has kept him alive—not terribly well; he has a wonky heart and forgets things and drinks too much—but still, alive."

"I see." He brushed off some ash that had fallen on his trousers. There might just be something in it—father/son identification, and certainly Brinton had been gravely irresponsible in allowing the boy to be so terrorized by his mother. At any rate, he was inclined to think that Kate really believed the danger of collapse possible. "And did you have it out with your father?"

"I tried. I went home for an early dinner this evening. I'd nerved myself to tell him that I *had* pushed Mummy down the steps. You see, although all these years I'd let him assume I was the guilty one, we'd never discussed it and I'd never admitted it." Slowly she came and sat down. She crossed her arms, one hand on each shoulder and stared silently at the fire. She sighed. "Actually, that's not quite true," she glanced quickly at Hugh, "and I suppose this is the moment for truth, isn't it?"

He said nothing, waited.

"You see, when we were sent up to Aunt Edith's after Mummy's death, Wardy wrote to me—a lot of chit-chat but in the middle of it all she said something like, 'Isn't it a shame they're going to put poor Maida away, everyone's saying she had something to do with your Mummy's dreadful accident but I say a poor dumb animal isn't responsible for what it does like us humans. . . .' I was absolutely devastated—more so than for Mummy's death, though I expect that sounds pretty callous. But I adored that dog, and Daddy too—I couldn't understand how he could let her be put away. But I guessed he was blaming her because he didn't want to blame me. So I wrote to him and said I'd killed Mummy—that it was nothing to do with Maida and he mustn't let her be destroyed. It wasn't really very brave of me—I knew they couldn't do anything to a twelve-year-old girl. Send me to a head-shrinker perhaps—but I wouldn't have minded that." She smiled vaguely at Hugh—or so he thought.

"He wrote back that it was already done—it hurt him more than it hurt me, sort of thing. I expect it did too, poor lamb. Maida was Sir Walter Scott's faithful hound, you know—not a poodle of course—and Daddy's always been mad about Scott; he must be the only person on earth who still ploughs through *Tales of a Grandfather* regularly once a year. Except Elaine perhaps—oddly enough Scott is about the one taste they have in common. So you can see he loved her very much—Maida, I mean, not Elaine. We never have talked about her since—but her leash still hangs in its old place in the back hall. . . ." She picked up her glass and drank—a slow, graceful motion.

Hugh sat absolutely unmoving, though the cigarette end was almost burning his fingers. In no way could he draw attention to himself, for this was the crucial moment of tension when to ask the obvious question—a question that was being silently demanded—would result in a defensive response and a false relief.

"I know what you're thinking," she said coldly, "you're thinking I probably did murder Mummy."

Hugh crushed the cigarette end between thumb and forefinger—an old army trick, a quick lance of pain of which he was hardly aware.

"Well, I didn't!" She was turned full face to him now. "I didn't. Though sometimes I wish to God I had!"

She too sat still and fixed, but he caught a glimmer of tears on her cheek. "Why?" he asked quietly.

"Because, don't you see? It would have been so much simpler."

"For whom?"

"For me. For Alex too, of course, although he doesn't know it yet, poor little chap."

"And for your father?"

"For him most of all." Yet there was an uncertain note in her voice.

"How did he react this evening when you told him you'd killed your mother?"

"I didn't tell him. He didn't really want to talk about it—didn't seem really interested. I don't mean that he was evasive exactly—actually he was calm and reasonable and kindly like the Daddy of old. Perhaps reasonable isn't quite the word, he said some odd things, like, 'I'm glad you didn't go into nursing, Kate,' and 'I was a lonely man when your mother was alive.' He said her death was probably an accident or 'perhaps Maida was responsible as they found at the inquest.' It seemed as though I was absolved, so I tentatively mentioned Alex, and he just said, 'Alex and I understand each other very well.' Apparently they'd had a long talk just before I came and—"

"Alex was there—at the New Inn?" He spoke mildly, but he was immediately worried.

"Oh yes, but I didn't have a chance to talk to him alone—I had to rush off and catch the bus back here to be in time for you."

"I see. So presumably he's still there now?"

"I should hope so—he wouldn't have passed a breathalyser if he'd tried to drive back to Carol. Why, is—"

"He was drunk?"

"Not staggering drunk, but distinctly shaky. I suppose Daddy had been feeding him whisky and he was drinking sherry all through dinner. He told a long pointless story about one of his ghastly public school friends. Elaine disapproved like mad of course, but he was all right really—quite harmless, just slightly silly."

"I see." He didn't like the sound of that at all, nor of Dr. Brinton's new-found calm. He absently slipped the dead stub into his pocket and lit another cigarette. "Your father didn't mention what had passed between him and Alex?"

"Nooo—it all seemed blessed harmony, a bit too cosy perhaps, but on the other hand, I've been thinking, maybe I've been wrong, after all it was a long time ago. Maybe she did just fall and then later Alex came downstairs and took a look and shut the door. Don't you think that was probably it?"

"No." And nor do you, he thought.

She turned her head sharply: "Why not—why couldn't it have happened that way?"

"Because according to the medical evidence at the inquest, the frontal bones of her skull were fractured—damage that could only have been inflicted by the cellar door slamming in her face."

"Oh. You—you've seen a report of the inquest?"

"I've read a transcript, yes." He hesitated, reluctant to mention the police; but if he were to get a more accurate picture of Brinton's state of mind, he was going to have to touch on her underlying fears. "The verdict was Death by Misadventure, but in fact I gather the police were not satisfied. The man in charge of the investigation did not accept the theory that the dog did it."

"Then who does he think did?"

"I understand you were all under suspicion. But working from motive rather than from circumstantial evidence, of which there was rather a shortage, I believe your father was considered to be the leading suspect."

"Daddy! That's absurd—he can't even swat a wasp without flinching."

"That," said Hugh in his most detached manner, "must be somewhat of a handicap for a medical man."

He thought for a moment she was going to hit him, but instead she gave a kind of half laugh, "You're trying to needle me, aren't you?"

"He had a lot to gain."

"So did we all! Me, especially. I hated the woman—and she me. I'd have done it cheerfully. Perhaps I did do it."

"You've said not."

"You trust me? You shouldn't, you know—I used to be known as a liar." She looked at him. "Would you still . . . would it matter to you if I were lying?"

"You are what you are. In my profession one has to get through a lot of lies before one comes to the truth of the matter."

"Truth? Isn't your business just substituting a workable set of lies for a set of lies that has become redundant, nonfunctional?"

"That's a way of putting it." He was tired. Her defences were up now. His head ached slightly more than when he came. He drank some of the rum, it was tepid and reminded him this time of the stale mornings with his father sleeping it off at the kitchen table in the period of his decline—disintegration, after the death of his wife. He shook his head—the real worry was Alex alone in that house with his father. Alone? "Er, your stepmother—I suppose she's at home tonight?"

"Oh yes—she never leaves the place, except for one of her gardening bees or whatever they are. Why, what makes you think of her?"

"Only that I have no very clear impression of her—from you, or for that matter, from Alex."

"Oh well, she's the epitome of unobtrusiveness, you know—like a first-class nurse whom you only notice when she brings you nasty medicine to take."

Hugh smiled. "There must be a bit more to her than that."

"Yes." Kate sighed. "She's calm, stable, sensible, decent, efficient, responsible, full of sanitary good works. In the early days I think Daddy would probably have gone to pieces without her. She hasn't any sense of humour of course, but then on the whole we're rather a humourless family. Her 'Favourite Author,' apart from Scott, is Jane Austen, and, as a matter of fact, she reminds me of Fanny Price in *Mansfield Park*—only Elaine got a doctor rather than a parson."

"You don't much care for her?" said Hugh, not having read any Austen, or Scott for that matter.

"No, I'm not fond. It's natural. Alex is her darling. The fire under the ice, as it were." She was speaking off-handedly, but suddenly there was an alertness in her tone. "You're not thinking that Elaine could have—no. No. Of course it would have been physically possible—she was out there gardening and could—"

"In the fog?"

"The fog? Oh yes, in the fog. Elaine would garden in a typhoon. No, she *could* easily have popped in to go to the loo or something, slammed the door on Mummy and slipped out again. But I don't see her committing murder, at least I don't think I do. Not that I think she'd object to the taking of a useless human life on principle—she would just sort of disapprove of it, like holding a teacup in both hands."

Hugh laughed outright. He stood up and going over to the fireplace, dropped his cigarette among the smouldering logs. "Well, I must be off."

"Did you come in a car?"

"Yes."

"I don't suppose you could give me a lift, could you?"

"Of course, where?"

"Home. The New Inn."

"With pleasure." Which was not altogether an exaggeration—the more people in that house with Alex, the better. He wondered whether the housekeeper lived in or not.

It was icy in the car at first, the leather clammy as dead flesh, the windscreen obscure with frost. But soon the dry heat washed over them with an odour of dust and old cigarettes, leavened by another, fresher scent—perfume perhaps that Kate wore, lavender or heather. Usually a day of heavy smoking deadened his sense of smell, but tonight the buds were open and delicately receiving.

He drove slowly, peering ahead. Oncoming headlights caught the cracked lens and sliced like a shining scalpel across his vision. Despite the effort of concentration, he was aware of Kate's intensity of silence.

"The New Inn—odd name for an old place," he said conversationally, "sixteenth century?"

"Early seventeenth." She seemed to hesitate, and then she began to talk and he sensed the relief behind the words. "It was opened in the year of Charles the First's coronation and they duly called it the King's Head. Then later when they chopped the head off, it was changed to The Case Is Altered."

He listened with half an ear to her rapid chatter. ". . . Restoration they compromised on the New Inn, which is what the locals had always called it anyway. . . ."

He would ring Alex in the morning—which was against his principles, but, after long practice, he knew enough sometimes to follow his instincts, however unprofessional.

". . . fashionable with young bloods going to and from Newmarket and too tired or too tight to make it into Cambridge. . . ."

On the other hand, if there had been any serious development, Alex would probably have phoned and left a message with Julia or on the message-taker. There must have been something to make the boy ignore his advice and go home.

". . . one of Ben Jonson's earliest comedies, and, oddly enough, *The New Inne* is one of his last. They're both of almost incredible intricacy—everyone turns out to be someone else, if not two other people . . ."

A black distorted shape loomed at the car and he swerved, then saw it was a gnarled tree ravaged by the flat country winds, the whipping branches unbudded, long dead.

". . . opposite sex, although I suppose it might conceivably be of psychiatric interest. You're going to turn right in about a hundred yards. It always terrifies me in the dark—just opposite the bus stop —it's almost invisible. Here, now."

He swung the car blindly into a huge black hedge and then felt the crunch of gravel under the wheels and saw a narrow black tunnel ahead.

"Here, this is it."

He stopped the car with a jolt and switched off lights and engine. At once it seemed colder, and the warm box was infiltrated by the chill noises of the night, the wind's cry, the creak of branches, the uneasy rustle of the hedgerow enclosing them.

"May I have a cigarette?"

"Of course." He felt the feathery touch of her fingers as she reached for the packet in the darkness. In the brief light of the match, close to her as he was, he saw the sharp lines of strain in her young face.

They smoked for a while in silence; clearly she was reluctant to enter the house, and he knew there was more she had to say.

"Do you want to come in?" she asked at last.

Hugh was tempted. If Alex was up, he could see for himself how he was; or if asleep, he could legitimately look in on him.

"Well," and then suddenly he pulled himself together—he was becoming as much of an old woman as Mike, infected even by Mike's taste for dramatics—"No, I won't, thanks."

"You could meet Daddy."

"I don't fancy I'd be a very welcome visitor." And yet again he felt the urge to say yes—a few minutes' conversation would undoubtedly be illuminating. "Anyway, I expect he'll be asleep by now."

"I doubt it. He usually stays up till all hours these days—working in his study." Her face showed dimly as she drew on her cigarette.

"What sort of work is that?"

"Oh, that's just a euphemism for whisky. All he does is sit and tipple. Sometimes he forgets to go to bed at all, and Elaine or Wardy finds him in a stupor in the morning." Then her tone lost its detachment. "It's much worse than I've told you really. He's terribly deteriorated. He's lost most of his patients, and the rest of them—the old faithfuls—well, he's incapable of dealing properly. Sometimes if there's a night call, Elaine has to prevent him forcibly from going out—it would be suicide, half sozzled as he usually is. I must say Elaine is good about it, doesn't complain, just copes. And Wardy pretends everything is perfectly normal—maybe she believes it really is. But it's like a nightmare slowly repeating itself. Oh God, Hugh, what on earth am I going to do?"

"If it's as bad as you make out, then—"

"Worse!"

"Yes—well." There was the force of true feeling at last—no concealment in this, no game for the moment. "From what you say, it sounds as though your father is a chronic alcoholic, or on the way there. In that case, no time should be lost in having him treated—which almost certainly means commitment."

"Daddy in your loony bin at St. Ethelbert's? He'd be better off dead."

"As a matter of fact, we don't have an alcoholic treatment centre at St. E.'s, though I've long been pressing for it, but—"

"And what would you do—electric shock treatments so he'd come out an amiable vegetable?"

"The treatment usually consists of various drugs combined with special therapy. But it's generally better if hospitalization takes place in quite another vicinity."

84

"Why? So we won't contaminate him with visits, is that the idea?"

"Something like that—although we put it in another way."

"I'm sorry. It's just that he's such a . . . he'd be destroyed in a place like that. I know, I know—you'll say he's being destroyed here and now."

"Why don't you talk to your stepmother? She's a nurse. She must be concerned."

"Yes. I suppose that would be the sensible thing to do, wouldn't it? But can I really trust her? After all, perhaps it *was* she who murdered Mummy. I seem to remember hearing there was something funny about her own father's death. Maybe she's one of those unobtrusive little souls who go about quietly murdering their relatives." Her voice caught: "Oh Christ!"

Hugh nodded silently in the darkness—for a moment he was entirely in sympathy with her. "Yet your impression this evening was that your father was—easier in his mind?"

"Yes." There was a vague movement and she blew her nose. "In a way—but he was, well, excited too, like a small boy with something up his sleeve. But God knows what—or whether it was anything at all. I can't really trust my impression of that—I can't trust him anymore. He lies, you know, about all sorts of stupid things." In the silence, the susurration of the surrounding night enveloped them, whispering of unquiet. Tomorrow, Hugh thought, he'd have to look up Stand again and have a serious talk about Brinton.

Kate stubbed out her cigarette. "Sure you don't want to come in and look at the scene of the crime, after all?"

"I think not, thanks."

"I expect you're wise. But don't you—do you ever find it odd that all these people come and talk to you about themselves, their background, their families, their ills—and yet you yourself never verify the context, never go out and visit the scene of the crime for yourself?"

"In some sense, the scene of the crime *is* the patient."

"That's—I see. Why am I running on like this? I'm so tired I feel I could sleep forever. But I don't suppose I shall at all."

"Would you like a pill?—I've got one in my bag, it might help."

"No thanks. Anyway, I can always pinch one from the surgery

if I really need it. But I'd rather not. Who said, 'Eternal vigilance is the price of sanity'?"

"Liberty, I thought."

"Oh yes—you're right. Not quite the same thing—quite the opposite in fact. Sanity is rather like being in prison. Sorry, I could go on for hours. And I believe you'd sit here patiently and listen to me—or rather, doctorly." She opened the door without warning and was out of the car in one movement, it seemed to him. "Good night."

"Wait a minute," he blinked in the light from the roof, "how do I get out of here?"

"Go on a bit farther and you'll come to a broader place by the paddock gate—you can turn there." And she slammed the door.

The gravel ended after a few yards and the car jolted in the rutted lane. The space to turn in, when he got there, was hardly bigger than the length of the car. Beyond it, the lane ended in woods and his headlight caught the reflection of a redly glinting eye—he wondered vaguely what kind of animal would be out on a night like this. Only mad dogs and psychiatrists. The wheels raced, churning up mud from the late rains. By the time he was round, he was sweating. As he came abreast of the gate again, on impulse he stopped the car. He wound down the window and tried to peer through the blackness of the night at the unseen house, invisible scene of the primal crime.

At Hillside the upstairs windows were dark—so Julia was asleep or perhaps waiting for him downstairs. He left the car at the front door and went in; he picked up the white phone and pressed the message-taker play-back button—but there had been no calls. On the salver there were two or three letters to go out, addressed in Julia's strong passionate handwriting, but no messages either. His sense of disquiet returned and he was aware of a vague disappointment that Julia had not stayed up to greet him—the waiting room was dark and, except for the wind, the house soundless. And yet that was surely a good sign; she must be less anxious about Kate than he had imagined. But Alex—might it not be possible that he had rung Mike Semple? Hugh reached for the black phone, then paused. Why not simply go up there? It must be late, but Mike was a night bird and boasted of getting in three or four hours' work after a dinner party. The thought of Mike's ironic frivolity, his chatter about Ferenczi or

Foucault, or even Zita and Zog, was suddenly appealing. He laid his broken glasses face-up on the hall table, as a reminder to have something done about them in the morning.

Then he went out, shutting the door behind him. He reached in and turned off the lights of the car. He had no compunction about breaking in on the Balkans. And the walk would do him good. He wondered momentarily why he was bothering to make excuses to himself. But then he was already trudging into the darkness, letting the bitter wind blow the Brintons from his mind.

And, although it was noticeably warmer, it was extraordinarily dark—the wind actually roared. A Witch's Night, Julia would have called it—when the riding demons rose at nightfall from the swamps to sweep and scour the souls of the marsh dwellers. Her fancy was that the strictured, flat-country conscience of the Puritans had been developed to combat those old dark evils. Suddenly Hugh's heart leapt and he stumbled and half fell into the ditch as something heavy and dark seemed to rush past him carried on the gale. Probably another dead tree.

He was glad to see the Semples' floodlighting still on, so that he could avoid falling in their pitted driveway. He knocked on the door and then turned to look at the striped lawn. He felt again a longing for flowers—not this perfect turf, or the rough one at home —even Henry Stand's tossing daffodils would do. Movement, colour, perfume, a dance for blind eyes.

"Hello, Hugh."

Startled, he turned to see a tentative, diaphonous Reg in the doorway. "Oh, er—I'm sorry, did I get you out of bed?"

"Come in, come in." Her thin garment billowed in the wind.

"Is Mike about?" He stepped into the hall.

"I just washed my hair."

"Oh quite." Her thin locks, black with water, were pasted to her head, giving her a more than usually elfish look. "I'm afraid it must be rather late."

"No, Mike's in town." She shut the door and slipped the chain on. "A two-day conference at the History Society. They usually are two days, aren't they, if not three?"

Hugh's heart sank. "I should have rung up."

"It's not late at all—I've been working for hours on the Artaud footnotes, I'm only too glad of an excuse to stop."

"Well, I just thought he might be free for a chat. . . ."

"Anyway, I dislike the telephone—so often when one answers all there is is breathing at the other end. After a couple of minutes of that I say 'Drop dead' and hang up. The other day I did it to the Master—the poor old blighter stutters, I expect you know, except in Latin, I'm told, and it takes him an age to get the first word out. Also he's got a thing about women. I expect he's got even more of a thing now. Does it happen to you?"

He had never known her say so much—intelligibly, that is. Slightly mesmerised, he followed her into the living room, where a fire burned briskly.

"No—I'm protected from that sort of thing. I've got one of these automatic recording devices, you know."

"Whatever Mike is doing now, I don't suppose it's chatting. Have some whisky." She handed him a tumbler three quarters full of neat spirit. "Is that what you call her?"

"Who?" He accepted the glass unwillingly; it had been a mistake to come.

"Why aren't you wearing your glasses?" she said, curling up in Mike's enormous wing chair.

"Well, as a matter of fact, I broke them earlier on this evening. You wouldn't happen to have any ice, would you?"

"Julia, I mean. You look much nicer without them. No. Mike is furious. The fridge is on the blink."

"All the same, I wish I'd had them coming up here; I practically had to crawl." He sat down on the other side of the fire. "Oh I see —no, it actually is a machine that answers and says, 'Will you please record your message. Doctor will call you later' sort of thing."

"Did you come on foot? How daunting."

"It was rather—like going through the Plague of Darkness."

"Or the Valley of the Shadow."

"What?"

"Oh I'm sorry."

"Sorry about what?" He was faintly irritated.

"I'm afraid that's what I call where you live."

"The valley of the shadow—of death? Why?"

"Because they look so grim as they bump along the shortcut and coast down to you."

"Who's—you mean, my patients?"

"The ones on bikes—cyclists to the trick-master."

"Perhaps they look a bit happier on their way back?"

"Not many of them come back this way—I expect it's easier just to continue on downhill." She smiled at him with a cheerfulness he'd never seen in her—come to think of it, he couldn't recall ever having seen her smile before at all.

"What do you do, stand at the window and count them?"

"My workroom's upstairs over the porch, so naturally I see them. Knitting at the foot of the guillotine. Why don't I ever get the machine when I ring up Julia?"

"It's on a special line for patients." He felt uncomfortable, inexplicably uneasy.

"Could I get one?"

"I expect so."

"You've got Madge Platten as a patient now, I see."

"Ummm." He didn't like this. He sipped the whisky, as nasty as he remembered. Was Reg one of these gossips who knew too much, but never enough, about everyone?—fleshing out an impoverished existence with vicarious scandal. Poor Reg.

"Poor Hugh."

"What?" He made an abrupt movement and the ash of his cigarette tumbled down his waistcoat.

"Don't you hate to go out?"

"Why do you ask?" A confused echo in his head.

"I do. I ride down into your valley—but that's only the beginning. Into the town—the crassness behind the mediaeval splendour, the total din and asininity, the raucousness—*c'est brutal.* Isn't it? I ride back at the end of The Lane. That monstrous deformity."

"I don't go out much myself," he said shortly. Then, aware of his ungraciousness, he made an effort. "A man of my profession tends to deal mechanically, I'm afraid. One's too busy for the world to impinge much."

"The alienated alienist?"

He stared at her nestled in her chair, quite unable to make out her expression. Was she—what had been Kate's expression?—*needling* him? Or trying to tell him something? He had a stronger feeling of unease, a kind of heaviness and—and dread. Perhaps the reason she didn't go out in the day was that she rode at night—behatted and cackling in her billowing robes on the wind. Perhaps it had been she who'd swept by him as he came up to the house—astride her broomstick.

He shook his head and arced his cigarette towards the fire; it bounced off the grate onto the carpet. For a moment he remained immobile with an immense lethargy; then he forced himself to his feet, moved the few necessary steps, and picked up the smouldering cigarette. He was close to her now, and he looked down at her small, sharp face, searching for malevolence or—what?—enchantment? With a grunt, he turned and tossed the cigarette into the fire. "I'm afraid it's made a mark on the carpet."

"One more scar won't make any difference."

"Well," he gave a meaningless laugh, glancing involuntarily at the water stain on the wall. "I should be going." And yet he made no move. He wanted to go home. He had a sense of alarm, almost of foreboding, although whether its source was at Hillside or here in this room, he couldn't tell; but its very irrationality made him reluctant.

"Would you have liked children?"

"What?" He blinked at her. "Oh—well, if it only required an act of will, we'd have had them long ago."

"An unconscious resistance?"

"Something like that." He nodded abruptly. But, there was a shift, a hope now. Perhaps one day there would be a rush of small feet on the staircase where now only patients sedately trod. He pulled his mind away—talking about Julia was for him a breach of confidence worse than chattering about his patients. He had the impression already that Reg knew too much. He hadn't come here for that. What had he come for? Alex, of course. He had a spasm of irritation at his dilatoriness. "Er, Mike didn't get a call tonight from any of his men, did he, by any chance? Alex Brinton specifically, I mean."

"No—no calls, no visits, no flowers."

"Er?" Suddenly he felt he should stay, talk to this lonely woman. He shook his head. "Well thanks. I really must go," he repeated.

"Would you like me to drive you back?" she asked him in the hall.

"Oh don't bother. Do you drive?"

"In an emergency." As she opened the door and he looked out on the night, there was a nyctophobic instant when he would have been glad of a lift.

The wind was as strong as ever and there was a smattering of rain, but he got home with no outward alarm. And there were no messages on the message-taker. He looked in on Julia—asleep in an attitude of utter abandon on her narrow bed. He undressed quickly in his own cold room; as he got between the chilly sheets, he realised he hadn't put away the car. Well, it was too late now. And, wondering vaguely what time it actually was, he too fell asleep.

Two

7

The committee was not due to meet till ten-thirty, but he had left the house early, parked his car in Queen's Road, and walked through to Beasely's the optician to deposit his glasses for repair. Old Beasely had promised them for Friday, then spent an inordinate amount of time adjusting Hugh's spare pair so they did not cut into his ears; he had succeeded at that, but now they had a tendency to slip down his nose. As he crossed King's Parade, Hugh had a vague sense of oppression and a slight headache; he had probably drunk too much of Reg Semple's whisky last night. And he had misjudged the weather—it was a balmy April morning—and his heavy tweed suit prickled uncomfortably. The prospect of taking the chair at the Special Projects Committee did not cheer him; the S.P.C. was a creation of the Director's to further his own pet schemes, but today, as frequently happened, Grantham was attending some more important function in London, leaving Hugh to fight a number of battles for which he had little heart. The only consolation was that Bantock would be there and could give him news of Bob Lummis.

Hugh stopped at King's Bridge and reached in his pocket for cigarettes, and then realised he had none. Julia had been asleep this morning and the usual box had not been on the breakfast table; and Mrs. Nance, who had arrived just as he was leaving, did not appear to know where the supply was kept. He thought of retracing his steps to buy some, but felt unusually lethargic. He could probably borrow a few from someone at the meeting. He breathed in the soft spring air without coughing. The vileness of last night had been the final cruel effort of winter to stay the approaching summer, and yet the brightness of the day was tinged and darkened by the dream from which he had woken sweating at dawn.

In the dream it had been real summer, hot and idyllic, the water blue as it seldom was in reality, and he heard music, which, instead of grating on his ear, sounded extraordinarily beautiful and harmonious. He was poling a punt in which sat Julia and Kate and Reg Semple, all wearing long old-fashioned summer dresses—perhaps the music emanated from their lips, he could not be sure. At first the river might have been the Cam, gentle and calm; and he was punting with an easy competence that both surprised and delighted him. And then the traditionally absurd accident happened—he dug too deep, the pole stuck fast and, instead of letting go, he held on to it and the punt drifted away. At that moment the scene changed to a river he did not know, broader and heavier and running swiftly to a wide, high weir, over which the stream plunged with an abrupt violence and towards which the punt was being carried with increasing rapidity. And Hugh had watched, clinging helpless and voiceless to the pole, as the women turned towards him smiling and waving and laughing at his predicament, quite oblivious of the imminent destruction that awaited them.

The dream itself was simple and even elegant with its clear equations and pole-arities: professional detachment and sexual impotence, guilt and aggression, the idealised and the disastrous. He was surprised at such a powerful reaction and recrudescence of, as far as he was concerned, such prehistoric fear and guilt. Of course every little boy wants to push his mother down (the steps) or over (the weir), but it was rare that he identified with a patient so closely as with Alex (man of the river). His own obligatory three-year analysis, though not thorough-going by Freudian standards, had been quite satisfactory in clearing away the necessary cobwebs; but perhaps, he reflected wryly, he was due for a refresher.

As he looked down at the untroubled waters of the real river and surveyed the promise of the summer day, he was inclined to be wary. Alex was the problem. He reached absently for cigarettes. All around clocks began to strike the hour. Time enough to phone Alex when he got to St. Ethelbert's. But all the same he turned and began to move more quickly towards Queen's Road. He saw at once a police panda parked beside the Rover and a policewoman trying the door.

"Good morning, er," what did one call a policewoman? "Can I help you?"

"Is this your car, sir?"

"I'm afraid so—what have I done wrong now?"

"Are you Dr. Hugh Welchman?"

"Yes, I'm Welchman." He was immediately alert, had a fleeting thought of Julia. "What is it?"

"I'm instructed to ask you to accompany me, Doctor. There's an emergency at the residence of Dr. J. Brinton."

"Right." He stepped quickly toward his car.

"In the panda, if you wouldn't mind, Doctor. It'll save time. My colleague can follow on with your car."

"Right," keys already in his hand, "I'll just get my bag." He unlocked the complicated double alarm lock of the boot, lifted out the bag, slammed the lid, and dropped the keys into the hand of the policeman standing quietly beside him.

As he ducked his head and squeezed his bulk into the front seat of the tiny car, the policewoman was saying into a microphone, ". . . got him. There in five minutes. Out." Then the car was in motion even before he had shut the door.

"Any idea of the nature of the emergency?" He sat awkwardly crouched with the black bag on his knees.

"No, sir." They sped up Queen's Road, into Northampton Street, and then she stamped on the brakes and went through the red light at the top of Magdalene Street into a skidding right turn under the nose of a lorry trundling down the hill. "The call was put out for you about twenty minutes ago, Doctor, that's all I know." She switched on the siren and accelerated down Bridge Street, whipped the wrong way into Sidney Sussex, and made a swaying left into Jesus Lane, which sent Hugh's glasses slithering down his nose. He pushed them back with an abrupt gesture.

The car entered the first roundabout into the Maids' Causeway at not less than fifty, and slid round the second still accelerating, the little vehicle rocking as they went into Newmarket Road and gathering more speed, through a set of lights fortunately green, and past the city cemetery. By the time they drew up at New Inn Hugh was feeling slightly queasy. The policewoman was out of the car and had the door open before Hugh had found the handle.

They went through a tall wooden gate in a high wall and up a wide brick walkway between round beds of scented white roses. The house was much larger than he'd imagined. Through the open front door a broad shaft of sunlight fell into a spacious hall, catching a ruddy reflection from a huge copper vase of yet more white roses. As Hugh entered, a heavy figure stepped out of the surrounding gloom.

"Dr. Brinton?" asked Hugh.

"I'm Chief Superintendent Ply of the Cambridge Criminal Investigation Department. Dr. Welch—"

"Where's my patient?"

"Brinton died in the night, or early this morning."

"Died?" Hugh's blood drained, then instantly surged back in anger. "What—"

"Is that Welchman there?" A voice boomed into the hall. "Welchman, is that you?"

"Stand? Yes, it's me." He could just make out the little doctor halfway down the staircase.

"Took your time, didn't you? Come along then, Welchman, come along. Alex is up here."

"Alex is . . ." He turned to the policeman impassively regarding him with pale grey eyes. "But I thought you said—"

"*Dr.* Brinton died in the night. Young fellow's all right, though taking it badly, according to *him.*" Without taking his eyes from Hugh, he made a slight motion of his head towards Dr. Stand. "But I'd like your opinion on that, Doctor. Why don't you hop up and have a look at him?"

"I will indeed." He crossed the hall swiftly and took the stairs two at a time.

"Oh, just one thing, Doctor," called Ply, halting Hugh in midstride, "I'd like a word with you when you come down. I shall be in the dining room."

"Very well." For a moment Hugh found himself looking down into a small passage with a heavy wooden door set in one side—this, he guessed, would be the cellar door. Then he turned to Stand. "What's the problem?"

"This way." The doctor caught his arm and half pulled, half guided him down a broad carpeted corridor with a single large sash-window at the end. "In here," he said, indicating the last door on the right.

"Hold on, you'd better fill me in first." In the light from the window, he saw that Stand looked tired, strained.

"Well, er," he cleared his throat, "Brinton died in the night, you know."

"I've just been told. How?"

"Quite. Oh, pretty obviously an O.D.; barbiturates, perhaps. Elaine found him about nine—that's Mrs. Brinton. I came straight over as soon as she phoned—good thing I did." He paused, tugging at an ear lobe. "I arrived just as Alex had been told—he was reacting badly, hysterics, shouting, thrashing about. Had quite a job to get him up here."

"He's quiet now?"

"Oh yes, like a lamb. I gave him a shot of Thorazine, had to—"

"You what?"

Stand's face tightened. "Intramuscular injection of Thorazine."

"I see. Dosage?"

"Five hundred milligrams."

Hugh opened his mouth, then shut it. He drew a deep breath and looked out of the window—beyond the wall one could just see the roofs of the traffic along Newmarket Road and the top of a red double-decker bus halted opposite the house. "Well, that would have quietened him down all right. Any other effects?"

"Heart action, blood pressure, etc., all quite normal. But he has an intermittent facial tic and seems to have some trouble moving his eyes."

"Talking?"

"No." Stand looked worried—and so he well might. "I suppose perhaps—"

"Who's with him?"

"Well, I'm here."

"What about the stepmother—I thought she was a nurse?"

"There's a bit of a problem there."

"I see." Hugh nodded shortly. He put his hand on the doorknob.

"Do you want me to—"

"No. Stay here, if you will."

Inside it was dark and stifling. Hugh pulled back the curtains and glanced round at the traces of disorder—the unmade bed, an overturned vase of flowers, a lampshade askew. Alex, in pyjamas and dressing gown, sat in a slightly hunched position in an armchair.

"Hello, old chap," said Hugh, taking a chair and sitting down facing him.

There was no response. Hugh remained still, watching him closely. The eyes were deviated downwards. He passed his handkerchief slowly backwards and forwards—the eyelids fluttered, but the eyes did not move. Suddenly there was a severe spasm of the facial muscles, that passed back into tonic immobility. The arm, when moved, was rigid. Hugh got his bag and began to examine the boy. Twice during the examination the facial spasm recurred, once the lips moved slightly as though he might be about to speak.

"Well?" Stand demanded as Hugh stepped out into the passage.

"When did you administer the injection?"

"About an hour ago—bit more, now. How is he, do you think?"

"He's suffering from some obvious Parkinsonian effects—chlorpromazine is likely to do that, you know."

"I see, yes, I suppose so. What are you going to do?"

"I'm going to hospitalise him."

"Oh—really, is that necessary? I mean, surely . . ." Stand's large grey eyes regarded Hugh fixedly. Then he screwed up his face with an expression of distaste.

"In the circumstances, I think it essential." He stared at the bluff little doctor and suddenly he was struck with the most extraordinary idea—if Stand's hair was black instead of grey and . . . He shook his head. "Perhaps you'd better tell me a little more fully what the circumstances are. But first, is there a phone I could use?"

"In here." He led Hugh up the passage and into a large bedroom with a green carpet, green chairs, a green satin-covered bed—and another immense vase of white roses.

He rang through to St. Ethelbert's and explained the situation to Jeremy Wilson: "I can't bring him in myself; I've got some business to attend to here. But I'd like you to have a look at him when he arrives."

"I'll do better than that, I'll come along with the ambulance myself—there's nothing much on this morning and anyway it's my coffee break."

"Excellent. Put me onto the Director's office, would you?" He had been lucky to get hold of Jeremy—not only brilliant and competent, but also pleasant, and a heavy smoker who'd be bound to have some spare cigarettes on him. "Oh hello—Miss . . ." With an effort of memory he dredged up the exquisite blond creature's slightly absurd name, "Miss Plenderlieth-Blunt. Welchman here. I've got an urgent case on my hands so I shan't be able to make the committee meeting this morning. Would you give my apologies to Mr. Bantock and ask him to take the chair for me?"

"Very good, Doctor. But the meeting has already commenced, with Mr. Bantock in the chair," she said disapprovingly.

"Then that's all right. Thank you." He smiled briefly as he

replaced the phone—she looked down on him, probably because he spoiled the image of handsome and well-dressed suavity that the Director cultivated so skilfully. Hugh was seldom introduced to visiting V.I.P.s. He turned back to Stand.

"All right—now I'd like to know exactly what happened this morning."

"As I said, I came straight over when Mrs. Brinton rang me about her husband. Alex was on the stairs wrestling with Kate and Wardy—Mrs. Warden. He was shouting and throwing himself about and—"

"What was he shouting?"

"Oh 'Daddy, Daddy'—that sort of thing. I gather he wanted to see Jonathan. And 'You bloody bastard'—that was to me. I had the deuce of a time getting hold of him. Then Elaine Brinton came into the hall and that seemed to start him off again worse than ever. He made a dart at her, nearly knocked me down the stairs. He was yelling, frothing at the mouth, you know, hitting out as hard as he could, so I—"

"What was he yelling this time?"

Stand hesitated, cracked a knuckle. "Well, I don't know, I—"

"Please, I want all the details. Obviously this might be important for Alex—in the treatment of Alex."

"Yeees. But it doesn't mean anything, you see, and . . ." He looked around the room, then back at Hugh. "All right. But this is in confidence, of course. He said, 'It was Nursey, I saw her, it was Nursey, Nursey did it!' Kept on at it in a high-pitched squawk."

"I see. 'Nursey' being Elaine Brinton?" And the high-pitched squawk an approximation, probably, to the voice of a small boy fourteen years ago.

"I suppose so—yes, that's what he used to call her before— before she married Brinton."

"And then?"

"I got a half nelson on him and brought him upstairs."

"And then you administered the Thorazine?"

"I tell you, Welchman, he was definitely manic; I've seen some cases in the army and . . ." He made a restless movement with his shoulders. "It seemed the right thing to do."

"Not medically."

"Now see here, I've—"

"Do you know anything about neuroleptic drugs?"

"Well I—I'm familiar with some of the literature."

"Then you should be aware that Thorazine is almost invariably given only in cases of severe psychosis; certainly not to a neurotic lad at a delicate, even crucial, moment in both his life and his treatment."

Stand suddenly looked like an old man. He walked slowly over to a chest of drawers and set a straying rose back in the vase. "You don't think—I mean, it couldn't have been in any way harmful to the boy, surely?"

"Certainly. It might quite easily have thrown him into a severely depressed state. I'm not sure. We shall have to wait and see."

"Very well," Stand cleared his throat with a rasping noise and braced himself, "I take full responsibility."

"That's excellent, but you don't have to bear the consequences." Hugh sighed—he badly needed a cigarette. "There's a bit more to this than you're telling me, isn't there?"

Stand turned away as if to hide his expression. "You don't understand. You've got to remember, Welchman—I've been here before. I did what I thought was best." He reached out and lifted a rose from the vase and, clutching the stem tight in his hand, sniffed at the delicate white petals.

"Yes. But in fact, you didn't want to quiet Alex down, you wanted to shut him up, didn't you?"

"I did my duty, as I saw it."

"All right. Now what about Brinton—barbiturate poisoning, you said?"

"I said perhaps. Some drugs plus a lot of whisky. There were powdery traces of the stuff in the bottom of the glass."

"He had a heart condition, I understand?"

"Faugh—a mild murmur when he was a boy. So he said. Didn't stop him getting into the army. Actually, he was as strong as a horse. Drank too much, of course. Fond of pushing pills into himself, like some ignorant old woman. But all the same," he frowned, "he was no fool."

"He was an alcoholic?"

Stand blew out his cheeks. "Getting on that way, I suppose." He wiped his palm on a handkerchief and Hugh saw blood on the white linen—he must have pricked himself quite badly on the rose. "But, as I say, he was always careful. A thorough-going hypochondriac."

"I see." Hugh hesitated, but this was not the moment to ask about paranoid tendencies. "In other words, you consider an accident unlikely. Then that leaves us with suicide?" And yet it didn't jibe.

"Shouldn't have thought so. Bit too fond of himself for that." He compressed his lips. "And there was no note. Jonathan wasn't the type to go out without leaving something to be remembered by. Still, it's the best we can hope for."

"What exactly are you implying?"

"I told you the situation was serious, didn't I?"

No, thought Hugh, it was I who told you. "Surely," he said slowly, "you're not suggesting there was anything criminal involved—"

"I told you to leave it alone, didn't I?" He blazed out suddenly. "I told you to let sleeping dogs lie. But you would come meddling, wouldn't you, like all your breed?" His face was suffused with blood and his hand curled and uncurled on the bloody handkerchief. "Meddle meddle."

"Pull yourself together, Stand. If there's the slightest truth in your suspicions, there's plenty to be done. It's not our job to apportion blame."

"No—that's for the police, isn't it? Each man to his appointed task, eh? And you with your dangerous damned innocence—"

"It certainly won't do any good being bloody-minded about it," said Hugh mildly.

"Good? Good?" The little doctor puffed out his cheeks again. He glanced down at the handkerchief he held, then thrust it into his sleeve. "Sorry," he muttered, turning his head away and rapidly blinking his long grey eyelashes, " 'fraid I must be a bit worked up."

Watching closely, Hugh had the same impression of deviousness he'd felt at the doctor's house. Stand's anger rang true all right —the natural reaction to fear, and yet it was being used to conceal that fear. Fear of what, for whom? Alex? If the drastic means he had used to procure the boy's silence were any measure of his fear, then Stand was a very frightened man indeed. "Right then," Hugh said, "perhaps you'd stay with Alex till Wilson arrives?"

"Of course."

"He ought to be kept warm by the way, and he'll need an overnight bag."

"I'll see to that." Stand quickly preceded Hugh to the door—once more his old brisk tough self.

The staircase creaked gently as Hugh descended, but otherwise the house was silent. With the front door closed, the hall was warm and dim; cracks of daylight escaped from the edges of the drawn curtains, gleaming on old wood and burnished copper. He stepped over to the cellar door and touched the polished ridges of the oak; but he restrained an impulse to open the door and look down on the scene of the crime. This is where it had all begun. *I've been here before, Welchman.* He frowned; perhaps because he'd not smoked this morning, his sense of smell was especially acute—furniture polish, woodsmoke, a faint trace of formaldehyde, but, above all, thick in his head, the morbid odour of roses. No, it had begun before that —with Arabella Brinton's alcoholism. But from what misery had that itself stemmed? He wondered whether her father, old Dr. Anstey, had been an alcoholic. He had a sudden sense of the family's inbred, almost proprietary, penchant for disaster—each fresh young plant brought to a malodourous flowering, clutched and warped and possessed. The stark cleanliness of Hillside was almost desirable by contrast. Julia—he ought to let Julia know at once. He dropped his bag beside the table and reached for the phone.

At that moment the door of the dining room opened and Superintendent Ply stepped into the hall.

"Ah Dr. Welchman? Finished your business upstairs?"

Hugh withdrew his hand from the phone. "I've examined young Brinton, yes."

"And how is the lad? When can I see him?"

"Not for quite some time, I should think. I'm hospitalising him."

Ply gave an almost inaudible whistle. "Bad as that, eh?"

"I'm not sure just how bad it is—which is largely why I'm sending him off to St. Ethelbert's."

"I see." The policeman stared at Hugh intently. "Well, in that case, perhaps you can spare me a few minutes."

"All right, but the ambulance will be here shortly, and I—"

"Oh, I'm sure we can interrupt ourselves for that. Come along, Doctor." He stepped aside to let Hugh pass ahead of him into a large beamed room filled with dazzling sunlight from a great bow window at the south end. "This is my assistant, Sergeant Ramm."

"Good morning, Doctor. Would you sit here?"

Hugh nodded at the man who'd risen as he entered. Then they were all seated—the policemen with their backs to the window, Hugh facing the light. He sighed at this ridiculous technique.

"Right, Doctor, could I have your full name and address and your professional description?" This was Ramm.

"My name is Hugh Welchman—with a 'c'; and I live at Hillside, The Lane, Cambridge. I am a doctor of psychiatric medicine and I qualified at St. Matthew's Hospital, London. I act as a psychiatric consultant at St. Ethelbert's Hospital, and I am director of the outpatients' Mental Health Clinic there. I am also in private practice as psychotherapist, which I conduct from my home." As he spoke, he looked out at the garden—a lawn sloping gently downwards, dotted with small beds of shrubs not yet in flower, or already done, an apple tree in full white blossom, and then a thick high hedge of yew, which must join up to the wall in front, he thought. A scene of peace and tranquility, and a house well hedged and walled about from the scouring winds off the Fens—and from the outside world. For a moment his mind returned to his dream—the three smiling faces drifting to disaster under the summer sun, the soft mockery of laughter, the approaching downpour, the culpable terror of—"Sorry—what's that?"

"Alex Brinton, Doctor—he is a private patient?"

"Yes, quite." He brought himself back to the present and unthinkingly reached for nonexistent cigarettes. "He was recommended to me four or five weeks ago."

"And who recommended him to you?"

"Dr. Stand."

"Are you well acquainted with Dr. Stand, does he often recommend patients to you?"

"No to both questions. He has never recommended anyone to me before, and, although I have heard of him, I met Dr. Stand for the first time last Thursday."

"Do you know of any particular reason why Dr. Stand should have chosen you?" Ply asked his first question—up to now he had been labouriously filling his pipe from a worn leather pouch.

Hugh hesitated—what had Stand answered to that question: "Heard he was a good man?" Well, there was no point in beating about the bush. "I believe he was friendly with my late father-in-law and at one time I understand he was the family G.P."

"That would have been old Professor Welling?"

"Yes." Ply obviously knew his Cambridge.

"In that case, although you didn't know him, I presume your wife knows him?"

"Obviously. Knew him, at any rate."

"Are you aware that Drs. Stand and Brinton were once in practice together?"

"I have recently become aware of that, yes."

"Who informed you?"

"I believe it was Dr. Stand."

"You believe?"

"It might," reluctantly, "it might have been my wife."

"Was your wife acquainted with Dr. Brinton?"

"I really don't see the point of that question, Superintendent."

"You don't?" Ply paused in the act of lighting his pipe with an ancient metal lighter. "But it's a perfectly simple question. I'm merely trying to establish the background of this case."

"Case?"

"Isn't Alex Brinton one of your cases?"

"All right." He damned his lack of nicotine—it was making him slow. "Yes, my wife was acquainted with Dr. Brinton—with the whole family indeed—but that was a long time ago. Before the accident."

"Oh, so you know about 'the accident,' do you?"

"Wasn't that the verdict at the inquest?"

"How do you come to know that—that was a bit before your time, wasn't it, Doctor?"

"I have read a transcript of the proceedings at the inquest." At least he had got the questions away from Julia.

"Have you now? And who gave you that?"

"Alex Brinton's tutor at Carol College."

"Then I presume you have discussed the case with Mr. Semple?"

"Obviously Mr. Semple and I—as the boy's tutor and psychotherapist—have a certain common interest in Alex's welfare."

"When did you and Mr. Semple last have occasion to discuss 'Alex's welfare,' may I ask?"

"On Monday night." He saw well where this was leading—there was no help for it. But he might possibly speed the proceedings up a bit. "Mr. Semple came to my house after his meeting with you and Mr. Mainwaring. In the course of conversation he mentioned your views concerning the demise of Arabella Brinton. Is that what you want to know?"

"Ah!" Ply puffed gently at his pipe. "I wondered what was behind all that. Came to report, did he?"

"Mr. Semple's meeting with you—just as his procurement of the transcript of the inquest—was entirely his own idea. Perhaps we ought to get one thing straight right away—I am not concerned with the legal aspects of Mrs. Brinton's death, nor am I interested in the manner of that death, except, peripherally, as it might have a bearing on the psychological state of my patient."

"And in your opinion, does it have such a bearing?"

"Any traumatic childhood event—and there can hardly be anything more traumatic than the premature death of the mother —is bound to have an influence on the patient's psychological make-up."

"Is that why young Brinton came to see you?"

"I'm not at liberty to answer that type of question—surely you must be aware what passes between patient and doctor in these circumstances is entirely confidential?"

"Could you tell us then, Doctor," said Ramm rather quickly, "what the psychological state of your patient is right now? We must be entitled to some explanation of why we are not being permitted to interrogate him."

"Fair enough." Hugh nodded. "Alex has received a severe psychic shock following the death of his father. He has reacted by going into a state of temporary withdrawal, which is to say in non-technical terms that he is not reacting to normal stimuli."

"You mean he's not talking?" asked Ply.

"Among other things."

"That's not what I heard. I heard he was talking nineteen to the dozen, had a regular outburst, in fact, is what I heard." Ply spoke holding his pipe between small blackened teeth, which gave an odd effect of ruin to an otherwise rather monumental face.

So he'd already been told, thought Hugh—by whom? Someone who had it in for Elaine Brinton—the housekeeper perhaps. "So Dr. Stand mentioned—a not unusual initial reaction."

"But didn't Dr. Stand give him a sedative?" Ramm.

"Yes."

"What?"

"A drug by the name of Thorazine."

"That's chlorpromazine, isn't it?"

"Yes," said Hugh, slightly surprised.

"Isn't that mostly used in the treatment of schizophrenia?"

"Yes, but it's also quite effective in the emergency treatment of some forms of mania."

Ply took his pipe out of his mouth. "You're saying the boy's a maniac?"

"Not at all, whatever that means. This sort of thing could just as easily happen to you or me, Superintendent."

Ramm smiled and said pleasantly, "What was the dosage used?"

"Five hundred milligrams."

"That's a massive dose, isn't it?"

"Fairly heavy—though I have myself administered heavier ones in my time."

"But in the present circumstances, would you have administered such a dosage of such a drug?"

"That's difficult to say—I wasn't on the spot."

"Can't you enlighten us a bit more than that, Doctor?"

"I—I would perhaps have been more cautious. But it depends what one has in one's bag, you know."

"In point of fact," said Ply, "it was the drug, not the shock, that knocked the lad out, wasn't it?"

"As I've indicated, Thorazine is likely to have a heavy sedative effect under the particular circumstances."

"What kind of pussy-footing ans—"

"One moment, Super, if I may." Ramm paused. "Doctor, has Brinton been subject to psychotic episodes?"

"Absolutely not." Hugh experienced a thin cold feeling somewhere along his spine.

"There would be no possibility, for instance, of a sudden onset of psychotic behaviour, last night, say, or this morning?"

"Positively out of the question."

"Can one ever be as positive as that in your profession, Doctor?" Ramm smooth, reasonable.

"In this instance, yes, I think one can."

"But are there not instances, well known in criminology, of people of otherwise calm and even gentle disposition suddenly resorting to acts of violence quite out of their normal character?"

"That's correct." Hugh smiled in a deliberately schoolmasterly manner. "But character, you see, is only one element in the make-up of the total personality, which is what my judgement is based on in Alex's case."

"By the way," Ply again, "when did you last see Alex Brinton?"

"Yesterday afternoon."

"Would you describe his mental condition as being normal then?"

" 'Normal' is an imprecise term I don't much—"

"All right, all right—was he especially excited—upset in any way—disturbed, as I suppose you'd say?"

"Excited?" Hugh thought fast—Alex had probably not told anyone else, except Kate, about his row with his father that morning. Kate would probably keep her mouth shut—but he couldn't risk it, and anyway, it would be better coming from him; as a last resort, he could always counter the unfortunate impression the encounter might give by making the point that Alex had that same evening made it up with his father. "No, not excited. He had had a bit of a—a dust-up with his father that morning, but I would describe him as puzzled rather than excited."

"What was this dispute about?"

"Misunderstanding, rather than dispute. But I'm afraid I can't disclose that."

"About his mother's death?"

"Sorry." Hugh waited for the next question, but it didn't come. Ply had knocked out his pipe and was now filling it again—he had rather long, delicate fingers, Hugh noticed. He looked out over the window seat, where Kate had sat on the afternoon of Arabella's death, at the summery garden, half expecting to see the second Mrs. Brinton pottering among the borders. The faint scratching of Ramm's pencil had ceased, there was no sound of traffic, and in the silence Hugh almost fancied he heard the hum of bees—or the murmur of the coming storm.

"You're not being exactly co-operative, are you, Doctor?"

"Ummm? Well, let me put it this way, Mr. Ply. The death of Dr. Brinton—and I presume that is what you are investigating—has undoubtedly had a serious, though I think temporary, effect on the mental health of my patient. But I am bound to say that I fail to see what possible bearing the mental health of my patient has upon the death of Dr. Brinton."

"You don't, don't you? Well, that's easily explained. Two

108

nights ago I'm invited over by my good friend Charlie Mainwaring to discuss the old Brinton case—I go because I've never been satisfied about it, and one reason I wasn't satisfied is that I was never allowed to question the two children involved in the matter. Not to put too fine a point on it, Dr. Welchman, it was always my view that Mrs. Brinton was murdered. And when I get to Mr. Semple's rooms I find he's young Brinton's tutor—and a good job of cross-questioning he does. And who's Mr. Semple's next-door neighbour?—the well-known Cambridge psychiatrist, Dr. Welchman, one of whose patients just happens to be Alex Brinton. That's Monday night. Tuesday morning, said young Brinton has a row with his father. Tuesday night—or maybe early this morning—Dr. Brinton's dead. And when I arrive on the scene, the boy has been knocked out by Dr. Stand, unavailable for questioning, *non compos mentis,* whatever you like—history may repeat itself all right, but that's a bit too much for me to take. I can tell you straight off, Doctor, that I'm not satisfied this time either."

"And your dissatisfaction leads you to the assumption that Dr. Brinton was murdered too, is that it?"

"I've got a nose, an instinct, Doctor—just like you have, I don't doubt. I don't like coincidences. I don't like concealments."

"All I can say to that," Hugh leaned forward, and his glasses promptly slid down his nose, "is that the one thing twenty years of professional life has surely taught me is the self-serving fallibility of instinct."

"That's very clever, but I—" he was interrupted by a heavy knocking at the front door.

Hugh stood up at once. "That must be my ambulance—you'll have to excuse me."

Ply was on his feet too and with remarkable agility had reached the dining room door before Hugh had taken a step. "That's all right, but I haven't finished with you yet, Doctor. I shall have to ask you to stay a bit longer."

Hugh had the sudden absurd impression that if he didn't agree, Ply would not let him out of the room. "Provided my colleague is with the ambulance, there is no urgent reason why I should go along; in which case I could spare you a little more time, although frankly I can't—"

"That's very decent of you, Doctor, very decent indeed." Ply opened the door.

8

The hall was no longer dim. The curtains had been drawn back and at the front door Kate was talking to Jeremy Wilson, behind whom stood two white-coated orderlies. As soon as she saw Hugh, she broke off and turned.

"Well, Hugh," she said softly after a moment's silence, "the case is altered now—with a vengeance."

In her black dress, her long hair neatly pinned up, she had an unfamiliar air of sad respectability. He felt a sharp pang of pity. "I hope not, Kate—not with a vengeance."

"Well, the policeman thinks so, don't you, Inspector?" She looked past Hugh at Ply, who made no response. "Or are you keeping us cooped up in the sitting room twiddling our thumbs just for fun?"

"I'd be obliged if you didn't go into the surgery wing or leave the house for the time being, but I don't mean to confine you to one room, miss."

"That's generous. Then can I tell Elaine she can see Alex, Hugh —before your friend carts him off to the loony bin, which I gather is what he's going to do?"

"Wiser not, I think. He's not responsive, and it would only be likely to upset her."

"What have you done—doped him to the gills?"

"Now, Kate, you—"

"As if we hadn't had enough of drugs in this house."

"Alex is going to—"

"And now you're dragging him away to give him a course of electric shock treatment, I suppose?"

"Nothing of the kind. He needs to be under proper professional observ—"

"Away from our wicked influence?"

"—observation. Which he will get at St. Ethelbert's. But you may tell your stepmother that he's going to be perfectly all right."

"When—in 1984?" Though her wide green eyes were steady, her face was drawn and her cheeks flushed. "Damn. I'm sorry, Hugh, I suppose you know what you're doing. I'll shut up—but for God's sake don't offer me a tranquiliser!"

"Of course not," said Hugh, who had precisely that in mind.

"Well, I'd better go and tell her."

"One moment, Miss Brinton," Ply said, "perhaps you could spare me a few minutes in here?"

"Another inquisition?"

"Just one or two points I'd like to clear up."

"As the Grand Inquisitor said to Joan of Arc." She smiled, but Hugh felt she was close to cracking. "All right then."

Hugh watched her enter the room and Ply shut the door—but there was nothing useful he could do. He turned to Wilson.

"Hello, Jeremy."

"Phew, she's a bit of a Tartar, isn't she?" Shock-headed, gangling, untidy, a perpetual half-smoked cigarette in the corner of his mouth, Jeremy Wilson was an able, even brilliant, psychotherapist. His origins were similar to Hugh's, but being half a generation younger, he had altered neither his native directness nor his accent. "What's up then, 'ughie?"

Hugh half smiled, despite himself. "She's my patient's sister—their father died unexpectedly in the night."

"And the rozzers aren't satisfied, eh? Will we need a stretcher then?"

"Something like that. Yes. Come along, I'll lead the way."

"Mickey, Bert—work, lads."

They made a little procession up the stairs—Hugh, Jeremy, Bert, and Mickey. Stand fussily pressed a small suitcase into Hugh's hands, "Suit, shirts, toothbrush, razor—though I don't s'pose you'll let him have that." But when they went downstairs, the little doctor remained behind.

The orderlies bore Alex along the garden path and slid him into the ambulance waiting outside the gate—the boy lay apparently asleep, the nostrils indrawn, the long lashes lacing the cheeks.

"The problem is the heavy dosage of Thorazine—there are slight Parkinsonian effects and we may have to use Artane to counter them. But of greater concern is the effect of the father's death—which in some ways reproduces an early childhood trauma. It's a fairly classic case of conversion hysteria. In the event that he fully regains consciousness, he may have an urgent need to talk, and I want it firmly impressed on Sister Arkwright that I am to be sent for at once. I'll come up in an hour or so—meanwhile I'm here."

"Suicidal tendencies?"

"All ordinary precautions should be taken. But I do want him fairly closely watched."

"Private ward?"

"Yes," Hugh nodded, then, catching Jeremy's glance at the house, he said, "they can certainly afford it."

"Coming out of their ears, I'd say. What was this bloke Brinton's line—stockbroker?"

"He was a doctor."

"Was he then?" He took the cigarette out of his mouth and gave a low whistle.

"By the way, Jeremy, could you let me have a couple of cigarettes? I'm out."

"A couple? That wouldn't hold *you* for five minutes. I've got a spare twenty somewhere—here we are, you better have it."

"Capstan Full Strength—I haven't seen these for years," Hugh took the packet gratefully.

"They'll stop you smoking, if nothing else will."

"Thanks." Hugh was about to turn away when suddenly he remembered and asked about Bob Lummis.

"Yes—knew he was a patient of yours, so I had a word with Bantock. Opened him up yesterday morning . . . generalised . . . nothing to be done. . . . Bantock says a month at most. . . ."

Bob Lummis, an old man by all standards of the calendar, but of a clear-eyed sanity, ready to reject all that had led him to those achievements for which he was so admired—success, money, respect—in order to see, to put off the old and put on the new. It was not often that Hugh admired a patient, but he had admired Bob; more than that, Bob had been the patient he had quite simply *liked* the most in all the latter years. He took off his glasses and looked up at the high drifting clouds; the sun was hot on his face and his balding scalp, and an angry bewilderment passed over him at such brutally unexpected news. He longed suddenly for a soft April shower.

"What you need is a holiday, 'ughie." Jeremy patted his back.

Hugh rubbed his eyes and put on his glasses. "Perhaps. Perhaps." Watching the departing ambulance, he tried to recall when he'd last had a holiday, but memory slipped like water through his mind.

He shook his head and stepped through the door in the wall. Facing the house, he paused to light one of Jeremy's cigarettes. It was easy to see how the brick-paved walk and the rose beds must once have formed the courtyard between the two wings—the left would now be the living room; the right must have once been the stables and, though it was windowed now and the doors bricked up, the old semicircular fanlights betrayed its origin. This then was where Julia had come to take Kate out riding on Maria and Beauty. No rose beds then perhaps, but it must still have been an amiable façade. At the open door Henry Stand was waiting for him.

"You're not going along then, Welchman?"

"I'll go later. Ply hasn't finished with me apparently. Wilson's a perfectly competent man, you know."

"No doubt, no doubt—though you wouldn't think so to listen to him." He scrunched up his eyes at the sun, which struck flecks of brilliant silver from his grizzled hair and long eyelashes. "The policeman, eh? Remember him from last time—nasty piece of work. What do you think of him?"

"I thought his reaction was a bit exaggerated," said Hugh carefully. "Have you talked to him yet?"

"Made a brief statement. He'll be back for more. Won't let you alone, that fellow—you'll see." He lowered his voice. "Keep him away from Alex as long as possible—for all our good."

"Alex is certainly in no condition at the moment to—"

"Quite, quite. And keep me posted about the boy, eh? Remember, he's my patient too." And then, with his normal briskness, "Well, come along, Welchman, there's someone I want you to meet." He drew Hugh into the hall. The blue-eyed policewoman standing by the dining room door gave him a smile—what was she doing: guarding the prisoner, or the telephone? He must phone Julia.

"In here, man." Stand led him through a door to the left into the living room—drawing room? sitting room? Hugh could never get these terms straight. "Elaine, my dear, I've brought you Dr. Welchman. Welchman, Mrs. Brinton."

A small blond woman sitting on the couch turned her head. "How do you do?" Her hands lay folded in her lap and she made no move to offer one to Hugh as he advanced into the room.

"Well, I'm off. I'll pop in this afternoon, Elaine."

"Thank you, Henry."

Stand was gone.

Hugh glanced round the long room, immaculately neat—beiges and mushroom pinks, flowers everywhere, a fire laid but unlit, brass tools gleaming. It looked unused. And Elaine Brinton looked unused to it, out of place; a ward sister, a bit of a terror, uncomfortable in mufti—an unbecoming black dress slightly too large for her. She would look attractive in uniform—just as Julia had always looked less attractive in hers.

"Please sit down, Doctor."

"Thank you." The delicate velvet armchair creaked at his weight, but held. It was not a room made for men.

"Tell me about Alex."

"As a matter of fact that's just what I was going to ask you." Hugh smiled, but got no response. How preternaturally still the woman was; except for a slight inclination of the head, she hadn't moved since he'd come in. He hesitated, then stubbed out his cigarette in a brilliantly shined silver ashtray. "Well, it's obvious that Alex has received a severe shock. In the last few days he's been in a state of rather delicate equilibrium—I expect you noticed that?" He paused momentarily, but again she gave no sign. "At any rate, we have been approaching a rather critical area, a critical point in the treatment. His father's death has come at a rather unfortunate moment. I'm sorry, that's a clumsy way of—"

"My husband nearly always got his timing wrong."

"I see." So she, at least, must think Jonathan committed suicide. "Well, the point I'm making is that Alex has undoubtedly suffered a setback, but I'm reasonably confident it's a temporary setback—we mustn't make too much of his immediate reaction of withdrawal, which is not an uncom—"

"It didn't seem like withdrawal this morning."

"The scene on the stairs, you mean? I wouldn't give that very much weight, Mrs. Brinton; I shouldn't pay any great attention to that."

He was interrupted by a knock on the door.

"Come in!" Elaine Brinton had a high, light, yet oddly flat way of speaking—a tone often found in orphanage children or cases of long emotional deprivation.

"I've brought you some nice fresh coffee then."

"Thank you, Wardy. Dr. Welchman, this is Mrs. Warden, our housekeeper."

"How do you do?" said Hugh, half rising.

"Pleased to meet you." Mrs. Warden cast Hugh a tight-lipped smile—except for a large rather bulbous nose, she gave an impression of tightness: Her hair was tightly drawn back into a bun, and her sober grey dress seemed to cling a little too tightly to her angular frame. She set a silver tray on the small table by the fireplace, surveyed it to see all was in order—silver coffee pot, milk jug, cups, a plate of biscuits, dainty little napkins—and then turned to Hugh, revealing yellowish teeth. "You don't know me of course, Doctor, but I know you. You married our Miss Julia, didn't you?"

"That's quite right."

"Then you're a lucky man. A lovely girl, she was, just lovely." She closely examined Hugh, and he was conscious of not coming up to scratch—no one in their right mind could ever have called *him* lovely (in fact, at the hospital, he was known as the Beast). "And could I ask," she lowered her voice, "could I ask how our young Master Alex is, Doctor?"

"He is," Hugh caught Elaine's cold impassive stare, "he's as well as can be expected."

"Expected." Mrs. Warden nodded sagely, as though Hugh had given her a pearl of great medical wisdom. "Well then—I'll leave you two together." And, without a second glance at the mistress of the house, she left the room.

"Coffee, Dr. Welchman?"

"Thank you."

"And how did you come to know about Alex's little outburst?"

"Dr. Stand informed me."

"I see." She paused, the coffee pot in her hand, then began to pour. "And I suppose you'll tell the police?"

"The doctor-patient relationship is entirely confidential as far as I'm concerned—besides which the incident is for me no more than hearsay. On the other hand, the police appear to know about it already."

"Wardy, of course. Sugar and milk? I wonder what mischief she's up to." She handed Hugh his cup. "It can't do Alex any—any harm, can it?" For the first time there was a hint of emotion—anxiety—in her voice. She must have been deeply wounded, if not by Alex's words, by the fury behind them, but she didn't show it.

"It depends what you mean by harm." He sipped the coffee—it was excellent. "Perhaps it would help if first you could tell me a bit about how Alex seemed yesterday, yesterday evening in particular, and something about his relationship to his father in general."

"Very well." She stared for a moment at the unlit fire. She just missed being a beauty—nose, mouth, eyes were perfectly formed but set in slightly too small a face—and was left with an oddity that might have been attractive except for her facial immobility. It was hard to imagine her laughing.

"I didn't actually see Alex until dinner, although I know he had come in a little earlier. He seemed rather excited—as though he was especially pleased about something. I thought he might have had a bit too much to drink. He sometimes does, I know the signs. Not often, you understand." She frowned.

"You disapproved of that?"

"Drink has been one of the curses of this house, Doctor." There was a faint tinge of colour in her cheek.

"Quite." Hugh drained his cup—hardly more than a mouthful of coffee. "And how did he seem to be getting on with his father?"

"They were rather—pally. Jonathan made some little joke about head-shrinkers and Alex laughed rather a lot."

"I gather Alex had a private talk with his father before dinner?"

"Who told you that?"

"Kate."

"Oh. Well, yes, it's perfectly true."

"You don't happen to know what passed between them?"

"No." She set her face—clearly she wasn't going to give him any more. And yet whatever had passed between father and son might well be the key to Alex's reaction.

"And after dinner?"

"Alex went up to his room. I heard his record player going until quite late."

"He didn't talk to you at all?"

"No. He usually makes a point of saying good night, but, as I say, he was—preoccupied."

"Yes. Now could you tell me about normal relations between Alex and your husband?"

"I'm not sure that 'normal' is the right word. They were not close. Katherine was his favourite. He was always rather austere with Alex. Most of the time he had very strict ideas about what was good for him, and then suddenly he would spoil him most dreadfully—like giving him that ridiculous sports car, which is really quite dangerous. He was not consistent, and I don't think Alex—even as a little boy—ever really knew what to make of him. He would have liked to look up to him, but unfortunately my husband was not a man it was very easy to look up to."

"Ummm." Hugh took out his cigarettes and lit one. "Mrs. Brinton, in your view, was your husband fond of Alex?"

"He hated him."

"Do you know why?" Hugh asked gently.

Elaine made a small motion of distress with her hands—the more poignant for its simplicity—and turned her head away.

"Then perhaps you could tell me a little about your own relationship with Alex?"

"Alex and I have always been fond of each other."

"Did you try to make up to him for the difficulties he had with his father?"

"Alex didn't exactly have *difficulties* with his father—unlike Katherine, who was always having rows with him then making them up. There was just this hostility—with an occasional interval of rather stilted affection. If Alex had any troubles or problems he would always come to me rather than his father."

"And did he have many problems?"

"No, hardly at all. Alex has always been rather even-tempered, you know, very polite and gentlemanly, even as a little boy—not given to tantrums or imaginary fears or anything like that. He always got on very well with everyone." So what did he need a psychiatrist for?—easy to recognise the accusation. And easy to see that he was the apple of his stepmum's eye—what a double blow the quiet boy's sudden rage this morning must have been.

"No nightmares?"

"Oh well—yes, he had nightmares. But then everyone does, don't they?"

"You didn't notice any serious after-effects resulting from his mother's death?"

"No, I don't think so. He was a very lovable little boy, you know—when he came back from Yorkshire, where he'd been sent for a few months, he was very much the same, a little more subdued perhaps. Of course he didn't remember anything about his mother's death at all, and we felt it best to leave it like that."

"And how did you feel about him seeking therapeutic help?"

"Does it matter what I think one way or the other?"

"Yes, I think so." Although the family had almost certainly never thought so; Alex might have confided a minor worry now and again, but never Kate, and probably not Brinton either. And yet Elaine was a force of a kind—a disapproving kind perhaps, but more than that too. Beneath that cool, self-defensive exterior, she would be strong, even fierce, in protection of someone she loved—of Alex. "Oh yes, I think it certainly matters."

"I was not in favour of it, no."

"Is that on general grounds or—"

"Oh no. You won't remember me, of course, but I used to attend your lectures at Matt's—I thought them most valuable."

"Did you, did you? No, I can't say I do remember you. But then perhaps you knew my wife—Julia Welling?"

"I knew her by sight. But I had completed my final year and was already on the wards. I just came out of interest."

"Ummm. Then exactly what was your objection to Alex coming to see me?"

"You really don't know?"

"No—though I might guess it had something to do with not wishing to evoke the subject of his mother's death."

"Yes, there was that. It hasn't had very happy results, has it?"

"I think I'd have to say the opposite. On the whole the prognosis is good—what Alex is suffering now is a temporary setback, as I've tried to make plain."

"But not so temporary for my husband."

"I'm sorry, Mrs. Brinton—I realise how painful all this must be for you." And yet she had not spoken from pain, he was almost sure —her entire attitude was characterised by a marked absence of grief. "But are you suggesting that there is a connection between your husband's death and Alex's present condition?"

"Alex would never wittingly hurt anyone, it's not in his nature. But my husb—" She stopped abruptly.

"Oh I don't know, Elaine—he could be a vicious little brat when he was a kid."

Hugh turned to see Kate smiling faintly. She had come in by a door he had not observed, that must lead directly to the dining room. She walked over and took a seat at the other end of the couch from Elaine. They were like two clean blackbirds at opposite ends of the same perch.

"That is rather typical of you, Katherine." Elaine's hands were clasped tightly together—her only sign of tension. "You know perfectly well it is not true."

"But I have a reputation to keep up as the family liar, don't I?" said Kate, with the same smile on her lips. And then she was suddenly serious. "If you're getting around to telling Hugh that

Daddy committed suicide, let me tell *you* that the idea is absurd. If it wasn't an accident, then he was murdered!"

"That seems to me rather unlikely, Katherine. There were plenty of people who disliked Jonathan, but one hardly murders for dislike."

"If I may interpose for a moment," Hugh said quickly, "it seemed to me that you were about to say something about your husband?"

"I was only going to say that he was apt to get quite disproportionately worked up over really quite trifling matters."

"Only when he'd had a few—anyone who's slightly well oiled is a disgusting object to my stepmother's teetotal moralism."

"You know perfectly well I often take a small glass of sherry before lunch on Sundays, Katherine."

"Mrs. Brinton, this tendency of your husband's to overreact—was this a comparatively recent development?"

"Recent?" She frowned as Hugh absent-mindedly threw his cigarette into the fireplace.

"Within the last three or four or five weeks, say?"

"Well, now that you mention it, I think, yes, it did become more marked recently."

"Oh come on, Elaine—Daddy's been a bit eccentric for years."

"For instance," said Elaine, ignoring Kate's interruption, "he developed something of a—well, I suppose you'd call it a mania for locking up. Is that the sort of thing you mean?"

"I'm not sure. Wasn't the house usually locked up at night?"

"Often not. But this wasn't just at night—it was all the time. Really extremely inconvenient. He couldn't bear to have the windows open either. I had to air the rooms behind his back. And in the study he actually screwed the window shut."

"I see. Did he got out much?"

"Hardly at all—recently in fact he stopped doing his rounds. He wouldn't even go out to have his hair cut. He seemed to be almost cutting himself off. He wouldn't even answer the phone—he actually had the instrument taken out of his study. He said he couldn't stand it ringing all the time."

"I feel exactly the same way myself," said Kate.

"I see." Hugh nodded. Probably neither of them saw quite where his questions were leading—but it made Kate, at least, clearly uneasy. "Is there anything else?"

"Well, I don't really understand it—of course with his drinking he'd been erratic for some time. I'm sorry, Katherine, but that's the truth." Evidently she sensed Kate's discomfort. "I think it must have been two Sundays ago—I had turned on the radio to listen to the service, which usually begins with church bells, you know. Perhaps I did have it on rather loud, but he ran into the room—this room—and he just picked up the radio and threw it into the fireplace. Of course it was smashed to smithereens."

"Elaine—you never told me that!"

"I didn't really think it was any of your concern, dear."

"Did he say why he did it?"

"He just said, 'those blood-stained bells again.' "

"The sound of the bells—I see. Were there any other noises he objected to?"

"He didn't like the rats scratching."

"You have rats in the house?"

"I don't think so, but lately Jonathan thought there were. He said he could hear them at night, whispering."

"A rat in the arras."

"He thought they came from the cellar. He even insisted that I call a firm of rodent exterminators, but when the man came, he wouldn't let him into the house. He said the man would steal the whisky in the cellar. I'm afraid he must have been quite rude, because later the manager rang up to complain."

"Dead for a ducat!"

Elaine turned her head slightly to look at Kate. "Is that very clever?"

"You're making all this up, aren't you, Elaine?"

"Don't judge others by yourself. I have no reason to make things up."

"Oh yes you have—if you can only make poor Daddy sound barmy enough, everyone will think it was perfectly natural for him to commit suicide. After all, all suicides are of 'unsound mind,' aren't they, Hugh?"

"No," he answered drily. "But Dr. Brinton's state of mind last night unquestionably has a bearing upon the nature of Alex's reaction this morning. I have been wondering if Alex didn't perhaps have a second talk with his father—after dinner."

"No." Elaine, quickly. "I told you he went upstairs to his room directly."

"Ummm." He refrained from pointing out that Alex could just

as easily come downstairs as go upstairs. It would be hard for Elaine to accept the idea that, when the crisis came, Alex went to his unloved father rather than to the woman who had cherished and guarded him and been his psychological mainstay through what could have been quite disastrous years. "Mrs. Brinton, I suppose you yourself didn't talk to your husband later last night, by any chance?"

"I—yes, I did. You sound just like the police, Dr. Welchman."

"I have no interest in the circumstances of your husband's death—my concern is Alex. I wondered if you had talked about him?"

"Briefly. I tried to make him understand that it was not a good idea to constantly be giving Alex whisky. He—well, it was not very edifying, I'm afraid."

"And then?"

"Then we went on to other things." She hesitated, then continued in a tone of stoic flatness. "I can't pretend that my husband and I were on good terms, Dr. Welchman—but I do think his last moments are due a little respect."

"Of course, but—"

"That won't wash with the police, Elaine."

Staring straight ahead, Elaine lifted her chin slightly, but made no reply to her stepdaughter. "Yes, Doctor?"

"Nothing." He shook his head. He was sorry for her. She had come as a nurse and stayed on as—not quite a wife, nor really a mother, nor yet, with Wardy in the house, ever really a housewife. Even now, sitting in her baggy black dress on the velvet couch, she had the air of an intruder—a guardian, a watchdog.

In the silence a thin trickle of smoke rose from the fireplace— by some trick of draft his cigarette end must have caught and kindled. Soon perhaps there would be a blaze.

As he opened his mouth to speak he was aware of the door behind him being opened.

"Mrs. Brinton?" It was Sergeant Ramm. "Superintendent Ply would like to see you."

Hugh glanced at his watch: eleven-forty. "What about me?"

"Oh yes, Doctor. Mr. Ply says he won't be needing you right away, but will try to contact you later—he apologises for keeping you waiting."

I'll bet he does, thought Hugh.

"Will you give Alex my love?" Elaine was on her feet. "If you think it advisable, that is."

"I'll do better than that. As soon as I have any news, I'll drop by and let you know how he's getting on."

"That would be very kind." She moved stiffly across the room and Sergeant Ramm shut the door behind her.

"I must be going." Hugh stood up.

"No—wait. Wait a minute." Kate smiled, then gave a little shuddering breath.

As Hugh sat down again, he thought how right she looked in Elaine's place—or Arabella's—in her well-cut black dress, her hair carefully plaited and coiled above each ear; elegant and correct, except for the bitten-down fingernails. Her mother's daughter.

"I suppose you think I behaved rather badly."

"I don't make judgements. It's my stock in trade."

"And what do you think of my stepmother—not exactly the mournful widow?"

"That kind of—of coldness is not an uncommon reaction to shock." He lit a cigarette. "Do you really dislike her so much?"

"I don't know." She sighed. "One's always maundering on about love, but the problem with someone like me is not lack of people to love—it's finding someone to hate. Ever since Mummy died I've been deprived of that—the hate object. Elaine doesn't really fill the bill." She picked up a biscuit and began to eat it. "But dislike—yes, she's easy to dislike. I dislike her quite a lot, Daddy disliked her. . . ."

"She mentioned to me that your father disliked Alex too."

"Did she?" Kate put down the biscuit. "Well, she would say that, wouldn't she?"

"I don't think I quite follow."

"To divert suspicion from Alex obviously—just in the same way she was busy making out the case for Daddy's suicide, which you seemed to be aiding and abetting."

"You're mistaken about that, Kate." In fact, what Elaine had recounted had raised some objections in his mind to the idea of suicide. "On the face of it—and I don't know much—I'd be inclined to think your father's death was almost certainly accidental. The combination of alcohol and certain types of tranquilisers, even taken in small quantities, can be extremely dangerous."

"But Daddy was always careful with drugs—which was why he was so careless. I mean he was so concerned about exact doses for himself that it never occurred to him that other people might be vague or stupid about it—which was why he never locked the medicine cabinet."

"Yes. On the other hand, alcohol impairs the memory function —it not infrequently occurs that someone who has drunk rather a lot takes several pills, imagining that each is the first one."

"Sort of psychosomatic suicide? But if Daddy had any unconscious self-destructive impulses, they were long-range—one doesn't drink oneself to death in a day, does one?"

"Nooo." He was curious that Kate and Stand were both so adamantly against the idea of an accident. What had Julia said about Kate?—*She'd die if anything happened to Jonathan.* The closeness of her identification with her father would give the idea of his self-destruction dangerous and ominous personal implications, which would have to be avoided on the simple grounds of self-preservation. Perhaps the only way she was going to be able to support his death at all was to find a scapegoat—a "hate object," as she'd put it. He had an unpleasant premonition of who this was going to be. It was delicate ground, but it would have to be trodden.

"Kate, last night you mentioned that your father seemed unusually happy, elated even—and that that made you uneasy."

"Yes, that's true." She brushed some biscuit crumbs from her lap. "But then doesn't happiness always make us uneasy? I mean this, today," she spoke slowly, "this familiar sorrow, or whatever you might call it, seems so much more normal. It's happiness that's aberrant."

"But mightn't that happiness have derived from a decision already taken?"

"Not the decision you mean. I'm not saying Daddy was particularly stable, but he was attached to his existence and to—to things in it. Why would he have killed himself, in the name of what?"

"You mentioned, you know, that if your father ever came to believe that Alex had been directly involved in the death of your mother that he would be liable to collapse."

"But not like that," she said quickly. "That's clever of you— but he would have just gone to pieces. Besides, I've rather changed my mind about that since this morning."

"Why?"

"You mean you don't know—you haven't heard what Alex said on the stairs?"

"Oh yes." The curl of smoke in the fireplace had gathered more body now. "But it would be a mistake to take what he said literally —I understand he was seriously disturbed."

"Why? It was a clear and direct statement. He *was* in a hell of a state, but that gives it more weight rather than less." She got up and took hold of a small pair of bellows, then knelt down and began to blow gently between the bars of the grate. "I'm not sure exactly how it worked. But you know how puzzled I was by Daddy's mood last night, his excitement? I think it might have been because of something Alex told him. Let's say that Alex had suddenly remembered seeing Elaine give Mummy the shove." The smoke rose in swirls now. "Which would have exonerated me, and Alex himself too of course. That would have made Daddy happy."

"But surely not Alex, and I understand he was rather merry last night. If what you say is true, wouldn't he have been more likely to have been seriously upset?"

"Daddy probably got him plastered on purpose—told him that it was some kind of misunderstanding or, at the least, a trivial accident, and that he'd clear it up with Elaine after dinner. Which of course wouldn't have been what he intended to do at all—he disliked, even hated Elaine, hated having to be dependent on her. Now he was sitting pretty—now he could get his own back all right, get rid of her, chuck her out. So they would have a terrible row, and then . . ."

"You think she murdered him?"

"Perhaps. It wouldn't have been as difficult as you think. She would just have said, 'You know you're being completely absurd, Jonathan. Of course I didn't murder Arabella; she was my patient. Now I'm going to get you a bromide to calm you down.' But instead of the powder, she'd have mixed a few tranquilisers or what-have-you in a glass and brought it to him. And he'd have quailed and swallowed it. You see, he did trust her—at least for things like that, her competence as a nurse, and he had the habit of obedience. It must be easy for nurses to get away with murder—doctors too, I suppose."

"I see." It had a certain superficial cogency. He coughed— Jeremy's cigarettes were harsh to the throat. "Don't you think you're rather allowing your emotions to colour your view of your stepmother?"

"What use are emotions if not to colour viewpoints?" There was a tiny flame now in the nest of kindling. Kate stood up and went back to the couch. "But actually I don't think that's what happened. I think it was Alex."

Hugh nodded—this was what he'd been afraid was coming. "Perhaps you'd better tell me."

"All right. Let's say Alex goes up to his room last night. After a while, perhaps he dozes off, he sobers up a bit—and the doubts that Daddy had instilled begin to get the better of him. He decides to have it out with Daddy, goes downstairs to the study door and then hears Elaine and Daddy having this row. He's quite used to creeping about the place and listening at keyholes. And of course he realises that Daddy is out to destroy Elaine. So he waits a bit after Elaine has left and then goes in to see Daddy himself. He pretends to be just as convinced as ever of Daddy's good intentions, suggests another drink. Maybe he's already prepared the fatal potion—or he could take the glasses out to the surgery for more water, Daddy always drinks—drank his whisky with water. And he wouldn't suspect Alex, you know—Alex is rather a wet after all, but he's always had a streak of sly viciousness that people don't recognise. And—he's not exactly a model of stability, is he?—perhaps an Oedipal fury gave him the guts, or pushed him over the edge." She smiled faintly, looking directly at Hugh. "That's what the police think, isn't it?"

"You have discussed this with the police?"

"No—there is such a thing as family loyalty, however fragile it is. But it's not hard to see the way Mr. Ply's mind is working— the police always prefer the obvious, I imagine, and Alex is very much the obvious suspect, isn't he, if Daddy's was what they are calling a 'suspicious death'?"

"The police are more or less bound to investigate the circumstances of a death whose causes are not immediately apparent. And they are not less prone—perhaps more prone—than the normal layman to assume that someone seeking psychiatric help is *per se* seriously unbalanced and therefore more liable to perform a criminal act. But that's not a view that ought to be encouraged, and in Alex's case I regard it as quite unwarranted."

"Yes, Doctor."

"Kate. I want you to be quite clear about this." He put a sharper edge to his voice. "If your father was murdered, it would not have been a case of simply seeing someone in a vulnerable position, giving a quick push or slamming a door on the spur of the moment without time to reflect; on the contrary, it would have been a cold-blooded act, coolly decided on and carried out; the murderer would have had to dissemble, to lull suspicion, to wait and to watch, and to—"

"Hugh—don't!"

"Very well. But the point is that it would have required a quality of ruthlessness that is extremely rare, and of which I would clinically judge Alex to be incapable." He hesitated, but he would have to go farther. "You've got to get some perspective on this. I feel the strong probability is that your father's death was accidental —but, whether that is so, or whether he died by his own hand, or by the hand of another—he is dead. That's the fact that you have to face as squarely as you can. And hypothetical attributions of guilt to others is not going to help you deal with that." She sat unmoving, staring at the fire, which had caught and was beginning to blaze now. He felt as though he were speaking to the air, or to himself —how much he wanted, needed, to talk calmly to Julia, cool and measured and uninvolved. Although, of course, Julia *was* involved.

Kate turned her head. "You imagine I'm blaming Alex for Daddy's death so as not to have to face my own overwhelming guilt feelings, is that it?" Her tone was mild, only faintly sardonic.

Hugh drew slowly on his cigarette—if he had not been a smoker, he would have sighed. In his experience, intellectual grasp of a situation was nearly always one of the greatest inhibitors of real progress. "I'm only saying that you have to be careful."

"For whose sake? Alex's? Or mine?"

"For both."

"But you really mean for Alex's—you're only really interested in patients, aren't you? Would I become more worthy if I were one too?"

"There's nothing dishonourable about seeking help."

"And I suppose you have someone up your sleeve. The man at the door, for instance."

"The man at the—oh, you mean Jeremy Wilson. Perhaps. He's extremely sound. But you'd have to come to the Clinic in that case —he doesn't take private patients."

"But don't you understand that I don't feel guilty—that even if I had killed poor Daddy myself, I wouldn't feel guilty. I feel," she opened her hands, "bereft. That's all I feel, Hugh—bereft." The gesture was one of bewilderment.

"In that case, I think you should put the question of blame to one side and—"

"Oh no. No. We must preserve our proper hatreds—just as we do our loves—or else we have nothing. Nothing. Isn't that why people commit suicide—because they have nothing?"

"Sometimes, though the psychological set would have to be one that permitted, or even encouraged, such a solution. But neglect *is* often an important factor, particularly among the old. However, there are usually a number of elements at work—not all of them irrational, by any means. Of course—"

"Neglect—but I did neglect Daddy, you see. I can't forget that he was in there last night—in his study—dead or dying, and I just passed by. I nearly went in—but he'd been in such an odd good mood when I left him and I thought, I was afraid, that it might have changed. I didn't want to—I wanted to go to bed happy for one night. But if only I had—had gone in, perhaps . . ."

"That isn't a very productive way of thinking. You might as well say that if I had come in—and you did ask me—and met your father, none of this would have happened. One can't afford to avoid reality in that way."

"How relentlessly sane you are. It must be uncomfortable at times." She spoke lightly, then gave a shudder. "I'm sorry. I'm afraid. You don't blame me for that, do you?"

"Of course not."

"I'm afraid of knowing what has happened—of what's going to happen." Her voice, which had been low and throaty—like her mother's, perhaps—changed to a quick intensity. "I hate this house —God, how I hate it! I've always hated it. It's doom-laden, beastly. We're cursed here in this blighted, bloody place. God, what wouldn't I have given to have been brought up in a house like yours —nice and modern and four-square, where nothing ever happens except to other people!"

Hugh stubbed out his cigarette. Here in a nutshell were all the passionate guilts and deprivations and hostilities that unconsciously afflicted her—or not so unconsciously, for there was, he thought, a clear element of calculation in the performance. It struck him too as a peculiar irony that the symbolical house of the flesh

Kate so reviled was the real house where Julia had come to seek a solace and stability she did not have at home.

"Well, you know," he said mildly, "all houses have their share of guilt and betrayal—even mine." Although, he added as a mental rider, it is not in fact mine, but Julia's.

She stared at him, coming to herself. "Oh for Christ's sake stop *analysing* me!" And then she laughed—and he was glad to hear it. "Well, I'll give you the vileness of your house too—though I don't believe it." She took a biscuit from the plate and ate it rapidly.

Hugh stood. "I have to be going."

"Where's your car?"

"I don't know. The police brought it along, I hope."

"I'll come with you."

He nodded and opened the door into the hall for her.

"Your car keys, Doctor."

"Oh thank you, Nurse—er . . ."

"Constable." The policewoman smiled. "We put your car in the lane at the back of the house."

"Thank you—Constable." Hugh picked up his bag.

"I'll show you," Kate said, "come on." She preceded him along the passage, pushed through the swing door into a smaller hall—the back hall, he thought, where Maida had scratched and whined on the afternoon of Arabella's death. Involuntarily he glanced round and saw the dog-leash on a hook beside a row of coats, a nurse's cape, boots, umbrellas. "That's the kitchen—and that's the service door to the dining room."

Hugh caught her smile. "I see."

"We go out this way. The back door."

It opened on to the north or north-west side of the house, and it was chilly out of the sun. They began to walk down a stone-flagged path.

"Have the police asked you where you were last night yet, Hugh?"

"Me? No—why?"

"They've asked me. At a guess, I'd say they're not sure when Daddy died, so they're checking up on our alibis."

"Well, you were with me until . . ."

"Until when? That's just it—twelve, one? I've no idea."

"I'm afraid I don't either." They passed the kitchen window and turned the corner of the house. "I didn't look at my watch—but it was certainly latish."

"Perhaps Julia noticed the time when you got in?"

"She was asleep." He hesitated to mention his visit to Reg—all these academic people knew each other and he'd had his fill of gossip for the morning. Anyway he couldn't see Reg as a time watcher. They were walking through a kitchen garden and he caught the warm summery scent of the boxwood hedges surrounding the beds.

"That's the patients' door there." She nodded at the lone door on that side of the house, with a little round window beside it. "I'll have to put up a notice, I suppose." She turned and opened the gate that led into the lane.

Hugh's Rover was parked a little farther up, neatly facing the main road.

Kate ran her fingers over the brass plate on the gatepost: *Dr. J. J. Brinton.* "This will have to come down too."

They had moved into the sun and Hugh felt himself beginning to sweat.

"It'll be the first time for over a hundred years there's not been a G.P. in the house. My great-grandfather Anstey put up his plate here in 1865, and then my grandfather at the turn of the century, then Henry, then Daddy. I wonder if Henry will come back—it wouldn't surprise me."

"Stand—here, to the New Inn?"

"Don't sound so surprised. I expect Elaine will invite him back—they always had eyes for each other. That's why Henry moved out when Daddy married Elaine."

"But I thought it was your mother Stand was engaged to?"

"Yes. He was once. Poor old Henry got a raw deal all round from Daddy. But I expect he'll get the girl in the end." She loosened her hair so that it fell about her shoulders. A gesture of liberation—and hadn't, in fact, her father's death liberated her in some way?

"Of course, the house is Alex's now—but he'll do whatever she wants, if he's not locked up somewhere. Even if he is. Sorry, Hugh—but it all really comes back to Alex, doesn't it?" She shook her head and the hair stirred. "I wish her joy of the rats." She sighed. "Oh yes, there'll be changes. No more whisky in the cellar. Henry pontificating in the surgery. Little Alex licking everyone's arse. Wardy out on her ear—unless she can think of a way to blackmail Elaine into letting her stay. No heat till Michaelmas or after Lady Day. I expect she'll institute morning prayers—or worship, as she calls it." She glanced sidelong at Hugh. "You see, I'm getting it out of my system—that's the healthy thing to do, isn't it?"

"Ummm. You know, Kate, if I were you, I think I'd go back to Lady Strange."

"Why? Nobody's going to murder me. Oh I see—you think I'll say something silly, or do something silly?"

"No one—and particularly no one under stress—is immune from doing foolish things. If you want to get hold of me, you know where I am—if not at St. Ethelbert's, at home."

"Yes, Doctor."

He took a last look at the house—how forbidding it seemed from this angle. He turned and held out his hand. "Good-bye, Kate."

The inside of the Rover was stiflingly hot, and the heavy sense of lethargy he'd felt earlier in the morning came over him again. His head was muzzy and he had difficulty in ordering his impressions. As an April cloud flitted across the sun, he was reminded of his own dream—for an instant he felt he understood it fully and that it bore a vital relation to this whole business of Brinton's death, and then it was gone. He wondered whether Brinton—*always popping pills*— had been in the habit of taking amphetamines. And yet, in the circumstances of his death, the hypothesis of amphetamine psychosis, like alcoholic paranoia, posed more problems than it solved. What kind of man had Brinton really been? Somewhere out of the past Hugh heard his father's voice: "an undesirable fucking type, laddie." Perhaps, but, apart from all other considerations, it was not generally the undesirable types that committed suicide.

He lit a Capstan and switched on the ignition. With a grating of gears the car began to move in a series of jerking hops. Hugh abruptly released the handbrake and swerved with unintended velocity into the main road, narrowly missing a bus.

9

". . . Yes, I think on the whole Kate's taking it better than one— or you—might have supposed. But I don't think being in that house is at all good for her."

"She never liked the New Inn," said Julia across the dinner table.

"No, and I can quite see why." He took a mouthful of anonymous meat stew—goulash or beef burgundy perhaps. Years ago he'd overheard one of Julia's bridge friends say, "Oh, I expect it'll be her usual grey mud again," and it had stuck in his mind, just as sometimes it stuck in his gullet. He said, "I suggested she go back to her rooms in college."

"That's what you said to Alex."

Hugh looked up abruptly and his spare glasses slid down his nose. "Yes. That's true—it was." He had come home late, tired, taken a bath and changed into an old grey flannel suit—yet Alex had remained with him, lying on the stretcher, his eyes shut in the bright sun, and, later, comatose in his private room, softly holding Hugh's hand. He decided to ignore the implications of Julia's remark. "I think Kate is going to be—sensible. At least, as far as she herself is concerned. What I really doubt is her discretion."

"I'm sure Kate can be discreet if it serves her purpose—she had a lot of practice as a child."

"Yes." He hesitated—he had only given her the bare outlines of Brinton's death, hardly more than she had known already. It seemed that Mrs. Nance was a friend of Wardy's and the grapevine had worked with such rapidity that Julia was informed of the death before Hugh knew himself. He thought she was looking particularly beautiful tonight—even in the rather harsh light of the dining room there was a faint glow under the ivory pallor of her cheek; all traces of yesterday's anxiety had been smoothed away and replaced by a tranquility, almost a contentment, which he did not wish to disturb. It was as if the bus had arrived, the ice really been broken; and he was aware of a new and stronger kindling of hope—that particular glow, that special grace, was often the first outward sign of pregnancy. He smiled, and she smiled back.

And yet, unusual for him, he wanted to talk. He had not been able to organise his thoughts properly in this afternoon's rush to catch up on a lost morning's work. Six hours of patients, all unusually heavy going; a pile of paperwork that had to be dealt with urgently; ten minutes with Jeremy Wilson; a nagging worry about Sister Arkwright, who was obviously under some kind of personal tension that was affecting her usual incomparable competence. And then a late summons to the Director's office, where he had been kept waiting by Miss Plenderlieth-Blunt and then rebuked by the Director: "I hear you let me down this morning, my dear Hugh. I particularly did not want Bantock to chair that meeting. You don't seem to realise . . ." With a touch of impatience that had surprised even himself, Hugh had retorted, "Well, John, you could try chairing your own meetings now and again if they're so vital, and sending me to the conferences." He had been cheered by the look of horror on John Grantham's face—Hugh was employed at St. Ethelbert's partly because of his hard-working competence, partly because of his supposed connection to higher psychiatric politics through his dead father-in-law, but mainly because he was unambitious and didn't make waves. Grantham didn't care for competition, or for brilliance—which was why Jeremy Wilson probably would not last long.

Hugh sighed. "Yes, but that's just it," he took off his glasses, "what if discretion does *not* serve Kate's purpose?"

"Hugh—is there some kind of doubt about Jonathan's death?"

"I'm afraid there is—or rather the police seem to think there is. I believe they're treating it as a suspicious death. In itself, that doesn't worry me, but—"

"But what does that mean?"

"I suppose, ultimately, it means murder. Of course it's far-fetched—if Brinton really did die of an overdose, it's extremely hard to imagine somebody administering it to him. But, after all, it's the police's business to be suspicious—and they're quite right in that the cause of death has to be determined. My only concern is with Alex—but unfortunately they seem to have a bee in the bonnet."

"About Alex?—but they couldn't seriously consider—"

"About Alex, yes—about the Brintons in general. Of course, in a sense it's no more than the usual foolishness about someone under any kind of treatment by a psychiatrist being automatically classified as 'dangerous.' Then unfortunately the investigating officer is the same man—Ply, by name—who was always convinced that Arabella Brinton was murdered. It's the same fellow whom Mike talked to on Monday night—and he seems to think *that's* a suspicious circumstance too. But the main problem is that when Alex was told about his father's death this morning—clumsily told by the woman they call Wardy—he created rather a scene, throwing himself about and shouting accusations. Stand put him under enormously heavy sedation—effectively putting him quite out of reach of help, for the time being, at any rate."

"Is it very serious—serious for Alex?"

"Serious enough to hospitalise him. The main outlines of the problem are fairly clear—but that doesn't mean it's going to be easily resolved." He took out a new box of fifty and lit a cigarette, glad to get away from Jeremy's gaspers. "I think Alex probably remembered something after he left here yesterday afternoon—he may well have been able to fill in that significant gap in his memory of the afternoon of Arabella's death, although I have no means of knowing that. But whatever it was, I rather think he told his father . . . I get the impression from what Kate says and from what Mrs. Brinton says that something had been resolved between father and son. Or rather, and this is more important, that Alex thought it had been resolved. He drinks a bit too much, happily though, not morosely, goes up to bed early, plays a few records, gets up latish —which leads me to suppose that he was not worried, but relieved. Then he is met on the stairs with the news of his father's death. His reaction is striking—literally, as a matter of fact. A frantic denial of responsibility in the form of wild accusations of another. What he is doing there—the mechanism—is unconsciously imputing magical powers of life and death to his buried, or not so buried, impulses, and furiously denying them at the same time. This is a classically critical moment—an absolute breakthrough leading to catharsis, if properly handled. And what does Stand do? He pumps him full of Thorazine and clamps the lid back on again." With an impatient movement he stubbed out his cigarette in his plate.

"You're angry, Hugh—I don't often see you angry."

"Yes. Yes, I am angry." He looked at her in surprise at his own unusual emotion—and at her gentle recognition of it. For an instant he saw her as in his dream and had a sense of illumination that was as instantly gone. And with it, his anger. "Stand couldn't have known it, but he may well have destroyed months of work. We have two almost identically traumatic events—both on the stairs— and one is likely to reinforce the other. We have farther to go now perhaps, and even to get back to the same place may take a long time or . . ."

"Or never? You're not saying that, are you, Hugh?"

"No, I . . ." Where did this feeling of bitter pessimism come from? He cast around. Lummis—Bob Lummis, of course. He shook his head. "No—I've been painting the picture too dark. It's equally possible that tomorrow—"

The phone rang, and he recognised the slightly shriller tone of the patients' line. "I'll go." He heaved himself up.

"Welchman speaking . . . What now? Tonight? . . . Don't you think it a little late, Mr. Ply? . . . I see. Very well then. Yes, as soon as you can, please." He dropped the shiny white instrument back into its cradle. White for the patients, black for the others. The policeman had called on the wrong line . . . or had he?

He returned slowly to the dining room—circumstances were again conspiring to prevent him talking to Julia calmly. To his surprise she wasn't there—the grey mud had been cleared away. He sat down at the table—plain scrubbed deal had replaced the polished mahogany of old Professor Welling's day. After his death, Julia had stripped the house of everything substantial and shiny and plush—and comfortable. It was not so much that Hugh disliked the modernity (or whatever it was), as that he was discomfited by the lack of warmth—the fleshlessness. Julia had achieved in *her* house a place unencumbered by memories or possessions (for those objects that surrounded them might have belonged to anyone), that "purity of spirit" that Kate so missed in hers. The emptiness of the house, of the garden, was partly explained by this denial of memory. He wondered if Julia even knew where her mother was buried. And he thought of his own mother's dutiful—loving—Sunday pilgrimages to her daughter's grave, an hour's journey by bus and tube each way: *Here Lies Harriet Welchman, Aged 8, beloved daughter of Albert and Dorothy.* How often had he stood there with her in the bleak cemetery with the cold drizzle falling. Once, when he was very young, he had asked her what Harriet had been like—"Oh not a bit like you, Hugh," she'd said, and even then he'd realised that she must have been lively and gay and pretty.

"Who was that, Hugh?"

He looked up at her in her slightly formal black dress. "That was the police—they're coming up in a few minutes. More questions, I suppose."

She nodded. "I've got some rice pudding, if you . . ."

"No, I don't think so, thanks." He lit a cigarette. "Let's go into the waiting room."

They were only halfway along the hall when the bell rang.

"That's quick work."

"Take them into my study, if you like, Hugh."

"All right." He watched Julia go into the waiting room, then opened the front door.

Half an hour later Ply, puffing gently at his pipe, said, "Look here, Doctor, I know you feel a conflict between your professional loyalty to a patient and your plain duty as a citizen to help the police in their enquiries. I respect that." He smiled his black-toothed smile; he had conducted the questioning in a reasonable, even genial manner, quite different from the morning's aggressive interrogation. "But you know as well as I that what young Brinton remembered about his mother's death may well have an important bearing on what occurred last night. Now you tell me I shan't be able to see the lad for several days—maybe even several weeks. Well, I can wait of course. Every policeman's second name is patience. On the other hand I'd like to get this matter cleared up as soon as possible. So just between you and me and the gatepost—off the record—can't you give me a hint of what was troubling the youngster?"

The phone rang, but as Hugh reached for it, it was answered, though not before he had recognised the ring of the private line—one of Julia's bridge friends, no doubt. They were sitting in her little study—Hugh and Ply at the plain table against the wall, Sergeant Ramm at the rolltop desk, typing up Hugh's statement on Julia's old Imperial. So it probably would be off the record—the written record, at least. Hugh had met the Superintendent's calm with his own deliberately slightly pompous professionality. But he didn't like the new Ply any more than the old—less, in fact. He knew that he was reacting to the image of his father, whom Ply so closely resembled—the same mixture of the jovial and the heavy-handed, of openness and cunning, the same easy reasonableness that could switch in a moment to a kind of savage bullying that had made his mother's life miserable, that could never be trusted. This realisation irritated Hugh, who was being pushed perilously close to a projective identification with Alex, an error that could help no one.

"Well, Superintendent, in all fairness perhaps I do owe you a slightly fuller explanation." He grudgingly admitted that it would be unreasonable to withhold all information; and it might help to counteract whatever absurdities Kate had confided in Ply—he didn't trust her promise of silence. "The problem on the face of it is a simple one, however there are one or two complications. Without going into detail . . ." He chose his words with care, but he was an old hand at giving apparently concise summaries without revealing anything of real significance or arriving at any concrete conclusion. Kate had been right about one thing—Ply had enquired closely into his evening at Lady Strange and the time of his arrival at the New Inn and his return home. Reluctantly Hugh had mentioned his visit to Reg Semple, but he had scrupulously refrained from asking the significance of these questions.

". . . rather technical, I'm afraid. But to summarise in plain language, I seriously doubt anything young Brinton remembers is going to elucidate his mother's death. We're unlikely ever to be able to unravel what he imagines he saw, or what he's been told he saw, from what he did see—if indeed he saw anything. From a clinical point of view of course, none of this is a major consideration." He put his cigarette out in a conch shell that he hoped Julia had meant for an ashtray.

Ply nodded, but made no comment. He had been smoking continuously—his pipe seemed inexhaustible—and the room was filled with the smell of his scented tobacco. Suddenly he said, "Nearly finished, Andy?"

"On the last para—won't be a tick, Super."

Julia's study was unfamiliar territory to Hugh. Occasionally he would pass the door and hear the same rapid rattle of the typewriter as now, but he seldom entered. There were days when he didn't encounter Julia at all, except at breakfast—particularly on Mondays and Fridays, the bridge nights. If he was home he would sometimes slip down between patients and get Mrs. Nance to make him a cup of tea. Tea, which in his own home had been such an important social rite, was reduced to something one drank hurriedly, standing up in the kitchen. And Julia would be off playing tennis or practising archery in the summer, or roaming the Fens on her Norton, or perhaps sitting silently in this room—he didn't know. Again he was oppressed with a sense of—almost of desolation. He had the curious idea that if he could draw back the oatmeal-coloured curtains that shut out the darkness, he would see the garden in full bloom of roses and bright sunlight. . . .

"That's it—here we are, Super."

Ply took the statement and gave it a cursory glance. "All right, Doctor, if you'd just read that over, I'd be much obliged. If it looks okay, initial the first page and sign on the second, if you wouldn't mind. Take your time."

Hugh smiled faintly at the admonition—so often in his own mouth. He read rapidly—his cautious answers seemed even less forthcoming translated into flat police prose:

About ten days ago I prescribed for said patient the mild tranquilising drug Librium in the amount of 500mg consisting of fifty capsules of 10mg each, three to be taken every day. To my certain knowledge Brinton had the prescription filled and took the prescribed dosage for at least two or three days. I do not know whether he continued to take the drug thereafter. Librium is a drug I prescribe for many of my patients showing symptoms of mild anxiety or stress. I did not prescribe any form of hypnotic or sleeping pill.

In fact, he was morally certain that by the third day Alex had stopped taking the Librium, which he blamed for the recurrence of his staircase phobia. But Hugh was concerned to combat the implied police equation: dangerous instability = need for drugs; failure to take drugs = dangerous instability. He jotted his quick indecipherable signature and handed the statement back to Ply. "Yes, that's all right."

"Thank you." Ply was already on his feet; he carefully folded the statement and stuffed it into one pocket and dropped his pipe in another. "That's been very helpful, Doctor."

In the hall he took his hat from the table. "Like me to mail these for you, Doctor?"

Hugh glanced at the sheaf of envelopes on the letter salver— Julia must have been billing the patients, though the top one, addressed in her strong passionate handwriting, was to Barker & Trentham, her solicitors. "Oh don't bother. I'm sure there's nothing urgent."

"No bother. There's a box at the bottom of The Lane, and I'm going to walk anyway. Andy, you take the car."

"Right, Super. See you in the morning."

They stood on the doorstep, watching Ramm's skilful U-turn and the taillight dwindling down the driveway and The Lane.

"Nice night," Ply said, putting on his hat.

"What? Oh—yes." It was too—clear and cool and moonless, faintly scented with spring.

The policeman seemed to hesitate, but then all he said was, "Good night then, Doctor." He touched his hat in the semblance of a salute and moved off down the drive with a measured regular crunch.

Hugh was in the act of lighting a cigarette when the phone

rang. He turned quickly into the house and picked up the white instrument. "Welchman speaking. Who? Bantock, oh."

"Look, Welchman—I gather Wilson has told you about your chap Lummis. Days rather than weeks, I'm afraid. I've just come from seeing him. He's heavily sedated of course, but there was a lucid interval in which he asked to see you. Wants to talk. I could taper off the medication tomorrow afternoon to give him twenty minutes or so relatively unclouded. Four o'clock suit you? Good. I'll have him wheeled over. Right. Not at all, not at all—nothing. Good night."

Hugh went heavily into the waiting room. He stood in front of the fireplace and let the gently poppling gas warm the backs of his legs. He carefully put a match to the dead cigarette in his mouth and stared down at Julia, who was sewing a double patch into the seat of a pair of trousers—threadbare buttocks being part of the price of his profession.

She glanced up at him. "What did they want?"

"What?" He blinked. "Oh—the police." He didn't want to talk about that—the police, the Brintons, the deliberate confusion of nebulous suspicions. He was about to shrug it off, when he was aware of a strained look on Julia's face. The whole business was not really his worry, except professionally, but it was, he told himself again, very much Julia's. He forced a smile. "Nothing much really —wanted to know more about Alex, when they could see him, that sort of thing."

"Hugh," the needle was poised in her hand, and he had a sudden sensation of menace, "they really *do* suspect Alex."

"Well, as I told you at dinner, I think the grounds are very thin for any kind of suspicion of that nature."

Julia slowly folded her hands in her lap. "Mike Semple rang up while you were in there with them. He says they've analysed the contents of the glass found on Jonathan's desk. It contained heavy traces of chlordiazepoxide, apart from the whisky. That's Librium, isn't it?"

"Yes." He frowned. "I thought Mike was in London. Did he ring up Mainwaring?"

"No, it wasn't Mainwaring this time. It was the police. Mike was called back early. They wanted to search Alex's rooms in college, and . . ."

"And?"

"They found an empty bottle of Librium prescribed by you."

"I see." Hugh sighed. What a devious lot they were. "It doesn't particularly surprise me. Alex gave up taking the Librium after a few days—he thought it made his staircase problem worse. I expect he threw the remainder away. It would be the natural thing to do. That's not very worrying."

"Mike's worried—I know you think he's an old woman, but that's not all. They found Alex's fingerprints on the glass too."

"Well, there's no mystery about the fact that Alex was drinking whisky with his father in the study before dinner. If Alex poured the drinks, obviously his fingerprints would be on the glass. Look, Julia, did Mike say he'd actually talked to Ply?"

"Yes, I thought I'd made that clear—it must have been not long before they came up here."

"Then that accounts for it, I think. Mike was impressed by Ply the other night, you know, a little too impressed. Now I believe he's simply overreacting. Ply wants him to be worried, wants us all to be worried—to create an atmosphere of mistrust and suspicion. Well, he hardly has to create that, it exists already in the Brinton family. Frankly I think it's a deplorable—and useless—method of proceeding, but it's not so uncommon. I see no substantial basis at all for believing that Brinton was murdered."

"You think it was—an accident?"

"It seems to me very likely. It's a common enough occurrence. The patient's excited, takes a pill as prescribed, then a drink, a nightcap say—definitely not prescribed. The benzodiapines rapidly potentiate the central depressant action of the alcohol, with its consequent effect on the memory. So the patient takes a second pill or capsule, under the impression it's the first—and so on."

"But Jonathan wasn't a patient, he was a doctor."

"Yeees. Of course, that's perfectly true." He frowned. Both Stand and Kate had emphasised how careful he was about dosing himself, neither believed in an accident. One could discount Kate, but Stand's view was a professional one.

"Hugh, why not suicide? Suppose, as you say, Alex did recollect something yesterday afternoon—filled in the gap in his memory. And told his father. And suppose it was something Jonathan simply couldn't face—perhaps that Alex had seen *him* slam the door on Arabella. Wouldn't that be a sufficient reason for suicide?"

"On the face of it, yes—but the trouble is that, from a police point of view, it would have provided an equally good, or even better, motive for Alex to have killed him."

"Oh God!" Julia bent her head; the black hair gleamed in the lamplight. His heart went out to her. "After all these years . . ."

"Mind you, I think that's very unlikely." He bent over and put out his cigarette. He took another, but his matchbox was empty and he began to pat his pockets vaguely, in search of a full one. "Suicide is a definite possibility, although there are one or two difficulties."

"You mean, he left no letter?"

"Well, there's that of course, although—"

"If there was one, I expect Wardy took it."

"What?"

"Wardy, the housekeeper. It's just the sort of thing she would do—particularly if he confessed to killing Arabella. She was devoted to Jonathan, she wouldn't want any blemish on the name of Brinton."

"But that would have been a most malicious thing to do."

"I don't suppose she thought of the consequences, although I think she's quite capable of being malicious. But anyway, once she'd done it, it would have been too late. There are matches in the box. Give me one of my cigarettes while you're about it, would you?"

"Yes, of course." He took the lid from the ebony box on the mantelpiece, handed her a cigarette, lit it and his own. "Yes."

"But you're dubious, Hugh—why?"

"Well, puzzled, at any rate. You see, there are some indications that Brinton had recently entered a stage of alcoholic paranoia. In fact, from what I heard from his wife this morning, I think that is almost certainly so. He felt menaced, persecuted, threatened—by what or whom we don't know, but in any case this is not a rational matter. And the problem there is that it rather excludes the kind of suicide you are talking about—a rational act with good cause and a full explanation. Besides which, though paranoid suicides are not uncommon, the means are generally violent—I would say almost invariably. On the whole, from what I know now, I should have thought it more likely that Brinton would kill someone else rather than himself. Of course, I never saw the man—I have only hearsay to go on. And even if I'm right, unexpected remissions do occur;

there might well have been a period of temporary lucidity. . . ." He looked down at Julia, wondering how she would accept this sketchy attempt at comfort—he hardly believed it himself. But it was as if she hadn't heard him. She sat, staring, faraway, the smoke from her cigarette drifting unnoticed into her eyes, slipping sideways, sucked by the slight heat of the lamp into the roseate cone of the shade.

"Well," he said as casually as he could, "what else did Mike have to say for himself?"

She didn't answer at once; and then she said, "Did you know Reg was once a patient of Jonathan's?"

"Reg? Mike never said anything about that."

"I expect not—he's a bit ashamed of it. It was a long time ago, shortly after they came to Cambridge; Mike heard about Arabella and—well, I suppose he thought it would be rather a lark to have a possible murderer as a G.P. But it didn't turn out as expected. Jonathan attended Reg a few times, then must have made a pass at her or something. Mike was furious, rang up the police, but later thought better of it and withdrew the complaint. But now . . ."

"Now what?" Hugh felt a sense of irritation at all this idiocy and deviousness. "Don't tell me that he's afraid Reg went off and murdered Jonathan last night? That's a bit far-fetched, even for a delayed reaction. Anyway, Reg didn't because I saw her latish last night, went up to the house."

"Oh. Then that's that." She smiled faintly, then was serious again. "Anyway, I think he was more worried about the police finding something compromising at the New Inn. They told him there were a lot of notes and billets-doux in Jonathan's desk— signed Mopsey and Poppet and Bunny Rabbit and that sort of thing."

"Surely that's hardly Reg's style?"

"No, but all the same he's anxious—on the phone he sounded slightly hysterical."

"I see." His tone was neutral, but he was suddenly angry, bitter even at such stupid mischief, such petty self-concern in the face of a man's dying.

He crunched out his cigarette and went over to the French windows and lifted the curtain and looked out at the clear night. It was not Brinton of course, but Bob Lummis's dying that evoked such a harsh, personal reaction in him. A pain of dying that entirely overrode any sense of the limited, ameliorative gains he sometimes achieved in the case of the living. This death, this loss was his own.

"Hugh. Hugh, there's something I want to tell you."

"What?" He roused himself, let the curtain fall back, turned to his wife.

"Hugh—what is it? What's the matter?" She stood up.

And as he saw her, beautiful, young, alive, a grief assailed him, winded him, so that he had to reach back and hold hard to the curtain.

"Bob Lummis is dying."

"Oh Hugh!"

He shook his head. "I'm sorry," he said. "Forgive me. I'm a damned fool."

She came slowly over to where he stood and laid her hand on his arm. "No, Hugh, it's I who should be asking forgiveness." There were tears on her pale, grave cheek.

"What is it you wanted to tell me?"

"Nothing." She smiled. "Another time. Nothing."

10

Alex sat on the bed, staring straight ahead, his hands clasped tightly on his knees. He didn't turn, but a flicker of his long eyelashes betrayed his awareness of Hugh's presence.

"Hello, Alex." Hugh held out his hand. "How are you feeling this morning?"

"Hello." Alex looked away, then back again. After a pause he raised his hand. "Sorry, but I can't get up."

"That's all right." Hugh took a hard chair and sat down.

"They've taken away my belt—and my tie!"

"That's perfectly normal procedure on the wards, you know."

"And they won't let me have my shoes. Look!" He thrust out his feet, which were clad in the regulation grey canvas slippers.

"That happens to everyone. Don't worry." Hugh made a business of taking out his cigarettes.

"And they won't let me smoke either," said Alex in an accusing voice.

"Well, you can have one now." He held out the packet and, after a slight hesitation, Alex took a cigarette. Hugh lit it for him

142

and got an ashtray and put it on the floor between them. The boy inhaled deeply.

"I understand you didn't take your pills this morning?" When Hugh had questioned Sister Arkwright about the notation *medication refused* on the chart, she had been unusually vague—she'd left it to a new nurse despite his instructions to pay special attention to Alex.

Alex had not answered.

"Did you have any particular reason for refusing them?"

Alex muttered something.

"I'm sorry, I didn't catch that?"

"I said," he licked his lips, "I didn't know what they were."

"They're just something to help you keep your equilibrium. You've had a bit of a shock, you know. Well, I expect you'll take them a little later on."

There was a long silence, then Alex swallowed convulsively and said, "Dr. Welchman, is . . . is . . ."

"Yes, old man?"

"Daddy is d-dead?" Then in a sudden rush, "They wouldn't t-tell me. I kept asking, but they wouldn't answer, they just kept saying . . ."

"Your father died late on Tuesday night. When you were told, you had a fairly violent reaction. Dr. Stand gave you an injection to calm you down, and then you were brought here so that you could have the proper care and help. That's why I'm here too." Hugh smiled. "Do you recall any of that?"

Alex nodded slowly. "I thought—I didn't know—I thought perhaps I'd d-dreamt it, or imagined it—I thought perhaps I was here because I was—I was m-mad."

"You are certainly not mad. You can be absolutely and completely confident of that. You've had a severe emotional shock, and what you have to do now is to come to terms with it; which, given a little time and care, I'm sure you will do perfectly satisfactorily. And there's another thing I want to emphasise: You are here as a voluntary patient, and any time you want to leave, there is nothing to prevent you. All you have to do is sign yourself out. I don't advise it, because I think this is the best place for you at the moment—and while you're here, of course, you'll have to follow the regulations like everybody else—but you're not in any way being confined or held against your will. Is that clear?"

"Yes," it was a whisper. "Can I have my shoes?"

"I'll ask the sister if she'll make an exception, all right?"

Alex nodded; he bent down and carefully dropped cigarette ash in the ashtray. "Dr. Welchman," he said, head still lowered, "how did my father die?"

"His death was probably due to an overdose of some tranquiliser, combined with whisky."

"Oh. I thought—I m-mean, it wasn't a heart attack?"

"No. As a matter of fact, although I know he complained about it from time to time, your father's heart was perfectly sound."

"Then he . . . but Daddy . . ." He wiped his mouth with the back of his hand. "Was it an accident or . . ."

"It's not certain how it came about. It may well have been an accident."

"But D-Daddy was always so careful. . . ." He frowned. "I don't suppose—I mean, he couldn't have done it on purpose?"

"Suicide is certainly a possibility, yes."

"And what," there was a small quivering smile on his lips, "what do the p-p-police think?"

So he'd been aware enough to register the presence of the police, even after the Thorazine. Or was it a memory of last time? "There is another possibility, yes," Hugh said carefully, but he'd already decided that it better be met head on now, "although I regard it as a remote one. It's possible that your father was induced to take an overdose by someone else."

Alex stared at him intently and began to tremble; his cigarette fell on the floor and he gripped his knees tightly but the trembling increased until his whole body was shaking with a violent ague. "Then it was her, it was her after all!" He gave a neighing giggle that rose to a higher and higher pitch.

Hugh leaned forward and took the boy's hands in his own, and the force of the shuddering laughter shook him. "Brinton!" He strengthened his grip. "Brinton!"

"Eh?" A hiccupping break in the high hysterical sound.

"Take it easy, old chap."

Slowly the giggling diminished and Hugh gently released his hold. He got up and sat down on the bed beside Alex.

The boy began to weep, softly at first and then with great heaving sobs—he wept in Hugh's arms, his head on Hugh's shoulder. The little apple-green room was almost unbearably hot, but Alex's hand was icy cold in Hugh's. And then, in their turn, the sobs died down to a low crooning.

Hugh took out the spare handkerchief he always kept in his

inside pocket and gave it to Alex. "I'll get you a glass of water."

"Don't leave—d-don't—"

"It's all right. The jug is here." He went to the little table and poured some tepid water into the plastic mug. He opened his bag and shook a couple of yellow pills into his palm.

"What's this?"

"Just something to calm you down."

Alex flinched, then his mouth widened in a smile. "That's funny—ha ha—that's very funny, ha ha ha—"

"Alex!" His voice snapped off the beginning giggle and Alex stared up at him, his mouth still open for laughter.

"Swallow these, would you?"

"I'm sorry. Of course."

Hugh replaced the mug, picked up the smouldering cigarettes that had burned two small scars in the linoleum, and sat down on the chair again. "I think it might help if you talked a bit, you know."

Alex nodded, made a helpless gesture with his hands. "I don't know . . . where . . . to b-begin. . . ."

"Just try to put your mind back to Tuesday—Tuesday afternoon perhaps, when you left me."

"All right." He sighed. "But it's done now, isn't it? It's too late."

"It's not too late."

"Have they—have they," his voice fell to a whisper, "have they arrested her?"

"No one's been arrested, Alex. Just tell me what comes into your mind. Who is 'her'?"

"M-m-m-Elaine. That's what she said, you see—'something to c-c-calm you d-d-down.'"

"When was this?"

"Last night. What d-day are we?"

"Thursday."

"Oh. Tuesday n-night then."

"Tell me about it."

"Well, it was when—it was after I went . . ." He took a deep breath. "All right, I'll try to begin at the beginning. Well, you see, after I left you, I thought I'd go for a drive. I went out to Ely and I, well, I p-prayed a bit there. There was no one else about. Then I went up in the tower and came down again—all those steps, you see, I wanted to be—to p-prove that it was all all right. And then I went home. I felt awfully tired, I remember. So I just went up to

145

my room and went to sleep. It's funny—I don't remember waking up, but suddenly I was standing by the door of my room, I *was* awake then and I . . ." He bunched Hugh's handkerchief tightly in his hand. "I knew what I would see if I opened the d-door and looked out. It was like the morning, only it was worse n-now. I knew I'd see N-Nursey . . . she was c-coming across the hall, you see, very quickly . . . she was wearing her cape with the hood up over her head and I was frightened then, I mean, because of course I should have been lying down. . . ." He hesitated, frowning, kneading the handkerchief. "So I remember I slipped back into the room and half closed the door and waited and waited . . . and then, well then I was d-down there and it was—well I've t-told you all that. Could I have another cigarette?"

"Of course."

"I could hardly believe it," Alex went on when the cigarette was lit. "What could it mean, I thought? What was Nursey—I mean Mother, of course—doing there? Because, you see, it was after I'd seen Mummy go downstairs, but before—before I was down there myself. I didn't know what to do." He broke off and fell into a kind of trance.

So there it was, thought Hugh: Elaine Brinton, Nurse Trotman, there in the right place at the right time—but was it the right time? With such retrieved memories, no time sequence could be trusted. "What did you do, Alex?"

"Eh? Oh, I went, I thought I'd go and see Daddy—I know you'd said to be, well, gentle with him. But what could I do? What could I *do*?" he cried out. "I couldn't talk to Mother—how could I?—if she, perhaps she . . . and she had done it. Oh God." He closed his eyes and a single shudder shook him.

"Take it easy now. *Did* you go and see your father?"

Alex nodded and opened his eyes. "He was in his study. At first he didn't want to hear—he didn't want to listen to me. 'If you're coming to me with more of that tarrydiddle, you can go away.' But I think I must have been rather d-desperate. I kept saying that I'd seen her and he kept saying nonsense and then suddenly it dawned on me that he thought I meant Mummy—so I said, 'No, not Mummy.' He'd been, well, pretty worked up, but suddenly he was quite calm. 'Who then,' he said, 'who d'you mean?' So I told him about Mother—Elaine really, then. He was very quiet for a bit, then he said we'd better have a whisky and so we did—I n-needed it. You see I couldn't believe what I'd been saying—what I'd seen. But he was very nice about it. He said he'd better tell me the whole thing. He'd always tried to keep it from me because it was all so d-distressing. The inquest had brought in a verdict against the d-dog —well, I suppose not exactly, but that seemed to be the conclusion. But he had always thought it had been Kate—of course he realised that he'd done her a great wrong. But I wasn't to be distressed because now he saw quite clearly how it must have occurred— Elaine must have come in from the garden, seen the cellar door open and automatically shut it, unaware of Mummy on the top step. He said that she must have realised only later what she had done . . . and no one could blame her for not speaking up. He said we had to be . . . very sorry for her, that she must have been suffering d-dreadful p-pangs of conscience all these years. He said I mustn't, shouldn't talk to Mother about it—because it would be just too awful for her.''

Alex puffed rapidly on his cigarette, then stubbed it out and sat still, frowning slightly.

"Tell me what you're thinking, if you can. What else did your father say?''

"He sort of—apologised really. He said he'd been terribly worried that I was going to start imagining that *I* had something to do with Mummy's death, and that's why he had been so rude this morning—that morning. And he said that now it was all cleared up, of course, there was no need for me to go on seeing—seeing you.''

"And what did you say to that?''

"Well I . . .'' He looked away. "I think we must have drunk quite a lot of whisky, I thought that was probably right—after all, it was all cleared up now, wasn't it? And it wasn't so—so very d-dreadful, after all. I thought, poor Mother, what a frightful time she must have been having—and I understood then why she always seemed so, well, unhappy really. A sort of secret sorrow, I thought.''

"And how did your father seem to take this?''

"Well he was pleased—relieved in a sort of suppressed way. He'd been a bit het up in the last few weeks, but now . . . and of course, I could see why. If Mother had done it, that meant that Kate hadn't . . . and he must have been happy about that; he's always preferred Kate to me, you know. I'm not blaming him—I've always been frightened of him, I suppose, at least I could never think of anything to say, and he wasn't a great one for conversation himself, but Kate, well, she could always talk nineteen to the dozen. . . ." He slowly wiped his face with the handkerchief.

"You're tired. Would you like to stop now?"

"No." He shook his head. "No. You see it was—it was wrong, it was all wrong, but I couldn't p-put my finger on it. I didn't *want* to put my finger on it. I'm a frightful coward, really, I know that. But, you see, it did seem as if everything were going to be all right —and, well, I suppose it might have been the whisky, but there I was having a decent conversation with Daddy for the first time for years, or ever, I think." Two large tears rolled down his cheeks. "And he *was* decent. He *was,* but then . . . and I thought, poor old Mother. Poor Mother! What a damn fool I was!" he said with a sudden viciousness. "God, what a blubbering idiot." He dried his eyes brusquely. "At any rate, I'm sure I'd drunk too much, because after dinner—I couldn't eat much and neither could Daddy, I no-ticed—I felt distinctly woozy, so I went up to lie down. I put on some records . . . and then the next thing I remember was Daddy calling me. . . .

" 'Come back . . . come back!' he was saying, in a terribly urgent kind of whisper—but I could hear it quite clearly above the Beatles —'come back!' And there was something about his voice that made me—well, that gave me the willies. I went out on the landing, I didn't want to go, but I went—but I couldn't hear anything except 'Penny Lane' in the background. I stood there t-trembling for a long time, but I knew I had to go—I had to; and I thought he must be in some kind of pain or . . . I don't know what. And then it came back, it all came back—I couldn't do it, I couldn't get down those steps, yet I had to . . . I must I must I must—I shut my eyes and it was like, like being swallowed up. And I did it. I did do it. Oh God I wish I hadn't. If only I hadn't . . ." His whole body was taut with urgency.

"If only you hadn't what, old chap?"

"If only I hadn't gone down there! If only I'd never said any-thing in the first place! If only I'd kept my blasted trap shut. If only I'd never come whining to you!" He glared with a halfhearted belligerence at Hugh. "It wasn't so bad after all—not so very bad, lots of people have worse, I could have left it alone . . . why did I have to go and smash everything up? I wish . . . wish I were . . ." He trailed off, staring fixedly at the barred window behind Hugh.

"You came to me because you needed help, Alex. No blame can

possibly attach to that. You were immobilised in the past, and it was absolutely necessary for you to find a way out. You can't hold yourself responsible for the actions—or reactions—of others. Do you understand what I'm saying?"

"I suppose so." A pause. "If you say so."

"Good. Do you want to continue, or would you prefer to—"

"I'd better tell you the rest—n-now I've got so far. Where am I?"

"You've just come down the stairs into the front hall."

"The front hall. I was standing there—I was what did you call it? Immobilised. I knew I couldn't stay there forever. . . . I wanted to run up to my room and slam the door and—but I knew I couldn't do that either. And just then, I think, the record ended and before the next one dropped, there was a silence . . . and I listened and listened but I could only hear the wind outside . . . and that—the silence—seemed worse than anything somehow. I crossed the hall . . . and, suddenly, I remembered what it was that was wrong about what Daddy had said. You see—he'd said that Nursey must have come in from the back hall, noticed the cellar door open and quickly shut it. But—I don't know if you know, but, you see, the cellar door opens out towards the back hall door—so if you were coming from the back hall you wouldn't see down into the cellar. But it suddenly came to me then that it couldn't have happened like that—because Nursey came from the other direction—she came from the door to the stable wing, the door I was standing in front of—and she'd crossed the hall *towards* the back hall. So, you see, she couldn't have helped looking down into the cellar and she m-m-must . . . must have seen anyone on the steps. So I knew that something was t-terribly wrong. I opened the door and went into the corridor and I had just lifted my hand to knock at the study door when I heard voices on the other side. I knew at once it was Daddy and Mother —but the door was too thick to make out exactly what they were saying. And after a bit there was a silence, then suddenly I heard Mother's voice close to the door—I heard her say, 'your beloved Kate'—and I realised that she was going to come out. For a moment I was sort of p-petrified and then I ran down the corridor and into the surgery—I didn't, I couldn't b-bear to see her. . . . I was just in an absolute p-pure funk. Then she must have opened the study door, b-because I heard her say, 'If you think you're going to use Alex to get rid of me, you're making a mistake.' And then she said what you said to me, you see, that's why I thought it was so. . . . She said, 'You're really quite worked up, Jonathan—I'm going to get you something to calm you down . . .' You see why I thought it was—f-funny?" He brought out the last word with a little gasp.

"Yes. But of course it's not really very funny."

"Not really. I can't b-b—I just can't b-believe that she . . . that she . . ." He put his head in his hands. After a while, he looked up.

"Try to keep talking."

"Well, of course I realised she was going to come into the surgery—so I hid behind the screen. There's a screen round the washbasin in there. She came in and switched on the light and I heard her at the medicine cupboard. Well, that's all. She didn't see me. Then she went out again. I heard her go down the passage and she said, 'There you are. Good night, Jonathan.' I didn't move for a long t-time, though I hate the surgery, I hate the smell of—what is it?—ether, I suppose, and floor polish and sort of general sickness. It's the same here. I could never have been a doctor." He rubbed his hands together slowly. "I didn't think about anything. I was in a kind of daze. I think I might have stayed there all n-night, if I hadn't heard the noise—a curious sort of soft little noise. I thought it might be mice scuffling, or rats—Daddy says there are rats in the house now . . . said." He gave a convulsive shudder, bit his lip. "So. I decided to investigate—besides I c-couldn't stay there forever, c-could I? I went along the passage—the study d-door was open and that's where the noise c-came from." Alex was gripping his knees hard now, his knuckles white. "I looked in and Daddy was sitting at his desk, just sitting there and chuckling—that's what the n-noise was. He was chuckling—very low, like this." Alex made a little throaty noise—a perfect rendering of private maniacal glee that Hugh recognised at once, had heard many times before. It went on and rose and then, suddenly, stopped.

"I see. And then?"

"And then?" He stared at Hugh and his whole face seemed to collapse, turn inward. He was wringing his hands and looked down at them as if they belonged to someone else. "I can't remember any more. . . . I can't . . . I promise I c-can't . . . can't . . . can't. . . ." Gazing at his writhing hands.

"Very well. Tell me about the next morning, if you feel up to it."

150

Alex raised his head, his hands still. "When I went d-down-stairs?" he said in a normal tone.

"Start at the beginning if you can, when you woke up."

"Oh. Well," he frowned with the effort of memory, "to tell you the truth I think I felt a bit of a fool. So I smoked a cigarette or two and tried to puzzle it out—I mean, these things always seem better in the morning, don't they? It didn't all seem so cut and dried. For one thing, I thought maybe I'd got the time sequence wrong. . . . And then, sitting there in the window of my bedroom and looking out at Mother's garden, I thought, she loves flowers—really loves them, and Mummy was like a flower, an exotic sort of flower, a tiger lily perhaps, I don't know, I'm not very hot on flowers, but you don't kill something you love like that . . . well, at any rate, I d-determined the only thing to do was to have it out with Mother. As soon as I'd decided that, I felt better and I didn't even wait to put my clothes on, and then . . . and then as I c-came down the stairs, Wardy was in the hall and she looked up and saw me and said, 'Oh, here's a d-dreadful thing, Alex, the Doctor's dead!' And just then Mother came out of the living room," he began trembling, "and suddenly I knew I'd just been making excuses for her. I *knew* then . . . again . . . And I can't—couldn't . . . it was like being swallowed up and I tried to fight to save myself and far away I heard myself shouting and everyone was attacking me and dragging me away and . . ."

"Take it easy. You're quite safe here, you know. Would you like a cigarette?"

"No—no thanks. Dr. Welchman, d-do you think I'll have to give evidence against her? I d-don't think I could d-do that."

"Look, Alex, while I'm not saying you didn't see your step-mother in the hall that afternoon long ago, you must remember that it was indeed a very long time ago, and, as you've said, the time sequence in your mind is quite probably confused or transposed. I think it's possible that you have superimposed another memory on this one. You remember telling me that when you ran those errands for your mother, you were always frightened of being discovered by someone—Wardy or the nurse or your father; and this could well be a memory of just such a narrow escape. Do you see what I mean?"

Alex nodded anxiously.

"What I'm saying is that I don't think you can draw any valid conclusions from what you recollect having seen. As to giving evidence, of course there's no question of that at all—the recollection of a five-year-old boy could never be accepted as evidence at this distance in time. I think your best way of resolving this particular problem is to quite simply and honestly ask your stepmother about it one of these days—not now, not immediately. But I'm sure when she realises how vital it is to you, she will tell you. And if it is the worst, Alex, well at least by that time you will be prepared."

"But what about Daddy? It must have been Mother who gave him the t-tranquilisers?" It was more a plea than a question.

"Well, as I say, I don't think that would have been very easy, not the way you describe it. But for the moment that sort of consideration is better left to the police—sometime soon they will want to question you, but I shan't permit that until you are up to it. There is no harm at all in you trying to remember as much as possible, and even in trying to piece it together . . . but you must realise you don't have all the pieces, so you must, insofar as you can, suspend judgement—it would be unfair to do otherwise." Hugh lit a last cigarette. "There is perhaps one piece of information I ought to give you, and that's concerning your father. I think there's reason to believe—I don't say it was so—but there is reason to believe that your father had recently been undergoing some kind of quite severe mental disturbance, quite possibly related to his drinking. You should probably only accept his reactions, both emotional and verbal, in the light of that fact—what he said to you, however normal seeming, was likely to have been the statement of a highly overwrought and even quite unstable mind."

"You mean I should take everything he said with a p-pinch of salt because—because he was m-mad?"

Hugh smiled slightly. "Well, we don't make much use of that word nowadays, you know. Let's just say unstable, and leave it at that."

"All right."

"Good. Now it's probably better if you don't have any visitors for a bit. But as you'll be here for a few days, I think you might participate, if you want, in the life here—most people in this section are in a not dissimilar situation to your own; there's a common room, one or two clubs, quite a good library, TV, all that sort of thing. You're not isolated, you see, and we're all here to help you. I shall pop in to see how you're getting on at least once a day."

"You sound rather like my prepper headmaster—'we want you to have a happy, healthy life here.'"

Hugh laughed. "Yes, well, but no sports, I'm afraid—not just yet." He stood up. "By the way, don't worry about your work, I'll have a word with Mr. Semple."

"That's very g-good of you, sir."

They shook hands. "And be a good chap and accept your medication, all right?"

In the sister's little office it was even hotter, if possible, than in Alex's room. Out of the window he could see the broad lawn of the hospital gardens, misty with drizzle, and he had a sudden longing for fresh air. "Very well, Sister, that's clear, I hope—positively no visitors and especially not his mother, Mrs. Brinton."

"Yes, Doctor, that's quite clear."

"And you understand my notes on the new medication?"

"Yes, Doctor," Sister Arkwright permitted herself a faint frown of impatience.

"And if there is the slightest cause for concern, I want to be reached immediately." He knew the danger of repeating instructions, but was impelled by his uneasiness at her vagueness this morning. "And I particularly want to know if anyone does ask to see him."

"Very well, Doctor."

He couldn't do any better than that. He turned to leave. "Oh, by the way, Sister, I'd be glad if you could see your way to letting him wear his own shoes."

"Very well, Doctor. If you insist."

Outside the ward he paused indecisively—uneasily aware that he'd handled Arkwright badly. He descended the staircase slowly and paused again. To his right was the corridor that led to his consulting room where a press of paperwork awaited him. In front of him was the door that led to the hospital grounds; he opened it with his private key and stepped out into the fresh air, hardly noticing the light spring drizzle. The paperwork would have to wait —there was a greater uneasiness on his mind than his concern for Arkwright.

Alex had been more open than he could have hoped, and yet Alex was blocking, not unconsciously, but consciously: *I can't remember any more, I promise I can't.* In such circumstances, a promise was always a lie.

He lit a cigarette. The grounds were ragged, unkempt now—once they'd been immaculate, beautifully kept up, the beds glowing. But two springs ago Milsom, the patient whose charge the gardens were, had slit his throat, overwhelmed perhaps by the beauty he had created. Now the only colour was the rich crimson blossom of a single young plum tree.

Normally such evasions didn't matter—in fact, their very transparency was often a positive sign. But this, he reminded himself, was not a normal situation. He couldn't put Ply off indefinitely—and an independent judgement might easily consider Alex fit enough to be interrogated now. And what he had to say about his stepmother was damning indeed, or would be so construed by the policeman. No professional caution would prevent immediate acceptance of Alex's frightened defensive indictment of her. Given time and patience there was little doubt that the conflicts of the boy's evidence would be resolved, without criminal prejudice to him—or to her. But there was not much time; not enough clinical time. And clearly Elaine Brinton had not been wholly truthful. In which case, the obvious course was to ask her—as he had advised Alex. There was time—it was not yet midday, and his next patient wasn't until two. And after all, he had promised to report to her on Alex's state.

And yet again, Hugh hesitated, suddenly aware of the dampness of the rain on his scalp, the unmoving blue spread of the great cedar tree above the ravaged gardens, the barred and watching windows at his back. As the soft drizzle gently bore down the drift of cigarette smoke, he had a feeling of deep dis-ease—an instinctive sense that he was missing something vital, that he'd touched on a personal blind spot. Then he braced his shoulders—there was no help there. A blind man is no less blind for knowing he cannot see. He dropped his cigarette and turned slowly along the unweeded gravel path in the direction of the parking lot.

By the time he got to the New Inn and drew into the little lane beside the house, the rain had ceased; and, as he stepped out of the car, the air was colder, the sky heavier, and there was a stillness—of coming snow perhaps. Julia always said that one could smell if it were going to snow; Hugh sniffed, but smelt nothing, instead was caught by a fit of coughing. As he pushed open the gate, he saw that Brinton's plate had already been removed—there was a clean rectangular patch on the wooden post where it had been.

He went up the flagged path between the low box hedges that enclosed the kitchen garden. On the patients' door there was a neat hand-lettered notice: *Dr. Brinton's private and panel patients are referred to Dr. H. Stand, 2 Meads Way.* They must be used to being turned away —on days when Brinton had been incapable of holding surgery or had failed to unlock the door. Beside it, the small round window regarded Hugh blindly. There was no mention of death—but they would know about that by now.

He followed the path along the blank north wall, turned the corner, passed the kitchen window, and stopped at the back door. There was no bell, and for a moment he was puzzled. Why had he come this way? And then the door opened abruptly.

"Good afternoon, Dr. Welchman."

"Oh—good afternoon, Mrs. Warden. Is Mrs. Brinton in, by any chance?"

"Mrs. Brinton?" The welcoming smile vanished. "No. She's off at one of her hortilogical lunches."

"I see—well, perhaps Miss Brinton?"

"Not her either, poor thing—she went back to that college of hers. There's not a blessed soul in the place but me." Again she smiled.

"In that case, I won't trouble you. Perhaps you'd tell—"

"Is it about our Alex?"

"Well yes, I thought perhaps—"

"How is he?" Stepping forward she put her hand on Hugh's arm. "How is the poor lamb, Doctor?"

"He's as well as . . ." *can be expected,* he had been about to finish, but it occurred to him that, now Brinton was dead, Mrs. Warden must know as much or more about the family than anyone alive. ". . . as well as might be hoped for in the circumstances—which of course are rather complicated, as you know."

"Complicated? I don't know as I'd say that." Her mouth was half open, exposing an array of yellowish teeth, and her breath came in small toothpaste-scented pants. "But here—a fine one I am, letting you stand out in the cold like this. Come in, Doctor."

Hugh allowed himself to be drawn into the dark little hall. He saw the dog-leash in its usual place, a basket of gardening implements—secateurs, trowel, fork—and a lone hat on a peg above the coats. That would be Brinton's—not yet removed.

"In here, Doctor—how about a nice cup of tea? I'll have the kettle on the boil in a jiffy."

"I can't stay very long, I'm afraid, Mrs. Warden." But he followed her into the kitchen.

There were frilly fringed lamps—unlit now—set about the place, china ornaments on the mantelpiece, a horseshoe above the door, and in one corner an old bakelite radio. *A real old-fashioned kitchen,* Julia had said, and she was right—it seemed immediately familiar, as if he had stopped here for tea many times before. There was a Welsh dresser, an ungainly piece of furniture he recognised as an Easiwork, and a cast-iron range in the chimney, with a glow of coals from the open door, bright in the dimness of the afternoon.

"Sit down, sit down, Doctor."

Nodding, he sat at the table covered with an olive-green baize cloth—also fringed. Perhaps where Julia had sat so long ago—with the nanny-cum-housekeeper bustling about just as she was now. He turned his attention to her.

"I gather you feel there's a simple explanation for Dr. Brinton's death, Mrs. Warden?"

"Simple? I didn't exactly say that." She poured some water from the kettle into the teapot, turned to face Hugh. "But I know the truth when I hear it—that's all I'm saying."

"I suppose you're referring to what Alex said on the stairs?"

Mrs. Warden merely pursed her lips and swished the hot water in the teapot.

"But you must realise that he was speaking under very great stress—he'd just had a considerable shock. We can't place any reliance on what is said in the course of an hysterical outburst."

"Shocked into telling the truth, I'd say."

"Would you?" Hugh took out his box of cigarettes and laid it flat on the table. It was she of course who had told the police about the scene on the stairs—and her intention was becoming increasingly clear. "In the circumstances, that's extremely difficult to estimate, and it may do a good deal of harm to innocent people if—"

"The truth hurts none but the wicked, that's what I've always been taught, Doctor." She emptied the pot, briskly dried the inside with a cloth, and put in four spoonfuls of tea. "There's someone in this house that's not all that's made out. I won't say no more."

"Unfortunately, what one says or doesn't say—or, in this case, what *has* been said—is liable to a variety of interpretations or misinterpretations."

156

"Misinterpretation? I don't see that." She sniffed. "Plain as the nose on my face—I'd say." She poured the boiling water into the pot.

"Not to all of us. Not, I think, to the police." He took a cigarette from the box.

"The police? I don't hold with the police—not usually—a nasty nosey lot, they are." With deft movements she placed cups, saucers, sugar, milk jug, teapot on the table. "But old Ratty Ply's a sharp one all right, *and* he knows his plain duty." She sat down.

"Quite. But from the police point of view Alex's outburst goes to show that he is seriously unstable—a view given more weight by the fact that he is under my care. Now, you see, if you have in the same house two people, one of whom dies in somewhat mysterious circumstances and the other of whom is imagined to be, well, what is popularly termed 'crazy,' the idea of a suspicious connection between them is bound to come up."

Mrs. Warden opened her mouth, then shut it. She stared at Hugh. "Alex? Why they wouldn't be thinking that our Alex had anything to do with . . . with the Doctor's death."

"I'm afraid that's exactly what they do think." He nodded shortly. "Of course I feel the idea's completely erroneous—but unfortunately there are one or two other rather worrying things. It's probable, for instance, that Dr. Brinton died from an overdose of a drug called Librium—and it so happens that Alex had just that drug in his possession, but doesn't now." He spoke with a studied lack of emphasis. "And another point is that the glass from which the Doctor drank has, in addition to his own fingerprints, those of Alex, as well. All this is probably no more than coincidence, but all the same, at least superficially it looks bad."

"Looks bad . . ." Mrs. Warden repeated automatically. She had made no move to pour the tea; she sat quite still.

"And then if Alex and his father were not on very good terms . . ."

"He was on good terms with everybody—everybody, except *her.* Now—but whatever's come over me, here I am forgetting our tea." She gave a quick nervous laugh and caught up the teapot. "Oh no, everybody loved the Doctor. Did you see that lovely notice in the *News*? 'Much loved local healer,' they called him, 'much loved local healer passes away peacefully at home.' I call that beautiful, and it's true. One or two sugars? Oh, he's going to be missed dreadful, he is. There you are, Doctor." She placed the cup in front of him.

"Thank you. Yes, of course—particularly in the family, wouldn't you say?"

"The family?" For a moment she looked nonplussed, then recommenced her rapid chatter—there was no doubt she was edgy. "The *real* family—yes. Kate now—she was always his little darling. Poor Kate, you can see how she's suffering, though she won't let on, of course. She always was a cool one, even as a little girl—on the surface, that is. But she takes everything very hard inside. Sometimes in the morning when I made the bed I'd find her hanky under the pillow still wet from her sobbing herself to sleep, but when I'd ask her if she'd been crying again, she'd say, 'Don't be so silly, Wardy,' in that prim little way of hers. Oh dear me yes—not a bit like my own two little ducks—they weren't afraid to make a fuss, but then, you see, my poor mites never had a daddy, not to remember like, and that makes a difference, specially to little girls, don't you think, Doctor?"

"Yes, I do indeed, quite so." He sipped his tea; it was good and strong—far better than Mrs. Nance's teabag brew. "On the whole it sounds as though this wasn't a very happy household?"

"Happy? Well, nobody's happy all the time, are they? But it was once. In the old days . . . Miss Arabella, she was a lovely, gay thing she was—that pretty it made you catch your breath. A great favourite she was with everyone, particularly with old Professor Welling, I remember—our Miss Julia's father."

"Really?" Hugh put down his cup. "Did he used to come here often?"

"Not here—no, he didn't come here. I don't think he got on with the old Doctor—Dr. Anstey, that was—towards the end. But Miss Arabella, she was often up there at Hillside, quite like a daughter to the old professor, she was. They had a lovely rose garden up there in the old days, I don't expect you remember that."

"Yes—I remember." He was surprised that Julia hadn't mentioned these visits—was it possible she hadn't known?

"Ah well, it's terrible how things change, isn't it? And our Miss Julia—she was a lovely thing too, but quieter—ever so good with the children—not like Miss Arabella, always so bright and lively she was."

Hugh smiled. "Julia hasn't changed much." He found himself

curiously touched by this kitchen gossip, eager to know more about the young Julia, even from the untrustworthy lips of this tattletale. But that was not, as C. S. M. Welchman was always saying, the object of the exercise. "And Dr. Brinton?" he prompted.

"The Doctor—he was as handsome as she was pretty. And always such a merry way he had with him in those days—oh dear!" She produced a handkerchief and dabbed at her eyes. "I'm afraid I'm a bit emotional."

"Tell me about him. Merry?"

"Well, in a quiet way—joking like, but never nasty. More like Kate really—and of course she's the spitting image of him. But you mean—well, he was a gentleman, I can't say more than that, can I? A proper gentleman." There was a tinge of pity in the look she gave Hugh—a doctor maybe, but not handsome, not very merry, and, to her discerning eye, rather obviously not a gentleman. "Of course he was never the same afterwards— after she died, I mean. It was a terrible shock. All the life went out of him. And now this! But he wasn't responsible—no, I mustn't say that. He was *too* responsible—taking it to heart like that, taking it on himself." She raised her cup and drank in quick greedy little sips, afterwards patting her mouth delicately with the handkerchief. She looked about the kitchen with darting glances, as if searching for something—or fearing an enemy. And then she looked straight at Hugh, "What I say is, the wicked should be punished."

"That may be right. But it's not right that the innocent should suffer, is it, Mrs. Warden?"

"The innocent . . . Doctor . . ." For once she was tongue-tied. "Yes?"

"I . . . will you excuse me a moment?" She stood up and went over to the dresser at the back of the kitchen. She came back with a large black handbag and sat down with it on her knees. For some moments she didn't move, then she undid the clasp, rummaged inside, and produced two sheets of typewritten paper. She slid them across the table to Hugh. "There, you read that, Dr. Welchman. Read it—that'll show you what kind of a man he was."

Hugh stubbed out his cigarette in the saucer. "What is this, Mrs. Warden?" But he already knew.

"It's his—letter. I—I found it."

"When?"

"Yesterday. Yesterday morning before . . . Please read it, Doctor." She stared at him with her protuberant eyes, her hands automatically opening and shutting the clasp of her bag—*click-click, click-click.*

Hugh slowly picked up the pages, and began to read:

My dearest children, my dear wife,

This is the last communication I shall ever address to you, and I write it in great sadness. Yet also with a sense of relief—relief that at last things will be straight between us as they should have been, but were not, these many long years. They were years poisoned for all of you, my dears, by ignorance and fearful suspicion, and for me by a terrible weight of guilt and deception. For it was I who, fourteen years ago almost to this day, killed my dear wife—your mother —Arabella.

In all that time I can truthfully say there has hardly been an hour when I've not recalled that afternoon. I came home a little earlier than usual, for the fog was coming down and it was already getting dark. As soon as I entered the hall I saw the door of the cellar ajar. I had been up all the previous night delivering two babies in succession, and although my fatigue does not excuse my anger at this breach of a firm house rule, it may help to account for it—for I am, or was then, an equable man. I strode forward and slammed the door. In the last second, I must have sensed a presence on the steps—and an instant later, hearing the dreadful thud of the body falling upon the stone and the splintering of the bottle.

This is the hardest part of what I have to tell you. I cannot explain it to you, least of all to myself—but I was possessed of an overmastering fear and, in dreadful neglect of what every duty called me to—as doctor, husband, and as a man—instead of going down on my knees to succour that broken body, I turned tail and fled. I ran to my surgery.

Gradually, standing there in terror and anguish, my sense of duty returned to me. You know then, my dear Kate, how I found you at the door—which added a second horror to the horror lying below, that you had seen it. And now I know that you, Alex, my son, saw it too.

That I held my peace then (and later) was not only out of fear for myself—at least so I have told myself—but also from a knowledge of the dreadful effect upon you both of having at one and the same time a mother murdered and a father for the murderer. No verdict of manslaughter would have prevented your having to pay that terrible penalty—a curse upon those years that should be years of joy, but that you would have had to bear without the love and understanding I have tried my poor best to give you.

I think you must by now have come to realise that your mother was in the last two or three years of her life a desperately unhappy woman. This is the most painful of the trials I bore then or have borne since. I know of course that there can be no forgiveness for what I have done. But I see now that you have a right to the truth, however terrible. And I realise now too that you at least, my dear boy, set as you are upon a course of self-discovery, will not (and should not) rest until you have that truth. I trust and pray that you will eventually be able to live with it in undamaged tranquility. You will be stronger than I—for I can no longer bear to live with this knowledge. Nor could I bear to see on your faces that judgement I see every morning in the mirror upon my own.

I wish you now to think of yourselves. If you can find it in your hearts to understand, not to condemn too harshly, then do so, and you will be the better for it. But do not grieve for me. My life and everything that made it worth living—the consciousness of duty gladly done, of honest service & innocent affection—was destroyed one day fourteen years ago. So what I now give up is no more than the sad ghost of a man long since dead.

I have been, I think, lately almost demented, but now tonight I feel quite calm. I can think of no phrase more fitting than the last words of Sir W.

And there it ended—no salutation, no signature. He had timed it almost right—caught only at the last moment. Tinged though it was with a weak man's mawkishness, the letter had a certain gentle grace that surprised Hugh. Most people die as they live—the complainer will whine even with his last short breath. Yet Brinton had died with a decency not consonant with his life—or at least not consonant with the last few weeks of his life. No alcoholic paranoiac intent on suicide could have written such a tranquil, old-fashioned epistle—it was certainly not the work of Alex's stealthy chuckler. That was the puzzle. It presupposed a sudden and remarkable remission—not unknown, but not usually occurring without provocation, an activating factor. But of course there *had* been a potentially activating factor—Alex, standing at the study door.

Hugh was inclined to think Alex had actually entered the room . . . in a state close to breakdown . . . and quite possibly the cathartic moment had arrived then, the final memory had surfaced—and had proved cathartic for Brinton too. Perhaps, but then what. . .

Mrs. Warden coughed and he glanced up.

"You see, Doctor?"

"Yes. I take it you came upon Dr. Brinton before his wife yesterday morning?"

"Yes, yes I did. I come in early often—that's when I don't sleep in the house, like. I went first thing to the study—the poor thing, I'd often find him there, you see, asleep on the couch or even in his chair, and I'd make him comfy and bring him a cup of coffee and that. So yesterday . . . well, I could see straight off he was dead— he was as cold as anything, though the room was hot and stuffy. There was nothing I could have done—nothing."

"And the letter?"

"It was right by his hand—the second page in the typewriter. So I read it and then I thought, that's not right, he'd never do a thing like that—not the Doctor, so I—"

"You don't think he would have committed suicide?"

"No, I'm not saying that. I mean, he did, didn't he? And in a way it didn't surprise me—he's been funny the last few weeks, not himself at all. But all that about pushing Miss Arabella down the cellar steps—a good kind man like he was would never have done such a terrible thing. I knew it wasn't him who did it—I *knew* that. He was just taking the blame for her. It wasn't fair—not after all she—"

"Yes yes—well, you needn't tell me all this, Mrs. Warden. You're going to have to tell it to the police, you realise that?"

"The police . . . but I didn't mean any harm—that's what I wanted to avoid, the poor Doctor made to look like a murderer, which he never was—the disgrace!—people will believe anything, I know that, and the nastier it is the more ready they are to give it credit. I thought if I took the letter, it would just look like an accident. . . ."

"But it didn't." He thought, and you did your best to see that it wouldn't look like one—ready to do any amount of harm to her mistress. Still ready. A dangerous woman, but fortunately a silly one. She turned her head away from him now, snapping the clasp of her bag again, backwards and forwards. "Well, Mrs. Warden, I don't have to tell you that you did a very foolish thing. But it's fortunate at least that you didn't destroy the letter."

"Doctor . . . the police . . . couldn't we, couldn't you . . ."

"I'm afraid not, Mrs. Warden. The police are going to have to know about this at once, and you are going to have to tell them."

She sat quite still, and then suddenly cried out, "What are people going to think of him?" In the premature dusk of the early afternoon, she might have been a woman of any age—a young beauty lamenting the loss of her beloved, or an old woman bitter at a wasted life of unrequited service.

"If you will get your hat and coat, I'll drive you down to the station right away."

"Very good, Doctor." She rose obediently. "I won't be two minutes."

When she'd gone, Hugh took off his glasses and rubbed his eyes. He was reminded of old winter afternoons in the kitchen at home, his father away at the war, his mother sitting preternaturally still in front of the small coke stove—IDEAL stamped on the cast-iron —and himself struggling to read in the dimness before the blackout was drawn and the lights turned on. How different that kitchen— and this one too—from the gleaming enamel and chrome of Hillside. How extraordinarily prescient Julia had been—*if there was a letter, I expect Wardy took it.* He closed his eyes.

He woke abruptly, staring at the black-clad figure in front of him, not knowing where he was.

"I'm ready now."

For an instant he had the illusion that this was his mother— so she'd stood, so she'd spoken, the very same words, on the days they made the long trek out to visit Harriet. Then he pushed himself to his feet and put on his glasses.

"Right." He slipped the letter into his pocket; the letter that was the answer to so many problems. And yet, as he led the way out of the house and through the garden to the car, he had no sense of relief. It was bitterly cold and had begun to snow—a few single flakes floating gently down in the utter stillness of the darkened afternoon.

"Unnatural weather for this time of year, Doctor."

"Ummmm." He shivered—a goose across his grave; a grave-yard chill. Well, in a sense they were bound for a burial—the burial of an old mystery.

11

"The Super won't be long now, Doctor. Meantime I thought you might like a cup of coffee."

"Thanks—thank you." He watched her place the cup on the table; there were three biscuits in the saucer and he felt a pang of hunger. This was likely to be the only lunch he would get. She was a good-looking woman in her neatly pressed uniform and starched white collar; there was something familiar about her that he couldn't place. Then he realised she was blushing.

"Sorry, I was staring." And then he had it. "It was you that drove me out to the New Inn yesterday, wasn't it?"

"That's right. I hope I didn't give you too much of a scare." There was a pleasant burr to her voice.

"No no—you're an excellent driver. You must be a local girl, Miss . . . er . . ."

"P. W. C. Brandt—or just Brandt." She smiled; she had fine china-blue eyes. "More or less—my folks have a bit of a farm out beyond Ely way."

"Ahh. I see." He wracked his brains for something to say—he was not a naturally adept chatterer. "It'll be cold up there tonight —it's already begun to snow."

"They do say." She lifted her head as if to sniff the weather. "I've known five or six inches fall sudden in April out on the Fens, but it won't lie long."

"No. I suppose, er—not."

"Well, if you're wanting anything, you just pop your head round the door and give us a shout."

And then she was gone and he was alone in the hot little room that smelled of fresh paint. They'd whisked away Mrs. Warden and her letter and asked him to wait "a few minutes." He didn't object; in fact, he was grateful for the warmth, and the ordinary clean anonymity of the place dispelled the shadow of anxiety at the back of his mind.

The coffee seemed to taste faintly of paint too. He ate a biscuit and thought of Julia riding out to the Fens on her big Norton in the afternoons—wild rides. Often she came back with her ivory cheeks ruddy, her sleek black hair bushy as an animal's winter fur, her eyes bright with a secret joy. A marsh sprite. It was that same air of secret joy occasionally breaking through her almost unnatural maturity of manner that had first attracted him years ago at Matt's. But he hoped she'd had sense enough not to go out riding this afternoon —any kind of hormonal imbalance might render such strenuous exercise dangerous in early pregnancy. Not that he knew of any such imbalance in Julia or whether indeed she was really pregnant. Yet he felt his instinct was not deceived. Tonight perhaps he could verify it; with Brinton's suicide confirmed, there would be no police interruptions or any other diversions. Even Kate would have to accept her father's suicide now—a difficult business, but not his problem; after all, she wasn't his patient.

As he lit a cigarette, he thought suddenly of Irma Monroe—who had been his patient. On her twentieth birthday Irma had swallowed forty aspirin in her rooms at Girton. She had fallen asleep and dreamt that she was "walking by the river and it was raining and the raindrops were puckering the surface of the water and softening the gravel of the path and the heads of the daffodils were heavy and still because there was no wind and nobody about just the close grey sky and the green lawns . . . and then in the distance there was thunder, far away at first and faint like an underground train and then louder and closer until a terrible clap came just overhead—and I knew it was the crack of doom. And I struggled and fought to wake up . . . and when at last I did there was the smell of spring in the room and water on my cheeks like a healing. . . ."

Irma had been lucky, she'd had the strength to get up and force herself to vomit and live for other springs. Maybe Brinton too had heard the drumming rain of blood in his ears, the grumbling thunder—if so, he'd been too far gone to do anything about it. Even if there'd been anything to do.

"Good of you to wait, Doctor."

"Mr. Ply." Hugh glanced at the electric clock on the wall—ten to one, he had plenty of time. "That's all right."

"Well, this is a bit of a turn-up for the book, eh?" Smiling, the policeman sat down facing Hugh—there was surely a touch of ruefulness in the smile.

"You've talked to Mrs. Warden?"

"I've listened to her. Always did like an audience. I was at school with her, you know. Betty Best she was in those days—she was good at her work, but always sucking up to the teachers, needed an authority figure, I suppose you'd say. A silly girl—and she hasn't changed."

"Probably not—but one would have to say that she's capable of being a thoroughly malicious woman."

"Got her knife into Mrs. Brinton, you mean? Yes." He grunted and took out his pipe and pouch. "How's the lad?"

"Better than I'd hoped, on the whole. And now this business of his father's death's cleared up, I'd say the prognosis is definitely good."

"Worried about it, was he then?"

Hugh smiled. "You could put it that way."

"When am I going to be able to see him?" Ply carefully prodded a few dangling shreds into the bowl of his pipe.

"Perhaps sometime next week—if you still need to."

"Oh yes, I think so—just for the record, you know." He put the pipe in his mouth and cocked his head to one side. "So his father's death being a case of suicide is going to make it easier for him, is it? Now why is that?"

"Not for the reasons you were thinking yesterday, if I read your mind correctly. But he did have some—rather odd ideas in his head."

"You mean like what he said on the stairs—that 'Nursey' did it?"

"Yes. There's generally a reason behind these—these ravings. Although not always the obvious one. Under severe shock, one tiny fact can easily be twisted into a monstrous certainty."

"You're right enough there." And again Hugh thought the policeman's smile was almost crestfallen—for that was exactly what Ply himself had done. "Thought his stepmother did his father in, I suppose?"

"That was his line of thinking, yes. I don't suppose there's any harm in my telling you now," he hesitated fractionally; but he knew it would be better to have Alex's accusation clearly and cleanly explained away. "The fact is that Alex overheard the tail end of a conversation between his father and stepmother that Tuesday night —I expect she's told you about it?"

"Yes—says she was upset about his drinking."

"Exactly. Apparently he was a bit upset too, so she mixed him a bromide to calm him down—as I understand was her habit." Hugh picked up a second biscuit and ate it.

"I see. And the boy saw her, I suppose, and jumped to the conclusion she'd put the doings in the glass instead of the bromide, is that it?"

"Yes, I think so." He took a sip of coffee—it was tepid and the paint taste was worse.

"Dear oh dear, and there I was thinking as how he was talking about the day of his *mother's* death—it was the *'Nursey'* that gave me that idea, of course, a baby name, I thought. Just shows you how wrong you can be."

"You weren't entirely wrong. I am more or less convinced that Alex did see his stepmother—Nursey—cross the hall one day when he was small, although whether it was that particular afternoon it would be impossible to say at this distance in time."

"Dressed in her nurse's cape, I suppose she'd have been?"

"Why yes—how did you know that?"

"Because Warden, one of the things she said on Wednesday morning, was that she'd seen Nurse Trotman that afternoon coming out of the back door—looking out of the kitchen window, of course. Eyes in the backs of their heads, these women."

"But why—"

"Why hadn't she come forward at the time? Trying a bit of blackmail, I wouldn't doubt—when you come to think of it, it's odd the way Mrs. Brinton kept her on all these years, with them disliking each other so much."

"That wasn't what I was going to say." Hugh felt a spurt of anger. "I was going to ask why you suspected Alex in the circumstances, rather than Mrs. Brinton?"

"Oh but I did—I do—suspect Mrs. Brinton."

"Do? Oh come now, Superintendent, don't tell me you're going to rake over the whole business of Arabella's death, now that Brinton's has been cleared up?" Hugh gave a little laugh.

"Ah—but has it been cleared up? The Doctor's death, I mean." Ply put a match to his pipe and sucked gently.

"I'm afraid I don't follow you."

"Well . . . you read the letter . . . anything strike you about it?" He blew out the match and dropped it in the ashtray.

Hugh frowned—what was the man up to? "I thought it clear and rational—perhaps more so than one might expect from someone in his condition. On the other hand, once a decision to take one's own life has been made, the cath—the emotions associated with the decision may subside and there is often an interval of great lucidity before, in this case for example, the drugs begin to take effect."

"That's very interesting. But what about the form of the letter —the typing, let's say? Not a mistake in the whole thing—and the spacing, perfect. My expert's taken a dekko at it and he says the pressure on the keys was remarkably even. Take my word for it, Doctor, that letter's the work of a professional typist, or as near as makes no matter."

"I suppose you're going to tell me that Brinton couldn't type," he allowed his irritation to show, "that he kept a typewriter for decorative purposes."

"Oh—he could type all right, in a manner of speaking. But he was a two-fingered pecker. Here, have a look at this." He put a piece of paper in front of Hugh.

Darling pussy-catty,

       here I am in my old study ,   wishing you were here
with   your soft paws   and pink   tongue   too
nestle next   to your old   shabby-tabby   and

"Got that from one of his floosies—that's his style, all right. Even in the first few lines you can see the spacing's all cockeyed, there's a spelling mistake, a comma misplaced, and you may not notice it, but the touch on the keys is . . . very uneven—the way someone uses a typewriter it's as good as a signature—and this one's Brinton's, all right. He could no more have . . ."

Hugh raised his eyes vaguely to the clock—one twenty-two.

". . . accounts and billings and things like that, just as I expect your wife does for you."

So they'd already been questioning Brinton's pathetic paramours. Hugh wondered if they'd got to Reg yet. And then he had another and colder thought—Alex: *always hands in his essays typed—professionally typed,* Mike had said. "Mr. Ply, are you saying that letter was written by someone else—not Brinton?"

"Not a shadow of a doubt about it. And it's got to be somebody close in the family, wouldn't you say? And a womanish work, in my opinion."

Hugh lit another cigarette, forgetting to stub out the old. "Are you going to arrest Mrs. Brinton?"

"Lord bless your soul, we haven't got that far yet. Though I'm not saying things don't look black for her. No, I'm not saying that —particularly now we know she was in the hall that afternoon, and did give Hubby a glass of something or other to drink on Tuesday night. She's got a mite of explaining to do, has our Mrs. Brinton."

168

Hugh felt physically sick—no lunch, too much tea, coffee. But it was his own stupidity that filled him with nausea. Sad, deprived, self-righteous, obstinate, Elaine Brinton might be, but she was not a psychopath. Inadequate she perhaps was as housewife, spouse, stepmother, but he recognised in her the quintessential nurse devoted to the preservation of human life, not its destruction. Her guilt was not psychologically plausible—but Hugh had put her in grave jeopardy by betraying a professional confidence, by smugly babbling to a policeman.

"Well, all this is very interesting," he stood up, "but I have to get back to my patients."

"Of course. Good of you to spare me the time, Doctor. Here, I'll show you out."

They walked down the corridor in silence. At the door Ply said, "Just one thing, Doctor. We've got a murderer on our hands, we know that now. I'd feel a lot happier if that lad of yours was forbidden visitors—all visitors."

"I've already organised that." He regarded the policeman with contempt—but he was, after all, only doing his job, and doing it better than Hugh was doing his. The contempt, he knew, was really due himself.

Outside the snow was coming down more thickly. Parker's Piece was already white and there were children breathlessly trying to trap the flakes; except for those cries of childish joy, the town had settled into silence and stillness. He picked the parking ticket from the windscreen and shoved it into his pocket. He knew what his job was, and where his duty lay now. He started the car and turned the heat full up. Peering ahead in the gloom and snow, he drove as fast as he dared towards the New Inn. After a while, he switched on the headlights, but they didn't help much.

He missed the turning into the lane and had to bump the car onto the grass verge in front of the house. At first the tall gate in the wall wouldn't move, but when he gave a push with his shoulder it opened abruptly and he stumbled into the garden, almost coming down on his knees.

He was shaken and stood for a few moments regaining his breath. He moved slowly up the path between the flower beds into the space enclosed by the two wings of the house. He stopped and put out a hand to touch a white rose, shut tight against the cold, the bud flesh smooth, the leaves sprinkled with snow. His breath too was white. Elaine Brinton had made this a place of natural tranquility, and he understood her horticultural obsession—the flowers in every room an assertion of sanity against the unnatural venom in the house. He was filled with a sense of peace—he thought of the foetus, tiny itself as a rosebud, a soft secret stirring, a whisper of long-denied life, a patient promise.

His feet made no sound on the fresh snow as he went up to the front door and knocked. There was no answer. He beat a rapid tattoo with the knocker, then tried the latch. The door swung open into the dark hall—the objects barely visible in the gloaming. No warmth flowed out from the house, only the already familiar smell of polish and copper, flowers and formaldehyde. His mood changed and he had a sudden premonition that he had arrived too late to avert some unknown calamity. He stayed still, gripping the door-jamb, staring into the darkness.

Then a light went on.

"Who's that? Welchman—is that you? What are you doing here?"

"Stand?" He blinked, although the single wall lamp cast only enough light to make the hall a place of shadows and dark corners. Stand was a dim figure by the door of the surgery wing.

"Well, come in, man, come in."

"Sorry." Hugh stepped over the threshold and shut the door. "I came to see Mrs. Brinton."

"Not here. Off to a flower show—in this weather!"

"Oh." He was nonplussed. He had no time to wait. But surely Stand could be trusted to relay a message to Elaine Brinton—*they've always had eyes for each other,* Kate had said. "Stand, there's a letter found and I wanted to—"

"Letter? What sort of letter? When?"

"What the papers call a 'suicide note,' I suppose," he felt suddenly muddled, thick in the head. "I mean—"

"Of Jonathan's? Suicide? Tommyrot. Don't believe it."

"Well no—that's rather the problem. Look, Stand—have you got a few minutes, can we talk?"

"If you like. I've got nothing on till surgery. Just clearing out Jonathan's effects—that's no joke, I can tell you. Man had no more sense of order than a spastic elephant. Come on back to the stables then."

"The stables? Oh yes . . ."

"That's what we call it. Appropriate, if you ask me. Jonathan was never much more than a horse doctor, nor his father-in-law before him. Come along."

They went along a narrow corridor, and Stand opened a door on the right. Farther on would be the surgery, where Alex had hidden on the night, and beyond that, the waiting room.

"This is the study. Sorry about all this." Stand gestured at the piles of papers on desk and sideboard and floor. "Police have been messing about in here too."

Despite the coal fire glowing brightly in the grate and heavy velvet curtains over the windows, the room was cheerless; oppressive with too much heavy furniture, and perhaps basically the wrong shape—too high and narrow for its width.

"Here, take a pew." Stand took a pile of folders from the chair and dumped them on the floor. "Well, what's all this about? But, first tell me—how's Alex?"

The little doctor's manner was brusque as ever, but he looked tired, smaller, as though the whole business had shrivelled him— pushed him, perhaps, round the last corner of middle age.

"In a sense, Alex is all right. The effects of the Thorazine are not in evidence, so you can set your mind at rest there. I had a long chat with him this morning. That in itself is a good sign—he's in adequate contact with reality. But he's obviously holding something back—and that's disturbing him a great deal." Hugh lit a cigarette.

"Any idea what?"

"I have the impression that he came in here latish on Tuesday night—after Elaine Brinton had been in—and . . . well, what? That's the problem. But I think something must have passed between him and his father . . . but, mind you, that's a guess on my part."

"And he's not telling?" Stand nodded with a grim little smile. "Well now, what about this letter of Jonathan's? Did it arrive in the post, or what?"

"No. Mrs. Warden had taken it; this afternoon she evidently thought better of it and handed it over to me."

"To you? Why to you?"

"I exerted a bit of pressure. You see, she imagined that by removing the evidence of Brinton's suicide, there was a fair chance that the police would conclude that Elaine Brinton had deliberately

171

murdered him—particularly after the episode on the stairs, which she also told the police about, by the way."

"Damned meddlesome old fool—up to her old tricks, is she? She nearly wrecked the whole thing last time, you know."

"She did—how?"

"What?" Stand began gently to massage an ear lobe; he sat opposite Hugh, on the other side of the fireplace. "Oh—told me she saw Elaine coming out of the back door at about the time Arabella must have had her fall. Well, why the devil shouldn't she? Not that I think she did—she says not. But it would have been a nasty coincidence. I shut her up of course—put the fear of God in her— told her if she ever mentioned it to the police I'd see she never got another job in her life."

"Well, she's told them now, you know."

Stand's head jerked up. "Has she? Has she now?" He sat quite still—only a small fall of coal in the grate broke the silence. Then he said slowly, "What's all this about, Welchman?"

"Let me just go on a moment." He rubbed his forehead—the room was stifling and his head had begun to ache. "Warden's calculations went awry—the police, as you know, did think there was something odd about the death, but they didn't suspect Mrs. Brinton—they suspected Alex."

"They must be insane," but he said it without his usual conviction.

"I don't think it was a balanced opinion—if indeed they ever really held it." Had it not actually been just some complicated maneuver of Ply's? "But at any rate, I passed it on to Warden, with the result that she produced the so-called suicide letter. She certainly didn't want to do any harm to Alex."

"So-called? What did it say?"

"I can tell you exactly, if you like." He cast his mind back to the kitchen and the pages in his hand in the dim light. He repeated the whole letter almost verbatim.

"*Sounds* like Jonathan, you know—just the sort of soppy stuff he would write." He turned his eyes from the fire and looked at Hugh. "Extraordinary memory you've got, Welchman."

"Not as good as it was. But the point is the letter is not authentic—according to the police. It was typed, you know, and it's something to do with the touch being much too professional for Jonathan to have written."

172

"Alex is a first-rate typist." Stand spoke softly.

"Yes, I know. But the police—that's not the way their minds are working." Hugh threw his cigarette into the fire, feeling the heat of the coals on his hand. He was extraordinarily reluctant to go on and had to force himself to speak. "But Mrs. Brinton is apparently an excellent typist too—and they've turned their attention to her."

"On what basis?"

"Largely owing to me, I'm afraid. You see, in my talk with Alex this morning, he told me a couple of things about his stepmother that . . ." As he slowly explained the situation, he felt the band of pain tightening round his head.

When he was done, Stand grunted. "And you told all this to the police, before you realised the letter wasn't authentic, of course?"

"Yes. But it was an unforgivable breach of confidence, all the same."

"Forgiveness—pah! We've got to deal with things as they are. I daresay you meant well." He heaved himself to his feet—it was a visible effort. "How about a drink? Only whisky, I'm afraid."

Hugh heard himself say yes. Yesterday he'd not hesitated to come down hard on this elderly, ordinary G.P. for his error, but now, with the situation reversed, Stand was giving him a lesson in professional decency.

"Will you take it neat? The police nabbed the soda siphon along with the decanter, but I can fetch some water from the surgery, if you want."

"No, neat will do very well."

"Here you are then. Cheers." Stand sat down and drank half his whisky in one swallow, then put the glass on the floor. "Let me tell you something, Welchman—about Elaine Trotman." He shaded his eyes, as though the light were too bright for them. "Mother died when she was eight. Tubercular meningitis. Little girl nursed her for a year—father wasn't any help. With the onset of *spes phthisica,* the mother showed all the usual symptoms—optimism, cheerfulness, et cetera—and the little girl thought she was going to get better. Had to tell her what it meant. She took it like—like a trooper, and joined in her mother's merriness right to the end. I'd hear them making plans together. . . ."

Hugh swallowed some whisky—disagreeable as it was, it at least burned away the paint taste in his mouth.

"Hardest thing I'd ever had to do. Of course I was a young man then—just before the war—Anstey had taken me on as a locum and general dogsbody straight out of Matt's. Trotman had a grocery shop in one of those little streets on the other side of Midsummer Common. Knocked the stuffing out of him when his wife died—not that he'd been up to much in the first place. Took to drink. Elaine ran the shop all through the war. Looked after the old blighter— nursed him through a couple of bouts of pneumonia. Managed the whole kit and caboodle. *And* did well at school." The fire flickering on one side of his face gave him a savage, inflamed appearance, quite at odds with the mildness of his speech.

"Couldn't do much. I was in the R.A.M.C. Burma, then in a Jap P.O.W. camp. Didn't get back till late '45, and wasn't fit for much for another year. A few months later old Trotman got tight one night while Elaine was at the pictures, pitched head first down the stairs and broke his neck. Girl left high and dry. Good thing for her actually—but she couldn't see it that way, of course. Guilt and all that, but quiet, decent about it. Nursing seemed to be the best thing all round. Managed to get her into Matt's." He fell silent. "And now I suppose they'll dig it all up again."

"Again?"

"Oh, don't think they didn't try it the last time—and when she married Jonathan, it was worse. Gossip, innuendos—you don't know what that does to a fine sensitive woman." His one red eye glittered fiercely in the firelight. "What in God's name are we coming to, Welchman?"

"And you brought her down here to look after Arabella?"

"That's right. Always used her when I had something difficult on hand—if I could get her. Best nurse I ever had. She'd had experience with alcoholics—knew just how difficult they could be. And Arabella wasn't easy. But Elaine has an instinct for care and a competence to go with it. D'you see? It's inconceivable that . . ."

"Yes, I see." He heard the wound—and accepted the doctor's knowledge. It *was* inconceivable. But not to the police, and perhaps not to a coroner's jury. There seemed no end to the harm that was being done here. Why had he meddled? Without the letter, Brinton's death could still have been thought of as an accident. His mind went to Alex . . . to Kate. . . . He finished his whisky.

Stand's eyes seemed to be shut, the long lashes resting on the cheek, the face as immobile as a mask. "Yes—I introduced Elaine Trotman into this house. Just as I introduced Jonathan Brinton—

almost thirty years ago now. We'd just got our commissions and were waiting for a posting. They gave us a seventy-two-hour pass. Brinton was alone, no people, nowhere to go—so I brought him down here. I was practically a member of the family then, you see —engaged to Arabella. I thought it would be a kindness." He smiled faintly and opened his eyes. "A kindness. Well, what do we do now? Are they going to arrest her?"

"I don't think so—not right away, anyway. I think she might be well advised to consult her solicitor. You'll pass on what I've said, won't you? I'm afraid I have to get off." He rose. "And you'll —you'll give Mrs. Brinton my apologies."

Stand nodded and stood up slowly. "I shall. Good of you to come. You're a decent chap, Welchman."

"For a head-shrinker."

"For a head-shrinker." There was a visible effort to Stand's smile. In the hall, he said, "Take care of the boy, won't you, Welchman?"

"I'll do my best." There was no more comfort he could give than that. The centre of this house had fallen apart, and there was nothing he could do about it. He opened the door.

The snow whisked more briskly now in the outside darkness. They shook hands and Stand held his grip for a moment longer than necessary. "Did you know I'm Kate's godfather?"

"No." Hugh hesitated in surprise on the threshold, waiting for something more. But Stand merely said, "Good day, Doctor."

"Good day."

12

He'd been late for the two o'clock session—the first time such a thing had happened to him—and he'd had a sense of hurry all through the afternoon, except for the visit from Bob Lummis, who had been wheeled in at four o'clock precisely.

"You should have let me come to you," Hugh said.

"I wanted to do one last thing under my own steam, so to speak." He smiled faintly. "I'm for it, all right. A matter of weeks, Bantock says, if I'm lucky. But I know better—so give me one of your weeds, Hugh."

"Of course. Bob, I'm sorry."

"Don't be. Wouldn't have missed it for the world—which I've had more than my fair share of, so I know what that's worth."

Hugh lit the cigarettes, then they sat in silence.

After a while, Bob said, "I've been thinking about Dotty. Odd, I never thought much about her when she was alive." Dorothy Lummis had tried several times to kill herself—with pills, the gas oven—and had finally succeeded in hanging herself from a tree in the garden. "Funny little bird of a woman she was. I've been wondering if she was ever happy. Are birds happy? She used to perch, you know—never sat down properly on a chair, even at the table she would flutter up and about. Used to annoy me. 'For God's sake, sit down woman,' I used to say. It was all right when I was working —I wasn't at home very much. But when I retired I was in the house the whole time—bringing her down to earth. All she wanted to do was to hop about a bit, but really I left her no alternative except to fly away forever. It's a silly fancy perhaps, but I like to think now that she went South for the winter. It was never really a very suitable place for her here. . . ."

Later on, between two patients, Hugh had briefly looked in on Alex. He'd been absorbed in a game of chess and his only acknowledgement of Hugh's presence had been a slight frown—and perhaps even that had only been a reaction to the game, where his queen was in difficulties. Hugh had been vaguely cheered, but said nothing. He'd snatched a couple of minutes to ring Julia, but there had been no reply—odd, because it wasn't Mrs. Nance's afternoon off. And, as he'd watched the snow getting heavier through the windows of his consulting room, he'd given way to the worry that Julia was rushing about the countryside on her machine. Of course there were many other things she could be doing—but what, for instance? It came to him again, as it had yesterday sitting in her study with Ply, that he knew very little of what she did with her time—or her thoughts. Had she gone up to see Reg?—they seemed more friendly than he'd thought. Or did she lie dreaming of the foetus within her? He felt a sudden imperative desire to know these things.

And yet now, as he peered forward to see through the snow dancing in the car headlights and his glasses slid down his nose, he was not headed home. For all the time, beneath his worry for Julia and his halfhearted attention to his patients' recitals, Stand's words tolled at the back of his mind—*I'm Kate's godfather.* The more he thought about it, the clearer it became that Elaine, a woman of little education and small imagination, could not have written Brinton's suicide letter. Alex might have done so; he had the literary ability, but surely not the cold-bloodedness, the cold intelligence to sit down beside a dead or dying man and type out such an epistle. But Kate had both the intelligence and the imagination—and the courage.

After the final patient left and he sat for a few moments smoking alone, Hugh became increasingly certain that Kate must have written the letter—though why, and what game she was playing he couldn't fathom. He struggled with his extreme reluctance to interfere, but he knew he would have to see her before she had the chance to complicate the situation even more dangerously; and also because—a factor that carried even more weight in his mind—it was up to him to do as much as he could to rectify the harm he'd already done to Elaine Brinton.

So now he was creeping towards Lady Strange, hardly able to see, fearful of a skid, of missing the mail box on the corner where one had to turn right. But he found it and two minutes later spotted the wrought-iron lamps that guarded the college's absurdly neo-Gothic portals—"like a set for a village hall production of *Marmion*," Julia had said once. *Marmion*—that was Scott, Brinton's favourite author—*the last words of Sir W. . . .* What had they been? Hugh put his foot on the brake and the car skewed slightly, stalled and stopped.

The porter's lodge was crowded with young women chattering, heads thrown back. He didn't attempt to elbow his way among them. If hall was over, Kate would be in her rooms—or in the combination room. He'd have to chance it. He hurried through first court, passing a flock of undergraduates moving soundlessly across the whiteness, their black gowns twirling in the floating snow, laughing and calling from covey to covey. The last of them were coming out of hall as he passed the open doors; the lingering smell of food wafting on the night made him feel slightly sick. He pushed across the stream and into second court until he came to the new building. He ran quickly up the shallow steps to the first floor.

Kate's door was shut and he stood nonplussed in front of it. There was nothing to ring or rattle or shake. Caught by an unreasoning anxiety, he lifted his fist and pounded on the panel.

"Here you—what do you think you're up to?"

"What?" Two girls were staring at him from the head of the stairs. "Oh—I'm looking for Miss Brinton."

"*Doctor* Brinton."

"Chasing her more likely," said the one in glasses.

"Well, can't you see she's sported her oak?"

"Oak?" He glanced at the door—it looked more like cheap pine. "Er—yes. Of course. But it's a matter of some urgency."

"Always is, isn't it?" Glasses.

"I should leave her alone if I were you." Nonglasses. "Her father's just died, you know." There was a kindly inflection in her tone.

"Yes, I did know, but—"

"What you ought to do is go to the lodge and get the porter to give her a ring."

"Yes—I suppose so. Well, thank you." They stepped aside for him and he went down the stairs. As he reached the bottom, one of them said in a clear bright voice, "Randy old beast."

And the other replied, "Well, he won't get far with our Kate."

The afternoon's headache had returned. He rubbed his forehead; despite the cold, he was sweating. Where on earth was she? With Julia perhaps. Or curled foetally behind that locked door, unable to face finally whatever it was that she had done. Why had he advised her to come back here alone? A flake of snow fell on one lens and for a moment he was half blind. He took a deep, steadying breath. The court was silent and deserted now—all the birds had gone to cover.

The porter's lodge was empty too. "Oh, I'm, er, trying to get hold of Mi—of Dr. Brinton. I've been to her rooms but she has apparently, er—sported her oak. But it's a matter of some urgency. I'm a doctor—a medical doctor—and I—"

"Like me to ring through for you, Doctor?"

"Thanks—thank you."

"Nope—not answering. Hasn't been answering all afternoon, as a matter of fact. Sorry, Doctor."

Hugh adjusted his glasses—his hand trembled, he noted. "I see. Look, er—"

"Jenkins."

"Jenkins. Frankly I'm a little worried about her—perhaps I ought to have a word with the, er, bursar."

"Worried about her, sir?" The man looked puzzled. "Well, of course if it's a medical matter . . . But she rang down to the kitchen only ten minutes ago—I put her through myself—and she sounded as right as rain then."

"She rang down to the . . ." An enormous weight was lifted from him. "Well, in that case . . ."

"These scholars—you know how they are, Doctor—like to cut themselves off from the world all right. But they never forget their food."

"Oh quite. Yes. Well, thank you, Jenkins."

"That's quite all right, Doctor. Would you like to leave a message?"

"I don't think that will be necessary. No—no message."

In the car, he lit a cigarette. He executed a smooth U-turn. The snow had slackened and he could see more clearly; and his headache was lighter, hardly more than a feather touch of half-forgotten pain.

That afternoon Bob had asked him about himself, and Hugh, seeking for a happiness to give the old man, had spoken about his hopes for Julia.

And Bob had nodded. "I remember my first—I had 'flu but I went along all the same. Dotty drank pints of tea, and I had a flask of rum. When Charles arrived, I was quite tight—staggered home from the clinic, miles it was, singing, exalted. He's been pretty much of a headache ever since—well, you know all about that." He laughed. "But he's happy in his way—and that's what counts. I shan't tell him about this—don't want him hanging about my death bed. As I did about his cradle. But that was a joy, a great joy—the best there ever is, I think."

Hugh accelerated slightly, eager to get home now.

As he turned into The Lane he shaved a black car parked half in the road, half on the verge. After a few yards he realised why: There were no visible tracks at all and the snow had drifted in little hillocks and hummocks across the roadway; the driving was impossible. The Rover slid gently sideways almost into the ditch, the tires lost their grip and spun uselessly as he raced the engine. He gave up and, taking his medical bag from the bag, trudged slowly up to the house—once sinking almost to his knees in a drift.

His hand on the door, he turned and looked back; beyond the semi-circle of light cast by the outside lamp, the snow stretched out into the night, obliterating all boundaries, immaculately concealing the life of the country. He had the odd fancy that nothing could go wrong as long as it lay like this—all the way to the Fens, out beyond Ely.

The door gave way under his hand and he turned, startled, to see Julia standing there in a long blue woolen dress, her black hair shining.

"How did you know I was here?"

"I heard you cough. Hugh, the police—why, your feet are soaking."

"The police? What about the police?"

"The same two, they're here, in the waiting room. They won't take off their coats or sit down. Hugh, what's happened?"

"I don't know." As he moved into the hall and shut the door behind him, he noted the solemnity of Julia's expression and felt a spurt of anger at them for invading his home, his tranquility. "Well, at least," he hesitated, lowered his voice automatically, "I suppose it must be to do with Brinton's letter. A letter's turned up—Mrs. Warden pinched it, just as you suggested."

"Oh. But then that—that's good, isn't it?"

"No—they're convinced it's a forgery. That Brinton didn't write it." He put down his bag and took off his glasses and wiped them—the change of temperature had misted them up.

"I see—so we're back where we started from?"

"Not quite." He replaced his glasses. "You see, now they're absolutely sure he was murdered." He watched her—there was a faint touch of rose on the ivory of her cheek. His heart was wrung. "Well, let's face the music."

As he went ahead of her into the waiting room, his feet squelched damply on the polished parquet. "Good evening, Superintendent."

"Good evening, Doctor." Hats in hand, they were standing by the glassed-in bookshelves, as though searching for "obscene material" among the medical literature or calculating the yardage for a quick sale.

"What can I do for you?" With Julia beside him, Hugh took up stance in front of the fireplace. "If you've come to enquire about young Brinton, I'm afraid I can't tell you any more than—"

"No, it's nothing like that, Doctor. Quite a different matter." His tone was heavy—with none of last night's false geniality.

"What? What's this all about then?" He took out his cigarettes.

"It's about Dr. Stand."

"Stand?" Hugh was suddenly uneasy, but he said calmly, "Has something happened to Dr. Stand?"

"Not happened, exactly. Doctor, am I right in thinking you saw Dr. Stand this afternoon?"

"Yes—that's quite true. I was with him for a few minutes." He shook out a cigarette and lit it. "Why?"

"Good. Then there's something I'd like you to listen to, if you can spare the time."

"I don't suppose I have much option, do I? What is it?"

Julia said, "Perhaps I should leave."

"I have no objection to your presence, Mrs. Welchman. All right, Andrew."

Sergeant Ramm took two paces forward and slipped some pages from an envelope in his hand. "The following is a statement made at the Central Police Station by Dr. Stand at five o'clock this afternoon." He cleared his throat, then began to read in a swift monotone:

I, Henry Harold Evelyn Stand, Doctor of Medicine, of 2 Mead's Way, Cambridge, do hereby admit my responsibility for the death of Mrs. Arabella Brinton on April twenty-sixth fourteen years ago and for the death of Dr. Jonathan Brinton last Tuesday, April twenty-first.

Being a partner of Dr. Brinton's and residing at the New Inn, I entered into a liaison with Mrs. Brinton some six years before her death. This affair was naturally conducted with the utmost discretion, and for all practical purposes it ended about a year before she died. Mrs. Brinton by this time was close to being a chronic alcoholic and at the same time was becoming increasingly exigent about her wish to marry me. On the other hand, I myself no longer had any interest in her, other than a purely professional one. However Mrs. Brinton never ceased to urge marriage and eventually began to use threats to achieve her aim. Matters were brought to a head after the introduction of Nurse Trotman into the household. Mrs. Brinton, entirely misinterpreting my long-standing friendship and respect for Nurse Trotman, became violently jealous. On the Thursday she told me that if I did not immediately dismiss the nurse and consent in writing to marry her, Mrs. Brinton, she would report my unprofessional conduct to the General Medical Council and see to it that I was "struck off."

On the afternoon of the twenty-sixth, a Friday, I returned from my rounds early because of the fog. I passed from my surgery to the front hall, intending to go upstairs to have a look at my patient. On my way across the hall, I noticed that the cellar door was open and the light on. I went to shut it and at once saw Mrs. Brinton on the top step with a bottle of whisky in her hands. I attempted to seize the bottle and we wrestled for a moment. Then suddenly realising that here was the solution to all my problems, I stepped back and slammed the door as hard as I could. I felt the contact, heard her fall and the bottle smash. I returned to my surgery to await developments. This was at about four-twenty. On being called by Brinton, I examined Mrs. Brinton, pronounced her dead and instructed him to ring up the police. He told me that he had found his daughter and the poodle bitch standing by the door. I myself remarked mud and claw marks on the wood. I therefore loosened the spring on the swing door between the two halls, which was always kept very tight to prevent the dog passing from one to another, it being my intention to give the impression that the dog had jumped at the cellar door and slammed it. I instructed Katherine not to say that she had been downstairs that afternoon, and I gave the small boy a heavy sedative.

I now come to last Tuesday. At about eleven thirty P.M. I received a very agitated phone call from Brinton summoning me to the New Inn at once. He would not say what it was about. I went down straightaway. I found him in his study. He was clearly in a highly nervous condition—in fact I thought him distinctly unbalanced. He .told me that his wife was trying to poison him and pointed to half a glass of cloudy looking liquid, which he identified as the poison. I picked it up and drank the contents. This seemed to calm him somewhat. He then began a long rambling discourse, which consisted mainly of accusations against his wife and son: His wife was spying on him, was conspiring to have him committed, was trying to prove he had murdered Arabella, had hired people to attack him so that he dared not venture out of the house. On his part he was convinced that Elaine Brinton had murdered his first wife and that Alex had seen her do it. His conversation was full of wild threats and illogical fears. He was clearly suffering from persecution mania, often associated with alcoholism. I judged however that his accusations might well be believed by an untrained listener, and I knew the harm he could do to his wife and son was incalculable. To myself too, because if any credence was given to his accusations at all, I would naturally be obliged to step forward and acknowledge the truth of the matter. I found myself in a position not unlike that of fourteen years previously.

I told him that if he were to do anything about his suspicions, he would have to do so in a more calm and rational manner and I suggested a sedative to allow him to sleep properly. To this he was agreeable. I went to the surgery. I dissolved the contents of twenty 10mg capsules of Librium in a glass. I knew Brinton generally dissolved his pills as he had great difficulty in swallowing them. In the study I poured a generous measure of whisky into the glass to take away the taste. He drank it down and in a matter of minutes he was comatose. I then typed a farewell letter to his wife and children in which I made him confess to the murder of his first wife. I am a very competent typist. I am completely familiar with his style of writing.

There is little more to tell. I emptied the dregs of the glass into the glass of whisky from which he had already been drinking. I cleaned and dried the first glass. I did not attempt to remove my fingerprints except from the typewriter, because I was confident that I would be the first to be summoned in the morning. I left the New Inn and arrived home at just after twelve A.M.

I have come forward because it is clear to me that my precautions were not sufficiently effective and that entirely innocent people are in danger of being accused of the crimes for which I am alone responsible. This is a full and true statement of all that occurred.

Signed: H. H. E. Stand

Hugh watched Ramm fold the document, reinsert it in the envelope, step back. But in his mind's eye he saw Henry Stand— Stand shutting the door on his visitor, going back to the study, sitting down in front of the coal fire, perhaps having another whisky; then working it out, making up his mind, and finally going straight down to the police station. Kate's godfather, Arabella's lover, Elaine's staunch friend . . . "What? What?" Julia's hand on his arm brought him to with a start.

"I said, what do you think of that, Doctor?" Ply spoke softly.

"Well, you've got your murderer now, haven't you?"

"Have I—have I?" The policeman moved forward, so that the lamplight fell on his face; his eyes seemed half closed. "What was the nature of your discussion with Dr. Stand this afternoon, Doctor?"

"We talked about young Brinton—our mutual patient." Hugh braced himself—he knew what was coming. His judgement had failed him and now he was in the absurd position of having to defend Stand against the accusation of innocence.

"Did you tell him—as you told me—about young Brinton having seen or heard his stepmother give Dr. Brinton something to drink?"

"I may have done. I don't recall."

"And that the boy had seen his stepmother in the front hall on the afternoon of Arabella Brinton's death?"

"It's possible, but I'm not sure I did."

"Or that Mrs. Warden had admitted to seeing Nurse Trotman emerge from the back door that same afternoon?"

"No." Stand had already known—his conscience was clear there.

"Did you inform Dr. Stand of Dr. Brinton's so-called suicide letter?"

"Yes, naturally I did."

"And that the letter was not in all probability authentic?"

"Yes. Look—"

"And you revealed the contents of the letter?"

"I expect I gave him the gist of it in passing, but—"

"In passing? Didn't you in fact give him a very detailed résumé of everything that was in that letter?"

"Look, Superintendent, our conversation was hurried, I was pressed for time. I really cannot recall the minutiae of everything that was said or not said."

"All right. May I ask *why* you went to see Dr. Stand at all?"

"I didn't go to see him. He happened to be there. I went to see Mrs. Brinton—she wasn't in."

"This was directly after you'd talked to me at the police station?"

"Yes."

"Why were you suddenly so anxious to see Mrs. Brinton?"

"There was nothing sudden about it. I had promised to drop in and tell Mrs. Brinton about her stepson's condition. I had tried to do so at midday, but she was out, and it was then I encountered Mrs. Warden, about which you know."

"I'm beginning to think I don't know very much—certainly not as much as you." Ply paused, slowly revolving his dark hat in his hand. "Doctor, isn't it a fact that most of the essential elements that make Dr. Stand's statement hang together were learned from you?"

"Nonsense." Hugh allowed himself to show an anger he didn't feel. "What are you suggesting?"

"I'm drawing your attention to the fact that conspiring to falsify evidence is a criminal offence."

The blood drained from Hugh's face. "That's a remark you may come to regret." He was really angry now, but kept his voice cool. "Let me give you a piece of advice, Superintendent: I think you're in danger of making a fool of yourself."

"Oh I am, am I?" Ply's eyes were wide open and his cheeks were flushed. "Well, if you ask me, someone's trying to *make* a fool of me. And I won't stand for that." The menace in his voice was clear and Julia's hand tightened on Hugh's arm.

"Superintendent, as far as I can see your business here is finished. So I'll bid you good night."

"I . . ." Ply closed his mouth tight over his little blackish teeth; he was not accustomed to being so brusquely dismissed. "Very well, Doctor." He nodded. "Come on, Andrew."

When Hugh had shown them out and shut the door and, for no very good reason, locked it, he came back to find Julia smoking one of her Turkish cigarettes.

"I expect you need a drink."

"I do, I do indeed." He managed a smile. "And some more cigarettes." While she was gone, he looked round the familiar room —it seemed changed somehow, perhaps by the presence of the policemen. Like them, he found himself staring at the bookshelves —as though he would find there the answer to this new puzzle. The leather volumes gleamed in fire and lamplight; Old Welling had had all the medical journals beautifully bound, the dictionaries, the texts, a shelf of forensic medicine. Like Brinton, Hugh had inherited the bulk of his library from his father-in-law—although technically it all belonged to Julia, along with the house and everything in it, of which she was to come into absolute possession on the birth of a child or at the age of thirty, now long past. But not too long; nothing was irreparable.

He was dithering—dreaming—mooning, when he should be grappling with what to say to Julia, how to allay this fresh thrust of sharp anxiety. Again he was filled with a useless exasperation at the Brintons' intrusion into their life together.

"What's this?" He looked at the clear liquid in the proffered glass. "A martini?"

"Yes, probably not as good as Mike's." She smiled and with a swish of her skirts sat down on the old leather pouf; she, too, was holding a martini, instead of the usual glass of sherry.

"No—it's good, just the right bite." He settled back into his chair and started to open the box of fifty she'd laid on the little table.

"You really should change those shoes—shall I take them off for you?"

"Oh, the heat will dry them." He stretched his legs out to the fire.

"The heat will ruin them." And then suddenly they both laughed. He was encouraged—as she sat, sipping her drink, the blue of her dress exactly matching the blue of her eyes, she seemed almost placid. Was it possible that she simply accepted Stand's confession, whole?

"Hugh—you're upset again, aren't you?"

"Ummm." He lit a cigarette, blew out the match, and carefully dropped it in the ashtray. "As a matter of fact, I've made pretty much of a fool of myself today."

"Because of what you told Ply about Elaine?"

"What Alex had said about her—yes. Ply is very astute and quite ruthless—he allowed me to maunder on making those damaging points against Elaine Brinton under the illusion that Brinton had committed suicide. I had no reason to doubt it—the letter sounded right, it had a placidness about it, with just the proper hint of self-pity. I thought it probable. I was wrong. I made a mistake."

"How did they find out it was forged?"

"The typing—too even apparently, it didn't match other samples of his typing."

"Yes, of course. But look, Hugh—have you really hurt Elaine in any way that matters?"

"Yes, I think so. I think I have—even if she is guilty. My profession isn't concerned with delivering people to the law in such circumstances."

"Isn't it rather to yourself that you've done the harm?" Her voice was so low he hardly heard it.

"That doesn't matter." He closed his eyes for a moment—he had a sensation of pain. "I took no oath not to harm myself."

"Do you really think her capable of having murdered Jonathan —or having murdered Arabella?"

186

"I don't know. I'd have said not." He would have to be careful here. "Of course I've only met her once. Don't you recollect anything about her at Matt's?"

"Not much. She was rather stern, forbidding, very professional. She didn't like me much."

"Why ever not?"

"I don't think she thought I'd make a very good nurse."

"Oh. Well anyway—now I'm rather nonplussed. Stand told me a rather unfortunate piece of her personal history. It seems that her father was an alcoholic; he died one night by falling down the stairs and breaking his neck—it was accounted an accident. And of course she did give Brinton something to drink on the night of his death, if Alex is to be relied on and," he said firmly, "I think he is. But I'm not sure all that holds much water—there's something missing."

"Henry must think she's guilty."

"Why—why do you say that?" He was alert.

"Because he came forward and made that statement." She was staring at the gas fire.

"I don't follow you, I don't see that."

"It's not another person's innocence one takes upon oneself, it's their sins," she said in a slow contemplative tone.

"Oh I see." He looked hard at her—he'd never heard her speak in such a way before. Was this the true voice of the Julia he didn't know? He suddenly had the unbearable feeling that she was unreachably far away, would never come home . . . and then, as she turned her head and smiled at him, he had a sense of such utter destitution that he almost cried out. "Yes, I see." He coughed and took a quick swallow of his martini and forced himself to consider her words. "Actually, there's no doubt in my mind, from the way he talked about her this afternoon, that Stand has a very great and long-standing attachment to Elaine Brinton. He would very naturally want to protect her." He'd spoken rapidly, now he paused. He was more than ever certain that it was not Elaine, but Kate, Stand was trying to protect; perhaps he'd always thought Kate had killed Arabella, and it would be a simple step to connect her—or Alex—with her father's death too. After all, he considered himself *almost a member of the family.* But these were thoughts he wanted to keep away from Julia at all costs. "Yes," he said, allowing a touch of ruefulness to words, "that explains the motivation, and as for the information, Ply was right—I gave him everything he needed to

make a plausible confession. I compounded one error with another."

"No one would blame you, Hugh."

"But I'm supposed to be able to do better than that—merely
avoiding blame. I did the very thing I detest—I gossiped like some
wretched old woman. Like Mike. I betrayed a responsibility."

"We all do that." She looked straight at him, but again he had
the impression of remoteness, that she was looking elsewhere. "Besides, your responsibility is to Alex." She smiled and was with him
again.

And to you, and to you, he wanted to call out. But instead he
said, "Of course we are both automatically assuming Henry Stand's
statement is entirely untrue."

"Yes, but you don't believe he's a murderer, do you?"

"I don't think so—not that I know him very well, but, after all,
he's a doctor."

Julia's laugh pealed out—he was astonished, delighted; a sound
he hardly ever heard.

"But all the same, he'll go to prison," he said perversely and at
once felt a bitter despair at his own uselessness, incompetence—at
Stand's futile, wasteful self-sacrifice. No one can rectify another's
mistakes.

"Perhaps it won't come to that." She reached over and touched
his hand. "You can't take it all on yourself."

"I . . . You're right of course. It's a bad sign. Detachment is an
essential condition of my effectiveness." He finished his martini—
tepid now. They sat in silence for a while. "Mrs. Warden told me
a curious thing this morning: She said your father and Arabella
Anstey were very good friends. Did you know?"

"Yes. Yes, I did. Though not then." She turned her eyes to the
fire. "Father told me about it just before he died. It was after dinner
one night; he'd brought out the '31 port, but after a sip, he pushed
his glass away. 'It's no good, Julia—it tastes like rot to me nowadays,
the odour of mortality. It's the same with the roses—they've got
that sweetish peardrop scent. Gas—I remember it on the Somme,
mixed with that curious smell the freshly dead have.' And then he
began talking about Mother—it was the roses that made the connection, I expect. He told me how after her death, he often thought
of suicide. He said one of the things that prevented him was Arabella's kindness. She used to bicycle up three or four times a week
to see him and they'd stroll in the garden and chat. About books

and music and places—Arabella always loved the mountains, and Father had been a leading light in the Alpine Club when he was a young man. She was engaged to Henry then, but was troubled about it, and they used to talk about that too. Then one afternoon in June—it was the day Hitler invaded Russia—'a radiant June day,' he called it, 'all our hearts were lifted because at last we had an ally.' Well, Arabella came up as usual and they walked in the rose garden and she told him she'd decided to break it off with Henry, he wasn't for her, et cetera. And he said, as he listened, he realised that he was in love with her, that she was what he wanted, needed, that he didn't have to be a lonely old man—'for a few moments I was dizzy with dreams of youth and the scent of roses.' But before he could speak, she told him of someone else she'd fallen for—young Dr. Brinton." She held out her hands to the fire. "So he was brought down to earth."

"Perhaps that's not such a bad place to be."

She smiled gravely. "Perhaps not."

"From one point of view, it was undoubtedly a lucky escape."

"A lucky escape . . ." For a moment he was not sure whether she was going to cry—but she laughed, gently this time. He was pleased—pleased that his incurable pedestrianism could amuse her —and touched that she had talked to him about herself, her father, the old days, subjects normally taboo. He was a little puzzled, yet reassured now. He felt in his bones that he was right—there was a turn, an opening, a fresh life free of that hidden hectic anxiety.

"I tried to reach you this afternoon, but no one answered."

"I sent Mrs. Nance off for the afternoon—she's been worrying herself sick about that daughter of hers."

Daughter—the word hung in the air. They'd not mentioned Kate all evening. He waited uneasily, but there was no reaction. Perhaps she really was coming to terms.

"And you—you didn't go out riding in the snow?"

"Yes, I did." She gave him a look of what—tenderness? indulgence? "It wasn't dangerous. I went to Ely."

"Ely?" Where Alex had gone *to pray a bit.* "You went up the tower?"

"No, I stayed down to earth. You know I'm afraid of heights." She laughed. "Hugh, I bet you've never been to Ely in your life, have you?"

"Well, I must confess I haven't."

"So I suppose some patient or other told you. What a vicarious life you lead. Are you hungry?"

"Well yes, as a matter of fact I am." He grinned. "And not vicariously."

She stood up quickly and left the room, before he had time to speak of that other hunger he had—for information, confirmation of his hope in her body. There was a change—there was no doubt of that—a new gentleness, mellowness. But perhaps it was as far as he should go tonight. There was all the time in the world to let it grow, infuse their lives with a new joy. He had the feeling that this place where they lived could become a home, after all.

13

The sky was brilliant and the sun glittered on the snow's crystalline crust; it was not more than a degree or two above freezing, but Hugh had remembered his overcoat this time and was even glad of the scarf and gloves Julia had handed him at the last moment. His visit to Beasely's had been abortive ("I really am most dreadfully sorry your spectacles are not ready, Doctor, but our young Mr. Chapman, who does all our best work, you know, came down with the 'flu yesterday morning, and it's set us all at sixes and sevens. A tragedy, no less, and he seemed in such a very fine state of health only on the Wednesday. Oh yes, quite at sixes and sevens we are."). So he had gone round to Heffers and added half a dozen books to his order list, throwing in the new Milmeyer monograph as a sop to Mike Semple.

Standing on King's Bridge, he sniffed the promise of returning spring in the still chilly air. On the bank below him a large black dog leapt and frisked with wild barks of joy round a young couple —she, pale and blond, lithely darting and dancing with the dog; he, tall and saturnine, frowning, clearly apprehensive of the gambolling animal. He was strongly built and his face was vaguely familiar— a celebrated hero of the football field perhaps, but wincing now with anxiety at the symbolic threat.

Hugh smiled. He had only the mildest of headaches. Last night after dinner he and Julia had drunk a bottle and a half of Arthur Welling's best port. In some way her reminiscence of her father had released Julia and she had talked about him easily and freely. And they had discussed the garden—she had been willing, even eager to replant the roses, which now that she had mentioned it, he guessed, had lost their "odour of mortality." She had described one of her bridge parties, and he had laughed a great deal. And yet her merriment had been gentle, as had their love-making later.

The dog suddenly bounded away from the couple, ran across the bridge and up the avenue towards Queen's Road—flushed and nimble, the girl followed in hot pursuit and then, after a desultory cry—"Oh I say, do stop, Jenny!"—the young man lumbered behind them. Hugh lit a cigarette and watched the dead match whirled away by the waters; the Cam was running high and discoloured with mud. Downstream the flood would be heavy over the weir. . . . Last night the nightmare had recurred—with a difference. This time he was naked on the pole, and the punt, if anything, had been closer to the falls, and the sky darker—a darkness that had remained with him as he woke, sweating in his bed. Listening to Julia's quiet breathing, he had gradually calmed himself. And then at breakfast —bacon and eggs, although it was Friday—Julia had suggested something he ought to have thought of for himself, something that gave him a hope, though it seemed almost too logical to be—

"Hugh, my dear fellow!" He received a slap on the back that made the glasses slither down his nose.

"Oh hello, Mike."

"I asked myself—now why does that funereal fellow on the bridge seem so familiar? Don't often find you among the cloisters of learning. Though close up, I see you're looking remarkably smug." Mike swept the tails of his gown about him—he was in his familiar leather-patched jacket and baggy trousers, with unpolished brogues and a wool tie slightly askew.

"Don't be deceived, that's merely the professional mask."

"Good—good!" Mike's laugh rang out heartily in the crisp air. "But you've got something to be rather smug about, all the same, haven't you? Charlie rang me up this morning and gave me the news."

"The news?"

"About Dr. Henry Stand! Who would have thought our old sourpuss G.P. capable of such passion and subtlety? Where are you off to? Come and have a glass of sherry. Come and have lunch!"

"I can't, thanks very much. I've got to get back to St. E.'s."

Mike laid a hand on his shoulder. "You work too hard, old boy. I'm worried about you. Definitely. And I'm not the only one." He nodded sagely. "Julia."

"Julia?" Hugh smiled. "Oh I don't know."

"But I do. The other night when I was moaning about myself on the phone to Julia, I did remember my manners enough to remark that of course it was difficult for you too. And she said, 'Yes, I don't think I've ever seen Hugh take a case so hard.' You see?"

"Yeees." Had it shown so much? He suddenly had no words —he was inexpressibly, stupidly moved.

"I've been worried myself, you know. About Reg—not just this Brinton business. That's all over now, thank God. But, well, I'm not sure I know exactly how to put it."

Hugh was immediately alert. "What's the problem?"

"Problem—I'm not sure there is a *problem*." He looked about him, as if to gather strength from the surrounding towers and spires. "But, well—Reg and I, you know—we go our own ways, as it were."

He spoke carefully, giving Hugh a quick half glance. And all at once Hugh did know—theirs was a marriage of convenience, academic convenience perhaps, but certainly sexual. And Mike's way led him to "conferences" in London, Paris, Toronto, all over the place, and to a painfully undue interest in his "men." And Reg? "Yes, Reg. I understand."

"Yes—the thing is, lately I've had the impression she isn't going anywhere. Do you know what I mean?"

"I think you'll have to amplify a little."

"I'm not sure I can." He passed his hand over his immaculate silver hair—there was not a finger of wind to ruffle it otherwise. "I'll try. Reg has always been one for retreating into her shell, you know. A crab, of course. But in the last few days she hasn't been coming out of it. I'm more or less sure it's a conscious decision—not, I mean, a depression—but I can't for the life of me think why, and it worries me."

"What exactly is it that worries you—her withdrawal, its effect on you, or your inability to explain it?"

"Blast—how can I expect you to understand? But, after all, you have talked to her, you know how, how—"

"Bewildering."

"Exactly. Bewildering it can be. Living with Reg, one always feels a bit like a seven-year-old trying to decipher the murkier parts of Blake without a key. Sometimes I've thought she has an apocalyptic view of life—at other times, a tragic or, more accurately, a desperate one: as if she sees all about her a—a horror." He had rested his hand on the stone balustrade and now he looked down at the heavy flood of waters. "A horror."

"Yes. I see. But isn't such horror an objectification of some unconscious terror? If I may make an analogy with Julia—I believe she too feels something of the same thing. Reg retires into her study, but she is intellectually active; though Julia is active in a more obvious fashion—bridge, tennis, archery—I think she finds her deepest solace in poetry, others' and her own. This may be partially escapism, self-defence at any rate, but there is nothing wrong with escapism as long as it's not incapacitating, as long as a reasonable contact with reality is maintained. And in such circumstances I don't think it's usually very productive to probe." He dropped his cigarette and trod it into the snow.

"In other words, the responsible course is to do nothing?"

"I'd say rather—to wait and see."

Mike laughed abruptly. "Do you ever go to the cinema?"

"Not very often. Why?"

"When did you last see a film?"

"Oh, I don't know—about a year ago."

"What was it?"

"To tell you the truth, I didn't see much of it. I fell asleep, woke up once—there were a lot of cars stalled on a motorway and people shouting and screaming—then I went to sleep again."

Mike smiled. "I remember seeing a film, it must have been just after the war, when I first came to England, you know—about a mad psychiatrist who, as far as I can recall, had gone about murdering his patients. It wasn't at all a good film, but in the final confrontation between the detective and the psychiatrist, the detective had a rather memorable line: 'You're not a doctor, Doctor, you're a patient.' "

"Ummmm." Hugh smiled dutifully—but he was interested, it was the first time he had heard Mike speak, even indirectly, of his antecedents. "Well of course there'll always be firemen who are pyromaniacs at heart."

"What?" Mike blinked at him. "Oh—quite."

"Look, Mike—is there something you'd like me to do about Reg?"

"Well, my dear fellow, as you ask so kindly—and as you've

already done it once—perhaps you could pop up and have a chat with her now and again? I'm out a good deal of the time myself, you see, alas."

"Of course, I will." To his mild surprise, Hugh found the prospect not altogether unpleasing.

"Splendid, splendid!" Mike's shoulders were straight now, and he waved vaguely at someone behind Hugh. The wave turned into a wagging finger. "Now, I want young Alex back, you know. I'm counting on you, my dear old psychiatrist. If he can break through all that conventional ice, maybe he'll turn out to be as bright as his sister." And then, as suddenly as he had come, he was gone—sprinting across the snowy turf towards Gibbs Building, his gown flowing behind him.

Not necessarily a desirable fate, thought Hugh. And watching that springy stride, he knew that Stand's confession had resolved Mike's immediate problems—including Alex—and had dissolved a little of his personal private darkness, whatever that might be. Just as Julia's suggestion this morning had dissolved a little of Hugh's own unease—was it not possible, after all, that one of them, son, daughter, wife, finding the man dead, had decided to write a last letter for him that would clear them all, liberate them all from the long years of suspicion and guilt and anxiety? Yes, it was possible. Plausible even—far more plausible than that Stand could have written it.

Hugh left the bridge and, as he walked up the avenue, he passed the dog-chasing couple—dogless now, reunited, arm-in-arm, laughing. He realised that his professional discomfort and his private happiness had never been so opposed.

"Sister, I'm just going to look in on young Brinton for a few moments. How has he been this afternoon?"

"Brinton, Doctor?" Arkwright's hyperthyroid blue eyes stared at him. "But he's gone!"

"Gone?" Hugh stood dead still. "What do you mean—gone?"

"Why, he left this afternoon with the nurse you sent to fetch him. There's nothing wrong, is—"

"I sent no nurse. What's all this about?"

"Well, I—why I . . ." She began to tremble.

"Now pull yourself together, Sister," said Hugh quietly, "and just tell me exactly what happened."

"Well, I wasn't on myself, Doctor. But apparently this nurse who came from—who *said* she came from you, that you wanted Brinton signed out for an hour or two as you urgently needed to see him at your house, so—"

"But I'm here on Friday afternoons, you know that."

"Yes, but Braithwaite's rather new. When Brinton was not back by six, I did ring your house, but there was no reply."

"Six? When did this happen then?"

"Ab-bout four. Just after four. Here, it's in the book, Doctor." Her hand fluttered over the page. "I'm sure it all seemed quite regular—after all she *was* a nurse."

Hugh frowned. "Anyone can dress up in a uniform and cape, Sister. Is Braithwaite available?"

"I'm afraid she's off, Doctor. But why would—"

"Did Braithwaite say anything to you about this 'nurse'?"

"Not really, just that she was, well, rather daunting."

"What did she actually say, Sister, please?"

"That she was a frozen little bitch." Arkwright smiled weakly, "I'm terribly sorry if there was any mistake. . . ."

But Hugh was no longer listening. That was Elaine Brinton all right. It would have been child's play for her to manipulate an inexperienced nurse, and easy enough to persuade a depressed and docile Alex.

"I'm going to have to use your phone."

"Of course, Doctor."

As he listened to the unanswered ringing at the New Inn, he felt the same unreasoning dread he'd had in front of Kate's locked door last night. Where on earth would she have taken him—and for what? No, he must keep his head clear of irrelevances for the moment. He tried Lady Strange—no, Dr. Brinton was not in; in fact the porter was almost sure he'd seen her on her way out about half an hour ago.

Then where? Aunt Edith in Yorkshire? On impulse he rang his own professional number.

"Dr. Welchman is not available at the—" Mrs. Nance's afternoon off, of course; and Julia's bridge night.

"Would you like a cup of tea, Doctor?"

"Ummmm." He stared at Sister Arkwright, her competence disintegrated into the nervous fidgets. Bridge—what had been the name Julia had mentioned in her bridge story last night? Celia something. Celia Scrope. "Hand me the phone book, will you, Sister?"

There was only one Scrope in the book—Frederick T., on the Trumpington Road. But there was no answer.

Hugh stared out of the little glass-sided office, hardly aware of Arkwright clinking the china at his back. He lit a cigarette, dismissing a quick, bitter reflection on his certainty that Alex was safe at St. E.'s—absolutely no visitors, particularly not his mother. Alex was in danger now. What had possessed the woman to kidnap him? No, a better question: To whom would she turn in such a situation? Stand, of course—Henry Stand. He reached out for the phone, then caught himself. No use ringing the good doctor, he wasn't at home, he was in custody—was there a notice on his surgery door directing patients to the Central Police Station?

"Your tea, Doctor."

He shook his head angrily. He was dithering. The fact was— Alex had to be found, wherever he might be, even if he were only eating cream buns in a teashop with a perfectly innocent stepmother. And Hugh had come to the end of his resources—his limited resources. His duty was clear.

He dialled the Central Police Station and asked for Chief Superintendent Ply and waited through a series of clickings.

"Dr. Welchman—speak of the devil! I've just been ringing your house, but your wife must be out and all I get is a disembodied—"

"Yes yes—it's her bridge night. Look, Mr. Ply, I am seriously worried. Alex—young Brinton—is missing." He drew a short breath. "Someone purporting to be my nurse was permitted to sign him out from here at about four this afternoon, without my being informed. And I've reason to believe that person might have been his stepmother."

"Yes, that's right."

"What do you mean?"

"I mean, it was her all right. As a matter of fact, she and your young scamp have just been down to see me."

"You?" Hugh was swept with relief. "How is he? Does he seem reasonably in control?"

"Oh he did, yes, I would say so. He made a very clear statement."

"Statement? What—statement? Have you—you haven't arrested Mrs. Brinton?"

"Arrested Mrs. B.? Lord bless my soul, no."

"Well," he frowned, "well, I must come down and see him at once."

"He isn't here now. I thought I made that clear."

"You let him go?"

"That's right. I saw no reason to detain him."

"No reason? Haven't you the slightest notion of the kind of stress that boy is under? It's totally irresponsible to let him wander about alone—he must be under medical supervision. I can't answer for—"

"Now take it easy, Doctor. Brinton was more sleepy than anything else after he made his statement. And by the way, I don't see what all the difficulty was about letting us ask him a few questions. He seemed perfectly normal to me. Anyway, nobody said anything about him wandering about alone."

"You let him go home with his stepmother?"

"Oh no. As a matter of fact I believe Mrs. Brinton had to go off to some horticultural do. She made a statement too, by the way."

"Superintendent," Hugh's anger was tight and lucid, "I don't care a jot about your statements or who made them, but whatever his appearance of normality, that boy needs help, professional help. Now, where did he go?"

"Well now, Miss Brinton was down here—Dr. Brinton, I suppose I should say—and she and her brother went off together, so I expect she took him over to her college. But, you know, Doctor, if you take my tip, it might be wiser to leave him alone for a bit."

"I don't think I need to advise you about my professional duty."

"Ah—boot's on the other foot a bit now, eh?" Ply chuckled. "Just one other thing, I'd like to pop up and see you later on—I've got a bit of clearing up to do down here first. Would around ten o'clock suit you?"

"Superintendent, I can't, of course, prevent you from coming to my house, but I won't guarantee I'll let you in." He cut the connection. He was breathing heavily and was caught by a spasm of coughing. What an utterly futile display of temper. He began to dial the Lady Strange number, then stopped and slowly replaced the phone.

"I'm going out now, Sister. I shall be bringing Brinton back in an hour or so."

Hugh's feet crunched on the snow in the car park, half thawed but freezing again now. He got into the cold Rover. His hand trembled slightly on the steering wheel. The aftermath of fear. He was seldom so sheerly angry. Or disquieted. And his anger had impaired his judgement; he should have asked Ply the nature of Alex's statement. And he heard his father's voice out of the past, "You made a proper balls-up of that one, lad, didn't you?"

He started the engine and let in the clutch. If Elaine had taken Alex to the police station—then his own fears were groundless. Elaine was in no danger, nor Kate, and Alex—*he seemed more sleepy than anything else.* The reaction to a crisis passed, and passed, despite all his precautions, when Hugh was absent. Something sufficiently critical had occurred to reunite the family, at least temporarily. Well, he would soon know.

"Dr. Brinton will see you in five minutes, Doctor, in the library—that's the west entrance in first court, the first door on the left."

"Thank you, er, Jenkins." His anxiety had tightened into a headache and, as he left the porter's lodge, he had to resist an exasperated impulse to go straight to Kate's rooms and force his way in.

In the library a faint illumination filtered through the stained-glass Gothic windows giving onto the court. He was unable to find the light switch. Standing in the centre of the room that smelt of old leather, he lit a cigarette. The flare of the match left him blind and, moving too brusquely, he hit his shin against some hard object. He put the spent match in his pocket. The library was cold; and silent—not even a mouse rustling among the dead books. The undergraduates would all be in hall. Eating.

He groped his way to a chair and sat down. Although he'd missed the canteen lunch, he wasn't hungry; but it seemed to him that he had been tired and cold for a long time. He wondered vaguely what he had done with his overcoat . . . and scarf . . . and gloves. . . . His eyes closed, his head lolled, jerked up, lolled again —his glasses slid down his nose.

The river flowed easily at first, softly shuddering the punt, a playful running, rocking. He clung nude to the pole—stuck stock-still on his stuprate stick. With muscular ripples of hidden strength, the white-speckled slipstream smoothly lifted—devouring punt cries and smiles of a summer's stricken day . . . too late his silent shout to the darkling sky, the furious river chuckling, chortling, mocking . . . too late, too dark . . . river and sky riven by lightning stab. . . . He cried out, struggled up into the light, half blinded—out of the dark they were calling him.

"Hugh . . . Hugh!"

"Yes? Yes?" Unseeing eyes wide open. "What's the problem?"

"Hugh—are you all right?"

"What? All right?" He blinked in the gladness of light, the dream destroyed, the woman beautiful before him—alive. "Yes . . . yes."

"What on earth were you doing in the dark?"

"I couldn't find the switch." He pushed his glasses back onto his nose and brushed at a long finger of ash that marred his waist-coat.

Kate went round to the other side of the table and sat down. "Here, use this as an ashtray." She pushed a pewter inkwell towards him. "I suppose you've come about Alex?"

"How is he?"

"He's all right."

"I'd like to see him."

"He's asleep."

"I'd like to see him all the same."

Kate shook her head decisively, "I don't think that's a good idea."

"Kate . . ." Hugh dropped his cigarette in the inkwell and there was a faint hiss. "You know as well as I do that he ought to be in professional hands."

"I don't agree—after all, your professional hands weren't very competent this afternoon, were they?"

"That's beside the point." He lifted his glasses and pinched the bridge of his nose between his fingers. "Our staff organisation might certainly have been better, but that doesn't alter the fact that Elaine's action was devious, irresponsible, and quite possibly dangerous."

"Why shouldn't he have left, if he wanted to?"

"Did he want to?" He let his glasses drop back.

"Who wouldn't?"

"That's not very productive, is it?"

"Productive! Christ, you and your bloody lingo. Do you think—"

"Kate, this is important. When I saw Alex this morning, he was certainly in—in no mood to leave hospital. He was simply not up to coping with the demands and terms of the situation, nor did he wish to. I'd be very interested to know what changed his mind—if indeed it was changed."

"Oh well—it was Elaine, of course. She can make him do anything she wants, the poor little twerp." She looked away, as if ashamed of the disdain in her voice.

"I doubt if it's as simple as that."

She was silent, then she sighed. "I expect she told him about Henry."

"I suppose we can assume she knew about that."

"Oh she knew all right—he left her a note. She rang me up this morning to tell me—or rather accuse me of having persuaded poor old Henry. I was able to convince her I had nothing to do with it, so I'm rather in her good books now, as you can see," she said sardonically.

"But you still can't guess at her purpose in removing Alex?"

"To assist the police in their enquiries."

"And how could he do that?"

"By putting the blame on someone else, pretty obviously."

"Who?"

"I don't know." She picked up a pen and began to scratch at the blotting paper. "You don't—you don't have any idea yourself?"

"On your father?" He paused, then softly, "on you perhaps?"

She raised her head and looked at him; her face was puffy with unshed tears—and for a moment he was sure she was going to tell him. And then she shrugged. "Perhaps."

The moment was lost. "I think I'd better go up and see Alex now."

"No."

"Kate, the boy is going through a serious crisis—it might be crucial. He needs professional care, which you are simply not qualified to give." In fact, rather desperately need yourself, he thought.

"No. I am not going to let you see him. And I am not releasing him into your hands. I mean it."

"I am his psychiatrist."

"And I'm his sister!" She lifted her chin, and her greenish eyes regarded him steadily. "I'm sorry, Hugh," she said as though she really were—there was a tone of regret, of melancholy that puzzled him. But he knew he was beaten for the moment.

She stood up; reluctantly, he rose too.

"Very well. But you'll let me know if he asks for me, won't you?"

She hesitated visibly. "I wasn't going to tell you this, but perhaps it's best, after all. About the only thing Alex has said to me quite clearly is that he specifically does not want to see you. I'm sorry." She paused, made a half gesture, arrested as soon as it was made. "Good night." She turned and left.

He moved to the long window and watched her lithe young figure as she crossed the court and disappeared. She must be cold, he thought idly, in jeans and a thin cotton shirt. The light from the stained-glass panels at the top of the window cast lozenges of ruby and gold and green onto the snow outside.

He had all the pieces—yet no picture. Unless the picture was his nightmare. What was it that had made Ply so genial, Elaine so nonchalant that she could leave her dearly beloved Alex in the care of her distrusted stepdaughter, that made Kate so ambivalently angry and mournful and withdrawn, and Alex so hostile? He knew that his understanding had been weakened by his own errors, and he also knew that wracking his brains would produce no result. In the last resort we all rely on instinct—but he had lost touch with it, mislaid it somewhere during the day, along with his overcoat and gloves and scarf.

Looking out at the empty court, he felt a curious ache, which after a while he recognised, with mild surprise, as a feeling of loneliness . . . of unaccountable loss. Personal loss. As if they had gone—the women—sucked down by the mighty rushing waters, and left him desolate. He stayed by the window for a long time until the cigarette burnt down to his fingers and brought him to with a start. Unthinkingly he dropped the stub on the floor and stepped on it.

In the court he was caught up in a stream of hurrying women just let out of hall—one he bumped into heavily, turned and he recognised the bespectacled undergraduate from Kate's floor. "Why, if it isn't the randy old beast!" Then she rushed on in a spurt of laughter.

He stood by the car, undecided, the thin wind piercing him to the bone. At home there was nothing but warmed-up soup and an empty house—Julia wouldn't be back for ages. What he really wanted, he thought, was a drink.

As he got in the car the college clock struck eight.

14

But as he entered the Blue Boar, he knew at once that it wasn't what he wanted. He'd been there once only—long ago when he'd been engaged to Julia and they'd had tea in a vast lounge filled with plants and palms and fat leather club chairs, a cavernous place of solid ugliness and comfort. But now it was all changed—miniaturised and prettified, glass doors, bright paint, false walls, and piped music—the geography entirely altered. He found a small plush bar and ordered a large port and lemon. Was this really where Alex had come for his double whiskies after his staircase ordeal? There were only four others in the bar—an elderly fellow, vaguely familiar, who sniffed audibly at Hugh's order; and an undergraduate trying to overwhelm his parents' timidity with cherry brandy and bursts of hearty laughter.

Hugh ate an olive from a small dish; it tasted of rubber. He sipped his drink and lit a cigarette and inadvertently caught the eye of the old man; as he did so, recognition came—it was he who'd rebuked Hugh for littering in front of the University Library. A don no doubt—who should have been drinking port in a combination room instead of gin in a cocktail lounge. Just as he himself should be studying that article in the new *B.J.P.*: "Experience of memory function after electroconvulsive therapy." Perhaps he should have ordered whisky. But neither study nor alcohol was going to cure what ailed him. What he really needed was company—not this desolate intimacy in a plastic world. If only he knew where Julia's bridge party was, he could have gone there, breaking all the rules, and accepted a drink and a sandwich (or someone else's "grey mud") and watched the women at play. For it was female company he yearned for.

Then why not Reg? After all, he'd promised Mike he'd look in on her from time to time.

Outside the hotel the cold blanched his breath; it was freezing hard and dangerous underfoot. But the main road had been sanded, the tires held well, and he drove fast. The Lane was more treacherous and, going past his house, he slowed to a crawl—but there were no lights, not even the outside lamp. Well, it had been a forlorn hope. Suddenly he was afraid that Reg would be out too, but almost immediately he saw the floodlighting of Hilltop. The potholes were plugged with snow and he came to a smooth stop. But getting out of the car into the full chill of the bitter night, he was struck with dizziness. He stumbled up the steps and caught hold of the knocker to steady himself. He took a deep breath against the roaring in his ears and the dimness before his eyes.

And then she was there, "Why Hugh!" and his hand was taken and he was drawn in. He let himself be led into the living room—lights bright, log fire blazing, the scar of his cigarette burned in the carpet. The geography hadn't changed here, at any rate.

"Mike's at a feast—he won't be back tonight. He's scared stiff of breathalysers." She took the wing chair.

He blinked at her—was that some kind of an invitation?

"Hugh—are you all right?"

"Ummm? Oh yes, yes. Just a goose walking over my grave. As my mother used to say." And when he'd first heard her say it, he'd had an image of clammy geese feet flapping across the little patch of neatly mown turf that concealed his dead sister.

"Help yourself to whisky."

"Well, I don't know, I . . ."

"I'll have one too."

"All right." His hand was steady as he poured the whisky, but he felt shaken. He gave Reg her drink and took the chair on the other side of the fireplace; he was glad to sit down, glad of the comfortable domesticity.

"You've had your glasses mended."

"What? Oh no—these are a spare pair." He reached up and removed them.

"Why do you take your glasses off when you talk to people?"

"Do I? I don't know—I didn't know I did. Not all people, surely. But I do spend a great deal of my time watching and listening —so I suppose it's a relief not to have to, a matter of relaxation."

"You mean it's easier to talk to someone when you can't see her?"

"Her?" He laughed. "Perhaps."

"Or is it your way of renouncing a false objectivity?"

"False? I don't think so. I always try to be reasonably objective."

"Doesn't that make things a bit drab?"

"Life is a bit drab—at least, a lot of it's boring. But in the end there isn't anything else—is there?"

"There's death. What's this sudden passion for Mike's company? I thought you didn't much like him. A lot of people don't."

"That's not very important. A lot of people don't like *me.*" He drank some whisky—it was unpleasantly strong.

"But you're paid to be disliked."

Hugh smiled. "I ran into Mike today, briefly."

"Did he mention me?"

"Well yes, he did—among other things."

"He's worried, of course. He's uncomfortable when I don't talk. It doesn't matter what—'Pass the cheese" is usually enough. Men like chatter, it makes them feel loved."

"Does it?" Yet perhaps she was right; hadn't Julia's unusual loquacity last night made him feel—happier?

"Not you, I expect. You're trained to listen to people being silent. Or perhaps you don't listen."

"I try to." He looked at the gold and red blur of the fire; without glasses, the world was a richer and more subtle place, more sensual and simpler. He had a quick acute longing to be at his own hearthside, listening to Julia's quiet tones. He cleared his throat. "Mike *is* a bit worried, you're right."

"He can't help showing off. He's missing a big toe, you know. He feels it very much." She laughed, but without malice. "You mustn't believe everything he tells you. He's an inveterate gossip."

"Yes."

"He's the son of a banker."

Hugh put on his glasses. Reg's expression was serious, almost demure. He had the feeling they were talking about something quite other, but exactly what he could not grasp. "You mean, he's unconsciously reacting against a father figure?"

"Something like that."

Hugh looked round the room and his eye caught the brown water stain on the wall. Like the holes in the drive—*a touch of dilapidation is very nice and English.*

"Of course he tries to be British, but he's not at home here. He's a romantic—his heart is in the Balkans. Like you."

"My dear Reg," he smiled, "I'm not in the least romantic, and as for the Balkans . . ."

"I mean, you're not at home here either. You're from the working class, that's like being a foreigner, isn't it?"

"It rather depends what—"

"All these strange bourgeois people you live among always concealing themselves, which is a dangerous thing to do even if you know you're doing it—and there you are, gamely using your professional competence to try to understand them."

"I'm beginning to think my professional competence is rather a blunt instrument. I seem to have made several avoidable misjudgements in the last day or two." He put down his drink and lit a cigarette. He had an urge to confide in Reg—yet wasn't it just such misjudged confidence that had caused all the trouble? On the other hand, she wasn't personally involved, she was intelligent and objective, she knew Julia. . . . "Reg, has Mike kept you up to date on this Brinton business?"

"He hardly talks of anything else. But it's all resolved now, isn't it—now that the G.P.'s confessed?"

"Well no—in fact the whole thing has become more complicated." He told her slowly, carefully of Alex's revelations, the appearance of the suicide letter, the talk with Stand at the New Inn, his confession, the disappearance of Alex and, finally, the abortive visit to Lady Strange College.

"So whom do you suspect now?"

"That's not really a word in my vocabulary—but, well, psychologically speaking, I don't really see how any one of them could have deliberately killed Brinton. There's something wrong—something that simply doesn't fit. I've been telling myself that it was probably an accident after all—and then one of them came along and wrote the letter. . . . Frankly, I'm in the dark."

Reg said nothing—a faint twitch of the eyebrow—but held out her tumbler. He stood up and took the two glasses to the sideboard and refilled them, just as Alex must have done on Tuesday evening before dinner. *Something wrong*—an irresolvable block in comprehension.

"Hugh?"

"Yes?" He brought the glasses back and sat down.

"Surely one thing that's upsetting you is that you're no longer simply an observer, you've become a participant."

"Yes, I'm aware of that. I know my judgement is not as lucid as it ought to be."

"Even about Alex. His refusal to see you, his hostility—"

"No, I'm clear enough about that. The sudden emergence of a negative transference is unfortunate, but understandable in the circumstances. It just means I'm probably of no further use to him as a psychotherapist."

"Don't you ever identify with your patients?"

"One tries not to, but obviously in some cases it's inevitable to some extent."

"Or treat them a little like the children you haven't got yourself?"

"I certainly hope not. Isn't that a bit facile?" But he felt himself flush slightly.

"Like you do Julia, for example—protect her, keep her away from the bad things in your mind. Don't you do—"

"Julia? Do I? But Julia's not my patient. I don't—"

"—don't you sometimes do the same thing for some of your patients? Isn't that perhaps what you're doing with Alex, for instance, and why you're so worried about having him taken out of your hands, of losing control?"

"You're suggesting that I'm projecting on him my own infantile fears?"

"Might that not be the thing that 'doesn't fit'?"

"Perhaps." He tossed his cigarette into the fire. He said slowly, "There's a penalty to be paid for that kind of thing. . . ."

"Of course—if the danger is unspecified, your fears are likely to point you in the wrong direction . . . or simply leave you in the dark. Which is where you said you are."

In the dark—up the pole. Those nightmare dangers were rather specific—and involved Reg herself. He drank some whisky and shuddered at the medicinal flavour. He turned his eyes away from the fire and looked at her. "I've not entirely excluded the possibility that Alex might in some way have been responsible for his father's death, you know."

She laughed—and suddenly he saw her in the punt, smiling and laughing in just such a way, in just such a white summer dress. He shook his head—too much whisky on an empty stomach.

"I knew Jonathan Brinton slightly once."

"What did you think of him?"

"Detestable. He had clammy hands and pawed you. I had to get rid of him. Actually I hit him in the balls with a book." She grinned. "A nice heavy copy of *Women in Love,* I remember. Later he had the gall to ring up Mike and complain I'd made sexual advances to him."

"That's interesting—it sounds as though he might have been showing paranoid tendencies even then."

"Perhaps—I'm sure he was more interested in punishing women than in loving them."

"Yes—I get the impression that he was rather a pitiable fellow."

"Pitiable? Not by me. Oddly enough, he looked physically exactly like his daughter—that Kate creature. Perhaps she bumped him off, have you thought of that? I should have done, if I'd lived with him any length of time."

"It would rather surprise me if she did."

"Aren't you ever surprised?"

"I'm sometimes puzzled. But surprised—no, I don't think so. One tends not to be in my profession. One—well, I won't say expects—but one allows for the worst, and is pleased by the best." He was aware of his pomposity—and yet there was an opaqueness between them. "To be taken by surprise is essentially unprofessional, you know."

"Poor Hugh, you and your profession—it'll be the death of you yet." Her laughter came again—and he was puzzled where to place it. He understood what Mike meant about her being in an unavailable world. Perhaps that was why he'd put her in the punt with Kate —and with Julia. He looked at his watch: ten to eleven.

"Reg, I must get back. Julia will be home soon."

"Oh—is she out too?"

"Her bridge night." He smiled, glad suddenly of that normality. "I'm sorry to have inflicted myself on you like this."

"Don't be." She rose and touched his arm. "I prefer solitude to other human beings. But I'm glad you came, even if Mike did put you up to it."

"Well, I . . ." He looked down at her, aware of sympathy. After all, he thought, she would make an extraordinarily interesting patient. "I'm glad too."

"Good night."

"Good night."

He sat in the car, letting the engine warm up for a few moments and watching Reg in the open doorway. He felt a pang of pity for her and his hand went to the window. He shook his head. She was not a pitiable woman.

He moved gently out of the drive, then let the car drift down the hill in neutral to his own home, the tires crackling coldly on the frozen snow.

As he turned in from The Lane his headlights shone on the large black car and caught two dim white faces behind the windscreen. He shut off the lights and got out of the Rover, clumsy with exasperation. At the same moment the police car's brights flicked on, and Hugh automatically threw up an arm to shield his eyes, his foot slipped on the ice, and he came down heavily on all fours. He heard his glasses skitter away on the hard snow, then saw them glinting a few feet away—but as he started to crawl towards them, all the lights went out.

"Look out for my glasses!" he cried, but the next instant he heard the crunch.

"Ooops—sorry about that, Doctor." A hand on his elbow heaved him to his feet. He shook himself free, mastering a blind impulse to strike out.

"That was a bit careless of you, Andrew." The lights went on again, on low beam. "Are you all right, Doctor?"

"Sorry about that, Super."

Hugh leant against the car, struggling for breath. "Was it— really—necessary—to turn up—your lights . . . like that?"

"Sorry, Doctor—knocked my elbow against the lever. Sure you're all right?"

"Yes yes." But he was shaken. Ramm had dropped to his knees and was carefully gathering up fragments of lens and frame. "Leave it, man—they're obviously beyond repair." The detective at work.

Ramm stood up. For a moment nobody spoke—and their breath blew white and thick in the night air.

"Hope you've got a spare pair, Doctor?"

"That was my spare pair."

"Oh—sorry ab—"

"May I ask—" his voice sounded too loud. He glanced up at Julia's room, but it was dark; he felt a sag of disappointment. "May I ask what you're doing here? I thought I told you on the phone this afternoon that—"

"Quite right. But there've been some developments."

Hugh pushed himself away from the car. "Is this an emergency?"

"That rather remains to be seen."

"Young Brinton—he's all right?"

"Brinton? So far as I know. Didn't you see him?"

"No, I went to . . . no." He was relieved, then his irritation returned in full force. "Well, what is it, then?"

He looked from one to another—without his glasses, they seemed utterly expressionless. He took out his handkerchief and dabbed at the stickiness on his palms.

"Perhaps we could go inside, Doctor?"

Hugh swung round and went to the door without a word. It was locked. After fumbling with three or four keys he managed to get it open. He stepped in and switched on the hall light. If anything, the house seemed chillier than outside. No Julia in the waiting room. He checked the impulse to check the message-taker—that could wait a few minutes.

"Well, what's all this about?" They stood just inside, but hadn't taken their hats off. "Shut the door, please."

Ramm moved with alacrity, and then they were both once again still—almost inhumanly impassive.

Then, "Wife not back yet, Doctor?" said Ply conversationally.

"Superintendent, I'm sure you haven't come here to talk about my wife. What is it, Alex's statement?"

"What time does she get back usually?"

"Just about now, but—"

"She normally rides a motorcycle—a black Norton 22cc?"

"Yes. What—" He felt a clutch of fear—Julia on these roads, in her condition. "Are you trying to tell me something has happened to my wife?"

"Not that I know of."

"Well, what is it then? Speeding, dangerous driving?—I can assure you my wife's an excellent—"

"Nothing like that, Doctor."

"Found the machine in a no-parking zone?"

"No, the machine's in your garage."

"Then in the name of all that's good, what are you making such a fuss about?" He felt a kind of feeble exasperation; too tired for real anger; too blind to penetrate their expressions, or pierce through the rigmarole to any sort of sense.

"Does your wife have any other means of transport?"

"She has her legs, Superintendent."

"She wouldn't walk in this weather, would she?"

"No—no, I don't suppose so. I expect one of her bridge companions gave her a lift."

"Do you know whose house she went to tonight?"

"No."

"Couldn't you ring round and find out?"

"The trouble is I don't know the names of—wait a minute, there's a Mrs. Scrope on Trumpington Road, but—"

"Mightn't she be there?"

"No. At least I don't think so. There was no answer when I rang earlier, but—"

"You rang Mrs. Scrope?"

"Yes."

"Why?"

"Oddly enough, I wanted to get in touch with my wife."

"What time was that?"

"Just before I phoned you at the police station, now what—"

"About half-past seven, Super."

"And did you eventually succeed in reaching Mrs. Welchman?"

"Obviously not, or else I'd know where—"

"Don't you have a housekeeper?"

"Yes—but Friday is her afternoon off. Now look here, I insist on knowing what all this is in aid of."

"We're interested in the whereabouts of your wife—and I'd advise you to be, too. For a start, I suggest you ring up this Mrs. Scrope at once."

Hugh's hand went automatically to his breast pocket for his glasses, then slowly he let it fall. "There must be something seriously wrong if you want me to phone a total stranger in the middle of the night."

"We have reason to believe that your wife may be in possession of information helpful to the police in the course of their enquiries."

"Information helpful to . . ." Kate? It could be about Kate—he was aware that Julia probably knew more about the girl than she'd revealed. "But that's absurd," he said weakly.

"That remains to be seen. Right now, let's try to find her if we can, eh?" The tone was less neutral. "I don't want to have to put out an all-points bulletin, if I can avoid it."

Slowly Hugh picked up the white phone. Grazed by ice and gravel, his palms were beginning to smart. With an effort of memory, he dialled the number.

"Scrope speaking," a sleepy voice answered.

"Mr. Scrope—my name's Welchman, Dr. Welchman, I'm—"

"Yes, Doctor?" The voice was suddenly alert.

"I wonder if my wife is there by any chance."

"Your wife?"

"If she is, I'd like a word with her, and if not, perhaps you could tell—"

"Is this some form of practical joke?"

"Not at all. I believe your wife and mine are—"

"You are from the hospital—St. Ethelbert's?"

"Well, yes, as a matter of fact I am, but that's got nothing to do with it. I understand our wives are bridge companions and I wondered if their party was at your house tonight."

There was a pause. "What's your name again?"

"Welchman. Hugh Welchman."

"Well, Dr. Welchman—and if you are a doctor, you must be a singularly incompetent one—it may interest you to know that my wife has been in your hospital for the last three weeks with a case of terminal cancer. Good night, sir."

"Not there, Doctor?"

"Er? No." He replaced the receiver—why had he chosen the white phone? "No, she isn't there."

"Didn't Mr. Scrope know where the party was taking place?"

"No. His wife's not playing tonight." He felt dizzy again, put his hand on the table to steady himself.

"Doctor, are you quite sure that *your* wife's playing?"

"Yes, of course, I—that's to say, I'm sure in the sense that she always . . . She's probably having trouble getting a lift back." He held his watch close to his eyes. "It's only ten past eleven. Where else would she be?"

"It's not possible she could be in the house?"

"In the house? Well, I suppose if she'd felt unwell . . ." A touch of nausea perhaps—that would be normal. He tried to think straight. The locked front door—an automatic reflex action before going to bed. "I don't know. Perhaps . . ."

"Don't you think we'd better have a look?" Beneath the gentleness—almost kindliness—in the question, there was an unmistakable urgency. Peering from one policeman to the other, he was over-come by a sudden irrational anxiety. "Yes. Yes, of course." He stumbled on the first stair, then took the rest two at a time.

She was not in their room. He hurried through the bathroom to her own bedroom, flicking on the lights as he went.

"Julia!"

In two strides he was at the bed and had turned back the blanket drawn over her head. She lay in a foetal crouch face to the wall, chin tucked down on the chest. As he turned on the bedside lamp, a book fell to the floor with a sharp bang.

"Anything I can do, Doctor?"

"Get my bag. Door to the right of the stairs, on the floor behind the desk." His hands moved rapidly over face and throat, cold, dry, to the wrist—pulse imperceptible. He slid an arm under her shoulders and gently turned her, pulling the pillows down to support her head. He leaned close—her skin had the characteristic faintly bluish tint of cyanosis.

"Your bag."

Lifting the eyelid with his finger, he examined the eye with the ophthalmoscope. Then, unbuttoning the high-necked green dress-ing gown, he applied the stethoscope.

"Is there anything—"

"Quiet, please!" He listened, waited; shifted, listened; shifted again, waited, listened—yes, something, an almost imperceptibly brief bird flutter.

"Right." He dropped the stethoscope into the bag and stood up. He moved into the bathroom, talking as he went. "Ring St. Ethelbert's—75420. Tell them we're bringing over a case of massive barbiturate poisoning. Oxygen, all that sort of thing, they'll know. Ask them to alert Dr. Wilson. We'll be there in ten minutes." He washed his hands, ruthlessly scrubbing off the dried blood and gravel ingrained in the heels of his palms.

"All right, Andrew, you heard that. Hop to it, lad. And you'd better warm up the car. She's alive then, Doctor?"

"Just." He dried his hands. "I'll need your help for a minute, Ply." He started to leave the bathroom, hesitated, then reached down and flipped open the lid of the white plastic wastebasket under the basin and removed a small brown-tinted glass bottle.

"I'll take that, Doctor." Ply neatly lifted the bottle from his palm. "Tuinal. Would it have been full?"

"Probably. Pretty much so. Come on."

He wrapped Julia in two blankets from the bed and a third from the cupboard, moved her sideways until her head was off the bed, supported by his hand and tilted slightly backwards so there was a horizontal passage from mouth to throat. "Hold her exactly like that, if you please."

"Right you are."

Hugh took the endotracheal tube from its sterilised plastic bag and slowly inserted it in Julia's throat. "This is to ensure a clear airway." He stopped when the cuff was almost resting on the lips. "All right now, Mr. Ply. You're going to have to carry her—I don't trust myself on the stairs without glasses. But she must be kept exactly in this position. Is that clear?"

"Got it."

"When we're downstairs, I'll get into the back seat and you slide her gently onto my lap. All right?"

"Right."

"Then you slip in beside me, so we can keep her level across our knees."

"Right."

"I'll give you a hand. Lift."

"Got her."

The car was warm, Julia small enough so that only her knees were slightly bent.

"All right, Andrew. Fast as you can, but keep it steady—no bumps."

"Okay, Super."

The car glided into motion without a tremor—down The Lane, the cold hillside, smoothly into the main road.

"Any idea how long ago she took them, Doctor?"

"Several hours certainly. No way of judging exactly. Mrs. Nance would have left at midday. Any time after that, I should say."

"We can do a bit better than that." The car gave a sudden rocking lurch—boat approaching the rapids. "Steady!"

"Sorry about that. Won't happen again."

"What do you mean, Superintendent?"

"Young Brinton saw her about four-thirty, I should say."

"Alex? Where?"

"At your house."

"I see."

The car took the long swooping curve that led to the hospital gates and Hugh felt the gentle pressure of Julia's head on his knees, her hair lank with past sweat under his hand.

"That gives us something to go on." If she'd taken them immediately at four-thirty or five—but why? No, no time for questions. Seven hours then, maximum. Three-quarter full—say, thirty 200mg: 6,000mg.

As they passed through the gates and up the curved drive through the bleak stretch of gardens, the sweat broke out on Hugh's forehead.

"Is this the Welchman O.D.?"

"Right—careful now."

Wilson was there.

"Jeremy—it's Julia."

"Yes, I know—the flatfoot told me. What's the situation?"

"Tuinal almost certainly—maybe as much as 6,000mg; maximum seven hours, minimum three, but that's a guess. Acute respiratory congestion, et cetera."

"Right. Want to come along?"

"Better not. Do your best, Jeremy."

"Of course I will, 'ughie. Listen, I rang Granny and he—"

"Granny?"

"Flyboy Grantham, our Director—he said to use his office. I've laid on coffee and that. I'll keep you posted."

With a wave, he was gone—and Julia, wheeled on the trolley down the familiar corridor, into the lift, the doors closed. No loitering. Pale wife.

He stood unmoving, unthinking. He became slowly aware of the heavy figures on either side of him. "Do you want to wait, Mr. Ply? It may be a long job."

"If you don't mind, Doctor."

"Come along then," he rubbed his blind eyes softly. "I expect we could all do with some coffee."

214

Three

15

Julia died at five fifty-eight.

The sun had risen with a soft fire, but long before that he'd known she was dying.

During the night he'd sat in the Director's chair smoking cigarette after cigarette until there were none left, listening to Jeremy's brief reports on the interphone, which came at longer and longer intervals. From time to time an orderly would enter soft-footed with cups of coffee and biscuits, from the outer office where the policemen waited. A little before five Hugh had turned off the desk lamp.

Now he stood watching the dawn. To his dim eyes the garden was milky, the icy ground rose-tinted—as though the neglected flower beds had sprung miraculously to life. Only the cedar was black against the lightening sky. There had been no call now for over an hour.

When he heard the door open behind him, he stiffened, but didn't turn. It was almost fully light, and it seemed to him odd that there were no birds in the garden—perhaps they were too small for him to see.

Then Jeremy was standing beside him. "She's gone, 'ughie," and he laid a hand on Hugh's shoulder for a moment.

Outside, the landscape swam and quivered, then slowly clarified and settled back to stillness. Hugh rubbed his face, the bristles rasping on his chin.

"Where are the birds, Jeremy—aren't there supposed to be birds at this time of morning?"

"They're round the other side—the nurses put crumbs out on the south terrace." He looked exhausted. "Haven't got a snout, have you?"

"No, I'm sorry, I've smoked all mine."

"Well, Granny must have some." He went to the desk and picked up a silver box. "Here we are." He offered it to Hugh, then lit their cigarettes with the silver desk lighter. "Does himself well, doesn't he? Silver fittings, wall-to-wall carpeting, and that's a Monet on the wall there or I'm a Dutchman. First time I've been in this place—and the last, I expect. Can't wait to get rid of me—'that oik Wilson' he calls me." He laughed.

Hugh's protest turned into a cough—he hunched his shoulders, but the spasm shook him, the air tearing at his throat. When it was over at last, he wiped the dampness from his eyes with his handkerchief; it was stained with the blood from his hands last night.

"He's quite—competent—you know—once," he was still gasping, "once you get over the—manner."

"Oh, he's a rare Beauty all right. Why do they all call him that —Beauty? It's sickening."

"It was just before your time—three or four years ago, his latest marriage. At the wedding they wanted a photo of him and me shaking hands—and as the flash went off somebody called out, 'Oh do look, Beauty and the Beast.' And it just, well, stuck. Of course, I was only asked because of Julia—Arthur Welling's daughter."

"Yeeeah. Well, you'll be dispensable too now—now that she's dead, I mean."

"I suppose so." He blinked. The harshness was unlike Jeremy —but he was tired, of course.

"Why did she do it, 'ughie?" the young man asked softly.

"I don't know." He looked down, surprised to see a cigarette in his hand. "You know, Jeremy, while she—while she lay dying there last night, at the house I mean, I was drinking port and lemon at the Blue Boar, chatting to a neighbour over whisky. If I'd gone straight home at eight, instead of gallivanting about Cambridge, perhaps she—"

"Cut it out, 'ughie. It's done, isn't it? You can't alter that—but why? That's what matters."

"Does it? I'm not sure. Why? I haven't the remotest idea."

"You're going to have to find out then, aren't you?"

"Well, I suppose . . ." He turned his head to the window. It had clouded over—the sun gone, the rosy light faded. It looked like rain.

"You've got to think about yourself now, 'ughie."

He heard the urgency, the strain; he turned back. "Yes," he said, and then more firmly, "yes, of course."

"You're the best we've got, you know." Jeremy nodded. "Do you want to see her?"

"Do I . . . ?" Hugh went to the desk and stubbed his cigarette out in the big silver ashtray. "Yes, yes, of course."

"I thought you would. She's not been moved. Benson's down there."

"Right."

"How are you going to get home? You came in the coppers' car, didn't you?"

"Oh, I'll manage. But the police ought to be told."

"I'll handle that. And look, I'll have one of the boys with an ambulance for you in front in ten minutes. Okay?"

"Thank you, Jeremy."

But twenty minutes later he was in the back of the police car.

They'd been waiting at the main door. "We'd like to examine the premises, with your permission of course, Doctor. So perhaps we can give you a lift back?"

He'd merely nodded and dismissed the ambulance driver. "These gentlemen are taking me home, so I won't be needing you, thanks very much, Bert."

Last night the landscape had been hidden and sharp and icy in the light of the headlamps, but now it was clouded over with soft rain. It was the first time he'd been driven, instead of driving himself, along this route—and he was aware of fields stretching away that he'd never seen before—trees and the flat vague sky and the grey beginnings of the town. He tried to concentrate on observation —the early morning bicyclists, the brown flood of the river, a posse of athletic students sloshing along the side of the road. Yet all he thought of was her face—lines from the mouth and beside the nose, always present masklike in her father but never before in her, deathly white of skin, the hair mean and scraggled back so that the delicate ears, usually concealed, gave her a childlike look; so that she seemed at once exhausted, yet innocent, young, yet wisened with age. And none of this, he had thought as he bent low over her, had he ever really seen—only the beauty, the grace of movement and stillness, the richness of ivory skin, the gleam of black hair, the blue eyes gravely regarding, now shut and sunken. And the foetus that he would never see or touch or watch grow to manhood. And, the thought crossed his mind as he fell into a light doze, he didn't even know if what he had lost had ever really existed.

He was woken by the crunch of the thawing drive's gravel as the car moved slowly between the flowerless borders up to the indifferent grey-stucco mansion that old Welling had built with the profits from his book, outdated now, useless, like the house itself. Hillside—Julia's home, and the place he had lived in for almost thirteen years. The *premises*—the *scene of the crime.* There was even a constable standing guard at the door—over what? The bird had flown.

"Good morning, Doctor."

"Er?" Looking closer, he saw it was the policewoman who'd brought him coffee and biscuits. "Oh, good morning, er . . . Brandt."

She and Ply and Ramm all followed him into the cold hall. They stood in a silent group, hats in hand, unmoving. For an instant he was sure that Julia was upstairs, sleeping peacefully, soon to wake up and . . . "What, er—what happens now?"

"We're going to have to go through all Mrs. Welchman's things, I'm afraid. That means her bedroom and the study down here. Is there any other room that Mrs. Welchman used habitually or where she might have left anything?"

"What have you got in mind?"

"Well, sir, a note perhaps—or diaries."

"I see. No, I don't think so. She wrote poems, but I don't believe she kept a diary. And a note—that would have been left in a fairly obvious place, surely?" He looked round uncertainly—on the letter salver, in the kitchen, on his desk upstairs?

"Yes, sir, that's usually the way. If you can think of anything, it would be a help. Then I'll want to go through the medicine cabinet—is there just the one?"

"I keep a few drugs in a locked cupboard in my consulting room."

"Right. We'd better take a dekko at that too. You'll have prescriptions, of course?"

"Yes." All neatly docketed, filed, entered in the ledger by Julia. "I'll look them out for you."

"Thank you. All right then, Brandt—you come upstairs with me. Andy, you can start in the study. Doctor, you have the right to be present, if you wish?"

"Oh no, I don't . . ." They didn't know what to do with him. He was in the way. Out of place in his own house—it was *his* house now. But it was still Julia's home—and she was there, somewhere, in it, a person he didn't know very well, had perhaps hardly known at all. He had his own search to make. "All right, I'll come along with you, Sergeant."

"Right you are, Doctor."

The old roll-top desk shone with polish as Ramm turned on the lights. Everything was neatly arranged in labelled pigeon holes—

Archery Club, Bank, Barker & Trentham, Bills misc., Borrowgrove.
. . . The only thing out of order lay beside Julia's ancient Imperial typewriter—Hyman's Seed Catalogue, a blaze of unlikely colour far too large for any of the slots. He glanced out of the window at the grey blur of the day—and tried to imagine the prospect of a summer rich and tranquil with roses and asters and . . . geraniums? Not the future—that was closed off now for good—but long ago, with a small girl reaching for her mother's skirts and calling . . . a small girl. He left the room and went slowly upstairs, holding onto the banister for support.

In Julia's bedroom, he drew back the curtains and opened the window wide. She would never have slept with it shut.

The room was austere to the point of barrenness—table, chair, chest of drawers, a shelf of books, the narrow bed, usually so neat, now so strangely disordered. But it was not this he had come to see. He bent and picked up a book from the floor, then turned to the picture on the wall: head and shoulders of a little girl with tumbling golden curls; a Monet—no, that couldn't be right—a Matisse, yes; pink of cheek, the girl's expression was quizzical, demure, enigmatic perhaps; the arms and hands that he had always thought vaguely deformed were raised in supplication. A child physically different in all respects from Julia, who herself had kept nothing from her childhood—though she had lived in this place all her life. Not even a mirror on the wall—unless the child was the mirror, the everyday truth of the matter.

From the bathroom he could hear the gentle litany of proprietary names as Policewoman Brandt read them off for Ply to note down: Luminal, Librium, Ativan, Integrin, Sinequan, Ponderax, Tacitin. . . .

He looked at the book in his hand, straightening the page that had crumpled when it fell:

> I saw their starv'd lips in the gloam
> With horrid warning gaped wide,
> And I awoke, and found me here
> On the cold hill side.
>
> And this is why I sojourn here
> Alone and palely loitering,
> Though the sedge is wither'd from the lake,
> And no birds sing.

He shut the book and moved to the window and leaned out. The soft April drizzle fell fine on his cheek, carrying a scent of freshness—this was how Julia smelled, her hair, her skin, unsullied by perfume or powder or unguents. There were no birds here either —had they too all gone to the other side to sing in the dreaming garden?

"Doctor?"

He came to with a shiver; it was icy in the room now. "Yes?" And it seemed to him that the golden hair of the girl on the wall coiled like serpents, the hands not open, but folded to guard a secret, disdainful heart.

"We're finished in the bathroom. I wonder if you'd mind un-locking the medicine cabinet in your room and getting out the prescriptions?"

"No, of course."

"Thank you. All right, Brandt, you go along with the doctor. I'll just have a look round here."

His room smelled stale, but at least it was warm with leftover heat, and the double glazing had kept out the frost. Long ago he had had the window raised and lengthened so there would be no land-scape to distract the patients—only the sky and clouds and the mist of rain, as now, against the outer pane.

Brandt coughed.

"Oh—I'm sorry," he said. He unlocked the little cabinet. "Here you are. And the prescriptions." He pulled open the file drawer—Prescriptions, Personal. He laid the file on his desk and looked down at the appointments book:

10.00	C. Savage
10.50	G. Pressman
11.40	M. Platten
12.30	A. Brinton

Alex wouldn't be coming—no doubt of that. And George Pressman would probably cut his session too—"I'm a busy man, Hugh; never relax, that's my motto—my problem too, ha-ha!" He reached out his hand to the message-taker, then let it drop. Mrs. Nance would be in soon, perhaps he'd ask her to do it. As he stood there, trying to decide, he found himself staring at Policewoman Brandt. What blue eyes she had—almost as blue as Julia's. But she hadn't Julia's even, ivory complexion.

"I'm sorry about your wife, Dr. Welchman." That pleasant Norfolk accent—up past Ely, from the Fens somewhere. A short ride on a motorbike.

He realised suddenly she was embarrassed. "Oh, that's all right. I mean—thank you, Brandt." He drew a steadying breath. "I think you should be able to match everything up from this file. But if you have a problem, I shall be in the kitchen making a cup of tea."

"Very good, Doctor."

In the kitchen he dropped the kettle in the sink with a clatter; he picked it up and refilled it, but his hand was trembling so much he could hardly light the gas. He needed a cigarette, but he'd no idea where Julia kept the supply. At least he could find the teabags, though it was Julia who bought them of course—Julia who made the breakfast and ordered the port and logs for the living room they never used, Julia who typed and filed and kept his appointments straight and bought his cigarettes and shampoo and mended the seat of his trousers, Julia who . . .

"Julia." The sound of his own voice startled him. This would have to stop—he must pull himself together. He made the tea with elaborate care. In the hall he put the cup down on the table and picked up the papers from the mat: *The Times, New Statesman, Poetry Review, Field.*

He took his cup of tea and *The Times* into the waiting room and sat down heavily in his accustomed chair, with his back to the window. It was cold here too, but he was too tired to light the gas. And too blind to read *The Times* properly. There would have to be a notice of course. How was it done? By phone—or did one have to write in? Julia would know—she'd done it for her father's death, and her Aunt Belinda's, and their marriage. . . . But he'd have to do this one alone. He closed his eyes and began to compose a notice in his head: *Welchman, Julia Judith (née Welling),* or *daughter—only daughter—of Arthur Ashcroft Welling? . . . and of Hugh Welchman, D.P.M., only son of . . .* no, *beloved wife of . . . Suddenly, at home . . . by her own hand . . . no messages . . . no—flowers . . .*

He sat up with a start and *The Times* slithered from his knees onto the floor. He rubbed his face. He was parched. He picked up the untouched cup of tea beside him and drank quickly—it was stone cold. What had woken him? A bell. Ten o'clock—of course, the first patient. He got to his feet and almost groaned—for a moment he hung onto the mantelpiece. Caroline Savage.

He opened the door of the waiting room just as Mrs. Nance came down the passage.

"Oh—oh Doctor!"

"Er, good morning, Mrs. Nance." He braced himself. "Mrs. Nance, I'm afraid I have some bad news to—"

"They told me—the police. As soon as I saw their car in the drive I said to myself that something dreadful had happened—oh, the poor lamb! What ever made her do such a terrible thing?"

"I don't know, Mrs. Nance, I only wish I—"

"And in such special high spirits she was, just the day before yesterday! Quite like our old Miss Julia, I said to myself. Oh Doctor —whatever are we going to do?"

"I don't—" The bell rang again—a long ring.

"A dratted patient!" She bustled forward and for a moment he caught the strange waxy odour that always seemed to hang about her. "I'll just send him away, and then we can—"

"No."

"No?" She stopped so close that he could see the puffiness about her little eyes. "You're not going to see *patients* at a time like this?"

"Yes, that's precisely what I am going to do. You see, what's happened has absolutely nothing to do with them," he tried to speak kindly, but he had never liked her, nor she him, he was sure.

"Well, I've never heard of such a thing!"

"I'd rather the patients were not made aware of my wife's death, this morning," he said, making an effort to conceal his irritation. "Whatever our personal feelings may be, Mrs. Nance, we must try to carry on in the ordinary way." He went to the stairs. "I shall be in my consulting room. Perhaps you could tell Miss Savage to come straight up?"

"Very good, Doctor."

He climbed the stairs carefully, ignoring the emanations of her disapproval below him, but quite aware that unshaven, unwashed, in crumpled clothes, he could cut an imposing figure to no one.

In fact, it was just these things that Caroline seized on immediately. "You're not wearing your glasses!" "I must say, you could do with a good brush." "Have you given up smoking then?"

He paid little attention, except to borrow her last five cigarettes —his own brand, of course. At first he had even been vaguely grateful for her background chatter: "I really think I'm getting better—I went through all yesterday without a single cry!"

"Why don't you marry him?" He was cutting through a half hour of simpering banalities.

"Whaaa . . ." Caroline gaped.

"Why don't you tell Reginald you'll marry him?" He'd had enough; he knew nothing he could say would make this pretty, pathetic woman's existence more pernicious than it already was. Who knows? He might even help.

"But, Doctor, he's not well! I can't marry him till he gets better! How can I? It wouldn't be a proper marriage—it wouldn't be fair."

"Caroline, I've told you many times that impotence is not an 'illness.' At least, not in his case, because you tell me he has taken the requisite tests that clearly show nothing organically wrong. It is almost certainly an anxiety symptom that would probably be alleviated by a mild dosage of anxiolytic sedatives."

"Well, I don't mean *illness* exactly—that's just the way I refer to it."

"Precisely."

"What do you mean?" She was still too nonplussed to have thought of crying.

"Do you think it helps him to refer to it as an illness?"

"But that's what—but what should I call it?"

"It's not a question of nomenclature, but of attitude. You call it an illness because you think of it as an illness."

"No, I don't—not really. I mean I'm just trying to be kind! After all, an illness isn't anyone's fault, is it? It just happens, doesn't it?"

"But this *is* his fault?"

"I've never said that—I've never even hinted that to Reginald."

"But it's what you think?"

"I . . ." Her cheeks became pink and she drew a deep breath, "Yes, I do! Of course, I think that! And it's true. It is his fault. He just does it to punish me—I know. Oh, of course, I admit it's all unconscious, but that's what it is. He hates me and he wants to punish me!"

"And what are you doing to him?"

"To him?" Outrage. "I'm not doing anything to him."

"Aren't you?"

"I don't understand—what do you mean?"

"He is punishing you by, literally, 'not doing anything' to you. If you say you are 'not doing anything' to him, doesn't it follow that you in your turn are punishing him?"

224

"Of course not! I *want* him to get better."

"But you're imposing a condition, aren't you? You're saying, 'Get better—then I'll marry you.' "

"But that's not a punishment, it's a reward!"

"A future reward, but a present punishment. You may be promising a reward, but what you are actually doing is punishing him for not doing what you want."

"Well, if that's punishment, he deserves it. Why *won't* he do what I want?"

"Perhaps in part because you are putting him under pressure which increases his anxiety which, in turn, reduces even further his ability to perform. But perhaps he *is* doing what you want."

"What—what does that mean? How can he be?"

"So long as he's impotent, he's no threat to you. What would you do if he suddenly became potent?"

"Why—I would be . . . but that's what I want," she said uncertainly. "I want a normal life, I want to have children and a family. Doctor?"

"The word 'potent' is the adjectival form of 'power.' So long as he's impotent, he has no power over you. But were he to become potent, logically he would have power over you. What does that mean to you, Caroline?"

"I—I don't. . . ." He saw her groping for the lessons learnt by rote. "Mother. . . ."

"Your mother. Yes?"

"Father. No—no, I won't. I won't! I can't!" The ancient grievous tears started from her eyes and, face plunged to protective hands, she sobbed, she wept.

"It's almost time, Caroline."

"Time?" She raised her head and looked at him. "I don't understand. You're different somehow—you've changed. I think you're, you're being . . ."

"Perhaps it's you who've changed, Caroline. At the start of this session, you said you thought you were really getting better. Perhaps that means you are ready to face up to certain things now, which you weren't before. And that, after all, is what you're here for, isn't it?" He stood up.

Automatically she rose too. "But I love you—him, I mean. I love him." She simpered fleetingly, bit her lip. "But what am I to do?"

"Think over what I said. You could always marry him."

"But I can't! How can I? He isn't—"

"Then don't. Tell him you're not going to marry him."

She was close to him, her face turned up supplicant—the mascara had run, so the tears had been real. Her breasts were actually heaving. "Do you really think . . ."

"I've told you what I think, Caroline." He opened the door. "Till next time then."

He watched her going down the stairs, awkward in her spike heels and, with no one in the hall to vamp, making no effort.

He ought to wash and shave, but he was still intolerably thirsty and he needed cigarettes—he'd finished Caroline's—and Mrs. Nance should know where they were kept. And he didn't want to go into the bathroom, the bedroom—not just yet. Anyway he thought lamely, perhaps the police were still there—searching. He descended slowly, aware that lack of sleep had made him more than usually clumsy, was in fact distorting all his perceptions.

As he reached the hall, he saw the letters had come. He picked them up—three bills, a circular, and an envelope on which he recognised the handwriting of Irma Monroe. This must be almost the last installment on the credit he had, somewhat unprofessionally, given her. And, with it, would be the usual glowing note, for she had got a part, was engaged—Irma was happy now, had put the storm behind her. The thunder had not been final for her.

"Dr. Welchman?"

"You still here, Mr. Ply?" The policeman must have just come out of Julia's study.

"Could I have a word with you, Doctor, if you can spare the time?" Unhatted and without his coat he looked oddly informal; and there was a note of respect—or commiseration?—in his voice.

"Well, I can give you five minutes, but I'm expecting a patient." But Pressman wouldn't show up now—he either came on time or not at all.

"That's all right. Shall we go in the living room?" Already he had the door open.

"The waiting room," Hugh corrected automatically. But there was nothing to wait for now. Mrs. Nance had lit the gas and switched on a lamp and taken away his dirty cup. *The Times* was neatly folded on the table. "Sit down, Superintendent. No, not there!" he said quickly as Ply moved towards Julia's chair. "The couch."

"Right you are."

Hugh realised he was still holding the mail; he put it on the mantelpiece. "Well. Did you—did you find anything?"

"Not anything you'd call material. No note, nothing like that. I found a loose-leaf folder of typewritten poems in the chest of drawers in her room. They're not signed, but I expect they'll be hers."

"Probably. What—what were they about?"

"You've got me there, I'm afraid." He took out pipe and pouch and began to fill the bowl. "They didn't seem to be very happy exactly. But then poetry is apt to be rather depressing, isn't it, Doctor?"

Hugh didn't answer, he stared at Ply's long fingers skilfully stuffing tobacco into the pipe.

"Sorry—will my smoking bother you?" He started to put the pipe away.

"No no—by all means go ahead. I only wish you had some cigarettes." There were Julia's Turkish ones in the box, but somehow he couldn't face those.

"Cigarettes? Well, I do have some as it happens—usually buy the wife twenty for the weekend, but of course I didn't get home last night." He held out a packet to Hugh.

"I don't want to deprive your wife of—"

"That's all right. I'll get her another. Keep it—what's left of it; Ramm smoked most of them this morning."

"It's kind of you." There were six left—Woodbines. The packet had changed since the old days when his father smoked them. He lit one, cupping his hands round the flame of the match, just as his father had always done. As he sat down and inhaled slowly, he thought what a dominant theme of his father's life cigarettes had been—producing packets miraculously from an unbulging uniform, nipping out for a quick smoke, pinching the end between his fingers at the last moment before the parade, and even at the end struggling to raise his head from the pillow, "Give us a snout, lad."

"Sorry, Superintendent?"

"I was just asking you if your wife seemed in any way depressed during the last few days?"

"I don't know. I don't think so. I . . ." But what value could any of his observations have had? "You see, my wife was rather a private person. Not a woman of moods. But I thought I detected a slight change recently." A crack in the ice—a hope, a signal. "I thought she might have been—pleased about something. More, well, contented than usual, more hopeful." He couldn't bring himself to say anything of *his* hope—as absurd now as the hope of blooms from the bleak untended soil.

"Was she generally a methodical woman?"

"Very. Yes. Why?"

"Ramm said he'd never seen anyone's affairs in such good order —anyone taken sudden like."

"Oh well, that wouldn't be unusual for Julia."

"I see. Doctor, are you aware your wife made a new will, two days ago?"

"A new . . . no." Two days ago—Thursday. What happened on Thursday? "But that's not very strange—that I shouldn't know, I mean. My wife had her own private fortune, you know, and we didn't interfere in one another's financial affairs."

"Quite." Ply's pipe was lit now and the blue smoke rose thickly into the air. "But you say she certainly wasn't depressed in any way."

"No, on the contrary." How could he explain the gentle merriment of their last night together, the tender passion, a promise, he'd thought, of something better, something fuller? But in fact it must have been only a kind of *spes phthisica,* not significant of a beginning, but fatally prefiguring the end.

". . . accustomed to taking drugs—tranquilisers, sleeping pills and what not, that sort of thing?"

"No—in fact she had an aversion to any kind of drug. She'd been a nurse, you know, and she'd seen the effects of . . . she thought . . . it doesn't matter."

"I'm sorry to have to ask you these questions, Doctor, it's not a pleasant proceeding, I know, but it has to be done."

"Of course, I fully understand that."

"Had anything of this kind ever occurred before, to your knowledge—any attempt on her own life, I mean?"

"No—oh. Well. Many years ago—but not seriously."

"Perhaps you could tell me about it?"

"It was just after I really got to know her, in London. She was staying with her aunt." Belinda Welling, a burly, brusque gynae-cologist, mannish, almost as big physically as her brother Arthur.

"She was quite ill at the time—bronchitis, high fever, that kind of thing. It had a depressive effect—not at all uncommon." All that week, morning and evening, he had come to the house with flowers and fruit and solace for her convulsive shivering, her speechless appeal. "She took a large quantity of—of aspirin, I believe. At any rate, her aunt, who was a doctor, found her almost at once, realised what had happened, and did all the right things." At the end of that week, they were engaged. Aunt Bel had said, "Well, if you're going to be one of the family, I suppose I'd better tell you—no good telling Arthur, an old woman if ever there was one. The first morning you came round—earlyish, couldn't sleep, went in to see how she was, found her gobbling pills out of the bottle like a pheasant after raisins. Silly girl. Mother was a silly woman. Got 'em all up. Keep an eye on her, that's all I'm saying."

"And there were no further incidents?"

"No, nothing like that. Nothing at all."

"All right, I've nearly done. If your wife was as methodical as you say, I don't suppose there'd be any other place in the house— an attic perhaps—where she might have kept old correspondence?"

"She cleaned out the attic when her father died, as far as I know there's nothing in it at all. She was not a sentimental woman—not given to keeping things. But what exactly do you mean—correspondence?"

"Letters—old letters." Ply rubbed his hand over his close-cropped hair—he would be tired too, of course. "I expect you remember telling me on Wednesday, up at the New Inn, that your wife had been acquainted with Dr. Brinton?"

"Yes—with the whole family, but a long time ago. You're not suggesting that Brinton wrote her letters?"

"That's just what I'm suggesting."

"Well, I don't know. I suppose it's possible he wrote her one or two, just as she might have written to him."

"Oh, she wrote to him all right—forty-seven letters in all."

"Forty-seven? Are you sure? When?" Hugh stubbed out the Woodbine, his fingers shaking.

"They're dated from just after the time she went to live in London until two weeks before Arabella Brinton's death."

"But—are they . . . are they signed?"

"They're signed 'Angel,' but there can't be any mistake; apart from anything else, the handwriting is hers."

"How do you know? Can I see them?"

"They were found in Brinton's desk, along with a lot of others, I may say. But I recognised the handwriting the other night—Wednesday—when I saw the letters on the salver waiting to go out. It is a very distinctive hand."

"And you took them—you offered to post them, and took them."

"I admit I did, Doctor," the tone was apologetic, "a bit underhanded, I expect you're thinking. But I'd have found out sooner or later, you know."

"I'd like to see Julia's letters to Brinton, Mr. Ply."

"I'm afraid that's out of the question—for the moment, at any rate. They're evidence, you see. Besides, I think in the circumstances, it might be—be wiser to, well, to wait a bit."

"You think there's something in the letters that would shock me? I doubt it very much, Superintendent. In my profession one's relatively shockproof. Besides, Julia—well, I know she had a mild schoolgirl crush on Brinton for a few weeks, but I really can't swallow the suggestion of anything much more than that."

"No, sir—Doctor. I'm afraid it was a bit more than a 'crush.' The letters are very, what you'd call, passionate—and frank. At least at the start; towards the end they cooled off—it's clear she wanted to get out of it, but the doctor wasn't having any, making things very difficult for her, he was."

"I see." But she had stopped, broken it off—or Arabella's death had broken it off—before she met Hugh, before, at any rate, they were engaged. "Was this why you came up here last night—you wanted to talk to my wife about the letters?"

"Among other things."

"Other things?" Out of his exhaustion, Hugh tried to grope for something concrete. "You said 'evidence' just now—evidence of what?"

Ply took the pipe out of his mouth and examined it; then very deliberately put it, still lit, into his pocket. "Look here, Doctor, have you got a solicitor? I'm thinking of the inquest."

"A solicitor? Yes, I suppose so. George Trentham of—but I don't understand. What have my wife's letters to Brinton got to do with her inquest?"

"Not her inquest, Doctor, although there's bound to be one, of course. I'm talking about Brinton's inquest—that's set for Tuesday. Your interests—your wife's interests—ought to be represented."

"What interests can the dead have, Superintendent? The exposure of an adolescent affair—if affair it was—with a middle-aged doctor fifteen years ago?" It could wound no one now—no one but Hugh. "I'm sorry, I'm in the dark—you'll have to explain a bit more."

"Very well." Ply paused, as if getting the facts straight in his head. "There is some evidence to suppose that your wife was involved in the death of Arabella Brinton and—"

"But that's impossible, she was in London that afternoon."

"Well, sir—we don't think she was. We have reason to believe that she was there at the New Inn at some time between four and four-thirty on the afternoon of Friday, April twenty-sixth. She was seen leaving the house by the back door by Mrs. Warden."

"But Mrs. Warden said that it was Nurse Trotman she saw."

"Mrs. Warden *assumed* it was Trotman, but what she actually saw was someone in a nurse's uniform. When she was questioned closely, what she described was a cape with a scarlet hood. And you know as well as I do that St. Matthew's R.N.s, which Trotman was, have violet hoods—it's only the student nurses that have the red ones. However it isn't only a question of Mrs. Warden's word, although she's a noticer all right. But there's also the statement that young Brinton made at the station yesterday afternoon."

"Alex," he had to make an effort to get the words out, "Alex saw her too?"

"That's what he states—he was quite clear, quite firm about it."

"But . . ." He searched his mind—what difference did it make if Alex had seen Julia rather than Elaine? He cleared his throat. "I don't think we can rely very much on that type of childhood memory—particularly when there is any kind of time element involved, it's apt to be quite unreliable, coloured, altered, even manufactured by later impressions, interpretations, half-heard stories and, and—and . . . other things." He forced himself to continue. "Anyway, we know from what Dr. Stand has admitted, that he was in the house at the relevant time—it's hard to c-conceive that he wouldn't have seen my wife, if she had been there."

"Dr. Stand has unreservedly withdrawn his previous statement."

"He . . . and you've accepted that? He's a free man?"

"Free in a manner of speaking. He's going to be in a certain amount of trouble for making a false statement to the police. But no suspicion for the murders now attaches to him, we're satisfied as to that." Ply's voice was firm, so calm as to be almost gentle.

"I—see." Hugh suddenly had a blinding headache—blinding? But he was already blind, had been for so long. . . . If only he could swear or throw up his arms, but he hadn't the little habitual gestures of other men—let alone the grand ones. His professional immobility had left him without recourse. "But it's inconceivable, Julia would never, could never have . . ." But that was no use—after all, what did he now really know of what she was or was not capable? "Let me p-put it this way: It's one thing to be there, if she was there, and quite another to have actually done—done the deed. Isn't it?"

"Yes. The boy didn't say he saw her push his mother, or slam the door. He just saw her in the hall. But he did *see* her—he made a very positive identification when he came up here yesterday afternoon with his stepmother."

"He saw Julia?"

"Yes. Of course, it's not proof, not something any jury would convict on. But we're not talking about that. Mrs. Welchman can't be tried now. Although, if she were alive, it probably would go to trial."

"And you think she would have been convicted on the word of a five-year-old boy's identification fourteen years later?"

"No, Doctor. But I'm very much afraid it's graver than that. It's only fair you should know here and now—though I expect I'll get in trouble for it. The fact is that young Brinton's identification didn't just refer to that afternoon fourteen years ago, it also had reference to last Tuesday night. That's the night of Dr. Brinton's death."

"Yes, I know." Hugh shut his eyes.

"Well, apparently young Brinton had been downstairs—what you told me about his having overheard his stepmother give Dr. Brinton something to calm him down is completely verified, both by the boy and Mrs. Brinton, by the way. Then apparently he went in and had a drink and a chat with his father, in the middle of which there was a phone call that his father took in the surgery. When he came back he was very anxious for Alex Brinton to drink up and go off to bed. Young Brinton duly left the study, but being curious, he secreted himself just inside the front hall, where he had a view of the patients' door and the corridor. After some ten minutes or so, a woman entered dressed in black trousers, boots, gauntlets, and a black anorak. He then went to bed—but this woman also he identified as being your wife. So you—"

"Yes." That was what Julia wore right enough, when she went out on her machine—always black. Black in the black stormy night, and he remembered the black shape riding past him in The Lane as he stumbled up to Reg Semple's. "Is it—your c-case that my wife murdered Jonathan Brinton, as well?"

"I don't have a case, Doctor. But Brinton was alive when the boy left him. Case? No, there's no question of a case. But what I'm trying to tell you is that all this is pretty much bound to come out."

"Yes." Hugh opened his eyes; the light on the table beside him was unbearably bright; he turned it off. "And you, Superintendent, do you believe that my wife committed these crimes?" He waited in the opaqueness of the room for an answer—an answer that suddenly assumed enormous importance.

"I believe she was there—both times. I believe she wrote the fake suicide letter. But as for the rest of it—I think the truth of the matter might well have gone with your wife to the grave." He stood up abruptly, as though he had overstayed his welcome, or said too much—or not enough. Then he said, "Unless, of course, something turns up."

"Quite." He pushed himself out of his chair. "Let me see you out."

"Thank you."

"By the way, those poems of my wife's," he said as he opened the front door, "am I to be allowed to see those?"

"The poems? I put them back where they were—in the chest of drawers—the top drawer on the right."

"And the will?"

"That's filed under Barker & Trentham in your wife's desk."

"Very well." It seemed warmer—the rain was only a thin drizzle making the day dim. Hugh could see two in the police car—Ramm and Brandt, waiting for their chief. "Well, good-bye then, Sergeant-Major."

16

Mrs. Nance had been at work in Julia's room too—the window was shut again, the lamp centered on the night table, the Keats replaced in the shelf; and the bed made, for all the world as if she would sleep in it again tonight. A faint odour of furniture polish in the air. He opened the window. There would be no perfume to remind him of Julia, only the fresh scent of the damp day, winter night thawed into spring morning.

The loose-leaf notebook lay in one corner; he touched it tentatively with his fingertips. *A private person*—and he'd never intruded on that privacy. Even her death had been private. But this is what he had come for—*You must know, 'ughie.*

He lifted it out of the drawer and, bending his head low, riffled slowly through the pages. Some were a whole page, or two, some no more than a few lines. A shorter one caught his eye:

Old child chant

old fields
old feet

 poppy-glutted
 running sweet

old eyes
old face

 summer-shuttered
 laughing place

old hands
old hair

 berry-bloodied
 plucked by air

old cheeks
old rain

 searching tears
 home again

old lips
old thighs

 moon-surrendered
 sleep-cool cries

old dream
old breath

night-enchanted
silly death

His black headache bore him down, and it was with an effort that he looked up. Arms folded, guarding her inner secret, the girl gazed at him aloofly from the wall. Stony as his unseen sister, dead and buried these fifty years—had Harriet Welchman known a laughing place? He thought of Caroline Savage's impoverished childhood and her uncertain lament, "I want a normal life, I want to have children and a family."

He put the book back in the drawer.

In the bathroom he took two aspirin and drank three glasses of water; he washed his face and hands, plugged in the razor and started to shave. He pressed it down too hard and nicked the little wart under his chin. The rose garden—was that the "summer-shuttered laughing place"? The blood had started out on his chin—he plugged it with a dab of cotton wool.

He tried to force something from the back of his mind—something about dates. On the side of the washbasin the razor buzzed like a trapped maybug. He switched it off.

As he went along to his room a smell of cooking rose from the hall below and he felt a prick of nausea. He sat at his desk and lit one of the last Woodbines.

Three minutes later Madge Platten entered in high spirits. "We had a lovely time last night, didn't we?"

"I don't think that's very . . . I'm sorry, Madge, what are you talking about?"

It turned out that she had phoned him and recorded a message, no doubt replete with all the usual obscenity—and now she was furious that he hadn't played it back. "You horrible arse-hole, you —if only I were Catherine the Great you'd be on your back soon enough, although you look too shagged out to do anything much. What have you been up to? Dipping your wick in the matrimonial cunt, I suppose, instead of attending to your patients . . ."

It had been a trying session and her phone call meant he'd have to listen to the play-backs himself, instead of getting Mrs. Nance to do it. But not now.

He sat waiting, fruitlessly, he knew, for Alex to appear. He stared out of the high window at the close grey sky, feeling nothing —only repeating stupidly in his head, *silly death, silly death.* Why

silly? He knew the numbness to be a salutary response, and yet
. . . he looked down at his hands, brown-spotted and nicotine-
stained on the immaculate white blotter. Slowly he made an effort
of will. He put out a feeler—a rod to divine the well of grief that
must lie hidden below ground—but there was no quiver. He was
being prevented, preventing himself. There could be no solace, no
healing until the extent of the wound was examined. There were
things to be done.

We have reason to believe . . . on the afternoon of Friday, April 26 . . .
He leant down and opened a drawer and took a packet of engage-
ment diaries that went back twenty-five years. He opened the relevant one—January, February, March, April: Saturday, April 27:
Julia, lunch 12.30 Brampton Sq. He leafed back—in March it was *J.W.*
and February *J. Welling:* two dinners, a concert, a ballet, theatre, once
to the Tate to see—what? Matisse? But April 27 was the first time
he'd been invited to Aunt Bel's house: "I'm afraid Julia's not very
well. Came home yesterday with a temperature of a hundred and
two. Put her straight to bed. Looks bronchial to me. Had a bit of
trouble with her this morning. Not usually a difficult child. Better
now. I don't suppose there's any harm in your seeing her for a
minute or two. You're a psychiatrist, I gather—like my brother, the
poor fish. Hasn't an iota of common sense. Hope you have—won't
be much use to Julia if you haven't."

Silly girl. Silly death. Yet it was Aunt Bel who'd had the silliest
death of all—six months later she'd been killed by a flower pot
falling on her head in South Kensington.

Hugh got up abruptly and fetched Julia's poems from her room.
He sat down again at the desk. There was something he had seen.
He peered at each page in turn—they were not numbered, there was
no index. Yes, here it was: *Green silk death.* He read it through
quickly, then a second time more slowly, concentrating on a single
passage:

> . . . sedulously I weave
> reflection
> to recollection,
> one to another
> in semblance
> of the forsaken—
> sunless the spring day—

who stood above her
at the cellar door
and sent her spinning
in green silk arabesque
to the rock floor below—
and so spun I
vertigo
into a stony nevermore. . . .

He sat on for a long time, all through the ghostly session. He began to have a glimmer of understanding. The clearing of house and attic, the desertion of the garden, the absence of mirrors except in the waiting room—which he had taken as attempts to abolish memory, repress the past, refuse all reminders and reflections, had been the very opposite: a divestment in order to rest more naked in a single moment. Mrs. Warden had seen her leave—but she had never left. For fourteen years she had stayed there at the New Inn on a foggy late spring afternoon, under the eyes of a brown-haired little boy. No wonder she had so sedulously avoided meeting Alex the patient—the true witness come into her own house. Yet she must have been glad to see him at the last, glad that it was all over. She had even made a new will . . . but that was before, before he came. The Thursday, not the Friday. Had she, then, seen it—him—coming? He could perhaps accept that Julia might have swung her hand and slammed the door on the enraged exigencies of her ex-lover's wife. One instant of blind horror. But the other!—the cold, determined murder of a man with whom she'd . . .

Hurrying down the stairs, he missed his step, staggered, slewed round, came down heavily, at the last moment catching at the banister to prevent a full fall. He got up, shaken. There was a sharp pain in the ankle as he put his weight on it. He hobbled lamely down to the hall filled with the smell of food, and stopped uncertain. Painfully he made his way into the waiting room—he looked round, it seemed quite unfamiliar. Was this where he wanted to be? In the mirror over the fireplace his image was blurred, softened out of recognition. And although his head was light and floating, he felt his body drowning in the heavy waters of a subterranean world he could not see. Dissociative symptoms. Julia smiling in red silk dress, Julia mocking. Julia leaving . . . What had Julia left? Nothing. No word for him. Unless the will—that would be near enough her last word.

In her study he pulled the envelope out of its pigeon hole—
Barker & Trentham. It was unsealed. On the face was written in her
clean passionate handwriting—*My Will.* He opened it and took out
the document and read:

This is the Last Will and Testament of me—

Julia Judith Welchman of Hillside, The Lane, Cambridge in
the County of Cambridge, Housewife, WHEREBY I REVOKE all
former Wills and Testamentary dispositions heretofore made
by me.

1. I APPOINT Katherine Amaryllis Brinton to be the Executrix of
this, my Will.

2. I DEVISE AND BEQUEATH all the real and personal property
whatsoever and wheresoever to which I shall be possessed or
entitled at my death to the said Katherine Amaryllis Brinton absolutely.

IN WITNESS whereof I have hereunto set my hand this twenty-
third day of April One thousand nine hundred and _____.

Julia Welchman

Signed by the said Julia Judith
Welchman the Testatrix as and
for her last Will and Testament in
the presence of us both being present at the same time who at her
request in her presence and in the
presence of each other have
hereunto subscribed our names as
witnesses

Dorothy Nance
F. G. Turner

"What?"

"I said I'll be leaving now, then, Doctor." She stood in the
doorway, a bulky grey figure in raincoat and head-scarf, shopping
bag in hand.

"Er, yes. Well, good-bye then."

"I've made you some nice goulash and mashed potatoes;
they're on the hotplate in the dining room."

"Thank you, that's very, er . . . of you." He could make out nothing on her moonlike countenance—she was as blank, as secretive as the house itself. "I'm sure I shall enjoy it."

"I'll be in on Monday at the usual time."

"The usual time . . ." Before he could think of anything else to say, she just nodded and vanished as silently as she had come.

"Thank you," he called feebly.

He wanted to go too—to get out of the house. He wrestled with the French windows, wrenched them open. Out of this doom-laden, beastly place. He stepped onto the narrow flagged terrace and hobbled slowly to the centre of the old rose garden and put his hand on the sundial for support. It was still raining mildly, almost invisibly. From the circle of turf where he stood, the bushes had extended out in eight sections to form a greater circle, each section containing a different colour or breed of rose. *Beastly, doom-laden*—Kate's words for her own home. He turned and looked at the grey house almost merging with the grey sky and the general greyness inflicted by the rain. Well, now it *was* Kate's—*nice and modern and four-square, where nothing ever happens except to other people.* A dream house—a dream of unsullied permanence. And Julia had instinctively known that— had given Kate what she yearned for in compensation for . . . for what she'd deprived her of? Had Julia really killed Jonathan too? Too? Her lover—always her lover, intransigent, paranoid, dangerous? . . . It was inconceivable—inconceivable. And yet hadn't he, ever so blithely, answered Kate—*all houses have their share of guilt and betrayal, even mine?*

His face was wet with the rain or, for all he knew, with his own tears. But he'd not weep for the house—it never really had anything to do with him in the first place. The shutters stood out black and forbidding against the grey stucco.

And then, standing there alone, he was shaken with a black spasm of rage against all that had been taken away, against all that had never been, the fondly imagined. Reaction to action. He raised his arm as if to ward off a blow—or strike one. And then it passed, and he shivered with the chill of the afternoon.

He limped back into the house.

He had his hand on the banister when the bell rang. He stood uncertain for a moment—the police? But he'd nothing to fear from the police now. All the same, when he opened the door, he was relieved to see the stocky figure in cloth cap and buckled Burberry on the step. "Hello, Stand."

"Afternoon, Welchman. Sorry to intrude at a time like this, but—"

"You know already?"

"Morehouse, the police pathologist, is a friend of mine. Look, just wanted a minute, but say the word, and I'll be off."

"No no. Come in. Let me have your coat."

"Thanks. I say, man, you're all wet."

"Oh am I?" Hugh took out his handkerchief and wiped his hands and face. "Er—would you like some tea?"

"Tea?"

"I suppose it is a bit early." He thought of the goulash waiting on the hotplate. "You've had lunch? Yes. A drink then? Port, sherry? No. Come along in then."

The waiting room was gloomy and cold—Mrs. Nance had turned off the gas. Hugh was seized with a fit of the shakes.

"Cold as a mortuary in here. I'd better light the fire.

"What did you want to see me about?" He had to cling to the mantelpiece to stop the trembling. The gas lit with a plop.

"There." Stand glanced up. "Welchman—you all right?"

"Yes. It's nothing—just twisted my foot."

"Umm, noticed you were limping. Let's have a look."

"No no, it's quite all right," but he sank down into the chair with an audible grunt of relief.

"Put your foot on this." Stand pushed the leather pouf under Hugh's leg and then switched on the lamp.

"Don't bother—after all, I'm a doctor myself and—"

"Don't be an ass, man. When did you last see a sprain?" He pushed back the trouser leg and dexterously unlaced and removed the shoe and rolled down the sock. "And that's what you've got. A nasty one. Hurt? Yes, thought it would. No dislocation though. How'd you do it?"

"Fell down the stairs."

Stand looked up, the beads of moisture on his long eyelashes gleaming in the light. "Did, did you?" He stood. "Well, stay put. I shan't be a minute."

"Where are you going?"

"Put a cold compress on it. That'll reduce the swelling. I'll bandage it up before I leave."

"Well, all right. You'll find the bathroom—"

"I know perfectly well where the bathroom is in this house."

240

He let out a brief cackle. "In half the houses in Cambridge, come to that."

Hugh closed his eyes—then opened them. There was something wrong about the room. He was facing the garden—sitting in Julia's chair. That was it. He made a half movement as though to change over to his usual place, then sank back.

"Right." Stand placed a bowl of water on the floor, and his black bag, and knelt down.

"I thought it was Brinton, not you, who'd been the Wellings' G.P."

"This was before Jonathan's time. Anstey was their G.P. really, but, as I told you, I was his more or less permanent locum for a couple of years before the war. The pull up the hill here was a bit stiff for his old nag, so I usually did the duty." He laid the compress gently on the swelling. "Matter of fact, I delivered Julia here."

"In this house? She never told me."

"Yes. Helen Welling's pains developed very rapidly and she went almost straight into labour. Only just got here in time for the delivery."

"I see." Hugh stared out at the blind garden. Slowly he struck a match and lit the last of Ply's Woodbines. "Stand, you must have known her reasonably well—what sort of woman was she?"

"Helen? One of the nicest women I've ever met. Beautiful to boot." He sat back on the couch.

"She wasn't—you wouldn't have called her silly?"

"Silly? Good heavens, no. Of course she was a bit—how can I put it?—ethereal, too good for this world, if you know what I mean." He cracked a knuckle. "Everyone liked her. Even old Anstey thought the world of her. Old Arthur was besotted about her. Surprised he didn't go off the deep end when she died—he was a passionate man under that rather monumental exterior. I wasn't here at the time—off at the war. But of course by then he had . . ."

"He had a daughter."

"Quite."

Hugh smoked in silence; he thought of the aging widower at the height of his reputation, surrounded by comfort, a difficult man, alone, trying to find things to say to his self-possessed little girl, eagerly awaiting his walks among the roses with the young Arabella Anstey. "Stand—the police think Julia murdered Arabella—and Jonathan too."

"Yes, I know." He cleared his throat with a rasping noise. "Welchman, I owe you an apology. More than that, in fact. I suppose if I were a religious man, I'd be asking your forgiveness."

"I don't follow you." Hugh looked at the little doctor sitting straight up. "What on earth are you talking about?"

"I see. I was afraid of that. You haven't made the connection." He tugged at his ear lobe. "Look—why do you think I sent Alex to you in the first place?"

"You told me—you said anyone who'd married Julia Welling couldn't be—couldn't be altogether a fool."

"Yeees. I'm afraid it was a bit more devious than that. Well, it's no good beating about the bush. Fact is, I always had a pretty fair notion that Julia was at the New Inn on the afternoon of Arabella's death."

"You . . . how?"

"Alex, of course. Look here, old man, are you sure you want to go into all this?"

"I think you'd better."

"Well, it was that afternoon. It was a few minutes before I got up to see Alex—I had quite a bit to do—and—"

"Altering the evidence?"

"Quite." Stand nodded brusquely. "Among other things. Jonathan went completely to pieces—typical. At any rate, I found Alex in a queer state, crouched on his bed, muttering about 'Nursey'— over and over again. I calmed him down a bit—hypnotised him actually. Always had a gift for that, you know. I asked him what he'd seen and he said, 'She was all black and red.' I thought at first he meant Arabella, but no, she was 'green and bare' he said. So red and black meant Nursey—well, that didn't fit Elaine, you see, because—"

"Yes. I know that part. The police told me. And obviously you knew Julia was a student nurse at Matt's and—"

"Of course I knew it. I arranged it."

"You? You seem," he found it suddenly difficult to breathe, "you seem to have had a hand in a lot of things."

"A meddlesome old fellow?" He gave a quick, unamused laugh. "I expect you're right. But in this case I was asked."

"By whom?"

"Welling. I wasn't the G.P. anymore, but I used to come up and drink port with Arthur now and again—a family friend, so to speak. Then one—"

"You're rich in surrogate families."

"You've every right to be bitter, Welchman. But please hear me out. Arthur rang me up one day in a fair old stew. He'd heard about Jonathan's goings-on, which were getting quite notorious by then and I'd had to warn him once or twice. Did he think Julia could be involved? I taxed Jonathan with it straightaway—he denied it, of course, but I knew the signs by that time. I felt bound to report to Arthur that it might be all for the best if she was sent away for a bit. He agreed, so I fixed things up at Matt's and she was duly packed off to her London aunt. Damned useful things, aunts."

"And you really thought Julia was the sort of person who could kill a defenceless woman like that?"

"I didn't know what sort of person she was. She was lovely and charming, but rather a quiet, intense girl, and as far as I was concerned totally impenetrable."

"But you believed she killed Arabella?"

"No. To be perfectly frank, I've always thought it was Kate— until now. But Julia's presence that afternoon—well, it worried me, nagged at me, that's all."

"But you sent him along to this house hoping that he'd recognise Julia?"

"It was a long shot, no more. I thought seeing her might jog his memory. One way or the other. I thought it better out in the open."

"Better for whom? Jonathan? Julia?" He kept his hands on the arms of the chair to stop the trembling.

"I'm sorry."

"It wasn't your attitude when I came to your house. 'Let sleeping dogs lie,' you said."

"I'm not trying to defend myself. I was not strictly honest. But I didn't think you'd take well to my encouraging you to probe—I suppose what I wanted to do was to whet your appetite."

"Whet my appetite!"

"I was concerned about the boy—damn it, man, can't you see that?" Stand cried out the words; now he turned his head away, as if ashamed. "He's been haunted by this," he spoke quietly, "of course, we all have, but he more than the rest of us. I knew perfectly well he's only been working on half cylinder. I knew the day would come when he'd have to find out what—whatever it was that happened. But I didn't want to prejudice you." Then, suddenly fierce again, "I wish to God it hadn't turned out like this! I wish to God it had been me!"

"Well, you did your best to convince the police that it was you." The other man's emotion seemed to have drained his own. He was desperately tired.

"What? Oh yes—though I'm not sure they swallowed it. Clever fellow that police chappie—went after me like a loose ball in the scrum. Caught me out on one or two. . . ."

Hugh stopped listening. His brain was muddled with fatigue, yet he was puzzled by the old man's depth of feeling, so uncharacteristic, yet so freely expressed. He stubbed out his cigarette.

"Stand, you thought that Alex killed Jonathan, didn't you?"

"It—well, it seemed possible. It was either him or—"

"Or Julia."

"No. I'd rather written Julia off—it just seemed too fantastic, although, mind you, I don't say it didn't occur to me. No, the only other person, I thought, was Kate. The difficulty there was that Kate adored her father; just as she hated Arabella. Still, it didn't really matter—Alex or Kate, I couldn't let either of them be implicated. I had to be quick about it, because if the police had got hold of Elaine, or arrested her or anything silly like that, she might well have taken the blame on herself—she'd do anything for the boy, you see. So I thought a bit and then buzzed down to the police station."

"You didn't for a moment consider that the police suspicion of Elaine might be justified?"

"Of course not."

"Why not? Because you're in love with her?"

"In love with her? Good God, no. I think very highly of her— I told you the sort of woman she is that afternoon. But in love with her—where did you get that extraordinary notion?"

"I thought . . ." Hugh rubbed his head. "Actually, I think it was Kate who told me that you and Elaine . . ."

"I shouldn't place too much faith in what Kate says, you know. She's always had a bit of a problem distinguishing the true from, well let's say, the fantastic."

"But not Alex?"

"Alex knows the difference all right—what d'you mean by that?"

"I mean," said Hugh slowly, "that we have only his word for it that Julia was at the New Inn on the night of Jonathan's death. And he's hardly a disinterested party."

"You're suggesting that he's *lying*—that he just, just fabricated the whole thing? No no," he lifted his head, "my boy wouldn't do a thing like that."

"I'm only saying that what he said he saw is not necessarily conclusive."

"No, Welchman, that won't wash. We know what we're talking about." He was silent for almost a minute. "Well," he said in a heavy voice, at last, "there's only one thing to do: We'll have to ask him."

"Where is he—at Kate's?"

"No—at the New Inn."

"Then I'd better go and talk to him."

"Are you sure?" Stand was reluctant. "Shouldn't I have a word with him? I mean, in your condition—"

"That's kind of you, but I must tackle him myself."

"If you say so. But I warn you, Elaine's there and she's a bit like a she-bear with a cub."

"Dealing with she-bears is part of my profession."

"All right. I'd better strap you up then."

"Thank you. And could you do me another kindness? I've broken my glasses and can't drive without them. Could you run me over to the New Inn?"

"Of course. You couldn't drive with that foot anyway." He was already kneeling, removing the compress, patting the skin dry. He strapped the ankle with quick delicate movements, found a gumboot for Hugh to wear and a stick from the hall closet for him to lean on.

As Stand was about to start the car, Hugh suddenly laid a hand on his arm. "Wait a moment. Stand—Alex, he's your son, isn't he, not Brinton's?"

The G.P. was silent for a moment, staring straight ahead, motionless. "Yes," he said then, "yes—how did you guess?"

"Back there, in the house, you said '*my* boy,' and then there's a clear physical resemblance."

"Noticed it, did you?" He gave his little old-maidish smile.

"So that part of your confession was true—about your having an affair with Arabella."

"Yes. More or less." He switched on the ignition. "Want me to tell you about it?"

"I think I do, if it wouldn't upset you."

"Good heavens, no." The car started with a brutal jerk and shot down the drive. "I was always in love with her, you see; there's never been anyone else for me, before or since. She was fond of me too, but she wasn't a very passionate woman—not physically. That's probably why she preferred Jonathan, though she pretty soon got disenchanted with him. She hated the whole business of pregnancy and childbirth, but she had to go through with it—old Anstey wanted a grandson, said he was going to leave his money out of the family if she couldn't provide a male heir. He would have done it too. Well, of course, they managed to produce Kate, but that wasn't good enough for the old man. The problem was by that time that Jonathan had pretty much shot his bolt. Couldn't get it up, in fact. Well, with Arabella not caring much for 'that side of things,' as they used to say, and Jonathan impotent, it wasn't surprising that nothing happened."

They'd got down into the town now, and Hugh was almost glad of his purblindness, for Stand drove with a kind of off-hand wrenching recklessness that scattered the Saturday afternoon crowds.

"Anstey was becoming more and more disgruntled—he could be unbelievably rude when he wanted to, and he did want to. It took the stuffing out of Jonathan, and it was partly why Arabella took to drink. And of course she hated Kate for being a girl. To cut a long story short, the old man hinted to me that maybe I should do the job—he knew I loved her, you see. And he told Arabella outright that she'd better look sharp and if her own stud wasn't up to it, find another. So there you are. It all went swimmingly and in a few weeks she was pregnant—that was the end of it for me, of course. I'd done my job, so there was no need for any of that anymore. Anstey was delighted—he was a frightful old curmudgeon and a damned bad doctor, but I always had a soft spot for him. He came through all right—left everything to Alex, in trust of course till he was twenty-one, which didn't please Arabella very much, I can tell you. Three weeks later he died."

"I see. Tell me, did Brinton know?"

"He must have guessed. But it saved his bacon, so he asked no questions. Mind you, he didn't like Alex from the first." They were on the Newmarket Road now; suddenly Stand swung out and scraped past a bus, causing an oncoming van to honk furiously. Hugh shut his eyes as the car lurched, nearside wheels well over the verge.

"After Arabella's death, why didn't you take Alex away, to live with you?"

"Thought of it. But he was better off with a mother. And say what you like, Elaine's been a good mother to him, even if she does dote a bit. Of course, she never made a go of it with Kate. One can't have everything. I tried to keep an unobtrusive eye on the situation . . . jolly old Uncle Henry, you know, rather an ass, but someone to come to if there was a bit of a problem."

"But surely Elaine didn't marry Brinton just to look after the children?"

"Oh no. She'd fallen for him—he was still good-looking in those days. And she was sorry for him—women were always sorry for Jonathan. Later all her affection went to Alex."

"And Alex has no inkling."

"None. But I shall tell him soon. Or you can, if you think it wiser."

"Perhaps."

They drove in silence; then suddenly turned with lightning speed across the oncoming traffic into the little lane beside the old house, and stopped dead.

"Thank you," Hugh said. He badly needed a cigarette.

"Nothing. Look, Welchman, you'll, er, let me know about Alex, won't you?"

"Yes, of course."

"I can't believe it." Stand clenched the steering wheel. "I don't believe it. I'm sorry, old man—but if Julia wasn't here that night, why did she commit suicide?"

"I don't know."

"Didn't she leave a letter or something explaining things?"

"No."

"But surely, man, you must have had some notion of all this?"

"No. You see, Stand, it seems I didn't really know my wife very well." He struggled out of the car, hampered by his stick. With the door still open, he hesitated. "Stand, there's one other thing you could do for me, not strictly professional but as you know Morehouse, could you find out from him if—whether Julia was pregnant . . . or not?"

"My dear chap! Of course, of course!"

As Hugh limped slowly to the gate, his gumboot squelching on the sodden ground, he heard the car reverse violently into the main road.

17

The single window stared blindly from the stable wall. Though the rain had stopped, a gutter dripped slowly. There was no other sound in the kitchen garden—the tide of traffic was far away and of a different time. The notice on the door directing patients away was curled with damp.

Hugh turned and hobbled along the flagged path, his body lethargic with fatigue, turned the corner, passed the kitchen window. He laid a hand on the back door, then paused, listening. The garden was misty and dim to his half-blind eyes—the individual flowers and blooms obscure, only the dark hedge and the vague form of the apple tree loomed out of the fog. And there was a smell of fog too—no freshness of spring earth and plants here—just as it must have been when Julia had stepped out, wrapped in her cape, and hurried along the path. And here the dog had pranced and gambolled for the last time—waiting for her beloved mistress who would not come out again.

In the back hall, coats and boots and sticks and gardening tools were all as before; the cape hung in its place, a peep of the mauve lining of the hood just showing. He raised the old dog collar close to his eyes; the engraved silver tag was brightly polished—*Maida: Brinton, New Inn.*

The swing door opened easily at his touch and then, as he moved into the front hall, swung back, sighed gently, and shivered to a stop. The burnished copper vase on the table was full of scarlet flowers—tulips, perhaps. They had no perfume, and yet, as he waited—for some sound, some sign, somebody—he fancied he caught a whiff of scent. He stepped back into the passageway between the two halls and touched the heavy cellar door; the wood was worn and rutted with age. Julia would have stood like this, for one instant, hand on door, as Arabella spun to the rock floor below, *green silk arabesque.* Perhaps, Alex would know. He raised his head and there on the staircase in the dead light was a white face looking down.

"Alex?"

"What are you doing here, Dr. Welchman?" Elaine's voice cut coldly through the dimness of the hall.

Leaning heavily on his stick, Hugh came to the foot of the stairs as she descended stiffly. "I came to see Alex."

"I'm afraid that won't be possible." She stopped on the last

248

step, looking at him with her head slightly on one side. She wore a close-fitting red dress—scarlet to match the tulips. The colour of triumph.

He shook his head. "May I ask why not?"

"For one thing, he's asleep." It was her scent he smelled—a thickish, musky odour.

Hugh hesitated. He was confused, pulled down with the intuition of defeat. "And the other reason, Mrs. Brinton?"

"I think you'd better come into the living room for a moment." She led the way, but her usual briskness was absent—there was a heaviness to her gait.

The fire was unlit and she made no move to switch on a light. There would be no offer of coffee or biscuits this afternoon—or even a chair. She closed the door, but stayed close to it, as though ready at any moment to make her escape.

"Dr. Welchman, you have caused a great deal of trouble in this house—you and yours. I do not intend to let it happen again. I may as well tell you that I'm not going to let you see or have anything to do with Alex—either now or in the future. I am legally and morally responsible for his welfare until he comes of age—at which time of course he may do as he likes." A little set speech, coldly and rapidly delivered.

"Mrs. Brinton, I don't dispute your responsibilities or your rights—but I think in the circumstances it would be foolish, if not impossible, to insist upon them."

"No, Doctor, it is precisely *because* of the circumstances that I *am* insisting on them."

"You appear to imagine that I am an undesirable influence on Alex. May I ask why?" His ankle pained him, and he longed to sit down.

"I shouldn't have thought you'd have to ask. Haven't you done enough harm already?"

"Alex is my patient. I've just been doing my job, as you well know."

"Only *too* well!" Her voice was sharp as a dart. "And your job's left the field strewn with corpses!"

Hugh shut his eyes and gripped his stick tightly. He had a sense of falling—of everything receding into the surrounding fog, leaving him alone, isolated in a formless world, a forsaken battlefield. Where had she found those words—Sir Walter Scott? Not in any handbook of nursing. He looked round the room—its colours muted, the elegance faded in the premature dusk. "Could we perhaps talk about this calmly for a moment?"

"Very well." Pause. "I'm sorry I said what I did, but—"

"Quite. Let me be perfectly honest with you—I'm extremely concerned about Alex. His recent experiences coming on top of the sudden death of Dr. Brinton are bound to have created a great deal of stress, which may well not be visible to the untrained eye, but nevertheless—"

"Alex is all right."

"Forgive me, but you are hardly qualified to—"

"Alex is all right. You *want* him to be unbalanced for your own purposes—don't think I'm not aware of that, Doctor."

"My *own* purposes? What *are* you talking about?"

"It's no good acting all innocent with me. If you can convince people Alex is unstable, you think you can prove his statement to the police was not responsible."

"I see. I won't deny that it is important to me personally, extremely important, to know exactly what Alex did or did not see on the afternoon of his mother's death—and on Tuesday night—but it is quite out of order to suggest that I would attempt to influence him in any way. That would be totally unprofessional."

"What he saw was plain enough—he saw Julia Welling slam the cellar door in his mother's face. He saw her enter my husband's study with murderous intent written on—"

"I question—"

"And you want to make him change his mind, you want to whitewash her, you want to make a plaster saint out of a wicked woman, you want to—"

"Mrs. Brinton, my wife is dead."

"And whose fault is that? Death doesn't alter the fact of what she was."

"What are you talking about, woman?" He hobbled a step towards her.

She recoiled, as though he were going to strike her. "Oh don't play so innocent. I was at Matt's when Welling was a student nurse —we all knew very well what she was like then. And she never changed, did she?"

"Will you please explain what you mean?"

"I mean your wife was a lesbian, Dr. Welchman—among other things. I can't believe you didn't know that, but I pity you if you didn't. She perverted Katherine, among others. They had a sordid little affair for years—I don't know when it ended, or if it ever did, nor do I greatly care. First Jonathan, then Katherine, and I wouldn't be surprised if she hadn't had eyes for Arabella at one—"

"You're making this up, you're—"

"An adultress, a pervert—and a murderess. That's what your precious wife was, Doctor. She did her best to destroy this family. But she shan't have Alex—not even from the grave." She said it all with quiet precision—but he knew now why her movements had been heavy: heavy with the weight of venom.

"Mrs. Brinton," with an enormous effort he kept his voice level, "you're speaking as a jealous woman."

"Jealous? And what have I to be jealous of? My husband's love?—he had no love to give me. My stepdaughter's?—my proclivities do not lie in that direction. Alex's?—Alex is the only uncorrupted member of this family, and Alex loves me. No, Doctor, I have no one to be jealous of." She spoke as if with a smile, but he heard in her words a winter of irreparable deprivation.

"You've not—I hope—spoken of this—to Alex?" he said slowly.

"No, of course not to Alex. I am not a malicious woman."

Something about the form of the phrase caught his attention. The pain in his head was almost intolerable, but he fought to keep his mind clear. She was the type of person whose fragile sense of security is maintained by dominating those around her—what better place for that than a hospital ward, or a house with a weak husband and a son who could be kept in a state of innocent infancy. Self-control was control of others. How she must have loathed Kate —or anyone who rebelled against her authority. Then suddenly he grasped it. "Mrs. Brinton, did you tell your husband this—about Kate and my wife?"

"Yes."

"You told him. You told him on Tuesday night—on the last night of his life—didn't you?"

"What if I . . ." suddenly defiant, "Yes, I did. I did tell him."

"Why? In the name of what?"

"Because he was threatening me—*me!* He said Alex had seen *me* that afternoon! He was trying to turn Alex against me. He said *I* had murdered Arabella and he was going to see that everybody knew it. He said I was—was a viper in the bosom of the family. He was going to throw me out, disgrace me, he said he'd see that I never got another job in my life. He said, without me they could have a

251

decent family life at last. *Decent!* I could tell him something about *decency.* Him and his daughter! So I told him—I showed him what kind of woman his precious Kate was, I let him know what sort of filth had been going on all these years. Like father, like daughter."

"Did it not occur to you that your husband might have been mentally disturbed—perhaps quite seriously disturbed?"

"That's a fine soft word for wickedness, isn't it, Doctor? Yes, he was sick all right—sick in the head, sick in the body, sick and putrid and stinking, an evil man in an evil house."

"But, Mrs. Brinton, our profession—yours and mine—is to take care of the sick."

"And do you think I hadn't taken care of him? Who do you think suffered his filth and his drunkenness all these years? Who do you think coddled him and protected him—protected him from the consequences of his irresponsibility and incompetence? Who do you think saved him from his errors and mistakes, who gave smooth answers to wronged women and turned away angry husbands and soothed neglected patients and saw that he was never charged with the negligence and malpractice and beastliness of which he was daily guilty? I did. Day in day out I did. For all our married life I never said a word against him. And he hated me for it. And then at last he thought he'd found a way to destroy me—and destroy Alex, who was no more his flesh and blood than I was, and which he hated him for, as much as he did me."

"You told him that too—that Alex wasn't his son?"

"*That* was no surprise to him. No, Dr. Welchman, there's a time to suffer in patience and silence the ills of this world, but there's a time to speak up against wickedness. It was my duty to do what I did—and I did it." Her words had been flung out like small sharp flints, and now that she'd done, she gave a kind of shuddering sigh, as though in release from passion long pent-up.

"And—he believed you?"

"Of course he did. I had the proof."

"The proof?"

She didn't answer, but went to the end of the room—walking with all her old briskness. She came back and held out a large brown envelope to Hugh.

He took it into his hand. "What's this?"

"The proof. I thought you might be coming round here, so I kept it aside for you. Letters, Doctor—letters to Katherine from your wife, may God forgive her. Read them, and you'll see the filth a fine lady can write. Read them and then, if you've got any decency, you'll burn them."

"How did you get hold of them?"

"I found them in the potting shed wrapped in an old piece of sacking—just before the end of Katherine's first year at the University. She was living at home then."

"And you just took them and kept them?"

"I had my responsibility."

"You call that responsibility?"

"You're a fine one to talk of responsibility. Read that crazy perverted filth—and tell me what you would have done. I was helpless in this house. But you—if you had taken your responsibilities seriously, you'd have had your wife committed years ago," she drew in a sharp hissing breath. "And that would have saved us all a great deal of unpleasantness, wouldn't it, Doctor?"

Hugh folded the envelope awkwardly with one hand and thrust it into his inside pocket. He limped to the door and opened it. Looking back, he saw her standing stock still, the scarlet of her dress turned muddy by the growing darkness. He opened his mouth —but there was nothing more to be said.

He went slowly into the hall and stood momentarily confused by the multiplicity of doors . . . at his back he was instinctively aware of Elaine Brinton watching him, waiting for him to mount the stairs.

Then, just as he moved, the swing door creaked softly.

"Doctor!" a barely audible whisper. "This way!"

He went along the short dark passage and pushed his way into the back hall.

Mrs. Warden grasped his wrist and thrust her face close to his. "Haven't you got a coat?" she whispered.

"Coat—no, I didn't have a coat," he said, inhaling her toothpaste breath.

"And you call yourself a doctor! Well, come on then." She had the back door open and she pulled him by the wrist. He tried halfheartedly to shake himself loose, but she only tightened her grip. Outside the fog had closed in and two yards beyond the wall of the house there was nothing to be seen.

"What's all this about, Mrs. Warden?" He was whispering himself in the clammy silence all around them.

"Sssh!" She opened the patients' door and pulled him after her into the corridor. "There we are," she was panting, "in the study —she'll never think of looking for you in there."

"You mean Mrs. Brinton?"

"That's right. I heard what you said about wanting to see our Alex and how she put you off. And I said to myself, he's the doctor, isn't he? He's got the right, hasn't he? So I popped up and gave Alex a shake and brought him down. He wasn't that keen at first, but I told him it was his duty."

"Well, I suppose I must thank you."

"I heard about your dreadful trouble. And I know what you'll be thinking, that it's all my fault for saying I saw her—but I didn't. I thought it was *her* I saw," a jerk of the head towards the living part of the house, "but they said it couldn't be, something about the colour of the hood. They worried it out of me."

"I'm not—not blaming you, Mrs. Warden."

"I know it wasn't her that killed Miss Arabella—why they were that fond of each other. We were all fond of Miss Julia. If only *she'd* have married the Doctor! A peck of troubles we'd have been saved. Oh, I'm sorry, I shouldn't—'

"No, that's all right."

"You're a good man, I can tell—just like the Doctor. And don't you go believing what *she* tells you—she's got a nasty point of view and no heart, nasty stuck-up creature that she is. And she's no lady, not like our Julia. I won't lock the door, so you can slip out easy."
She touched his arm lightly and then she was gone, and he was alone in the narrow lightless passage. Weariness was closing in on him. He fumbled fruitlessly for a cigarette, then braced himself and moved towards the study door.

Alex jumped up from the old leather couch. "Dr. Welchman!"

"Hello, Alex." He held out his hand.

The boy took it awkwardly—his palm was damp. "I s-say, sir —you've got a stick. Are you all right?"

"Just twisted my ankle. Shall we sit?"

They sat down side by side on the couch. Hugh gave a little grunt of relief at getting the weight off his foot. "Well, and how are you feeling, old chap?"

"Oh—not so b-bad, thanks." But his hands were clenched tensely on his knees. "I—you . . . I expect you're a b-bit m-miffed

254

with me, aren't you?" He rubbed his lips quickly as if to wipe away the stammer.

"No—no, I'm not." There were no piles of papers on the chairs, no fire in the grate, no bottle of whisky on the sideboard—all was in good order now. As neat as Julia's own study. As dead. Only the lights were too bright for his weakened eyes. "Tell me about it."

"I d-don't—I m-mean I'm n-not sure. . . ." He made a jerky gesture of embarrassment.

"Why don't you begin in hospital? Your mother came to take you away. That must have been rather a surprise, wasn't it?"

"Yes, oh yes, rather. Seeing her in the nurse's uniform, you see they said—I was just d-drinking a cup of tea—they give you an awful lot of tea in that p-place—and they said, 'Dr. Welchman's n-nurse to see you.' And then, you see, she c-came in, with her cape on and the hood up, and she just said, 'Well, was it m-m- . . . was it m-me?' She m-meant was it her I'd seen on the—"

"Yes, I know. And was it?"

"N-no!" He drew a small tremulous breath. "I kn-knew it wasn't the same at all—for one thing she was too small, and another was the hood, it hadn't been m-m—sort of violet, it was red, b-blood red and then her hair was the wrong c-colour. Do you remember I t-told you about a dream once about a woman in a c-cape falling on the ski slope?"

"Yes. The fallen woman had dark hair—which caused a confusion of identity in your mind."

"Confusion of identity," he repeated the words eagerly, "that was just it. I was puzzled, you see, and I was trying to explain it to M-Mother when she said we must go to your house and I must tell you at once. I said I'd told you, but she said you must have m-misunderstood. And then suddenly I wasn't sure whether I had told you or not—or what I'd told you. And I—so I . . ."

"So you decided that you did want to see me?"

"Yes. Well no, not really, I didn't really want to, but it seemed the sensible thing to do and—and it all happened so fast. I just signed this form—Mother knew exactly what I had to do—and then we were in the car, you see. . . ."

"Now I'd like you to tell me exactly what happened when you arrived at my house."

"Well, I . . . I rang the b-bell. . . ." His hands shook and he began to blink rapidly.

"I realise this is difficult for you, Alex. Just take your time. Put out of your mind that I'm anything but your therapist. Try taking a deep breath."

"All right." The breath, when he let it out, was a long sigh—but it calmed the trembling of his hands. "I rang the bell. Two or three times. But there was no answer. So I went back to the c-car and told Mother there was no one at home. She said I should t-try the door. Well, I—I m-mean I didn't want to very much, but I did—and it opened. And then—then I didn't know what to do. But Mother . . ." his voice trailed away.

"What did your mother do?"

"She said if the door was open, that meant you were b-bound to be at home and that I should go and have a look in your office."

"And that's what you did?"

"I—well, I knew it wasn't right to b-barge in like that but I . . ."

"It's not such a terrible thing to do."

"You don't think so?" He blinked, then smiled—and the large grey eyes, the long lashes, the quick gentle smile were clearly those of Henry Stand.

"No, of course not. Go on."

"Oh—well, I went upstairs and I knocked on your door and then after a bit I looked in, but you weren't there, of course. So I came out—out of your room, I mean. Well, I was just about to go down the stairs, when a door at the end of the hall opened and your wife c-came out."

"You recognised her?"

"Yes—and n-no. I m-mean I knew it was *her.*"

"The woman you'd seen in the hall the afternoon of your mother's death?"

"Yes." He nodded—an awkward convulsive movement. And then, in a whisper. "B-but not just that. You see, I'd seen her on—on the n-night Daddy died as well."

"Alex—exactly when did you recollect that you had seen her—or someone—on Tuesday night?"

"*Then*—when I saw her. It just c-came to me. But it *was* her—I knew it was her because she was dressed in the same c-clothes. She was all in b-black—a b-black—polo-neck, black trousers and b-boots, and a black leather jacket."

"I see." She must have been just about to go out—or have just

256

come back. From Ely perhaps, or the Fens. Five minutes too early, or too late. "Alex—on Tuesday night, what exactly happened? When I saw you on Thursday morning you told me that your last memory of that evening was watching your father from the study door—watching him chuckling."

"Yes . . . I kn-know." He looked away, and then down at his hands resting on his knees. "That's right, well then you see I thought it very funny and odd and I—but I didn't go in or anything. I started to go upstairs and then I came down again, there was something about the way he was laughing that sort of drew me back and so I stood just inside the door between the front hall and the p-passage to the surgery you know," he was speaking so quickly it was hard to catch every word, "to the surgery I don't know why I mean I stood there, or for how long I was just sort of frozen and then —and then the door, the patients' door opened and she came in, just like that all in black she didn't make any noise I suppose the boots must have been rubber-soled and she carried a skid lid and she just sort of slipped into the study and shut the door—it was only a second, two seconds that I saw her but there was no mistake she didn't see me because it was dark in the hall and the door only ajar." He raised his head and looked at Hugh with an open countenance.

"Yes—yes." It was convincing as far as it went, but he was too familiar with that rapid glibness, that honest regard, not to realise that something had been altered, something left out. Or something put in? But he knew that any attempt to get at it now would be futile. And it was quite possibly entirely trivial. "So yesterday afternoon you recognised her at once?"

"Yes." Alex gave an audible sigh. "But it wasn't until she spoke that I really remembered. We were standing there—she at the bottom of the stairs, me at the top—and then she said, 'Hello, you must be Alex. I'm Julia. It's a long time since we m-met. You used to call me "Yulia" when you were a little boy and I'd come to tea at your house. I don't suppose you remember that.' But I *did* remember— I remembered that lovely soft voice, so different from Mummy's, you know. I remembered her sitting at table with Wardy and Kate, and how glad I always was when she was there—she never used to pay me much attention, but somehow I always sort of felt she noticed me and liked me and was kind and, how can I put it?— would never be demanding, nice one moment and horrid the next like Mummy, or . . .

257

"But then as I started to come down the stairs, I thought how could this be happening? What was *she* doing *here*? And I was afraid, I was walking down into some kind of nightmare, I could hardly manage the steps, and I kept thinking she'll go away suddenly and everything will be all right, like she did before—but she didn't. And all I wanted to do was to run back to my room—to your room—and shut the door and I—I . . ."

He put his face in his hands and shuddered and began to rock very gently backwards and forwards.

"Take your time, old chap," Hugh said automatically. He waited through the soundless sobbing, keeping his mind blank.

After a while Alex took out his handkerchief and wiped his palms and face.

"And what happened then?"

"Mother came into the hall. I'd left the front door open, you see. And she just looked at—at your wife and said, 'Good afternoon, Welling.' And Julia said, 'Hello, Trotman.' And I came down the stairs and she told me that she was your wife and, well, we said good-bye."

"Do you recall exactly what she said?"

"She said, 'Good-bye, Alex. I don't suppose we'll meet again. By the way, I'm Mrs. Welchman, these days.' "

"And then?"

"Then we left. We got in the car and Mother asked me if she was the one—the one I'd seen. And I said yes—but I was sort of d-dazed, I couldn't see what it meant, until Mother . . ."

"Until she explained it to you?"

"Yes. I mean, if she was there that afternoon, she m-must—she must have . . ."

"Alex—did you actually see Julia slam the cellar door?"

"Well, no . . ."

"Or hear it?"

"No, but I was frightened, you see, I knew I shouldn't be there and I ran back to my room and shut the door and p-put the pillow over my head. It wasn't till later—it seemed like ages—that I went d-downstairs to see what had happened to M-Mummy and—"

"Yes, quite." He knew he couldn't bear a great deal more of this.

"But Mother says she must have . . . if she'd been there, I mean . . . and then again on T-Tuesday." He frowned anxiously—caught between hope and horror. Then he whispered, "It can't be true, can it? Not your wife!"

Hugh hoisted himself to his feet and went over to the fireplace —no mirror above the mantelpiece here, only a sporting print. He gazed for a moment at the impossibly angular horses and deformed huntsmen. Then slowly he spoke the bitter words of comfort to his wife's innocent betrayer. "I'm afraid it may well be true—yes."

"Are—are they g-going to arrest her?"

A fire of pain in his ankle as he swung round. "Are . . ."

"I m-mean—I'm sorry, I shouldn't . . ."

Alex didn't know! Of course, Elaine would have shielded him, and perhaps she was right—for the moment. In five seconds he had to make a vital clinical judgement and his mind was numb, frozen as the horseman's whip hand. All he knew was that he was vaguely against bloodsports . . . and murder . . . and guilt. No, he was suddenly sure—Alex couldn't stand that kind of punishment, not now, not this minute. "No, Alex—they're not going to arrest her."

"Oh I'm so glad!" Then, hesitantly, "That doesn't m-mean that later—"

"It means nothing!" and before he could stop himself he cried out, "nothing nothing nothing!" And he felt the veins in his forehead swell and he shut his eyes to block out the anguished brightness of the narrow room.

"Dr. Welchman—are you all right? Dr. Welchman?"

He opened his eyes—Alex was beside him, peering, patting his shoulder.

"Sorry," he managed to say, "Sorry about that, old chap."

"Would you like a glass of water?"

"No, no thanks." He cleared his throat. "You haven't got a cigarette, by any chance?"

"Of course," he took out a packet and lit Hugh's cigarette with a flick of his lighter.

"There's one other thing you might do for me." Hugh inhaled deeply. "That's call a taxi. I had to leave my car at home."

"Yes, of course. I'll do it at once."

Hugh's head was beginning to clear. He was aware of the vague murmur of Alex's voice in the surgery, but even with the door open no individual word was distinct. He was going to have to make some preparation, lay some foundation, however rickety, for when Alex would hear, or overhear, the news of Julia's death.

"You're in luck. There's a taxi just leaving Fen Ditton, it ought to be here in five minutes—ten, even in this fog."

"Thank you."

"Of course, I'd have been glad to take you myself, only . . . well, you see, it's Mother. I mean, she's very good at hiding it and all that, but she's a bit possessive about me really. And with Daddy gone . . . I think she really needs me. I'll stay here for a few days, I expect. I can do my swotting just as well here as anywhere else."

"Alex—last night, if I understand it correctly, you rather definitely did not want to see me—am I right?"

"Well—yes, you see I w-was—"

"Yes, I perfectly well understand why. But I want you to be absolutely sure in your own mind that no blame or guilt attaches to you in relation to—to my wife. Or to anything else. I am first and foremost your therapist and, as such, accept whatever you are and whatever you do without judgement or criticism. I in no way blame you, even—even as a human being." He managed to smile.

"That's frightfully d-decent of you, sir. I do understand that now."

"Good. There's just one other thing, and I want to be as direct with you as I can. There may come a time when you need a bit of help, someone with a clear head to talk to—and when I'm not available or when you will feel you'd rather not approach me."

"I c-can't imagine that."

"Nevertheless, it may be so. If it is, I would very much recommend that you have a chat with Dr. Stand."

"Uncle Henry?" He frowned.

"I think you'll be surprised to find just how open-minded he is. He's certainly sound, and I believe he's rather a wise man too. Anyone who survived three years in a Japanese prisoner-of-war camp is likely to know quite a bit about the rough side of life."

"Henry in a Jap P.O.W. camp? Are you sure?"

"Quite sure. Now I think I'd better be on my way, the taxi will be here shortly."

"Yes yes—quite," Alex said vaguely; he was looking at Hugh with a puzzled expression. "Dr. Welchman, you're not trying to tell me that I can't go on seeing you, are you?"

Hugh hesitated. "Alex, I won't disguise from you that such a problem may arise. But just at the moment, I don't think it's something we need to go into. I'm there to be called on, if you need or want to do so."

"That sounds a b-bit om-ominous," he gave an anxious little smile.

"Not ominous—just sensible."

At the patients' door they shook hands ceremoniously.

"Oh. Alex, just one other thing—do you have any Librium left?"

"I—well, n-no. As a m-matter of fact I chucked it away. I don't think I really n-need it now, do I?"

"Perhaps not. If you do, phone me and I'll send round a prescription."

"To t-tell the truth, I'm a b-bit off drugs." There was a pause. "And whisky t-too."

"I see. Well, good night, Alex."

"Good night, Dr. Welchman."

At the gate in the little lane, Hugh looked back, but the fog had thickened and there was nothing visible left of the house at all.

He waited by the door in the wall, leaning heavily on his stick. The pervasive chill numbed the ache in his head, dulled his mind. Yet he felt the house at his back, an almost palpable presence—the old inn harbouring ancient hatreds that coiled and turned back on themselves. The case is altered—*with a vengeance.* Even Elaine, immunised with white roses and radio church services, had taken her long revenge at last—ripping apart Brinton's last possible illusion of paternity, contemptuously flaunting the dual betrayal of his daughter with his once-beloved. What food for his ravenous paranoia she'd served him. From somewhere behind him he seemed to hear the man's chuckle, and he half turned.

"You the party for the taxi?"

"What? Oh yes. I am." He got in awkwardly.

"Where to then, Guv?"

"Where to?" He slammed the car door. Home—where else was there to go? "Hillside, The Lane—do you know it?"

"Yeah. I know. It'll take a bit of time in this—not in a hurry, are you?"

"No—no hurry." As he shifted his stick, he felt the bulk of the envelope in his pocket. "Driver, would you mind turning on the roof light, or would it bother you?"

"Nahh, no bother."

"Thank you." He opened the envelope and took out a thin sheaf of papers. Angling the pages to catch the light, he bent his head and began to decipher Julia's strong, passionate script.

It didn't take him long—there were only seven letters—not long in time. But as he dropped the last one in his lap, he had come a long way. They were nothing like he'd expected; but what had he expected—Elaine's "filth"? No, not that, but not the gentle appeal either—*Come back to your own, come home to tea, where you belong, to me.* . . . Nor that same sad, muted voice of the poems: *I'm secret in the fen fog waiting to be torn by the cold breeze of a dead morning stripping the little moment of hugged comfort . . . and then if I cannot hide myself, I can't hide you. . . .*

He looked up. The fog close against the windows was oppression, not comfort. "Where are we?"

"The cemetery, Guv. They'll be walking tonight."

"I expect so." He leafed slowly through the letters again; there was one passage—yes, this was it.

I am not old, but I feel old—not old in body, which can still rise and reach and spring—but old of another time. I am like the last wolf on the edge of the forest, wise with an instinctive ancient cunning that is totally alien and irrelevant to the ordered fields and tractors and combine-harvesters of the modern mechanical world without sheep that lies in the valley below. I am in this time here and now, yet not part of it. I feel my being—my doings and thinkings—to be a temporary ensconcement in my body, like the stub of an old candle in a ruined and long-forgotten crypt. However I move or run, I remain unmoving among old dark legends, beset by ancient spirits and long-gone dangers. If I could believe in any kind of redemption, I should be a nun. So you must guard yourself, my dearest, even against Julia—who loves you.

"You can turn out the light now."

Redemption. *You've got to know, 'ughie*—did that need redeem his invasion of her dead privacy? This was a Julia he didn't know; these letters were not for him. Those *ordered fields* were where *he* existed, but it wasn't there that she rose and reached and sprang. She'd ridden out to the Fens to find herself, and not *come home to tea.* The bleak enamelled kitchen, the waiting room, dead garden, bare bedroom—had not been home. Then where—the past, *the stony nevermore?*

"Driver, I've changed my mind. I want to go to Lady Strange College."

"Okay, Guv—that's easy. Have you there in a jiffy."

Kate would know. This was Kate's Julia, not his. He fought a rush of bitterness at the idea that she might have sought solace for the mother's murder in the daughter's love.

"No no," he said aloud.

"Changed your mind again, have you?"

"What? No, sorry, I was just . . ."

"That's good, 'cause here we are."

He fumbled for his wallet, paid, heaved himself onto the pavement, reaching back for his stick.

"Take it easy then, Guv."

"Yes. Thank you. Good night."

His rubber boots made no sound on the flagstones as he passed through the court shrouded in the quiet fog, and only the gentle tapping of his stick gave any sense of motion. There was no one about, no lights visible, only a dim radiance from an unseen source. In second court, he felt his way along the wall, counting the doorways—one, two, three. Each was a moment of light immediately vanished; he knew that if he did not concentrate, he would be lost. At the fourth doorway he could barely see the arch above his head, let alone the lettering. He entered and moved close to the board—*Gamworthy, W. F.; Prince, M. L.; Brinton, Dr. K. A.* He mounted slowly, his limbs weak, his breath short.

He stood in front of the door, waiting for his heart to slow, then knocked with his stick. After a minute or two, he tapped again, restraining an impulse to pound furiously on the panels.

"Go away." From behind the door.

"It's Hugh," then louder, "Hugh Welchman."

"Who? Why can't you leave me alone?" The door opened abruptly on her words. "Oh—Hugh!" She stood there—a narrow figure in black shirt, black leotards, hair pulled back—straight and shorn of ornament. Yet it seemed to him she swayed slightly and when she stepped back to let him enter, the movement was clumsy. As he passed her, he smelled the whisky on her breath—the whole room smelled of whisky. He sat down on the blue couch and laid his cane on the floor.

"Do you want a drink?"

"No, I don't think—yes. Perhaps I do." He watched her pour

from the bottle on the white table—refill her own glass and drop ice from a wooden bucket into both.

"Have you got a handkerchief?"

"Here," he passed her his spare one and she used it to wipe up a puddle of spilled whisky.

The fire was almost out, only a faint reddish glow in the ash. He stretched out his hands, hoping for a little heat; though he knew the room was warm, its stark modernity chilled him. She would be at home at Hillside.

"Kate."

"Here you are—here."

"Oh thanks." He took the glass, and she sank down cross-legged on the floor in front of him. He took a quick gulp of the whisky, the smell of it made him shudder.

"Hugh—was it . . . I mean, she would have gone gently, wouldn't she? She wouldn't have regained consciousness or," her voice shook, "or had second thoughts or heard . . ."

"The final thunder? No, it's unlikely."

"Thunder?"

"One of my patients—a long time ago now. Took a lot of aspirin, went to sleep, then had a dream—must have been before she went into a coma—a dream of walking in some gardens in the soft spring rain and hearing far away a growl of thunder coming closer. Unconscious warning of the death she thought she wanted, but she woke up—managed to make herself sick, did all the right things, and knew that's not what she'd wanted at all."

"Oh Hugh!" Her voice was blurred with tears, and whisky. "Oh Julia—oh the poor love. The spring—and she's going to miss the summer."

"Kate." Instinctively he stretched out his hand and she held to it tight. "You're right, it would have been—gentle."

She bowed her head and wept with slow wrenching sobs—he recognised the exhaustion of it; she had already wept long, here alone in the room, all day perhaps. She, who'd not wept a tear at her father's death. He glanced down at her hand in his—on the wedding finger there was a ring, a green stone gleaming in the lamp-light, set in twisted gold. An emerald held in a snake's jaws —he didn't have to be told it was Arabella's, the ring that had cracked against the skull of a terrified little boy.

"Kate," he carefully let go of her hand, "I've got something that properly belongs to you."

"To me?" She reached out and took his handkerchief from the table and wiped her eyes.

"These are Julia's letters to you." He gave her the envelope.

"Julia's letters . . ." She looked at it, then up at Hugh. "The ones I lost—but where did you find them?"

"Your stepmother gave them to me this afternoon."

"So she did steal them. The bitch! I always knew she had." She hugged the envelope to her, "Oh Hugh, oh Hugh," she half cried, half laughed, "so now you know too . . . or didn't you read them?"

"Yes, I read them."

"Well, I don't mind. They're so precious, and I thought they'd gone forever. She didn't write to me much, you see—I mean, not after we . . . She didn't like me writing to her either, except when I was abroad—that was all right. Do you know I went to Rome once for two weeks, just so I could send her a letter every day?" There was a quick catch in her voice. "I don't suppose you've found any of those, have you?"

"No."

"No, I expect she destroyed them. She wasn't in the least sentimental, I used to make frightful scenes about that—I didn't understand then, you see. Or perhaps I did, but just didn't want to accept it. . . ." She lowered the envelope to her knees and looked beyond Hugh.

Then she began to talk, softly—a barely audible musing, every now and again touching the envelope with a little protective caress. "You can't know what the coming of Julia into my life meant to me when I was a girl. You don't know. Nobody does. How can I explain? She was aloof, I thought at first. But it wasn't that. She was cool—cool like the evening breeze after a summer's day on the beach, like the spring rain—a seductive, dulcet beauty, a mistress of quiet longing. . . ." She fell silent, then roused herself. "I didn't want human contact. That's the whole point of dogs and horses for adolescents, isn't it? If you can ride, run with a dog—that saves you. It was her father, old Professor Welling, who suggested to Mummy that Julia come and teach me to ride. And Julia did teach me. Then —I think—Julia saved me. She was everything Mummy wasn't. She even taught me to read—really to read. I'd always been good at school, but before Julia everything had been a mechanical exercise. I was always a shy little girl—devious, if you like—but I lost my heart to Julia. She gave me poetry."

"Keats. That day in the dining room window seat, it was Keats you were reading, wasn't it? Did she give you that?"

"Oh no, she couldn't *give* me anything in those days, you know. Mummy would have found out and there would have been questions and scenes—Mummy was fantastically jealous. I used to have to pretend I didn't care one bit about Julia—that was the hardest part of all. But even then, Mummy sensed it and she used to snatch Julia away into the sitting room for glasses of sherry and long talks; she could be honey sweet when she wanted to. No, Julia introduced me to Keats—to everyone. But I meant her own poems—she gave me them sometimes. Hugh . . . you haven't found any of her poems, have you?"

"No." His response was automatic and, to be pedantic, accurate: the police had found them. He didn't want—didn't want to share that with Kate. It wasn't a question of jealousy. All their years together he'd known Julia wrote poetry; and he'd always hoped, been sure, that one day she would show the poems to him, when she was ready, when the break came. She had been ready only in death—but she *had* left them for him. He could hold on to that, the poems, even if he couldn't understand them. He had nothing else.

". . . a dreadful shame. There's nothing left then. You see, I—I burned mine." Her voice shook; she picked up her glass and drank quickly—a practised, easy motion. "It was after Mummy's death. Julia wrote to me about it—it seemed ages after, but it could only have been a few days. About how sorry she was and all that—but in the same letter was the news she was going to marry you. I was —stunned. I'd never thought of Julia marrying anyone, except perhaps Daddy, I used to dream of that sometimes. That's when I really began to hate you, if you want to know. I told you I had to have someone to hate—and you were it, for years and years. Until—well, I suppose until I met you."

"And do you hate me now?"

"Only in principle." She laughed vaguely, a little drunkenly. "Although I hated you more later. I used to think it was because of you that Julia wouldn't go away with me. I was always trying to persuade her, you know—once, I got an offer of a job in Vancouver, but she wouldn't come. Of course, it wasn't your fault really, but I did all the wrong things—I knew it but I couldn't stop it—I shouted and wept and carried on like, well, like Mummy! I think it was because of that Julia finally broke off with me—I accused her of wanting a daughter, not a lover, I said. . . . God knows what I didn't say."

"Kate, when did—"

"I'm telling you, aren't I? I'm *telling* you! Well, after that letter about marrying you, I burned all her poems, the letter too. I was absolutely desolate, but I was proud. I never wrote back—though she wrote to me once a month for ages. For a long time it was all I had to look forward to, those letters—but when I'd read them, I burnt them. I was away at school most of the time, but when she married you and came back here—although she still wrote—I told myself I'd put it all behind me. I'd become the intellectual pet of the school, you know—at least of Miss Marshall, the headmistress. I played hard too—hockey and tennis and dance, even archery. I came up on a major scholarship, and that made everybody happy —at school, I mean—including me, I thought. Then one day my first term—it was a misty rawish November afternoon—I popped into Heffers. And I turned a corner in the seventeenth-century section and there was Julia—and I realised that all those years since I'd seen her I hadn't been happy at all, I hadn't been even half alive, I'd just been waiting for the day I'd run into her. And when it happened, it was perfectly natural and we just fell in love right away, without having to say a word almost. At first she tried to resist, and of course it was more difficult for her than for me—I couldn't understand that she had anything to lose, you see, at least not anything that mattered. She was very reluctant, and then she'd forget and it would be marvellous and then, just as suddenly, she'd withdraw again. It wasn't for a long time that we . . ." She stopped, shook her head brusquely. "So you see why these letters are so important, with those she wrote me in the next two years—eleven of them—it's all I have left of her."

"Not quite." He took a sip of whisky; what he really needed was a cigarette. "Before she died—a few days ago, Julia made a new will. By that will, you are the sole beneficiary of her estate—and the executrix. Which means the house is yours, her money, personal effects, everything. . . ." Everything, he thought suddenly, that doesn't matter. The past—left to Kate. Of course—by that will, Julia had sought to free him.

"The house? Oh . . . oh!" She put her face in her hands, but looked up almost at once. "Then she hadn't forgotten . . . she loved me . . . Hugh, I'll try to," she touched his knee and he had to brace himself not to flinch, "I'll try to be worthy of it."

"Er, quite. You don't happen to have any cigarettes, do you?"

"Cigarettes?"

"Oh well, it doesn't matter."

"No no—where's the box?" She got up, clutching the envelope, lurching slightly. She went round behind the couch, but came back at once. "Here."

"Thanks." He opened the silver box, took a cigarette and lit it. He glanced up at her still standing in front of him.

"She was too gentle . . . too gentle to live." Then the cosy, musing tone changed. "But why—why didn't she stand up to them?"

"Them?" He frowned. "Do you mean—Alex?"

"And Elaine. It was Elaine who persuaded him, stole him away . . . took him down to the police."

"Wait a minute, Kate—did you know last night, when I came here, when we talked in the library, did you know Alex had gone up to Hillside and later told the police he'd seen Julia at the New Inn?"

"Yes—I—I had to shake it out of him he was so sleepy, but—I did know."

"Why on earth didn't you tell me?"

She looked at him, chin slightly lifted, mute for once.

"Didn't you have an idea what that confrontation with Alex might have done to Julia? Did you have no inkling at all? Weren't you faintly worried?"

"It was none of your bloody business!"

His head was pounding; with an enormous effort of control he kept his voice calm. "Kate, I left here at exactly eight o'clock last night. If you'd told me, or even given me the faintest hint of what Alex had said, that he'd been to Hillside, I would have gone straight home. Julia was dying there then—but she was not beyond saving, not then. She might be alive now."

"Whose fault is that?"

"I'm not interested in finding fault—or laying blame. I want to know why you chose not to tell me. I want to know the truth." Then, looking at her—silent, straight, unmoving—he grasped it, with a kind of horror. "Kate—did you want Julia to die?"

"It was what *she* wanted, wasn't it?" She gave a long, sensual sigh. "She died that I might live."

268

Hugh staggered to his feet and, wincing at the pain, went over to the fire and rested his hand on the steel hood. He dropped his cigarette into the last winking embers. All right—she was entitled to her defences, entitled to protect herself, but she was taking a long step down the road her mother had taken, her father too. . . . He turned and looked at her; she'd not altered her position.

"I think you're going to have to explain that remark."

"I should have thought it would have been obvious even to you." She made an impatient gesture. "By dying, she has taken the guilt upon herself—no police suspicions can be proved now. No Kate to foist the blame on, no innocent poodle bitch. Julia has said the last word, don't you see that? The case is closed."

"It may not be quite as simple as that," he said slowly. "I've talked to the police. But be that as it may, are you saying you believe Julia killed your father?"

"Of course not. Elaine did it—but that wouldn't have stopped them from suspecting me. If it hadn't worked with Julia, I'd have been the next scapegoat."

"But Julia was there on Tuesday night—or don't you believe that either?"

"Of course she was there, why shouldn't she be? She loved Daddy too. Besides, who else could have written the letter?"

"You could have done."

"There you are, you see—you're just like all the rest. If it wasn't Julia, it must be Kate. Don't you think she didn't know that, don't you think that's why she—"

"All right! What about Elaine then—if she killed your father, as you seem to think, why shouldn't she have written the letter?"

"Elaine? She's semi-literate."

"Oh come, you told me she read Scott and—"

"Oh for God's sake—she reads him to feed her prudish little shrivelled soul obscenely dreaming of rape by knights in armour. Really, Hugh."

"And Elaine killed your mother too?"

"No, I did—don't you remember, I wrote Daddy a letter confessing it?" she said, harshly sarcastic. "I've no doubt Elaine's kept that too. What does it matter who killed Mummy? Mummy—Mummy—the word sticks in my throat. What if Julia did kill Mummy? If she did, I'd be glad. She knew how vile Mummy was, she knew how I suffered—if she did it, she did it for *me*." But the rage was somehow halfhearted, the contempt automatic, weary.

Seeing the flash of the snake ring as she reached for her whisky, hearing the thickened speech, he felt that perhaps, at long last, Mummy was finally being assimilated.

"Don't you think you're exaggerating a little what one person will do for another—or to another?"

"I've lost the only two people I've ever loved because of the two people I've always hated." She tilted the glass and swallowed.

"Two—who?"

"Elaine and Alex, of course. Did I say two? Three—I mustn't forget you." She laughed. "What a trinity—two males and a neuter."

"Kate—do you know why Julia went to the New Inn on the day of your mother's death?"

"You think you're being very clever, don't you?"

If he'd had his glasses he knew he would have seen the greenish eyes narrowed, the lips drawn back from the vixen teeth.

"My poor Hugh—it's not for Julia you grieve, is it? You're grieving for your lost innocence. Finally, after all these years, she's stopped protecting you from the reality you always tried to avoid by shutting yourself up in your consulting room or stalking the wards of the demented. Your vanity's injured, isn't it? Your professional pride wounded—an unsatisfactory termination of the case, is that what you'd say?"

"Julia was my wife—not my patient."

"So the negligence was personal rather than professional—does that make it the more—amusing?"

"Ummmm." There was nothing he could do here—nothing that anyone could do. It was time to move on. "I must be going." He picked up his stick.

"This is yours too, I think." She held up his handkerchief by one corner.

"Thank you." He thrust it into his pocket. "One other thing, Kate—do you know what Scott's dying words were?"

"Of course I do—or rather I know what Daddy always said they were, he repeated them often enough. 'God bless you all—I feel myself again.' Is that what you want?"

"Yes. Yes. Well, good night, Kate."

"Good night." And then, just as he was opening the door, she said, "Oh, there's one thing for you, too. I just want you to know that you can stay on at Hillside for as long as you wish—within reason."

As he went down the stairs he heard the lock snap. *Leave me alone.* Well, he had left her. Julia had left her. Jonathan had left her. What had he imagined she could know of Julia? She was as blind as he—blinder. Clutching her lies, like the old love letters, to her bosom, she was locked in with her pathetic bridal dead. Perhaps irrevocably. It was only a question of time before the memory of Mummy too became a celebration. In all probability she *had* killed her mother, she had certainly killed Julia; her existence now would be pitiably devoted to their ghastly resurrection.

The fog in the court was denser than at his coming, colder, more choking. He shivered. His headache was worse.

18

He rested his weight on the gatepost and struggled to get his breath. The fog formed into droplets on his face and trickled down under his collar to mingle with the sweat of his body. There'd been no buses, no taxies: "If it's an emergency, sir, you should call the police." He had walked an endless distance, each step a spear of fire in his swollen ankle. Now there was nothing but the lonely closeness of the fog, no house, no light, no wind, no dark shape rushing down The Lane. . . . Then suddenly shockingly in the dead silence, a bell rang. Hugh swivelled—the sound seemed to come from behind him—*ring-ring, ring-ring.* The phone!

He began to run then, a hobbled, agonising half jog up the drive. The front door was ajar and for a moment he paused in uncertainty despite the insistent ringing. Then, he launched himself across the dark threshold, his stick caught in his legs, he tripped, stumbled, put out his hands and caught the hall table just before he fell, rocking the instruments in their cradles. And the ring stopped. As he stood there, trembling, it came to him that it had been the private line, the black phone, nothing urgent—nothing private was urgent now.

He leaned over and switched on the light. He wiped his face carefully with his handkerchief, sodden with whisky and Kate's tears. He knew there was something he ought to do, something to do with the phone, but he couldn't remember, so it couldn't much matter. He dropped the handkerchief onto the letter tray. He had plenty of time to remember—all the time in the world, in this empty, silent house.

But not quite silent. There was a sound. He held himself breathless unmoving. There!—a kind of snuffle from somewhere inside the house. A ghostly sob—he glanced up the stairs. Nothing. It came again, this time more of a scraping, a dragging—definitely downstairs. One hand to the wall, the other grasping his stick, he limped softly down the passage, past the kitchen, past the closed door of the living room. He took three swift hobbled paces and switched on the dining-room light.

The dog on the table lifted its head and bared its teeth, growling; it was large and liver-coloured and its muzzle was covered with Mrs. Nance's goulash.

He jerked the stick up and lunged at the animal and, missing it, swept dishes and hotplate to the floor with a crash. The dog leapt down and out of the door, cannoning into Hugh's legs and swerving into the passage. Staggering, he turned and swiped vainly, then flung the stick with all his force as the white-tipped tail whisked out of the front door. The stick clattered harmlessly along the polished parquet. He picked it up and hung it on the banister.

Outside the dog was yelping in convulsive fury. Hugh took hold of the door and slammed it with all his force. The barking was cut off.

He shivered again. It was bitingly cold. He put his hand to his face. Black dead frost in the place, tears on his cheek. He shook his head—*pull yourself together, laddie.*

Taking hold of the banister, he hauled himself slowly up the stairs, his strength almost failing him. But once there, he felt better —as if moving to a higher level had cleared his head. He went to the bedroom and changed his gum boots for heel-less leather slippers. He was shocked at his appearance in the bathroom mirror— black streaks on the cheeks, bloodshot eyes, dark stubble. The Beast, indeed. He washed himself carefully, scrubbing the nicotine stains from his fingers with pumice, brushed his teeth, then shaved —the insect buzzing of the razor was soothing. He combed the remnants of hair, straightened his tie. He opened the medicine cabinet—Librium, Sinequan, Mandrax, Tuinal. . . . No. He had homework to do.

He switched on the light in Julia's bedroom. It too was full of fog. He shut the window and drew the curtains. He lifted the poems out of the drawer, looked up at the little girl's sardonic smile—she had watched it all: dogs, horses, Keats, sleep, nightmare, death, and not one golden ringlet was disarrayed.

Downstairs, he went past the waiting room and into the almost unused living room. Living room?—no, sitting room, Julia called it. *I passed the time redecorating the sitting room.* It would not be redecorated now; it was already like a museum and Kate wouldn't alter it—the winter landscapes, the stark metal lamps, the skeleton chairs, the dead gaze of the TV. A shrine. Suddenly he wanted noise—loud blasting noise. A military band—a fight—a football match. He went to the set and jabbed a button— ". . . bring you our early evening in-depth study on rabies—how near is the menace, are our island shores protection enough or—" He switched it off.

Slowly he moved to the table—the only wooden object in the whole room, except the logs in the fireplace. He sat down and opened the notebook.

> The function of nightmare
>
> The function of nightmare
> is to disguise with
> terror true delight
> to prevent sweet dream
> of enemies stone dead
> of you and your
> paramour abed.
> In lethargy of fright
> you go to the door
> to shut out
> lover ascending
> heart's stair into light.
> Trembling later alone
> you lie till dawn
> in gratitude at grief
> for the still unknown
> undead unborn,
> high on the dry reef
> of separate safety
> you celebrate and sorrow.
> But my self having met
> my sister arising
> and having put her down
> there is no longer

273

any dream-devising
solace for tomorrow
and promise gone.
Pain is no opposite
of pleasure, nor
wounds, of joy;
guilt is the disconsolate
destroyer of hope of days
and heart's delight
afoot on the dark stair.
Reality is always
worse than the nightmare.

Hugh raised his head. There was not the faintest rustle of sound in the whole house—no scratching of rats in the wainscoting. Only the dry desolate whisper of her words: . . . *having met / my sister arising / and having put her down* . . . He searched his mind, back to his student days . . . *artistic ability is intimately connected with sublimation, but we have to admit its nature is inaccessible to us.* . . . Jung? Ferenczi? No, Freud. But that didn't help—what did imagination do to reality, or nightmare?

He longed for the patter of raindrops on the window. Or the crackle of logs in the grate—and the warmth. But he knew he had to read this cold. Again he bent his head close to the page: *Sister no sister . . . At gaze . . .*

At last he finished. He turned back to the first one he'd read —*Green silk death*—and at that moment the phone rang. Rising, he knocked the folder onto the floor, the spring clip popped open and the poems scattered. He stopped and started to gather them, then turned and lumbered into the hall.

"Welchman speaking."

"Stand here. Been trying to get hold of you. Well, did you see him?"

"Sorry. I, er, got lost in the fog. Alex, you mean. Yes—yes I saw him. We had quite a long—chat." He took a long breath. "I believe he's telling the truth. I'm bound to say I think—I think he did see Julia at the house on the Tuesday night."

"I see." There was a pause. "I'm sorry, old man."

"However, there is a—a bit of a problem. He doesn't know about Julia's death. I didn't tell him—I felt, in the circumstances, coming from me . . . he feels responsible enough as it is. But he's got to know sooner or later and I'm—I'm uneasy."

274

"Of course. I understand. Quite right. Better do it myself, what?"

"I think it would be wise, perhaps tomorrow morning—"

"Right you are. I'll get over there first thing, before the papers." He cleared his throat. "Look, I, er, had a word with Morehouse. Your wife wasn't pregnant—so there's no need to worry about that. As a matter of fact, old man, she was wearing a coil, so there doesn't seem to have been much possibility in that direction."

"I see. No. Well, thanks."

"Not at all. Er, how's that ankle of yours holding out?"

"Ankle? Oh—oh, it's all right, thanks."

"Keeping it up, I hope? Won't do it any good to go running about the place, you know."

"Yes, quite. Well . . ."

"Well, good night then, Welchman."

Running about the place—*however I move or run, I remain unmoving . . .* unfecund . . . infertile . . . sterile. Unconceived—inconceivable. He smiled. And then his whole body began to shake. Clasping the table he sank slowly to his knees. How long since he had knelt— or prayed, like Alex in Ely Cathedral? Not since he was eight: *No, Ma, I won't, I don't believe in it!* Later, *All right, lad, we know it's all a load of balls, but you don't want to upset your mother now, do you? And look at it this way—there's just an outside chance it might be true. There's always an outside chance. So you might as well be on the safe side.*

And that's all there'd been—a very outside chance. On the safe side—that's where she'd been, where she'd put herself, and made of him, of hope, a rank outsider. Julia, Julia—she who had lain *till dawn / in gratitude at grief / for the still unknown / undead unborn.* He was wracked by a spasm of dry sobs—dry, *dry on the high reef / of separate safety!* Dry, deceitful, deliberate, lying, defeating . . . And Hugh Welchman, faithful husband, deceived, defeated intruder in the forever empty womb . . . the fond forever dreaming fool . . . no birth, but death—death all around him . . .

After a long time he lifted his head and saw the handkerchief lying on the salver. Whisky tears, Welchman. Whisky. With infinite effort he pulled himself up. He held out his hand—it trembled gently. No, a cigarette was what he needed. Even one of Julia's Turkish gaspers.

In the waiting room he switched on a lamp and, reaching over to the mantelpiece, opened the ebony box. Something crackled under his fingers—an envelope. He looked at it—*Hugh,* the one word in green ink—and his heart leapt.

The letter inside was typed:

Friday

Dear Hugh,

I have not written you very many letters in our life together, and I am sorry that this one—the last I shall ever write—has to be of such a squalid and miserable character.

I'm sure that in your own quiet way you have noticed a change in me the last few days, although I have done my best to disguise it, but even you could never have guessed the dreadful reason for it. Now I am at the end of my tether.

It was I who killed Arabella Brinton fourteen years ago, and I who murdered Jonathan on Tuesday night.

I fell in love with Jonathan when I was just sixteen, and I think, in some complicated tenuous way I have remained in love with him ever since. At first, for almost a year, our relationship was passionate and happy, though by its very nature, furtive. But after I went to London as a student nurse, things became increasingly strained and difficult. More difficult for him than for me—because I was in a sense becoming absorbed in a new life. But as his loneliness, his lack of resource became worse and worse, the more passionate, demanding and at times suicidal his letters to me became. Finally, one Thursday evening he phoned to say that Arabella had discovered and read my letters to him and was threatening divorce, to have him struck off, etc. He was beside himself.

Early the following afternoon I caught the train from King's Cross. When I arrived at Cambridge, the fog was so thick there were no buses, no taxis. I took a bicycle from the station yard and rode out to the New Inn. I had warned Jonathan to expect me—but I had not expected him; he was more or less incoherent with terror, trembling, more than half drunk, I thought.

I must speak a little about my own position at that time. I loved Jonathan, but I was young, I had—I thought—my life before me. I was deeply attached to the whole family, and devoted to Arabella, who had always been kind, gentle, mysteriously exciting to me. If I were to marry Jonathan—and I had, through my mother, enough means to do so—I knew that not only would the Brinton family be

276

irretrievably wrecked, but also my own father would be shattered and appalled. Nevertheless, I was determined to offer him marriage —and did so.

I remember his answer—"No no, Julia—she'd rather kill me than that!" And he started to talk of her viciousness—her insane furies in private, her smooth public face. No one could believe what she'd done, was doing to him, to the children. If he left or was forced out she'd ruin them . . . he went on, desperate, terrified, terrified that I would be found there in the house. It would be useless to talk to Arabella, he said, worse than useless. He almost thrust me out.

He'd opened the patients' door when he saw Henry Stand coming up the path. "Quick, quick—the back way," he said. As I hurried through the back hall I glanced up and saw little Alex looking down at me. I pulled up my hood, but, as I know now, too late. He vanished at once. Then, as I turned I saw the cellar door open and Arabella standing on the top step. She gave me a look of the most horrible malevolence I have ever seen on human countenance—she said nothing, but sort of hissed at me. Without thought or hesitation, I slammed the door on that hatred. I heard her fall, the smash of glass. I went on, without pausing, out of the back door, picked up the bike in the lane and rode back to the station, caught the next train.

The rest you know, Hugh—better than I. Of how you rescued me. Of how you stayed there always, beside me, not questioning, undemanding—but there, solid, kind, devoted, sane.

I have no way of explaining—far less of excusing—the fact that some years after I came back to Cambridge as a settled matron, I took up with Jonathan again. Even then, he was—pitiable. Perhaps that was the reason. Perhaps some kind of due self-punishment, some idea of penitence for my crime. He used that—of course. He knew I'd killed Arabella, though he'd not seen it. So there I rested —in unfaithful anguish. Year after year.

Until one day Alex Brinton became your patient. I think I knew at once my days were up. I might of course have warned you that I was acquainted with the family. But then Alex would simply have gone to another psychiatrist—and told his tale to a stranger. I knew he'd seen me, I knew eventually he would remember, which is why I contrived to avoid meeting him. But at least it would be *you* he told. Perhaps I could have faced *you.* One clings to the faintest hope as long as one can—but daily, almost daily, I saw it fading.

So I was not really surprised on Tuesday night—when you

were out—that Jonathan called me. He spoke so quietly I could hardly hear him, yet I caught an immense suppressed excitement in his voice. He didn't say much, just that I was to come at once, something had happened—"we're going to be happy at last."

I rode out, parked my machine in the copse at the end of the lane, and went into the house by the back door, as I'd done almost exactly fourteen years before. Then, he'd been terrified, white with anguish, almost incoherent. And yet this time, though he was superficially calmer, it was far worse. Then, for all his anxiety, he'd been sane; now, I saw at once (and I'd not seen him for a few weeks) that he'd passed some borderline of sanity. "Julia, my dear, we've had a bit of luck"; he spoke reasonably enough, but when he touched me I could feel the trembling tension in his body. And there was a kind of menacing brightness in the mechanical smile he gave me. He started talking at once rapidly but with the excitement well under control. Alex, he said, had recovered his memory of that afternoon but had got it slightly wrong—he remembered seeing a nurse pass through the hall, but he thought it was Elaine, not me. "He's sure *she* killed Arabella now. You see what a chance that is? We can hang her on it!" He chuckled. "Oh I don't mean literally— the police won't accept a boy's word—but once the word gets out, she'll be done for, I can chuck her out, divorce her, stop her vile plots against me, and Alex will be on my side!" That last was vital, because in eighteen months Alex was due to inherit the house and the money his grandfather had left, which up to now Jonathan had enjoyed the use and control of. And he still could, with Alex's support and connivance—"and Wardy will back us up too"—and get rid of Elaine too and her "machinations against me," and we, meaning him and me, could live together happily ever after. And suddenly he went off in a tirade against Elaine—how she was trying to drive him out of his mind, spying on him, opening his letters, listening to his phone calls, bringing strange men into the house to examine him, poisoning his food so that he couldn't eat any meals she prepared, even hiring detectives to spy on him if he left the house.

When he paused, I said all that was very well, but what guarantee did we have that Alex wouldn't eventually remember that it wasn't Elaine he'd seen, but me? It was a stupid thing to say, but I had to stop that sort of cold mad rage. It did stop him. "That's clever of you, Julia," he said and then he was silent for quite a long time. "Well," he said at last, almost meditatively, "then there's no alternative—we'll have to kill her." He had a plan, as if he'd thought it all out before—and perhaps he had. He'd take Alex's old Scout knife and stab her to death as she slept; he'd fix the details to look as though Alex had done it—and Alex had the motive, revenge for his mother's death. And everyone knew he was round the bend, under psychiatric care—whisky and Librium had turned his head and in a fit of crazy vengeance he'd done the deed. He'd be put away of course—criminally insane—and he, Jonathan, would then be undisputed master of the house. "We'll kill two birds with one stone." He made it all sound quite rational and casual. "Well, no time like the present," and he stood up, actually rubbing his hands.

He had always been a pitiable man, but he wasn't now, and for the first time I was frightened of him. I knew he meant it—meant every word he'd said—and would do it. Yet, to an outsider, he was not obviously mad. He had to be stopped immediately. I suggested that we have a drink and plan it properly, so that nothing was left to chance. "You always were the sensible one," he said. I made us each a stiff whisky and went to the surgery to fill the glasses with water—I found Librium in the cabinet and quickly emptied eight or ten capsules into his glass. When I went back to the study, he had sat down again at the desk and had a pad of paper and a pencil ready; and from time to time, as we planned the murder of his wife and the incrimination of his son, he would make a note. I thought he would never drink his drink, but he did at last, picking up the glass and tossing off the contents in one. He put it down, gripped hold of the edge of the desk and, staring at me, died there and then. Instant rigor, I think it's called.

I wrote the letter, did the necessary cleaning up, and left. I don't need to tell you what followed—you know more about it than I do, in any case. I knew there was no more than an even chance, if that, of the police accepting a suicide. In the last resort, rather than let any member of the family be wrongly suspected, I had determined to do what I am now doing. Perhaps I had little hope even at the beginning, but, as each needle point of suspicion and anguish swung from one to another, I knew all chance was narrowing.

Alex has just left. This was a denouement I hadn't expected, but I'm not sorry. If I don't do what has to be done now, the police will come to the house and it will be too late. So I'm locking the door against them—against you. I'm sorry for that, for all the incalculable harm I've done you. I'm sorry, I'm tired. I've had enough.

Forgive me if you can,

Julia

He looked up at the dim whiteness of his own image in the fly-specked mirror—Welchman, solid, kind, devoted, sane. The blob wavered, featureless, unformed, blind. He reached for a cigarette and sent the lid of the box clattering to the floor. He lit the cigarette tremblingly, and the match too fell, spurted, died—*dead candle in the ruined crypt.*

So this was it, this bleak document—the truth of the matter. Alex had not lied, she had been there—*why shouldn't she be? She loved Daddy too!* In the back of his head he heard the phone ring. Credulous fool.

"Oh shut up!" he shouted at the impatient instrument. Suddenly the taste of the Turkish tobacco sickened him. He threw the cigarette on the floor and stamped on it and the pain lanced upward so that he cried out "aiyeh!"

"Aiyeh!"—limping into the hall, to the last remnant of duty, he lifted the white phone. "Yes," he whispered, "Yes?"

"Oh Hugh, I'm so frightfully sorry—I've just heard the news—I'm absolutely disgusted with myself—I—"

"Who—who's this?"

"Madge—Madge Platten. But then how could you recognise me not spouting my usual filth? Darling, I'm such a dreadful beast, I—"

"Yes."

"You sound so cold. But of course you're cold, I *was* so utterly vile this morning—if only I'd known—I could literally kill myself, I—"

"Splendid idea."

"Whaaa—what?"

"Go ahead, kill yourself, you miserable promiscuous whore you, take a dozen Librium and a large whisky and—"

"Why, Hugh—I didn't know you cared!"

"You treacherous bitch—fuck off—fuck off—fuck off!" He smashed the instrument down and it broke into two even pieces across the cradle. *Beep-beep,* it said, *fuck-off, beep-beep.*

He needed a drink, a real drink—port. He pushed Julia's letter into his pocket, took a quick step forward, and groaned with the sudden agony. He leaned against the wall, panting. *Keep your foot up, Welchman. Won't do it any good to go running about the place . . .* He gave a quick little chuckle. Run! He only wanted to get to the cellar.

He unhooked his stick from the banister and half hopped along the passage into the kitchen. He pushed open the cellar door and stood there shivering. He descended the short flight with the utmost caution, clinging to the wooden rail, forcing each step. At the bottom he sighed with relief and gave another giggle. Where was the whisky? No—port. He hobbled along the rack—the '31, that was the best, Mike said. He seized a bottle and pulled it out and held it up to the bright light over the table. Looked all right. He gave it a quick shake. He took hold of the corkscrew and jabbed it into the top of the bottle, twisted rapidly and pulled. Fragments of cork fell out. He tried again, worse this time. He attempted to push the cork into the bottle, but it was stuck fast. He flung the corkscrew on the floor, picked up the bottle, and cracked the neck against the side of the table. Port spurted over his hand, but it had broken cleanly. He shut his eyes, put the bottle to his lips, and filled his mouth. Long ago the Sergeant-Major had taught him the trick of opening the throat and sinking a pint without drawing breath. He did it now.

He opened his eyes and wiped his mouth with the back of his hand. "An act of reverence," he said and laughed and waved the empty bottle. He rested his buttocks against the table and surveyed Welling's treasures—*worth a fortune at today's prices.* A fortune for Kate—she'd be a warm woman. Warm?—cold as a witch's tit. Old Welling would turn in his grave if he knew. Britain's answer to Freud. Fuck Freud. He threw the bottle at the wall—smash! One for Arthur—poor old Arthur, prince of psychiatrists, come to this, stub of an old candle, all his treasures left to a titless lizzie. And like tits the necks of the bottles protruded from their racks—stuprate nipples yearning for consummation. Hugh leaned forward, and with his stick struck off a tit. The bottle gave a little jump of life and the wine flowed gurgling, making a crimson patch on the dry sand. Excellent. He struck again—three at a time—'34—even better.

He shifted into the centre of the little cellar, putting his weight on his good foot, and began a methodical decapitation, slow at first—four here, two there, half-a-dozen at the top—then gradually faster until he found a quick swinging rhythm. The cane flashed, bottles bounced, glass shattered and the port flowed out like blood—'55 and '31, '27, '48—excellent strong, rare superb, very fine, wonderful! Thirty dozen or more—not less. He stopped at last, leaning on his stick, watching the old professor's substance chuckling to the floor—a monstrous menstruation.

He waited until the last gurgle was done, the sweat of his exertion clammy to his skin, the crypt icy—*ruined and long-forgotten* now all right. "There you are, Arthur—that's a start." But only a start—there was work for filial piety still. Give the old man a cigarette—*give us a snout, lad*—give him fire and smoke. Burning.

With care not to slither on mingled port and sand, Hugh mounted the steps, slamming the door with a back-handed thrust, leaving a trail of sticky crimson across the kitchen floor. Ignoring the ringing in his head—*ring-ring*—he hurried as fast as he could into the living room. He knelt in front of the grate—paper, kindling, light logs all ready for burning. His hands were numb with cold and the matchbox fell to the floor and the matches scattered across the hearthrug. He scrabbled for them; two broke against the side of the box, but the third he managed to light and touch to the paper. He seized the bellows and began to blow gently at the small flames and then, as they caught hold, harder and harder until he was panting and the sweat ran down his face and his cheeks burned with blood. He scooped up a handful of spilled matches and flung them into the blaze, popping and flaring—percussion to the ringing in his head. Bang-bang, trumpet and tuba—he began to hum the old cracked off-key splendour: "We are the boys of the old Brigade. . . ." Torch to the burning—but not enough, not enough. He tried to rise but his head swam. So he crawled on all fours, grabbing the strewn pages all over the floor—gathering the—*the filth a fine lady can write.* See a fine lady on a white horse—*sister no sister. And if you've got any decency you'll burn them.* Three more, two more—*old child chant.*

He crawled back to the fireplace, laid all the poems flat, pulled the letter from his pocket and smoothed it down on top.

282

Then slowly he bent forward, lower, bowing—*you're a decent chap, Welchman*—and gently, with both hands offering leaves to the flames, he placed the pile of pages into the heart of the new fire. Crouching, rocking ever so slightly, half crooning—rings on her fingers, bells on her toes—he softly rubbed the singed hair from the sticky backs of his hands. The heat struggled valiantly with the mass, the little flames darting, edges browning, ears curling, words groaning, the wind's moan rising in sob and shriek.

Shriek? He clapped his hand to his mouth, but not before he'd recognised that piercing demented cackle that stabs the rustling silence of the senile wards.

He shook his head violently, but the ringing would not cease. With one quick motion he thrust his hands into the fire and snatched out the papers, beat at the smouldering pages with his palms. As he heaved himself to his feet and hobbled into the hall, clutching the letters to his chest, the smoke rose rank in his nostrils and watered his eyes.

He picked up the black phone—the white lay, a broken albino beetle, disconsolately buzzing.

"Hello—Welchman here—who's speaking? Welchman speaking. Who's that? Cambridge 4521. I said . . ." He carefully put the receiver down. No one. Too late. He laid the singed documents on the letter tray. He knew what he had to do now. He started to chuckle, but checked it abruptly. Information that would assist the police in their enquiries . . . irresponsible to withhold information. The station—no, not the station. Ply wouldn't be at the station—he'd be at home enjoying a Woodbine with his wife, his trusted spy-spouse.

He pulled out the drawer of the table so that it fell to the floor. Christ his head ached, hours to put it back—slot it into the right twat—slot. He pored over the phone book—P for Pry, Pie—easy as —Ply, R. H. There it was. And the number. But what did H. stand for? Hercules? Hero? A heroic figure in his way, one had to admit that. But not satisfied, never satisfied—well, he'd be satisfied now, satis-fucking-fied.

"Oh, hello—Mrs. Ply? Might I have a word with your husband, spouse, you know—the Superintendent, Chief Superintendent that is, of course. Welchman—like Englishman, as it were, Doctor Welchman."

He listened to the murmuring in the background—smiled—patted the papers on the salver.

"What's all this? Who's this?"

"Ah, Mr. Ply. This is Welchman—Hugh Welchman—here. Dr. Welchman, you know."

"Well, you sound like him. You're not drunk, are you, Doctor?"

"Certainly not. Wish I was. What an idea! A professional man like me? No no no no no no. No. What I'm ringing you up about, Mr. Ply, *why* I'm ringing you up is that I have—might have, that is —some, er, information, that could possibly be useful to the police in the course of their enquiries. Is that right?"

"I see. May I ask what's the nature of this information?"

"The nature? Ah—that's the difficulty, my dear Chief Super. *Exactly* the problem—is it natural, is it unnatural? No good speculating about that of course—have to look at the statistical evidence. For instance, my late father-in-law would have said—"

"Evidence? You have something in the nature of evidence?"

"Do I? Do I not! Lots of evidence, loads of evidence."

"In that case—"

"No no—not a case. A box. A black box, to be precise. An ebony box."

"Listen here, Doctor, why don't you ring me back in the morning? It seems to me you'd be better off—"

"No, look, wait a minute. I want to—to—"

"Yes, Doctor?"

Hugh looked round the hall, it swayed slightly—he took a deep breath to steady it. "Brinton's inquest. Are you going to c-call Alex?"

"Young Brinton? That's not up to me, you know. But in view of his statement of yesterday's date, the coroner will be pretty much bound to call him. Yes."

"So in other words—my wife will be, I mean . . ."

"You'll have to be a bit more precise than that."

"Very well. I mean, what I mean is—it'll be taken as m-murder, I suppose?"

"I think there'll be a strong presumption that way, yes. I'm not talking professionally now, Doctor, but in view of the forged suicide letter of Dr. Brinton's, I can't see that any jury is likely to bring in a verdict of anything but murder."

284

"Verdict against m-my wife?"

"You're putting me in a very difficult position, Dr. Welchman. As I told you this morning, there's nothing in the nature of conclusive evidence. It's too tenuous."

"So what will the verdict be?"

"My guess would be, murder against person or persons unknown. But you never can tell with a coroner's jury, you know."

"Yes, quite. Sergeant-Major, just one m-more thing: Do *you* believe my wife killed Dr. Brinton?"

"What I believe is neither here nor there, Doctor. From a police point of view all I'm prepared to say is that I'm not satisfied." There was a pause. "Now see here, if you can produce anything in the nature of evidence that will satisfy me one way or the other, I shall be much obliged. But it doesn't seem to me you're in any fit state to decide this evening. Why don't you sleep on it—ring me in the morning, if you want to? Right?"

"M-morning . . ."

"Listen, Doctor, you're all right, aren't you?"

"Oh—yes, yes. Don't worry about m-m-me. . . ."

"Okay, Doc. But what you need is a good kip. You're dead beat, aren't you?"

He put the phone down gingerly, sliding it softly onto its cradle. The top page on the letter tray was a short poem, or end of a poem. He bent down and read:

> I cover recover
> and cover again the days
> by guile
> alone
> I stand at gaze.
> When will the hunter come?

Dead beat. Mortally tired. By the light from the living room he could see the marks of his footsteps in the passage, blemishes on the polished parquet. He moved a pace, two, took hold of the banister and began to pull himself up.

He sat on the bed and pushed off his slippers. For a moment he fought against sleep—the last time he had woken to thunder, the return of the nightmare. *The function of nightmare/is to disguise with/terror true delight.* Where was the delight? Where—had—it—ever been? Where was . . . he lay down and drew up the eiderdown. An instant before he fell asleep he realised he'd forgotten to ask Ply what the initial *H.* stood for—could it possibly be *Hugh*?

19

He sat in the University Arms dining room and slowly ate a large breakfast—porridge, tea, bacon and eggs, sausages, tomatoes, toast. A rain squall against the windows had woken him cleanly at nine o'clock. He'd bathed, shaved, restrapped his ankle with a steady hand, and dressed carefully in a dark pinstripe suit and black tie. With the Sunday papers on the hall mat he'd found a sealed box —inside, his glasses and a note:

> Dear Dr. Welchman,
>
> Our Mr. Chapman was able to come in yesterday afternoon after all. I had him attend to your little bit of Business first thing and am taking the Liberty of sending my boy round with your Spectacles, being fully cognisant of what lack of proper ocular aids means particularly to a Gentleman of your Profession. Looking forward to seeing you at your Earliest Convenience for adjustment of the Frame and
>
> > hoping to continue to Serve you,
>
> > > N. F. D. Beasely

Before leaving the house, he'd taken Julia's last letter and two of her poems from the papers on the hall table.

Now, smoking his first cigarette—he'd bought a hundred on his way into town—he looked across Parker's Piece to the grey block of the Central Police Station, half masked by the trees whose still-damp leaves glittered in the sun. He had only to walk across the green, enter the portals and say, "I've come to make a statement." Ply mightn't be there, but Sergeant Ramm would do just as well, or even P. W. C. Brandt—*I'm sorry about your wife, Doctor.*

No wife. No child.

It was a temptation; it was, after all, why he had come—to

show those sad dead pages. Yet he was resistant; he was not ready for it. He needed to think—to feel.

He stubbed out his cigarette and paid his bill and left the hotel.

In Mill Lane he drew the car slowly into the curb and switched off. He sat still, with his eyes shut, for a few minutes—*grief//for the still unknown/undead unborn. I'm sure in your own quiet way you have noticed a change in me the last few days* . . . Oh yes—he'd noticed all right; the little flags on the steepening descent to discomfiture, desperation, defeat, decease, he blind-eyed self-deceiving, had seen as a break, a thaw, approach of spring, a quickening. . . . In each sign of the demise, he'd seen deliverance. With his fantasy of pregnancy he'd sought to ward off the imminent sense of death that had been daily all about him.

Not for nothing in his nightmare had he willed her dead.

He got out, took his stick, locked the car.

Ten minutes later he sat on the wall, the sun warming his baldness and the tankard of bitter cool to his hand, his mind blank, listening to the undergraduate chatter.

A flurry of wind freckled the water and sent a girl's light white summer hat spinning and her companions chasing. All laughed. This was the serene and normal Sunday world. Was he going to have to start again and learn it all anew—or stay stuck up a pole as everything vanished over the weir's sill?

He shook his head violently and the beer sloshed over the rim of the tankard.

"I say, you ought to watch out what you're doing, you know."

"What—what?" Hugh blinked in the bright sun.

"You've spilled beer all over this young lady's frock."

He stared at the stain seeping across the green silk thigh.

"Good heavens! Do look!" came a lilting voice, "if it isn't the randy old beast!"

"I say, Sylvia, has this bloke been annoying you?"

"He's always hanging about the college, barging into women and trying to break down doors."

"Well, I should watch out—he looks as though he's going to pinch your lovely bottom any minute now."

"Oh, it's not me he's after—it's Dr. Kate."

"I thought she was queer."

"Oh shut up, Tony."

"I say, you know, don't you think you ought to apologise?"

"Leave him alone—it doesn't matter."

"What—oh, I'm sorry," Hugh cleared his throat, "I hope I haven't . . . very sorry."

"Well, I suppose you'll have to be content with that, old girl."

They drew away a little, chattering.

"Tony, must you go shouting it all over Cambridge?"

"What on earth's wrong with being queer? Some of my best friends are as gay as mudlarks."

"And about as filthy."

"Don't tell me she hasn't come out of the closet?"

"Perhaps he's her latest?"

"Do shut *up*!"

"No, I mean a transvestite, like that chap—"

"Beauty disguised as the beast?"

"Shut *up*!"

And they all broke into giggles.

Hugh stood up shakily, with the vague intention of moving, but instead leaned on his stick and stared up at the sky flecked with tiny white clouds.

A gentle touch on his shoulder made him start; the glass slipped out of his hand and shattered on the cobblestones.

"Christ, the poor old bloke's as pissed as a newt!"

"My dear Hugh—I'm frightfully sorry!"

"Oh hello, Mike. That's all right." He could feel the beer soaking into his shoe. "I didn't really want it—just habit."

"You didn't? Are you sure?" Mike's face was quite white; he was almost absurdly distressed. "Let me get you something else. What'll it be?"

"Oh—whatever you're having."

"Gin—gin and tonic. Right. Wait here—don't go away." He went off, weaving skilfully through the summery crowd, though with less than his usual spring of step. But when he returned a few minutes later—a distinguished figure despite the careful insouciance of baggy trousers and patched jacket—he seemed to have regained a little of his poise. "Well," he said, handing Hugh a glass and raising his own, "I need this."

Hugh took a sip, remembering how much he disliked the taste of tonic.

"I thought I might find you here—or rather, Reg did. She wants you back for lunch, we both do, that is, if . . . ."

"Lunch?" He thought of Reg's odd foreign dishes, then realised he was hungry enough to eat anything. "Thank you, I should like that very much."

"Good. Hugh, my dear, I just want to say how desolated I am, we are, about Julia. It's a—a most dreadful shock." His face whitened again and his lip trembled. "Charlie told me this morning about . . . and Alex phoned too."

"Alex—what about?"

"Just to say he's coming back into college tomorrow. Do you think that's all right? Is he up to it?"

"I'm not sure, Mike. I think we'll have to wait and see. Did you get the impression he knew about Julia?"

"I didn't—I assumed . . . Hugh, Charlie said, but I can't . . . I mean, is it true he went to the police and accused Julia of, well, of having . . ."

"He didn't accuse Julia of anything, Mike. He just said he'd seen her at the New Inn on both occasions."

"Isn't that pretty, well, damning?" He drained his glass quickly.

"It depends. Not necessarily." He looked out across the dazzling pool, with its ducks and velvet-headed drakes, to the three budded willows on the little bank under the bridge. "It's a complicated story."

"Perhaps you don't want to talk about it?"

"Yes—I think I do." But it was Reg he really wanted to talk to —the last of the trio his unconscious had assigned to the fatal punt. "But not here."

"Of course, of course." He took Hugh's glass and put it together with his own under the wall. "Have you got a car or—"

"Yes. But, Mike, do me a favour, will you? I want to walk a little—would you take the car round and meet me on the other side of King's Bridge? Here are the keys, it's in Mill Lane—the Rover, you know it."

"Of course I will," then as Hugh took a step, Mike seemed to notice the stick for the first time. "But, my dear chap, you're lame —are you sure—"

"Yes yes. Nothing—just twisted the ankle slightly."

Mike smiled faintly, "How does one do that in your most sedentary of professions?"

"I fell down the stairs."

He limped slowly across Silver Street Bridge and followed the path across Queen's Green. There was an air of gaiety about the scene, the scent of Sunday food, a shout of merriment and a light ripple of answering laughter, couples in blazers and flannels and pale summer dresses, a big-bottomed bicyclist earnestly pedalling back to Newnham, green leaves rustling, the ice-cream man doing a rapid business from his van.

Once a dog lurched across his path, hunched in pursuit of an invisible prey.

Once he thought he saw the ancient anti-litter academic, but it might have been any old man mumbling.

Leaning against the stone balustrade, he forced himself to recollect the happiness he'd felt here just two days ago. Just as his mother had gone out each Sunday, come rain or sun, to tend the grave of her dead daughter, his unknown sister, so he had come to this place. Harriet had died of diphtheria, and Julia of no less ugly a disease. And Hugh, who had devoted himself to reparation of his father's crimes—ignorance, neglect, arrogance, brutality—had ended by committing those same crimes himself, more subtle but no less punishing, and in the same place: home. The haven had been a trap; protection—constriction; respect of privacy—another name for deprivation.

He did not know where Julia would have chosen to be buried —perhaps beside her father in the city cemetery, on the road to the New Inn. But, for him, her real grave lay here on the crown of King's Bridge, where the river ran in a glittering moment of remembered joy—down to disaster.

"No, not in there," Mike said as Hugh turned into the living room, "we go along here." He led the way down the hall, through a small untidy library, and out onto a long sun porch, with straw mats and wicker furniture and a whole row of potted geraniums running the length of the window.

"What a nice place."

"Nice? It's a horror actually—ruins the line of the house, but as Reg and I are seldom in the garden to see the beast, we decided to leave it. Sit sit. I must just pop out to the kitchen—I'm the cook on Sundays." He smiled. "Don't worry—my style's roast beef and Yorkshire. But I have got a rather curious little Auxey-Duresses that

I think might go well. Still, I don't see why we can't have a dry martini if we want—or would you prefer sherry?"

"Martini, please." The chair creaked gently as he sat. The porch was warm and earthy with the scent of geraniums and, though it was bright with sun, blinds were set to prevent the direct dazzle. He lit a cigarette.

They came in together—Reg in jeans and an old shirt and her hair drawn tight at the back, so that she looked like a child. She bent down and put her cheek against Hugh's for an instant, then took her place beside Mike on the long wicker couch.

"Mike says you want to talk?"

He nodded, but again he felt a reluctance. He took a sip of the martini and felt its icy shiver at the back of his neck. Carefully he set the drink down on the glass-topped table beside him. "Yes, but before I do, there are a couple of things—three actually—I'd like you to read." He took the papers from his pocket and passed them to Reg. "The letter I found last night. The poems, I don't know—they were probably written a fair time ago. There are several others, but these two are the relevant ones, I think."

Reg had her legs curled under her; Mike sat, hunched forward a little, elbows on knees. There was no sound except the faint rustle of paper as they passed a page one to the other and, now and again, the faint play of wickerwork as Hugh shifted to tap the ash from his cigarette. Above the scarlet line of the geraniums, the countryside, half glimpsed through the bushes and old apple trees in the garden, lay green and unmarred and open—spires and clock-towers brought close by the clarity of the day; but still dominated by the stub of the University Library in the foreground.

"Hugh—I'm at a loss." Mike was white-faced, a tremor in his voice. "I can't believe—"

"Of course you can't," Reg said quickly, softly, "none of us can, can we, Hugh? Not this—this missive."

He felt a flush of unease—doubt? gratitude? guilt? "Well, I think . . . if it wasn't for the poems. It's the poems that worry me, Reg. Not the *nightmare* one so much perhaps, although that bit about *having seen my sister arising and put her down* is—"

"*Put down* is current idiom for reject. *Put* isn't *push.*"

"No, well. I do know that. But it's the other—*Green silk death*—that I find, well, difficult."

Reg glanced down, shuffled the pages, then read aloud; but

after the first few lines, she raised her head and looked out of the window.

Eat a green apple
under a spring sun
and smile at remembrance
of how the seasons come
to furnish the trees
or make a flower dance,
of how the winds fleece
the sky or bare a branch
or toss a roof tile
onto a flagstone.

As a blind woman
must every day retrieve
what night has taken,
so sedulously I weave
reflection
to recollection,
one to another one
in semblance
of the forsaken—
sunless the spring day—
who stood above her
at the cellar door
and sent her spinning
in green silk arabesque
to the rock floor below—
and so spun I
vertigo
into a stony nevermore.
Shut out of season—
no weather here no time—
such doing is never done
undoing undone
there is no
rhyme or rhythm no
reason that can restore
green apple smile
under a fallen sun.

She spoke the words in an ordinary, almost casual manner, but now, as she ceased, they rested, a live thing in the room.

"Reg—you know that poem."

"I know all Julia's poems." She smiled. "What troubles you about this one, Hugh?"

"Well—*the forsaken . . . who stood above her/at the cellar door/and sent her spinning*—isn't that a clear admission that she did push Arabella?"

"Only if you assume two things: first that Julia is the 'I' of the poem, and, second, that Julia was the 'forsaken.' But Julia wasn't forsaken; if anything, she'd done the forsaking. She forsook Jonathan, who in turn of course, with all his little affairs, had forsaken Arabella."

"Jonathan?" Hugh slowly stubbed out his cigarette. "Then you think after all that—that what Julia wrote in Jonathan's suicide note *was* the truth of the matter?"

"It might be. But there are those words *in semblance,* which implies a very close identification with the forsaken, who is the one who clearly did the pushing."

"Kate." Hugh frowned. "Yes—certainly Julia did identify with Kate to some extent. And I suppose one could say that Kate *was* forsaken by Arabella. . . ."

"And by Julia too, eventually," Reg said sadly.

"Then—then you know about Julia and Kate?"

"Yes. And now you've found out too?"

"I—I have been told." He took off his glasses and rubbed his face, his eyes. "I've seen evidence." The town had disappeared, all he could see was a vaguely moving mass of variegated greenery. "Julia changed her will just before she died—she left everything to Kate."

"She what?" Mike's voice was scandalised. "My dear fellow, how simply . . . but I'm sure that can be challenged, in the, er, I mean, in the circumstances . . ."

"Unsound mind?" Hugh smiled faintly. "I don't care about all that, Mike."

"There's another very obvious point that implicates by omission," Reg said, "and that's that Julia's letter makes no mention of Kate at all."

"Yes." Hugh finished his martini and lit a cigarette. "I went to see Kate last night." Had it only been last night? There must have been an unfelt current of air on the porch, for the smoke moved languidly to the left, twisting and unravelling in the rays of the sun.

"And?"

"Ummm? The prognosis is none too good. I'm afraid she's

rather badly out of contact with reality. I'm thinking of what the poem says—the *stony nevermore. . . ."*

"I hope you're wrong," Mike said. "Scholars like her are not two a penny."

"Don't be a fool, Mike," Reg said gently.

"I'm sorry—I . . ." He looked from Reg to Hugh and back again. "But aren't we then to conclude that Kate murdered her mother and her father, and that Julia . . ."

There was an absolute silence, a perfect stillness.

"Well?" Mike cleared his throat. "Am I wrong? Isn't that what Julia's letter is all about? Well—isn't it?"

Hugh was aware that they were both looking at him. "I believe Julia was there at the New Inn that night, Mike," he said slowly. "Alex saw her—I'm satisfied of the truth of that. *Before* I brought Kate home. And I'm pretty sure Julia wrote Jonathan's purported last letter."

"But then you're saying that Julia . . ." He made a quick gesture that spun his glass from the table—an instant flash of gin—unbroken onto the straw mat. "Look," he said, "couldn't Brinton have been dead or dying when she arrived—why *not* suicide, or an accidental overdose?"

"He commits suicide," Reg said, "and then someone conveniently arrives to write the note he forgot to leave?"

"I know that sounds fantastic," he picked up his glass, "but surely . . ."

"I don't believe in suicide," Hugh said. "It doesn't fit the clinical picture. He thought he had everything to live for. He was triumphant—euphoric. And that's heavily against it being an accident, as well—besides he was a careful man about medication."

"But if it wasn't Julia . . ." Mike was gripping his empty glass tightly. "Surely to God you're not suggesting that—that Alex had anything to do with it?"

"It has to be considered," Hugh said reluctantly. He put on his glasses. "We must remember that he'd just suffered a series of shocks—he thought he remembered seeing his stepmother in the front hall, that therefore she'd killed his mother, been assured by Jonathan that it must have been an accident and *then* overheard him threatening Elaine with exposure. For Alex, Arabella was no more than a half-recollected figure out of a menacing past. But his stepmother is his closest, perhaps his only, affective connection, his stability rests largely on her. Whatever the crimes he imputed to her, he loves her."

"Hugh—Hugh, that's too unbelievably pat!" He gave a short harsh laugh. He blinked rapidly, then took out a handkerchief and began to dab at the few drops of gin spilled on the glass table-top. "I can't believe it," he muttered, "Alex? That gentle boy, model of English decency—a decent chap, a thoroughly decent chap . . ."

"Mike, oughtn't you to look at the beef?"

"What? Oh—the beef. You're quite right, Reg." He stood up. "I must attend to the lunch. I must open the Auxey." But he stood there for a moment, as if not sure of which way to turn.

When he'd gone, Reg said, "May I have one of your cigarettes, Hugh?"

He gave it her, lit it. "Reg—were you in love with Julia?"

"I loved her."

"I don't think that's quite what I mean."

"But it's more important than what you mean. Yes, we had 'an affair.' Of course I was in love with her! But she was unattainable. That was part of the condition—one couldn't possess Julia. Which is what Kate Brinton didn't understand. You realise of course that whole business in her letter about a continuing affair with Jonathan is a simple substitution—Jonathan for Kate?"

"Yes, I suppose so." He looked out over the countryside rich in spring with a sensation of desolate relief. "And it was after Kate that you . . ."

"I tried to help her to 'get over' Kate, yes—me among others —but I never knew the nature of the obstacle. . . ."

"Others?"

"It wasn't always bridge or tennis, you know. I'm going on the lines that it's better for you to know the facts."

"The facts," he murmured. "But what—I mean what was she looking for?"

"Hugh, I tried to prepare you a bit the other night. It's a different territory, this—from yours. You'd talk of borderline schizophrenia, apathy, flattening of affect—"

"Reg. I think you underestimate me."

"Perhaps, but she was suffering—she wasn't looking for anything. She was living it through, easing a consuming pain. I think at heart she wanted to let go, but she wouldn't. She was courageous with a gentle passion. But I'm not sure any of us were much good to her. I think she was happiest alone." She blew a long blue plume of smoke and Hugh watched it buffet the window and curl and cling to the glass. He felt at a loss—they were talking about someone he didn't know—but not betrayed.

"And yet," he said, "she did let go."

"I don't think so. That's what I'm trying to say. Her death isn't a de-defeat," for the first time there was a quaver in her voice, "only a defeat for us. She had a purpose."

"The letter." He sighed.

"You're going to use it, aren't you?"

"It will clear them all." He picked the olive from his glass and ate it.

Reg looked down at her hands, turned them palm upward. "The dead are most obliging scapegoats—they neither suffer nor protest. People will say she was 'a bit of a bad lot.' 'Welchman,' they'll say, 'picked a dud, poor chap.' How simple to denigrate the dead, and what will we suffer?—nothing more than a little dishonour."

"It will clear them," he repeated.

"And what about the truth of it?" she said bitterly, clenching her hands, "what about that?"

Hugh dropped the olive stone in the ashtray. "Truth," he said dully, "even if we knew what it was, is not necessarily therapeutic. Not for the living."

20

The sky was heavily overcast as he left the Semples, but he reached home before the rain. In the hall he hung his stick on the banister and took Julia's poems from his pocket and put them with the others on the salver, her last letter on top. He was lethargic with food and wine, the oppression of the day, reluctance to pick up the phone and dial the police. He was filled with the desolation of that decision.

He opened the waiting room door. On the floor by Julia's chair was a towel and the bowl of water Stand had used to bathe his foot —the lid of the ebony box, the cigarette he had stamped out. Slowly he went from room to room—the dried bloody footsteps in the kitchen, the cellar's churned crimson sand, the reek of wine, broken plates and smeared goulash in the dining room, the living room's burned-out fire, the beige hearthrug speckled with the scars of fallen sparks. In Julia's study the French windows were open and rain had stained the polished parquet and wind flurried the bright seed catalogue to the floor. Who could have believed so much ruin in so short a time?

As he mounted the stairs he felt the full force of the strangeness of this house—of his strangeness in it. And even more so in Julia's bedroom. *A different territory, this—from yours.* He had inhabited it, but not known it. The little girl regarded him from the wall, enigmatic, unattainable—*that was part of the condition.* But that wasn't acceptable. He'd been drawn into the wound and now . . . now what? Where was he to start? He moved close to the bookshelf. Keats? Blake? Marvell? Sexton, Bishop, Plath—Scott?

A quick flicker of rain against the window roused him. He limped along the passage to his own room—there at least he knew where he was. There was a cure that had never failed him yet—work. Two days of messages on the tape. He sat down, lit a cigarette, took pencil and pad from the drawer, and depressed the playback button.

"This is Dr. Welchman's residence. Dr. Welchman is not . . . leave your name and . . . Doctor will ring you back."

The tape hissed dustily for a moment and then:

"Hugh—this is Julia."

The pencil snapped in his fingers.

"When you hear this, I shall be dead. If not, then I ask you not to try to revive me, let me go—for I'm already gone in spirit.

"First, practical matters. In my black cigarette box on the waiting room mantelpiece there is a letter—it's addressed to you, but of course it's meant for the police, or the coroner.

"Then my will. I've left everything to Kate. I know you're absolutely uninterested in possessions, but all the same you will be hurt. Don't be. Your hurt will be far less than Kate's. For her, perhaps, it will convey some meaning, some solace—some hope. At any rate, it's the best I can do.

"My poems are in the top drawer of my chest of drawers. They are for you. If you find difficulty with any of them, ask Reg—she has helped me with most.

"Now for the hard part—the truth." There was a pause of several seconds—Hugh sat staring at the recorder—then she continued, a little huskily at first. "Whatever the truth may be—there is none of it, or very little, in my letter. I shall try to keep it in order, to begin at the beginning. . . .

"The beginning." She gave a sigh—or a smothered cough, restraint of tears. "It was the New Inn of course, as I've told you. The Brintons—such a large family and so lively, or so it seemed to me who was used to impassive days with my lonely father. I loved them all at once—from baby brother to the handsome, noble doctor, from Kate with her secret smile to the mother beautiful and mysterious, secluded in her shrine of a drawing room. To my unblemished innocence, they were everything the heart could desire. Falling in love with Jonathan was hardly more than an extension of this feeling—the excitement, the secret trysts, the sense of womanhood, even the sex were not measurably more important to me than the long winding afternoon rides in the autumnal mists with Kate talking and laughing or the huge teas in the glowing kitchen or the gruff heartiness of Henry Stand or a sudden smile from the quiet little boy beside me. But what *was* more important, or gradually became so, were the times I was invited to drink a glass of sherry with Arabella, or, later, to spend long summer afternoons in her cool chamber.

"Last night, I told you of what Father had said, had felt, about Arabella. In a slow, vague innocent way I came to feel the same thing. It was a feeling of a different order to all the rest. Of course, by this time I knew how vile she was to Kate, how she disdained Jonathan, ignored Alex, even how casually cruel she was to the dog. But that was beside the point—she fascinated me quite beyond that. I was breathless in her presence. Suspended. It was not just her words, but her every movement of head or hand was charged with significance. Then one day she happened to touch me on the arm, above the elbow—just like that, a gesture. Now I feel sure it was calculated, but then—then I was brought alive! Her fingers on my bare flesh—I was wearing a short-sleeved linen dress—changed me into a different being. Just that, just that touch—I trembled for days, I understood nothing. It was as if before she had been *describing* music to me, but this contact was like the open chord of a great symphony. It opened a new world to me—a new heaven, I thought. How was I to guess that it would turn out to be a hell, from which I would never escape?

"I said nothing to her; I was afraid she would laugh lightly and dismiss it. It didn't dawn on me then that she might be puzzled, unhappy at my lack of response. And then suddenly I was sent away—I've often thought that it might have been Arabella herself who told Father about Jonathan and me. For that had continued—as if in another, quite separate existence—although now it had to be carried on by correspondence. Gradually I tried to withdraw, but as I did so, he became more exigent, but I saw the falseness of his feeling—and of my own. I came back one Christmas, and, as he and I made love for the last time, I thought only of Arabella. I saw her too—she was ill, haggard, terribly deteriorated. I smiled and said nice words, I kissed her cheek on parting. I was convinced that it had meant nothing to her, she had forgotten me, I had never been more than the idle companion of her empty moments. Other vacations I was hardly at home—I went to Vienna, Venice, Prague. All the places she had talked of, the churches, museums, music—and yet their beauty cut me to the quick, it stabbed me sometimes with an actual physical pain. As I was discovering the world, so I was losing it. The richness made me only the more desolate.

"When Jonathan phoned me one evening at Aunt Bel's to tell me Arabella had found my letters to him, I was angry at first—he wasn't supposed ever to phone me. And then he went on and on, urging me to come down—he was frightened—'you've no idea what she's capable of,' he said, 'she's maniacally jealous.' Jealous! I said all right, I'd come. As I put down the phone, I felt a strange stirring —I can almost feel it now. I knew what Arabella felt for Jonathan —nothing—so it was not him she was jealous of. And then it burst over me—like sudden sunlight on a grey sea, glittering, breathtaking. She was jealous of me! She loved *me*! I remember standing by the phone, dazed. I couldn't sleep that night at all; I played music softly and danced to myself, I laughed, I wept with joy, from my bedroom window I watched the darkness pass into dawn in the square below . . . it was the happiest night of my life."

Her voice was full of that joy; she paused, and Hugh found himself absorbed in her memory—that slow dance in the shadowed room, alone. They'd never danced together; he didn't know how, had never learned.

"It was Arabella I went to see that afternoon. Arabella—Arabella. I would do anything, be anything she wanted—I'd go away with her, care for her, cherish her, give her the rest of my life. I was elated, transported—I felt like a bride—and, as I cycled from the station to the New Inn, the fog secretly wrapped me like my love, silent, total, obscuring all else.

"And then he wouldn't let me see her! He was terrified, beside himself, I should never have come, he said. When he saw Henry coming up the garden path, he simply panicked, bundled me out of the surgery. But then as I was halfway across the hall he called me —a harsh whisper: 'Come back, come back!' Perhaps he'd seen the open cellar door, I don't know. Oh, if only I had listened!" It was a sudden sharp cry.

"But I didn't. I saw the white flash of Alex's face, then looked down into the cellar. She was at the bottom of the steps, hunched over, clutching a bottle; but something, some instinct, or Jonathan's whisper, made her raise her head. I've never seen such malevolence on the face of a human being. 'Get away—get out of this house!' The words were soft, slurred, but they pierced me like daggers.

"I could hardly manage to push open the swing door—I was in a nightmare of slow motion. I stood in the back hall paralysed—I wanted to run, but I couldn't. I might have screamed, but I had no voice.

"At that moment Kate opened the door of the dining room. 'Julia darling—why whatever is the matter? You look as though you'd seen a ghost.' And then I was filled with an overwhelming fear—fear for her, fear for myself. All I could do was babble: 'Get back and shut the door, get back to whatever you were doing. Don't go into the front hall, you mustn't go into the front hall. Keep away, Kate, keep away!' And she looked at me in that cool green-eyed way of hers and said, 'All right, Julia, if that's what you want, I shall. I was reading Keats—at least *he* won't run away without saying hello properly.' I watched her go back and shut the door. And then I was off and running. And I've never stopped running since—until now."

There was a silence except for Julia's laboured breathing; then a thump and a scraping sound—laying down the receiver, pushing the chair back. And no sound at all. A minute—two. Three. He'd lost her.

"Julia!" he called, "Julia—come back!"

He took off his glasses and covered his eyes with his hand.

And then she came. "Hugh—sorry, but I was feeling dopey. I fetched a glass of whisky. Better now.

"On the ride back the fog throttled me, I thought it would never end, and in the rain the heat was choking. Aunt Bel took one look at me and pushed me off to bed with aspirin, hot water bottles, blankets. I burned and froze and froze and burned. I don't remember the night, but in the early morning the fever cleared. I crept down to the hall and phoned the New Inn—I had to explain to Kate, I told myself, but there was a deeper dread compelling me. I knew she was usually the first up, and she answered at once, as though she'd been waiting for the call. 'Mummy's dead,' she said. 'She fell down the cellar steps. But it's quite all right. It was only an accident. I'm not supposed to say anything about it. They're sending us away to Yorkshire. I—oh bother, that awful nurse thing's coming. I'm sorry, I'm afraid you have the wrong number.'

"I went straight upstairs and started swallowing aspirin as fast as I could—but Aunt Bel caught me at it. Did she ever tell you? I thought she might have perhaps—anyway, suddenly there you were—serious, earnest, upright, with all the sweet simplicity of daylight. I couldn't have managed those days without you—you were so patient, kind. Not just days—without you, I'd never have managed all these *years*. You've *always* been so kind. So kind. Oh Hugh—and how have I rewarded you? I . . ."

"It's all right, Julia," he said gently, "it's all right, my dear."

She paused, as though she had heard him, and when she resumed, her tone was firmer. "Those next years, I tried to push it all away. I tried to be a—a good wife. I wrote to Kate regularly, I had to do that, though she never replied. Because all the time I had to fight against the fear that Kate pushed Arabella—I didn't *know*, I told myself. I tried to take my stand on the evidence—that Maida had done it—oh yes, I knew all about the inquest. Or Jonathan— he was a compulsive door-shutter. Or Elaine—or even Wardy. *That* was not frightful. I clung to my ignorance, and sometimes I almost believed it. I struggled to keep the distance between the illusion of Kate's innocence and the weight of my own guilt—a distance into which so much of my life sank silent without a splash.

"I know you would say that the loss of Arabella was closely related to the loss of my own mother—the lost world of childhood love. But Arabella was my lover, my hope and chance of total passionate involvement—lost at the moment of discovery, never to be recovered. I've heard you say sometimes that most of life is boring most of the time. Well, I thought, perhaps he's right. There is nothing more. And I accepted it, tried to accept it." She gave a little laugh—of bitterness, regret, irony? He could not tell.

"And then one day it was all blown away—pouf! I ran into Kate in Heffers, a raw foggy afternoon just the same as when Arabella died. Kate isn't at all like her mother physically—she takes after Jonathan—and yet there's a grace, a gesture now and again, a turn of the head so like Arabella's it would make me gasp. And it leapt into my heart that I'd found her again, found Arabella—and in loving Kate I could undo all I'd done, repair it, recover the past, retrieve my life. In a way I knew this was perfect madness—but I'd been sane too long. And oh the burden of that sanity!"

And Julia laughed then—gay, carefree. And suddenly he thought her there, in the room—he half stood, then sank back again.

"My nightmares vanished. I forgot them—pushed them away. I ignored the faintly fearful corner in my mind, and I *was* happy. Happy in the way the whole world lifts as you see your love come tripping . . ." She paused. "I'm sorry—I don't mean this to be a love story—God knows it's not that—and even less to pain you unnecessarily. But it *is* necessary that you understand I was capable of another kind of happiness to the calm companionate one we've shared so long: a wild joy, a mountain madness. . . ." She coughed. And then she went on more calmly.

"Of course I never told Kate about Arabella. I never even told her how much I loved her, Kate. I exercised restraint. And perhaps I was wise, for one day I came tumbling down the mountain of joy —down onto our old flat Fens where the witches ride in the night. It was in London—I'd gone up to shop and spend one of the rare nights Kate and I had together. We stayed at the Cumberland, in suitable anonymity among the tourists. We'd been to see a performance of *The Magic Flute,* I remember, and gone to sleep smooth with love. Then in the middle of the night I suddenly came fully awake —Kate was sitting up in bed beside me with a strange little smile on her face. I knew at once it was a nightmare. 'Kate,' I said, 'Kate.' 'No,' she answered, 'No, I won't help you up.' Then she raised both hands palm outwards: 'Down you go!' she said and made a pushing motion, 'down among your dirty old bottles!'

"So then of course it was not just her nightmare, it was mine too. After a minute or two she woke up and turned to me and said, 'Julia, whatever is the matter? You look as if you'd seen a ghost.' It was that—that same phrase—that struck the heart out of me. I shan't try to describe the rest of that night—but she told me in the end. Imploring her not to go into the front hall was the very thing I ought not to have done. Of course she went—by the door that gives directly into the front hall. Arabella was almost at the top step, panting, labouring, and she begged Kate to give her a hand. And then . . . Afterwards she went back to the dining room; then she heard Maida whining and scrabbling, and let her through the swing door and there saw Alex.

"Well, all that was five years ago now. It was over for me then and there in that faceless little hotel bedroom. I still loved her—still do—but all passion was killed stone dead. I could hardly bear to see her anymore, although I did once or twice. It wounded her dreadfully. I could never tell her now what Arabella had been to me. And I couldn't bear to hear her justify what she'd done—she couldn't understand, you see, that it was wrong. I couldn't bear the hate, the venom that," her voice trembled, "that reminded me so much of Arabella, and that eventually turned against me. But worse, I think, was her puzzlement—'I can't think why you mind so much, Julia —Daddy knows I did it and he doesn't care.'

"So there it was. Reality—worse than any nightmare. I was returned to the place whence I came—as they used to say to the condemned prisoner."

She was silent, and he saw her in her study staring out at the icy waste of the garden.

"I have never been—been like other people. Even flowers . . . torture me. I am overpowered.

"In those years that followed, life was almost unbearable. I found a momentary solace, forgetfulness sometimes in riding out to the remorseless Fens, where there is no beauty except for the occasional windmill—but even they are stark, their sails static for decades now. Often I thought, as I crossed a humpback bridge, of making a quick turn into the dark waters of the dike. Death had a beauty, but a beauty without meaning. I had no claim on such poignancy. Despair doesn't kill us—it keeps us alive. Death was a reward I did not deserve—I was too much in debt. To Arabella. To Kate, still. And, Hugh, of course to you.

"When I saw the name of Alex Brinton in your appointments book—I had a strange feeling of premonition, as if I foresaw this moment now. But I was also frightened—oh not for myself. I was frightened that if he recognised me, it might touch his memory and he would recall everything about that terrible afternoon—recall having seen Kate slam the door on their mother. For neither I nor Kate knew whether he'd observed her. That's why she came here that Sunday morning, to probe me, to try to convince you that Alex had done it himself.

"So I had to say nothing to you, or as little as possible. I had to wait and be watchful—and lie to you. Dissemble, lie, pretend. Smile, disguise my dread. For I knew that if Alex brought it home to Kate, I would come forward and take Arabella's death on myself —where in truth it has always really belonged. I was, I told myself, prepared.

"So I was not really surprised by Jonathan's call on Tuesday night. But I was shocked when I saw him—bald and bloated and stoop-shouldered, a caricature of the man I'd known. He was—well, I've described how he was in my letter; although I have altered the conversation. Elaine had told him about Kate and me and he was —well, he was delighted. Elaine was to be sent away and as for Alex —'I've fixed him,' he said with a sort of snuffling chuckle. 'Anyway, he's Henry's son—not mine—no loyalty there, eh?' Kate and I were to come and live at the New Inn—'all my loved ones around me,' he said.

"He didn't offer me a drink, but he had a full one of his own —and there was a second glass on the side table. He went rambling on. Then suddenly he picked up his glass and drank the whole lot down. He began to talk again, but after a few words he stopped abruptly and clutched at the desk. He was staring at me, his eyes wide open. 'My God,' he said in a surprised voice, 'the little bastard's done for me!' He gave a convulsive shudder—and he was dead. I thought at first it was a heart attack, but when I touched him he was already stiff. Then I found the tiny granules in the bottom of his glass. I knew someone else had been in the room with him because of the second glass. Alex—'I've had a long talk with Alex,' he'd said.

"I stood there beside him for quite a long time trying to puzzle it out. Alex—why Alex? And then I remembered he'd said, 'Elaine will have to be disposed of.' Had he told Alex that? And had Alex taken immediate steps to stop it—doped his glass? I didn't know enough about the boy's mental state to know whether he could do such a thing. But I had no time to ask, to find out. The danger was here, now. I knew Jonathan's habits about pills, I knew no one would accept it as an accident. It would have to be suicide. So I simply sat down and wrote an appropriate letter. I was careful about fingerprints, I removed the spare glass, and I left. I didn't know I'd been observed a second time.

"And I think at that moment I was ready to tell you everything —when I rode back and saw the Rover in front of the house and knew you were at home, I was filled with a wild hope. When I couldn't find you, I became slightly demented—I ran through the house calling your name. Then I pulled myself together and drank some whisky; I undressed and sat on my bed to wait for you, my golden girl keeping me company. And then, perhaps because I was sure I wouldn't, I fell asleep. In the morning you were already gone.

"And by then it was already too late—although there was one more moment of weakness when I was on the edge of telling you —I think you sensed it—but I drew back. For I think I had already decided to do what I am doing now. And I didn't want to be deprived of death. I felt a kind of serenity I can't ever remember before, a clarity, an ease, even a gaiety. I bought a seed catalogue and turned the pages looking at the flowers with pleasure—they didn't hurt me now, no beauty had that power now.

"I have wanted to be dead for a long time now—ever such a long time, Hugh." She sighed, and there was a tremor in her voice. "But I didn't deserve death, I hadn't earned it. But now, do you see? I have earned it—this is a death in hope, a death that pays my debts to the living. It is purposeful, useful—to them, to Kate, to Alex, to Henry, to them all. Their need, their safety, their liberty is my entitlement. Duty fulfilled—joy embraced. Both. At last I have been given the password, so that I can enter where I've longed to be. I'm entitled to go to my long regard now—aren't I, aren't I? . . ."

He heard her choke then—heard her tears—and he clutched the edge of his desk. "Julia . . ."

"Well then, an hour ago, a bit more, he came—Alex." Her voice was thick. "I was just back from my last ride. From my study I heard the bell ring, someone going up the stairs—so I had to come out. He was dazed, poor kid, when he saw me. I explained who I was and he said, 'It was you I saw.' I said yes, that I'd been there that afternoon. And then he said, 'But I saw you on Tuesday night too.' I knew then that it was all meant to be like this and I felt a queer kind of elation—his having seen me is perfect supporting evidence for my confession. He stood there blinking at me, the tears running

305

down his cheeks. He came quite naturally into my arms. And I held him and I told him everything would be all right and that he was to do exactly what his stepmother told him.

"And that's how Elaine found us. 'Good afternoon, Welling,' she said in that cold way of hers. 'Hello, Trotman,' I said. She gave me such a look of jealous hatred. A sort of icy fury of distaste. And yet she'd liked me once, you know—when I first went to Matt's, Henry asked her to look after me a bit, and she did try. I think she even developed a slight lech for me, though no doubt an unconscious one—but I could never stand that kind of moralistic self-righteousness with its undercurrents of crawling sentimentality. I was sorry for Jonathan when I heard they'd married.

"So they went—and she's taken him off to the police station, I've no doubt. So I locked the front door and wrote my letter and phoned you—black phone to white. In a few moments I shall go upstairs." She stopped, and for one agonised moment he thought it was the end, and then she came back.

"Hugh—I'm sorry. I've made a hopeless muddle of it, haven't I? I've hurt you and betrayed you. You gave me a dignity I wasn't worth. You gave me unquestioning acceptance, I gave you lies. You gave me bread and I gave you a stone. 'She wasn't up to it—she wasn't worth it.' You're entitled to say that. But don't pity me, Hugh. I couldn't bear to see you looking at me as a patient, to be one more case in your files, and a stranger to your heart.

"Oh Hugh, there are so many things I want to say to you now . . . and yet none of them matters anymore. I want to say that I cheated you out of children, husband. I always took 'precautions.' I could never have been what they call 'a fit mother.' Perhaps I was just cowardly about it—as I am a coward, or so some will say, in what I'm doing now. But I didn't want to be responsible for giving pain, for causing yet another being to leap into what has been, to me, for so long, a dangerous world. I didn't want to groan or you to weep. I'm sorry, my dear—my darling—we never used even the simplest endearments, did we? Oh what respect and care you had for me, my sweetheart, my poppet, my lovely man, my tree, my . . . I'm wandering. I must end now, or I shan't have the strength to get up the stairs. Goosey goosey gander, whither do you wander? Upstairs and downstairs and in my lady's chamber. That's where you'll find me, Hugh. Don't wake me too early. Good night."

And that was the end. Except for the faint rustle of the continuing tape: "This is Dr. Welchman's residence. Dr. Welchman is not available. . . ."

The sky had darkened and there was a smattering of rain on the window. He leaned over and pressed the stop button.

Then he went to the top of the stairs and looked down into the gloomy hall. *Hugh! Hugh!* He heard her calling in the dark, running round the emptiness, searching for him when he wasn't there. And he never had been there.

He went slowly down the stairs and switched on the light at the bottom. . . . *one more case in your files, and a stranger to your heart.* He remembered as a boy hearing his mother's friends speak of "a little stranger on the way"—a curious manner of describing the child of one's own womb. The wife of one's bed. But it was he who'd been the stranger to her—a kindly but preoccupied, faintly daunting figure, who hadn't the habit of talking, let alone of confiding. Even more—a stranger to himself.

As he picked up the basin and towel in the waiting room and took them into the kitchen, he longed for someone to talk to. But there was no one in whom he could confide. He had no friends, only colleagues and patients. Wrapped in professional discretion, he'd lived almost entirely alone.

He found a dustpan and brush and a broom and a mop and began to clean up the house. Alone, and on his own terms. Terms entirely irrelevant to this situation—of grief and emptiness, of tears blurring the eyes so the lights danced, and a raw sobbing cough. As he went down on his knees and started to drop dollops of old hash and bits of broken glass and china into the spread-out newspaper, he thought of the grim little kitchen in Hackney, the emotional poverty of a house where the only demands had been for quick satisfaction—food, drink, and a brief rough tumble in the narrow parental bed—met with resignation and long suffering. The demands so few, the giving so little—love to the dead daughter rather than to the living son. Hadn't he spent his whole life symbolically succouring his mother's anguish—and rejecting his father's brutality? But in terms of human reality, demanding nothing, accepting nothing, giving nothing. Helplessly—but deliberately, for it was *his* dream—letting the three smiling women drift down to their death.

He stood up, the bundle of newspaper clutched in his arms, like a baby—or a bottle of whisky.

And what was he doing now if not trying to remove all traces of himself from a place where he'd left no mark except of ignorance and neglect?

Hugh, Hugh! he heard her calling again.

Where am I? he was tempted to answer. Who am I?

He shivered—a goose on his grave. He went to the kitchen, dumped the paper in the bin and turned up the thermostat on the central heating that was only used in the very depths of winter. He made himself a cup of tea and stood holding it, warming his hands.

Then he went back to cleaning. He'd almost done when the doorbell rang. He hesitated, but perhaps this was someone to talk to. He went almost hopefully to the front door.

"Hello, D-Dr. Welchman." Alex's smile flickered, and, far away, out of the corner of his eye, Hugh saw a flash of lightning slice the sky. The rain poured straight down. He mastered the impulse to slam the door.

"Come in, old chap." He cleared his throat. "You must be wet."

In fact he was soaked, his hair plastered to his skull, the water from his raincoat making puddles on the parquet in the hall.

"Take your coat off—you know where to hang it." He glanced upstairs, at the waiting room door. "Let's go in here," he led the way past Julia's study door into the living room—it was tidy enough and, though he hadn't been able to do anything about the burns on the hearthrug, he had cleaned out the grate and laid a new fire. He bent now and lit it.

"Your leg's better."

"Yes. No not there—on the couch." And as Alex took his place, he sat down beside him. "Well, what is it you wanted to see me about?"

Alex took out his cigarettes and lit one with a match—not only the leather pouch, but the lighter too was gone now. Hugh removed his glasses and started to clean them with his handkerchief.

"You didn't tell me she was dead!"

"No. Who did? Henry Stand?"

"Yes. He came to lunch and afterwards . . . I came straight round. Dr. Welchman, I—it was m-my fault, wasn't it?"

Hugh stared at the fire—it must have caught now, but he saw no detail of flame or spark, only a shimmering dance of yellow. The familiar unexamined beauty, all he'd ever wanted to see. "Fault?" He put on his glasses and turned to look at Alex. "No, it was not your fault that Julia killed herself. These things are seldom due to a single direct cause—one might say they're predetermined, over a long time." He waited, found the way in which to go on—the best were simple words. "I must tell you, Alex, that Julia wrote a letter —a letter in which she confessed to murdering both your mother and your father." As he spoke he felt the pain of the words—an acute pain that seemed to come from outside but invested him, was drawn into himself.

"But that's not true!"

"Oh?" Hugh winced and made a quick movement to cover it, bringing out his own cigarettes.

"I mean at least n-not with, with—*him.*"

"I see. Don't you think you'd better tell me about it?"

"Yes, that's what I came for. I killed him." He stared straight at Hugh, but his hand holding the cigarette trembled slightly. "Or at least I think I did."

"You'll have to explain that."

Alex nodded quickly. "When I told you I saw him sitting there chuckling that night and then just went away and waited by the front hall door—well, that wasn't quite t-true. I went into the study. The instant he saw me he stopped laughing, and glared at me. Then suddenly he was all smiles, delighted to see me, I must sit down and have a drink. And he leapt up—he moved in an odd jerky sort of way—and poured two large whiskies. 'No soda, damn,' he said, 'I'll get some water from the surgery' and he was out of the room with the glasses before I could open my mouth to offer help. He was away quite a time and I was beginning to wonder if anything had happened to him when he came back, handed me my tumbler and sat down with his own at the desk. 'Cheers!' he said and we both took a sip and then he began to talk, burble really, I could hardly understand what he was getting at—something about a shadow being lifted from all of us at long last, how happy we were all going to be, which I thought peculiar in view of what I'd heard of his conversation with Mother. But he hardly seemed to be paying any attention to what he was saying himself, and then suddenly in the middle of a sentence he bounced up again, 'Sorry, urgent phone call,' and rushed out of the room. I thought he'd probably had one too many—or several. I took another sip of my whisky and it tasted odd—faintly bitter, not that I'm a connoisseur of whisky. And then I thought that perhaps he'd given me the glass with Mother's bromide in it by mistake—and when I held it up to the light I could see tiny little floating bits in the liquid. So I simply changed my glass for his. It sounds funny, I know, but—"

"It seems to me a perfectly normal thing to do."

"Well, yes. Perhaps. Anyway, then he came back, and this time he was even more jittery. 'Young Grigson—bringing his wife in for a shot, broke the needle the silly fellow. Drink up, drink up, they'll be along any minute now.' As far as I knew the only patient he had called Grigson was a lorry driver who'd been killed about three weeks before in a frightful smash-up on the M4, but I didn't say anything. I just sat and listened to him waffling senselessly on about what a marvellous couple the Grigsons were—and trying to get down my drink, which he kept urging me to finish. I did at last and he more or less hustled me out. That's actually why I waited behind the door—if it wasn't the Grigsons, I wanted to see who it was. I was a bit puzzled when it turned out to be Julia, but I didn't think much about it, until the next morning when Wardy told me he was dead and then I thought . . . I thought Mother must have done it, given him something else, not a bromide, but a poison of some kind. . . ."

"And now?" Yes, this was going to fit all right—whether it was true or not hardly mattered. It was a basis on which they could build.

"I don't think the bromide's got anything to do with it. He put something in the glass himself, something—Librium or whatever it was—that killed him, but was really meant for me."

"Yes, I think that's quite likely. Simply on psychological grounds I think we could probably say your father was capable of—"

"He wasn't my father!"

"So Stand told you that too, did he?" The little doctor, at least, had done his duty.

"It was a bit of a facer at first." Then Alex gave his gentle, Stand-like smile. "But actually I think I rather like the idea."

"Good. Then the man you've always thought was your father, we'd better call him Jonathan—or the Doctor?"

"Jonathan. God, he was a bastard—I simply hated him. It makes it all easier now—I mean it's not so bad hating someone who wasn't one's father." He stubbed out his cigarette in the clean ashtray. "But all the same, I can't believe he really tried to kill me —and then I killed him instead."

"I'm not sure that's a very good way of putting it. In fact, he killed himself. No possible kind of responsibility or blame for his death can be attached to you."

"You don't think so?"

"I'm positive about it."

"I see." Alex lit another cigarette automatically. Then he got up and dropped the match into the fire. "In that case," he turned to face Hugh, "hadn't I better own up?"

Hugh gripped his knees tightly. He looked down at his hands, the liver-spotted skin, the tobacco-stained fingers. *Too late, too late!* he wanted to cry out, and the untasted words flew about in his skull like wounded birds.

"Alex," he said, and his voice sounded thin and distant to his own ears, "what you have told me seems to me to hold water. But that's because I know quite a lot about you, the sort of person you are, and about the situation. But it is based on certain psychological factors that are not easily explained, and there are certain things it doesn't account for, such as your—as Jonathan's false suicide letter."

"But Julia wrote that, didn't she?"

"Yes. But once that's introduced, together with the fact that she was there—and you've made a statement to the effect that you saw her—well, then some considerable doubt is going to be thrown on your story."

"But it's true."

Hugh turned his hands palm up and raised his head. "I don't think we can count too much on truth winning through."

"But that's not fair!" He came back and sat down. "You—you haven't g-given her confession to the police, have you?"

"Not yet."

"Then don't! Why should she be the one to bear the blame for something I did, if anyone did it? What do people's suspicions and gossip matter against that—against her good name?" Leaning forward, he put his hand on Hugh's arm.

"I don't think . . ." He wanted to jerk away—away from what had suddenly become a temptation. In his mind he heard the verdicts—Murder by Person or Persons Unknown, or, even possibly, Death by Misadventure, and Suicide while the Balance of her Mind was Disturbed. And then he could return to the house with a certain kind of peace. He could even hear the lawyer's soft phrases, "In view of the verdict, Doctor, I have little doubt that the will can be successfully challenged, if you be so minded." He would continue his practise, here, as if nothing had happened—another unsuccessful case, an inevitable prognosis unhappily fulfilled. But he had never expected to be happy.

"Dr. Welchman—did she, did she *want* you to give her confession to the police?" He frowned.

"Yes. I—I believe she did want that."

"So that I wouldn't be . . . she said everything would be all right, that's what she meant—she did it for me."

"No!" he said in furious vehemence against that echo of Kate's words—*She died that I might live.* Then, "no" more calmly. He lit a cigarette. Why was he protesting so violently? "She did it because of the sort of person she was."

"Then what sort of person was she—I mean, really?"

He looked at Alex, at the fire. *I don't know,* he'd said to Henry Stand; but he knew now—the clinical picture. He sorted through his mind, shuffling the cards of the professional pack for the layman's consumption; but this was a patience that would never come out, a game of Unhappy Families where no two cards matched. "In my job, Alex, I try to get people to adjust to an everyday world—for psychotherapeutic purposes we call it the 'real' world and accept its boundaries and its limitations as valid demarcations within which a certain minimal satisfaction and personal fulfillment can be achieved. We do not encourage high expectations; all things are very far from being possible. We are reasonably successful at dealing with the grosser symptoms, but this is not a world in which people are much changed, or transformed, or transfigured. On the whole people improve or deteriorate or, the most that can generally be hoped for, they manage a certain kind of equilibrium, often with the aid of drugs."

"It sounds pretty b-bleak." Alex moved restlessly.

"Er?" He had lost awareness of the boy; it was a lecture he was repeating by rote—the next point to be made was that it wasn't really so bad. "I suppose so." He hadn't answered the question, couldn't answer the question.

It was the wrong question.

"Please—tell me what you're thinking. *Are* you going to tell the police?"

That was better. He pushed his glasses onto his forehead and rubbed his eyes. He nodded. "Yes," he said. "Yes—I'm sure it's the right thing to do." It was the only course, he realised, on which Julia's compassion and his own pragmatism would agree. That was comparatively easy. But he had to do more than that, much more.

"I'm sorry—b-but if you really think . . ."

"I do." And the words shook him with the memory of an old vow. But now he really had no option—he was going to have to force himself to enter a world of which he knew little, without professional tools or protective armour of prognoses, alone, un-armed, empty-handed.

"And—and us, sir. Can I keep on as your p-patient?"

"Ummmm?" He looked at the boy vaguely, blinked—focussed. Alex, last of the Brint—but no, not even a Brinton. And he saw the strictness of mien, the strength of bone under the still-childish softness of cheek, purpose within the beauty. This—this was something rescued out of the general disaster. He felt a sudden great sense of yearning—he understood Julia, he knew, recognised, for a moment *was*—and then it passed. "No," he said, "No, I think not—better not."

"But I want—I mean, I have to understand, I—"

"There are no solutions, Alex."

They were both standing now.

"Then what?"

"There are—mediations. There is work—a great deal of hard work."

"But you don't want—you say—you're deserting me. . . ."

"By no means," he smiled faintly, "but I shall see you're in good hands—far better than mine, Alex. You'll have to work hard." He took Alex by the arm and guided him down the passage, tread-ing cautiously, favouring his injured foot.

"Hard work—well, I've n-never been frightened of that."

"No," said Hugh, "no."

They shook hands and he watched Alex get in his car, switch on the lights, drive cautiously away. The visibility was almost nil —and almost immediately he was lost to view. And there was no lightning now, not even a hint of distant thunder. No sound but the drumming of the rain.

Hugh turned into the house and shut the front door.

He picked up the black phone and dialled the number automatically.

"Cambridge Central Police Station—can I help you?"

"Er? Oh," he took out a cigarette and put it in his mouth. "This is Dr. Hugh Welchman. . . ."